100
av/h

11

A LITTLE LOVE

A LITTLE LOVE

C.C. Medina

WARNER BOOKS

A Time Warner Company

Grateful acknowledgment is given for permission to reprint "El Dia Que Me Quieras" by Carlos Gardel and Alfred Lepera
© 1935 (renewed) Editorial Musical Korn Intersong SAIC (SADAIC)
All rights administered by Rightsong Music, Inc. (BMI)
All rights reserved. Used by permission.
Warner Bros. Publications U.S., Inc., Miami, FL 33014

Warner Books, Inc., 1271 Avenue of the Americas, New York, NY 10020
Visit our Web site at www.twbookmark.com

 A Time Warner Company

Printed in the United States of America
First Printing: July 2000
10 9 8 7 6 5 4 3 2 1

Library of Congress Cataloging-in-Publication Data

Medina, C.C.
    A little love / C. C. Medina.
        p. cm.
    ISBN 0-446-52448-4
    1. Hispanic American women—Florida—Miami—Fiction. 2. Female friendship—Florida—Miami—Fiction. 3. Miami (Fla.)—Fiction. I. Title.

PS3563.E2396 L58 2000
813'.54—dc21
                                                                99-051757

For Nicole and Sonora

Acknowledgments

First, profound thanks to my agent, Janell Walden Agyeman, who was loca enough to approach me on a city sidewalk one fine tropical evening. More thanks to Diana Baroni, my editor at Warner Books, for her diligencia, support, and incredibly good advice, and to my copy editor, Jennifer Comeau, who has tremendo ojo for details. To my friends and first consejeros Betty and Jorge Gonzalez, Tessie Fraga, Michelle Hospital, Joe Mauro, and especialmente Amarilis Acosta (a little love around the corner?) for their enthusiastic encouragement and astute observations, mil gracias. Thanks to Linda Duarte, Sandy Mantooth, Linda Mackay, Betty Park, Margaret Fitzgerald, Nancy Weiss, Norma Soto, Teresa Vega, Cary Ser, Cathy Rosenfeld, Ann Rose, Martha Zamorano, Ricardo Pau-Llosa, Marta Magellan, José Blanco, and to all of my colleagues at Ransom Everglades School and at Miami-Dade Community College for putting up. Thanks to Jodeen Boggs and Grace Wang for taking care of me during a crucial moment, to Joan and Howard Lenard for their tip, and to Paul Royall of Little Palm Island for taking care of paradise. Carolina, chapter 21 is for you. To Nancy Fink, thanks for being a real "happy maker" in my life, and to Belkis Cuza Malé, gracias for staying on the front lines of Latino literature all these years. A very special abrazo to Jan Coppola for her generous corazón in sharing Tony (as if . . . !). Gracias with all my heart to my New York familia, Carmen and Eddy and everybody. My love and appreciation to my Miami family and friends for their apoyo (mira que hay que aguantar!), you too Alberto and Enrique. A gigante thanks to my daughters, Nicole and Sonora, for their patience, their amor, and their everlasting influence—hugs and kisses. And finally, I wrote this book! For Christ's sake!

A LITTLE LOVE

Chapter 1

Isabel Landon

*F*orgive me, Father, for I've had sex."

"When was your last . . ."

"Four years ago."

"Your last confession was four years ago?"

"No, Father, I had sex four years ago."

"Were you married?"

"Yes."

"Where's the sin in that?"

"The sin is in not having had any for four years."

That was my last confession with that priest. A good Cuban girl doesn't talk that way, especially to a priest. I was a good Cuban girl. Ay Dios! How many years with David. Mrs. David Landon, that was my title. No, it was my name and I loved him. David was everything I wanted in a husband. He was tall, fair skinned, broad shouldered, and with a faraway look in his eyes, not a dreamer's stare, but a hawk's. David always knew where he was headed. I like that in a man. But David has been out of the picture for four years now. Well, I still have pictures of him all over the place. The kids insist on that. Every time I see his face in their bedrooms, in the family room, and in the bathroom, I want to tear my heart out; I can't get to his because he doesn't have one. I have to stop thinking about him.

What was I thinking with that priest? Coño, I've been trying to get back to the church. My little cousin Mercy got me in this parish, Saint Anthony of the Lost Souls, what a name. I'm not lost. But it has a great school. "Isabel," mami always says, and I'm translating here, "a Catholic education is money in the bank and love in the heart." I received a good Catholic education, up in Connecticut. Lots of discipline and much mia culpa, guilt all over the place. That's good for the soul, but hija, can it make a mess of your love life. So I put the kids in the best parochial school in Miami. It has two priests. One is really an Irish Monsignor; he runs the place like a CEO of a Fortune 500 company. They call him Father Rambo. Gets it all done ahora. And then there's sweet Father Paquito, still wet behind the ears. And what an accent! It took me a month to figure out that "Leh-oh-pay" meant "Let us pray." That's what you get when you mix a Cuban with a Puerto Rican. He'll have to do my confessions from now on.

I've been doing everything since the divorce. Why is it that they never get the kids? Perdóname, Dios! Don't get me wrong. I love my boys, but if you add up everything I do for them—the baseball games, the play rehearsals, the guitar lessons, the homework assignments, the driving to and from places that if they can't get to they'll just die, plus the summer trips to Kansas to stay with their father, and those damned pictures of David—where am I? Not in Kansas. Gracias a Dios for that! Imagine a Cuban in that place? Everything is so flat. "There's nothing flat about you," so says my little cousin Mercy. "With those curves you'd have every farm boy trading their pickups for Ferraris." Well, it serves him right, with that big Great Plains face of his, to end up in Kansas. I loved that face, such a sonrisa, from dimple to dimple. When you squint your eyes he looks like Kevin Bacon. I fell in love with David the first time I saw him smile in chemistry class at the University of Connecticut.

Connecticut is where I lived as a kid. My parents left Cuba in the early sixties; we stayed in Miami for a week, and then, thanks to the generous Americano volunteers at the Freedom Tower, we were given three winter coats, two hats, and three one-way train tickets to Meriden, Connecticut.

The Freedom Tower, I see it every day on my drive to work. Now it's an exclusive office building with a Moroccan ballroom in what used to be the basement. We've all gone there, all the Cubans, to dance in our Oscar de la Renta dresses and our Anne Klein shoes. Raising money for the Cancer Society or some other cause. When I have the time, I attend a few of these a year. A good Catholic Cuban divorced mother, setting a good example for her boys.

I can still feel the sting on my hand from the example mami gave me in that same basement when we were refugees. We were waiting in line, something papi swore he'd never do after leaving Cuba, waiting for some canned cheese and powdered milk, when I noticed the janitor emptying the garbage can next to me. Being curious, I peered inside it. At the bottom was a nickel, an American nickel! Not a day in America and I was already making money. I dove into the can, stuck my arm out with the palm open, and yelled out, "Dinero!" The nickel went flying along with my tears. "Isa," mami growled, "free food is charity, an act of God; free money is mierda, take it, and you're mierda." With that, this small unassuming woman yanked me out of the garbage can, wiped my tears, and gave me an incredible hug.

I have never taken money, not ever, even though my lawyer said that the way David was feeling about this divorce I could've walked away with everything and David wouldn't have lifted a lawyer's pen against it. I never accepted alimony. It's garbage money. I take David's child support and school money, but that's different.

Mami was never against revenge. "Ojo por ojo," she'd often say. She had another favorite saying; it went something like "Whenever you're in the company of strangers, put on your Son-of-a-Bitch-Ometer, and if it starts buzzing, run like hell." Coño, for fifteen years I had that Bitch-Ometer off. Something else went buzzing the minute David walked into that chemistry class and smiled at me.

Sex was never a problem with us. David was an athletic lover, an all-American letter earner. But that was later. We both married virgins. I was a virgencita, untouched by desiring hands and other dangerous body parts. All through high school, papi was my chaperone. His idea of a good date was the school's athletic games. I went to every basketball, football, baseball, and swimming event the school competed in. Always by my side were my pimply date and my enthusiastic papi. With every score made, papi would whoop and holler; my date would sulk with limp hands and something else. I would sweat like a pig at a luau.

"Americano boys, you can trust them. Cubanitos, olvídate. Never date a Cuban boy! Mucha mano en la masa!"

"Sí, papi," and I never did. I never did anything with a boy. You can imagine my honeymoon night with David. Being trained engineers, we bought three sex manuals and a racy video titled *Orgasmic Universe*.

"No, not that way. Look at the picture on page seventy-four."
"Which book?"

We finally settled on *The Joy of Sex*. It took me six months to figure out the joy part. After that, well, put it this way, if sex were a sporting event, papi would get laryngitis from all the whooping and hollering he'd be doing. David and I loved the chemistry between us.

And we both loved our chemistry classes. For me, there is something about putting my hands into the basic elements, the things that really matter, and then building something new out of the old stuff.

I got this love for chemicals from papi. After we arrived in Meriden, we lived in an old three-story schoolhouse; an old Irish priest converted each classroom into two-room apartments. Ten Cuban refugee families lived in that schoolhouse. The adults had quickly made it into a little piece of Cuba. I remember seeing some potted palm trees next to the steam-heat radiators in a few of the apartments as the snow fell outside. And each evening, after the men had their black beans and rice, they would sit along the grand staircase, in the center of the building, drinking their Cuban coffees, talking, or I should say shouting, island politics. Papi could not often join them. He was too exhausted from the shift at the foundry. My father worked like a mulo. He was the supervisor of the day shift, which at least three times a week would turn into the night shift as well. He never said no to his bosses. Once in a while, when I had a day off at the public elementary school, he would take me to the foundry. I'd stay there the whole day watching the men mix the sand, the iron, and the carbon, heat it all up, and pour it into various molds. The men had big hands, with big veins crawling all over them. Hands big enough to take bits of powders and metals, and re-cast them into something useful. Papi made sure the men did their job right. But he was always tired. I think he looked tired from the day he left Cuba. Mami worked at Napiers, Inc., a costume jewelry maker. She assembled the earrings by hand. All the Cuban women of the schoolhouse worked there. "Isa, never work alongside of your friends," mami would repeat often like a Hail Mary on a rosary. There were days when the men would be full of island talk, and the women could not stand each other.

As soon as my parents could afford it, we moved to a respectable townhouse development (really remodeled row houses, all brick) on the edge of town, and I went to the all-girls' Our Lady of Sweet Charity Catholic School. Because I belonged to a minority (my maiden name, de la Llama, gave me away) and because of my high grades, I eventually got a full scholarship to the state university.

There's where I met David. We married the year we graduated, each with our own M.S. degree in Chemical Engineering and a desire to leave the cold. We left all right, and fifteen long Third World years later, he went off to Kansas, transferred at his request by Texaco Oil, the company he worked for in the Dominican Republic. And when I clicked my heels, I ended up in Miami, except that I got the kids and he got, as he put it, "kinfolk." I landed in the City of Exiles with both feet running and a banana peel under each heel, as mami likes to say. I was slipping, sliding, and running my way to the top of the heap. And as any decent, divorced, professional Latina would tell you, I am doing all this for the boys.

They're good boys, a couple of caballeros. David Jr. is fifteen years old, he looks like a Latino version of his father, and Sam is fourteen, he looks like me. We had the boys back to back. We planned it that way. I can tell you right now that the rhythm method works, that and celibacy. That's what I've been the last four years: celibate.

Here in my office, right behind my head on the credenza, there's a picture of the boys fly fishing somewhere in Kansas. El comemierda. Who's got time to fly fish? Maybe if there was one of those *A River Runs Through It* streams next to the Palmetto Expressway I could find the time to fish. The traffic is so backed up each morning and afternoon that I could fill up my Ford Expedition with trout and make a killing at Normita's Fish Market in Little Havana. Instead, on my Express-jammed way to work, I put on a "Books on Tape" and listen to Burt Reynolds read *The Frugal Way to Riches*. Don't get me wrong; I'm not struggling economically. My job as Senior Engineer for Boxer Medical Technologies pays me well, about $100,000 a year. I read in *Parade* magazine the article about how only 2 percent of Americans earn $100,000 or more a year. Well, ahí estoy yo. I buy what I need and what I want, but with two teenagers about to drive, my parents living with me in the house I just bought in Pinecrest Village, and the fact that I'm alone, I always feel like I'm on thin ice. So I buy a few nice things for myself, put some away for the future, and the rest goes to the everyday living expenses of two growing boys, two aging parents, and a big house. I'm the sole breadwinner in this family; I wear the pantalones around here. My favorite style of dress is a pantsuit but with a Latin twist. Sharp creases on the pants with a bolero jacket on top. Always in navy blue and black, or when I want to make the men in the office nervous, blood red.

Add to this high heels and a touch of jewelry—a diamond tennis bracelet I bought with the company Christmas bonus, 18-karat gold loops on the ears, and my ex's solid karat diamond engagement ring (for protection against intruders)—and I'm ready to produce. I work long hours in a leading-edge company. I have a nice office with thirty people under me and two on top, and I still have a long way to go before I sleep. I can't have it any other way. No time, no love, and definitely no hombre.

Enter Rubén

My dearest Isabel,

The moon was radiant last night, like your smile. I savored a cup of chamomile tea sweetened with honey, the color of your hazel eyes. I am in your power, Isabel. I feel a warmth when I think of you, a warmth I haven't felt in years. Your auburn hair flows like autumn leaves. As they float, I want to caress each strand with my very hands. Though we have hardly spoken, the words you have sprinkled on me have taken root. I feel I have known you for a lifetime. You are delicate in size, like a monarch butterfly, yet your strength has given me the courage to pour out my heart. Please be kind to someone who has the purest of intentions. Accept these flowers, fragrant like you, and answer me not with gestures but with words I can read and re-read until eternity. Your admirer,

Rubén

He sent the flowers to work. Everybody saw them being delivered to my office. No doubt the coffee-break talk will be about me and the damned flowers. You spend four years putting everybody in their place, "I'm the boss and you're not," and now a bunch of— what are these?—"Butterfly Flowers Bouquet by FTD"—can put you back in the caveman days. I could just see my male underlings getting their clubs ready. I gave the letter one last look. Its sappiness was giving me sticky fingers.

"Dorothy!"

"Yes, Ms. Landon."

"Dorothy, type this up for me and send it ASAP."

TO: Mr. Rubén García

FROM: Ms. Isabel Landon

RE: Flora

     Received your flowers in good order. Thank you for the words.

                Regards,

                Isabel Landon

"Dorothy!"

"Yes, Ms. Landon."

"This matter stays in the office. Comprendes?"

"Sí, señora. My lips are zipped!"

I like Dorothy. I hired her because she speaks fluent Spanish. She's a bilingual gringa; it throws everybody off around here when it comes to office gossip of the multilingual kind. She's also as loyal as a toothy terrier on a pant leg. Pero este Rubén is a dog of another kind wanting something else with my pants.

"So qué pasa with that?" Mercy, my little cousin, is saying to me on the cellular, as I'm making my way back home. "After four years of living like a nun and working like a man you get a little attention of the love kind and you freak out! Estás loca or what?!"

"I don't need a man in my life right now."

"You may not need one, but don't you want one? It's been four years, Isabel."

"So now you and a priest are experts on my sexual status."

"A priest came on to you también?! Oye, is it that obvious? You better get to this Rubén García before the Pope visits Miami again!"

"Qué graciosa estás, Mercy. This is serious. I see this guy at the monthly meetings of the Chemical Engineers Association of South Florida (of which I'm a sitting board member). All we ever do is talk strategy. Not once have I given this guy a hint of any possibilities."

"What does he look like?"

"He wears gray suits."

"And?"

"And black shoes."

"That's all you can remember about this guy?"

"That's all I notice."

"Well, notice his words. Caress, warmth, flood—this guy is a romantic, your very own Pablo Neruda. What's the harm in going out with him? He's a Latino, no?"

"Sí, I think from Chile."

"There! You've never been with a Latino man, your own kind for a change. You might like it. Just don't jump all over him on the first day. Wait for the first night!"

Traffic got moving again on the Palmetto and I hung up on Mercy. My own kind, that's what David said to me when he wanted out. He left me for a culture. What am I supposed to do, feel threatened by every McDonald's that comes my way? Qué carajo kind of a reason is that to break up a family?

It was past seven and I had enough time to get some take-home food before the boys got off to their rooms to interact with Nintendo, and before my retired parents retired to the TV room for their nightly novela.

"I'm home! Who wants the Big Mac with cheese?"

Chapter 2

Lucinda Portes de Colón

Lucinda sped through the Toledo hand-wrought iron gates in front of the house in Cocoplum driving her midnight-blue Jaguar XK8 convertible. She looked forward to returning home after dropping off Roberto and Brenda, her two children, at Ransom Preparatory School, the most exclusive school in town. By the time she got back, her husband had already left for work. He was the president of the Banco Dominicano Ltd. It was Tuesday, and on Tuesday mornings Lucinda read her favorite weekly supplement, *Vida Social*, included in the daily *El Nuevo Herald*.

Back in the house, she walked through the Poggenpohl-designed kitchen and poured herself a cup of coffee, brewed by Rosario, her maid. With the coffee cup in hand and the newspaper under her arm, Lucinda went to the conservatory, a greenhouse she had built at the edge of the bay, by the seawall.

"Por favor, Rosario, bring some of those señorita pastries over to the greenhouse," she called back. These were leftover desserts from the dinner party she hosted last night.

"Sí, Doña Lucinda."

Rosario brought the flaky custard-filled sweets on the buffed silver tray to the greenhouse. This was Lucinda's favorite morning space. The Amdega conservatory was hand made of glass and

lightly stained wood. It housed her enormous orchid collection.
She had started it with just a few phalaenopsis bought by her husband. But after taking a few courses at Fairchild Tropical Garden,
where her husband was a board member, Lucinda became good
at growing orchids. Twice a year, she attended the Garden's orchid
exhibits and bought exotic varieties for her collection. It grew so
large she could give away the many repeats as gifts for her few
friends. Lucinda savored the coffee, looking back at the orchids.
Orchids always reminded her of her homeland, with its tropical
colors and its variety of people. If only she could get rid of the excess people in her life, as she did the orchids, she thought, sitting
on the chair.

The greenhouse included a small solarium with a plantation
teak patio set she had picked out for herself. As the sunlight filtered through the opaque glass and the light morning breeze
blew from the bay, Lucinda drank her coffee and pored over the
Vida Social. She was the wife of Carlos Colón, a bank president,
so she had to keep informed about Miami's busy social life. It was
different in New York, thought Lucinda as she read the magazine.
In New York, they were busy only with each other.

Lucinda and Carlos moved to Miami from New York after
Brenda, their second child, was born. It was then that her father-
in-law, Don Carlos, made the attractive offer. But to Lucinda, it had
felt like un macuteo, a typical bribe back home. That was ten
years ago, yet she still missed New York. It was there where Carlos and Lucinda fell in love, though they first met in the Dominican Republic. Their families belonged to the same small social
circles of wealthy Dominicans.

The Portes family was part of the elite landed aristocracy in the
Dominican Republic. They owned sugar plantations and cattle
ranches in the interior of the island. The family prided itself in
tracing its roots directly back to Castille in Spain. Each spring the
family vacationed in Madrid and from there made excursions to
most of Europe's capitals. Lucinda had a collection of keepsakes
from these family vacations in Europe. Her favorite was the

wooden statue of Don Quixote her parents had bought her on the first trip to Madrid. It was really a present from her father, Leonardo Portes. He liked the way Don Quixote made a life for himself, "even if it was a crazy one," he was fond of saying. Her father believed you had to live your own life, no matter what others said. Her mother, Doña Rosario, who demanded everyone call her by that title, always expected Lucinda to marry into another distinguished Hispanic Dominican family. In that, she wasn't disappointed.

Carlos was the firstborn of an established banking family, Los Colón from Santo Domingo. They owned the largest domestic bank network in the country. They claimed direct lineage to Don Cristóbal Colón, the founder of the New World and what was then called Hispaniola, now the Dominican Republic. The first thing a visitor saw when entering the family's three-story Spanish colonial mansion was the Colón coat of arms. It was a huge shield carved out of dark mahogany with its lions and its castle towers crossed by two stainless steel gold-embossed swords. Don Carlos was the patriarch of the family and its business empire. When Lucinda and Carlos married, he insisted on personally giving them an authentic replica of the Colón coat of arms.

The two families had formal business relations and also met at many social gatherings. As children, Carlos and Lucinda often exchanged glances of boredom at the numerous family birthday parties and get-togethers at the Yacht Club. Carlos was a few years older than Lucinda, and it was during their teenage years that they lost contact with each other.

A few years later, while home for the summer after studying at the Pratt Institute in New York, Lucinda had reluctantly accepted an invitation to a family brunch on the ranch. She wanted to rest, not socialize, but Doña Rosario insisted that she maintain her social duties.

When they met again as adults, Lucinda was instantly attracted to Carlos' striking good looks. He was fairly tall, like Lucinda, with tanned skin and light brown wavy hair combed back. His mustache, of medium bulk, accented his chiseled facial features. Lucinda was taken by his dark eyes. They hinted at a tenderness uncommon in the young men of means who were always around her. They were always after money and sex, and a tolerant Doña for a wife who would put up with both.

As soon as Lucinda saw him, she regretted not having dressed more elegantly. She had carelessly tied her long brown hair into a ponytail and thrown on a pair of blue jeans with a white cotton shirt. She hadn't even bothered to put on any makeup. At first, she didn't recognize Carlos. He looked at her from across the room and caught her eyes. She was self-conscious as he approached her.

"Lucinda Portes, you have grown into a woman."

"I'm sorry, but do I know you?"

"Don't you remember me? Carlos Colón. I haven't changed that much, have I?"

Lucinda remembered him and was surprised by how familiar he was to her.

"Your mother tells me you are studying in New York," continued Carlos. "I'll be moving there next month."

"I've been there for three years."

"How do you like it?"

"I love it, especially for the snow," Lucinda said, smiling.

"Not me, I've been up to my ears in snow living in Chicago."

Carlos earned his degree in commercial photography from the Chicago School of Design and accepted a job in New York with Vanidades International, one of the leading Hispanic magazine consortia in the United States.

"I'll have my own photography studio. But not yet, I need the technical experience and the contacts Vanidades can give me."

"I'm hoping to finish my fine arts studies by next year. I'd like to have a painting studio, and I'll probably do some teaching on the side."

That day the conversation lasted long after the guests left in the late afternoon. A brunch visit turned into a dinner stay, and Carlos and Lucinda spoke of many things. They agreed they were true artists and made definite plans to see each other often in New York. They had one more thing in common; neither wanted to work in the family businesses.

That summer they fell in love, and after a proper home courtship at the insistence of Doña Rosario, and intensive dates in New York, they married. The event was noted and photographed by all of the important society pages in Santo Domingo. Lucinda didn't pay attention to these back then.

In their seventeen years of marriage, life seemed to unravel itself as smoothly as an anchor line. Their lives fell into place. Carlos worked for a few years learning the ins and outs of the commercial advertising business; Lucinda got a teaching job and painted at night. There were no kids, no parents, and no social obligations. To Lucinda, life was simple. They strolled a lot, dined out a lot, made love a lot, and talked a lot into the late hours of the night. When Lucinda got pregnant for the first time, her mother demanded they move to Santo Domingo. Doña Rosario couldn't accept having her only grandson so far away in such a cold place. She could help raise him, and Lucinda didn't have to work at all. But Lucinda didn't want to return to Santo Domingo. In New York, she wasn't part of the Portes/Colón families with all of their hierarchies and social duties and family intrigues. In New York, in the dead of winter, she was herself. The snow was like the walls of a Spanish fortress, thick and immune to attack. In her snow-protected tower, she was a painter, a teacher, a wife, and now a mother. She was also Carlos' lover. Back then they always made love with their eyes open. On their first night as lovers, they made a promise never to miss seeing all of each other. She would watch as his tender eyes directed his hands to the faraway places of her body. His hands would caress the nape of her neck, the smooth indentations behind her knees, the cool basin at the small of her back, and in her eyes he would see her falling to a secret place. They stayed in New York despite her mother's constant reminders.

The birth of Brenda was a surprise to them. Carlos was getting tired of taking pictures of flowers, furniture, and cars for ads in magazines like *Vanidades, Good Housekeeping,* and *Cosmopolitan.* He wasn't doing any of his own work. Whenever they got together with friends and relatives, all she'd hear about was how petty and frustrating his work was, especially for a family man. And his family would add, especially for a Colón. He never liked the cold weather. He had stayed in New York to please Lucinda. But with two babies, they just weren't getting anywhere financially.

It was at this moment in their lives that Don Carlos stepped in with his offer. The family had decided to open a branch of the Banco Dominicano Ltd. in Miami. They needed someone trustworthy to manage it. Being their firstborn, Carlos came to mind immediately. He was open to the idea.

"We'll be living in Miami, not Santo Domingo," Carlos told Lucinda. "The weather is nice down there. The kids will love the beaches, they'll speak Spanish. And you don't have to work, you can paint full-time. I'll be in charge at the bank. I'll have more time for you. My family needs me and they're willing to help us."

With Carlos feeling the way he did, and with the pressure of raising two babies and the offer from her father-in-law, Lucinda conceded to the Miami move.

At first, she was surprised by Miami. Expecting another American city, Lucinda found a typical Latin American one instead, especially in its social circles. She was also surprised at the ease with which Carlos and she fit in. Her father-in-law made sure of that, as he made sure of everything involving his family and his business.

Always in control, Don Carlos told Lucinda on her wedding day, "In our family there is no divorce." The words had sounded more like a threat than a reassurance.

Rosario interrupted Lucinda with a fresh cup of coffee.

"Gracias, Rosario. Please remember to leave the dining room spotless."

She always made sure the house was ready for any last-minute business or social dinners Carlos might arrange. The dining room was beautiful, as was the entire house.

The two-story house, done in the Neoclassical style, stood in a corner lot in Cocoplum, an exclusive gated neighborhood by the bay. Lucinda preferred an apartment on Edgewater Drive by the canal, but Carlos insisted on accepting the house. It was bought and furnished by the bank. Lucinda remembered the young realtor who showed them the house. She turned out to be her friend Isabel's cousin. All roads lead to Miami, thought Lucinda.

Apart from the five bedrooms and four and a half baths, the house included a grand living room with marble floors, appointed with impressive large French Empire painted paper grisaille screens and two silvered and gilded wood chandeliers. The furniture pieces combined mahogany with off-white satins and wools. The dining room continued the Neoclassical theme with a solid mahogany table for twelve. The foyer had as its central focus the Colón coat of arms her father-in-law gave them on their wedding night. Lucinda would have preferred a less serious look in a house, especially for one with two kids and an entire tropical bay for a backyard. But she had to admit the house had been tastefully furnished by the bank's interior decorator.

The corner back bedroom facing the water, however, Lucinda remodeled herself, turning it into her own private art studio. Light was important to her, so she gave it careful attention. She settled on three different light sources. Natural light flooded into the room through a large window, a French door, and a skylight she had built. The other two sources were a desk lamp with a fluorescent tube, so as not to cast a shadow, and track lights aimed at her wooden easel. She had cabinets put in to hold her many paints, tools, and brushes. And she had an elevated wooden floor built to ease the strain on her back while painting standing up. Finally, she had the silver-lined wallpaper replaced with an off-white textured paint. Back in New York, Lucinda would have died for such a space. Now, after ten years in Miami, she only found the time to paint occasionally.

On top of the detached three-car garage was a storage room which she had converted into a darkroom for Carlos' photography. He didn't use it much anymore. It was covered with dust. Lucinda never had Rosario clean it.

Lucinda's time was mostly taken up by the children and by Carlos' social obligations. Unlike her own upbringing, she tended to her children's needs so that Rosario was mainly the housekeeper and not the nanny she used to be. Lucinda had inherited Rosario from her mother. It was no coincidence that she carried her mother's name. Doña Rosario liked it that way, but she made sure there was never any mixup as to who was the real mother.

When Roberto and Brenda were babies, Lucinda nursed them herself. She also made it a point to take them on their daily strolls around the neighborhood. She organized weekly family outings, usually on Sundays, to various places the children enjoyed. They were regulars at the Science Museum, the Miami Seaquarium, and Shark Valley in the Everglades.

Whenever she could, at the children's pleadings, Lucinda drew charcoal sketches of them in imaginary adventures based on the books they were reading. The children conjured up scenes of themselves flying on a unicorn or battling giant dinosaurs. As soon as Carlos arrived home from work, if they were still up, the children would run to him with her sketches. He loved to hear their tales and always complimented her drawings. On nights like these, she could tell Carlos missed the children most. And Lucinda missed him.

He used to take many pictures of them. Hanging on the walls of the family den were his photographs from when they were babies and toddlers. Some were candid shots, taken by surprise; others were formal portraits, carefully posed and lighted. Few of them were of the children as pre-teens. Lately, the bank and its social affairs had become his life, and hers as well.

This social life was chronicled in the *Vida Social,* which Lucinda was reading. She slowly turned the pages and found herself next to Carlos at the cocktail party for the Easter Seal Ball. For this occasion, she wore a strapless blue taffeta dress which highlighted her firm shoulders and her smooth back. The five-tier pearl choker accentuated her graceful neck. Carlos wore a black Hugo Boss double-breasted suit. They were a handsome couple in the picture. On a following page, she saw Carlos at the Bankers' Breakfast at the Grand Bay Café in Coconut Grove, surrounded by his colleagues. Many of her friends appeared in the society pages as well. Lucinda and her friends used to call each other over the phone and talk of all the attention they were given, especially the Colóns. They were young, well connected, and Dominican, an intoxicating brew for the Miami establishment. But for Lucinda, it was now all part of the scene, good publicity for the Bank, as Don Carlos referred to it.

She was about to close the magazine when something on its last page, the Miscellaneous Shots, caught her attention. In the collage of smaller photographs, in the lower left-hand corner of the page, was a small black-and-white image of Carlos and two women. The caption read, *Carlos Colón, of the Banco Dominicano Ltd., and Yolanda Sandoval with daughter, the sculptor Gabriela Sandoval, at the Lowe Art Museum, University of Miami.*

In the photograph, Carlos stood stiffly between the two women; on his right stood the older woman, squarely facing the camera. On his left was the sculptor, her slender body slightly leaning to him. Her face was toward Carlos, while her eyes glanced at the camera. Lucinda was used to seeing Carlos with women in these society pictures. Many of them were business types or wives of business associates. All of them betrayed their desire to be seen with a bank president at their side. They were photographed with an arm around his waist, grabbing his elbow, or locked arm in arm, always facing the camera, as if saying, "Look at me with so and so."

But there was something different in this picture, thought Lucinda. The young woman was not posing. She looked like she was not worried about appearances. Lucinda read what the young woman did. She was a sculptor. In the picture, she was dressed in a light-colored, thin-strapped summer dress with raffia sandals. Her hair was bunched into a loose bun just off the back of her neck.

Lucinda bit into the last sweet pastry from the tray. Looking out to the bay, she noticed its flat sea, the morning breeze having subsided. The mid-morning sun settled over the low hazy clouds. The humidity in the greenhouse began to smother her, and suddenly coffee was not appealing. Rising with the magazine still open to the last page, Lucinda focused on Carlos. He looked vulnerable.

Lucinda tore out the image of her husband, dropping the magazine on the table. The cup spilled over, the dark coffee staining the pages of the *Vida Social*.

Chapter 3

───∞∞∞───

María Mercedes Virtudes (Mercy)

Thank God for Cuban mothers: they never stop mothering around with you. If it wasn't for mamá's daily wake-up call this morning, I'd have been late to the penthouse sale. You know what I felt like this morning? I felt like an eighteen-wheeler with five tons of frozen Big Mac all-beef hamburger patties had run over me. I looked like roadkill in bed. I stayed out too long last night. Where was I? Club Hades on South Beach, the current "in place" for this season on Ocean Drive. My mother would freak, get taquicardia or something if she would ever step into such a place. That's why I bought the house way out in Kendall for her and the rest of the family. I live right on South Beach. Once in a while I go sleep over at mamá's. But I have a great ocean view from my place and the club scene está fantástico. Last night was Latins from Hell Night at the club. Ramón, mi novio—my cousin Isa calls him Mr. Momento, the boyfriend of the moment, but I know he's for real—insisted we go even though it was a Wednesday. I never party on weekdays, except for Thursdays and Fridays, but these count as the weekend here in Miami. On Wednesdays, Club Hades offers a three-for-one drink special if you show proof that you have Latin blood in you: what a gimmick in a place like Miami. Who's not Latino down here? Oye meng, even the *Miami Herald* had to bite the bullet and come up with *El Nuevo Herald*. Now you tell me who's supposed to read this, the Brady Bunch crowd? They're all packing their bags and moving north to Orlando. The color down here is getting too local for them. I myself don't like pasty-looking guys. They look like raw dough, limp churros with no sugar on top. I like mine nice and toasty with plenty of sugar all over them.

Ramón is like that. He's real sweet to me. What does he call me? Mi amor. Now you tell me that doesn't make you feel like a Corín Tellado/ Harlequin Romance queen. It does me every time he says it close to my ear. He gets close to my hips every time we dance, let me tell you. I love the way he sways his hips, especially on the slow dances. He's got good hips, the small kind with wide shoulders on top. He's lean and long muscled también, like a baseball player. His dark skin is smooth as honey, and let me tell you, so are his kisses. They feel like when you swallow a spoonful of honey, thick and easy on the mouth. Every time I dance with Ramón, I feel light and thin like one of those neo-anorexic supermodels everybody loves to see in *Ocean Drive* magazine but no one wants in a Cuban family. And the man can talk as smooth as he dances.

Last night the music was hot and so was Ramón. He just didn't want to go. But at three in the morning, with a ten a.m. appointment at the penthouse the next sunrise, I knew it was time to take off my glass slippers and go home before I crashed. Pero qué me pasó? Ramón tightened his grip on my waist and signaled to the DJ. The music got real slow, a nice drippy bolero about some lover waiting in the bohío for his little peasant girlfriend to return from the field. His hips started to sway and my heart started to go Ka-pung pumping the six rum and Cokes I shouldn't have had on a Wednesday night into my brain faster than Superman and that speeding bullet. "Let's not go yet, I got something else for you, mi amor," he said. So I didn't go. Let me tell you, he took me to a dark corner of the club, holding my hands real tender. I never felt so delicate in his hands, like a puppy in its mother's jaws. I was drunk, I was dizzy, and I was hoping that this time reality would stick. I saw the little black box in his hands, precious by the way he held it. "Look what I got for us," he said. I closed my eyes, swallowed my dream, and took a deep breath. I do, I do, I do. Then I looked. Qué carajo, I took two of the black pills from the little black box. The box disappeared and my hurt took a dive as I rose to the occasion. It was showtime! The music got hotter and so did I and so I stayed out too long for a Wednesday. But it was Thursday morning and my head was still in a haze, like when you've been under water too long and everything seems thick around you.

In the end I'm a pro. And after barely hearing my mother bless me on the phone, "Que Dios te bendiga!" like she does every morning, I made it on time to meet with the client and I was in the thick of it in the penthouse wishing I had said I don't, I don't, I don't.

"How many bat-rooms?" asked the Arab man, Lebanese I think he said.

"Excuse me?"

"How many bat-rooms?"

Qué carajo is this guy saying? Bat rooms, bat, bathrooms?!

"Six bathrooms. Plenty for your family, no? One for each kid and the big one for you and your wife."

"And how many bete-rooms?"

Jesus, here we go again. Was I this bad when I got to this country? I came to this country as a kid, no father, no brother, no sister, but a gluey mother and an aunt with three cousins, and what's the first thing I said in English? Coca-Cola. It was the only English I knew. I said it real carefully, like I didn't want to waste a drop of it. "Co-ca-Co-la." I said this to the big American Coast Guarder who rescued me from the sinking boat my Resident Alien uncle bought with a loan using his house as collateral to go to Cuba and claim his family. In 1980, this was possible. Let me tell you, to an

eleven-year-old, everything seemed possible in America. My
mother was always singing the praises of los Americanos. "In
America, no comunismo, no Fidel, and you can fart without having a comemierda reporting you to the neighborhood police." "Sí,
Mercedes, in America everything is sweet because there is a lot of
sugar everywhere! In the cakes, in the pies, in the coffee, in the
ice cream, in the bubble gum, and in the soda pop, especially in
the Coca-Cola!" I dreamt of this on a leaky twenty-foot boat in the
middle of the Gulf Stream in the dead of night. I said my prayers
and crossed myself. And when I was rescued from this dream, I
asked for a taste of America. And I got it! Ahí mismo on the water.
I still have the Coke can the Coast Guarder gave me that night. It
was my first taste of America. That sweetness in the can, coño,
mamá was right. After that, I made it a point to learn other important English words like c-a-n-d-y, F-r-i-t-o-L-a-y, b-o-y-f-r-i-e-n-d,
and m-o-n-e-y. Back then I didn't know a word of English from Arabic.

But, let me tell you, in real estate money cuts through all ac-
cents. I was trying to convince these Arabs that a penthouse on
Brickell Avenue with a panoramic view of the city and the bay,
close to the downtown financial district, and a short drive to the
Freedom Tower, which this guy owned, was the ideal place to
raise a large family in America. I opened the refrigerator and offered the kids Cokes. It gave me a few minutes to think. What was
it he was asking me?

Bete-rooms, betting rooms, game rooms?!

"There is a large den which we can turn into a game room," I
said, pointing to the room with the huge city view.

"Only one bete-room? This is no good." He was pointing to his
five children as he was saying this.

What did this guy want, a game room for each kid? Man, the
rich, especially the Arab rich, are different from you and me. This
presentation was going nowhere, I could tell. I was sweating the
details too much. I usually wrapped up a sale in under an hour
and on the spot, but with that guy and my headache and his lady

in black . . . All I could see were her eyes. I freaked out. Why was she all blacked out? Whenever I party I wear black. Black makes me look thinner. It's not that I am overweight, I'm just chunky, curvy chunky. Ramón calls me "La Voluptuosa." I like to accentuate my curves by wearing tight black miniskirts with black sleeveless turtlenecks. I always wear my metallic gold high-heeled sandals to dance. These are easy to take off when the dancing lasts into the morning hours and my feet swell up to where the skin hugs each strap as if holding on for dear life. Dangling from both my wrists midway to my elbows I wear at least a dozen gold bracelets and rings. I like the way these clink when I dance. They also catch the spotlights on my arms and I know everybody is looking. Last night was no different. I partied hard like I work hard. Except the next morning my head was still messed up. I wasn't working too well. I was having a hard time understanding the guy from the Land of Araby.

"One game room is not enough?"

"No game room. Bete-rooms, bete-rooms!" the Arab pointed at the kids, closing his eyes and tilting his head.

"Bedrooms! Of course, excuse my lack of concentration. It's just that I am recovering from a very bad cold and my ears are still ringing," I lied in my perfect English. "Let's see. There are seven bedrooms including the master bedroom."

"Show this master bete-room, please."

"Yes. Follow me." I walked toward the east wing of the apartment.

As we entered the room, I drew their attention to the one wall entirely made of glass, opening onto a terrace overlooking the sea. They were impressed by the breathtaking view. Miami always looks good from above. It looked good to us from below in Cuba. They noticed the love seat and the recliner facing the bay and the luscious king-size bed on the opposite side of the room. I led the man into the master bathroom, which also had a glass wall view. The Roman tub in there was large enough for six people. Maybe the entire family could take a bath together as they watched over the city. I looked at the lady in black and wondered how she took showers. I could've used a cold shower myself to shake off the night's blackness. I was highlighting the gold-plated faucets when a sun ray ricocheted off one of them and struck my right eye. I was blinded for a few seconds when I heard a crash back in the bedroom. Three of the kids were using the bed for a trampoline. One of them even did a backward flip in midair. That's when I noticed the broken Tiffany lamp on the floor.

"No problem. We pay," said the Arab. "Jasuf! Sit down!" He grabbed one of the boys by the arm and sat him straight up on the bed.

"As you can see, it's a strong bed," I said, taking advantage of the opportunity. "Now if you'll follow me to the gourmet kitchen."

Let me tell you, I was about to leave the master bedroom when the little girl started screaming her head off in the bathroom. We all ran back in. She had one hand in the black porcelain toilet. Her other hand was pointing to her older brother, in the Roman tub trying to hide.

"What did you do, Imran?" yelled the father, pulling the boy from the tub in one clean lift like a magician pulls a rabbit from a hat.

"Jamille, what wrong with you?" he said to the bawling girl.

It turned out the boy had flushed the little girl's gold and emerald bracelet down the toilet. Qué escándalo! The father started to yell in Arabic and I couldn't understand ni una papa of what he said. But let me tell you, his loud voice, the screaming girl, the sobbing boy, and the silent black sentinel of a lady were too much for my aching head. I excused myself from this domestic foreign scene in the bathroom only to run into the three boys in the bedroom making swan dives off the headboard into the bed.

Coño! Esto es de locos, I thought to myself. I made an exit to the living room balcony. I needed fresh sea air to clear my mind. I tried to get back my focus. This was a big deal for me. I could clear at least $60,000 on this sale alone. These didn't come a realtor's way too often, let me tell you. I maybe got one or two of these a year. I'm used to selling condos on the beach and single-family houses in the suburbs. But once in a while, I get a few plums, like that penthouse listing. But what's $60,000 compared to a million-dollar headache? Never had I had such a bad one. Never. What the hell was wrong with me? I've always gone partying on the beach, coño, I live on the beach for the clubs and the men. The contacts with the rich and famous have made me a nice amount of cash. I have a knack for selling to people with a busy social calendar. I am always busy myself, looking for the right property for the right client and, if I'm lucky, the right guy for myself. But right then what I needed was the right head on my shoulders. Something was not right with mine.

Coño, Jesús, María y José! Those stupid pills Ramón gave me to keep me going. Pa' qué carajo did I take them? I pulled out my lightweight Sony cell phone and called mamá.

The phone rang but no one picked up.

I kept pounding the redial button.

"Mamá!"

"Mercedes! Qué pasó?"

"Where were you? I've been calling forever."

"Was that you? I was talking to your Tía Clara about Pepe's kidney stone. I heard the beep but I didn't know what to do."

"Ay mamá, I've explained it to you a million times!"

"Sí, but you know I hate all these fancy machines. En Cuba phones were so simple."

"Mamá, en Cuba the phones didn't work. I don't have time to talk about Cuba right now."

"Bueno, y qué pasó? Where are you?"

"I'm at the penthouse in Brickell and I'm feeling sick. I don't think I can go through with this."

"María Mercedes Virtudes, pull yourself together."

"I can't, mamá. These people are crazier than the nuts from that crazy house Mazorra. Además, I don't understand the man's English. I can tell he doesn't like me, una pushy Cubana. You should see his wife dressed in black, all covered up, never talking."

"Mercedes, you have dealt with all kinds of clients before; since when are you worried what they think about you?"

"Mamá, my head feels like a horse is trying to kick my brains out of it. I can't think straight. I'm just going to call the whole thing off."

"You will do no such thing! You are not a quitter."

"I know, I know, but this is different. Anyway, I have to go. I just wanted to know if I could come over today to spend the weekend."

"But it's only Thursday."

"I know, but I don't want to go back to the empty apartment."

"Claro que sí, mijita. This is your house. You don't have to ask. I'll have your room ready."

"OK, mamá, I got to go. Call you later."

I took a deep breath. That's what I like about living in Miami, the air was still clean on most days and the ocean salt was good for my Cuban lungs. I was ready to go back in. I glanced at my watch and noticed the time. I might as well wrap it up as a lost morning. But not before the guy paid for that Tiffany lamp. As for the girl's bracelet, well, he could just hire Roto-Rooter and snake the entire thirty-floor sewer pipe. "No problem, we pay," I could just hear the guy saying.

"My father wants to see you now," said one of the boys, rushing on the balcony. Great, what next, the lady got frozen in the walk-in freezer? I imagined a giant black Popsicle standing three feet behind this guy, the kids taking turns making her disappear with every lick. I wished I could disappear from this scene too. In these situations, I knew how to disengage. I would shake hands firmly, smile, and offer to meet at another more convenient time with them. The send-off was just a delayed done deal. Mamá was right; I never quit on any client. But that day I just wanted to get the hell out.

I followed the boy to the dining room, where the rest of the family was seated waiting for me. The man wore a stern look on his face, the kids were straight-backed on the chairs, and for the first time, the lady in black was looking at me square in the eyes. Now I am in tremendo lío, I thought to myself; this had to be bad news.

The Arab placed his leather briefcase on the table, opened it facing me, and said, "How much for deposit?"

The cash in the briefcase caught me by surprise. Even my headache forgot to ache for the moment.

"A deposit? Well, yes, the deposit. That's perfect. But we can't do that here. We need to schedule an appointment for that at the office." I was scrambling for words.

"Soon, we want move in soon," insisted the man.

"Soon, yes, very soon. Talk to your lawyer. I'll call you Monday morning. I'll have all the paperwork ready." I was rushing through this. There was no need to please this guy anymore; I had to get out.

With that and a last quick look around the penthouse, we shook hands and parted, the father leading his five kids with the melting mother picking up the rear.

I always have my emergency overnight bag in the trunk of my yellow Miata. With a pair of blue jeans, my oversize Miami Heat sweatshirt, my red sneakers, my Victoria's Secret nighty, an extra pair of panties, and my bathroom stuff, I'm ready to drive anywhere anytime. But right then, I needed to go to mamá's in Kendall. I needed to get away from the Beach scene. That night was too much, too much booze, too much Ramón, and too much messing around with my head.

In Miami you don't need street signs to know where you're going. All you have to do is look at the passing store names. On the Beach, you see Calvin Klein, Armani, Dry Clean USA, and Bagel Emporium; as you head west, you get Sedano Supermarket, Perez Auto Repair, Latin American Cafeteria, and Nena's Casa de Belleza hair salon. I was home.

"Hola, mamá."

"What do you want to eat? I have arroz con pollo on the stove and I can fry some sweet plátanos for you . . . pero, hija, you look terrible . . . I'll make a Spanish stew . . . Pepe is going to the hospital for his kidney stone . . . I'll put some kidney beans in the stew . . . Y Ramoncito? . . . Did you make a lot of money on the penthouse?"

Chapter 4

━◦◦◦━

Julia Velásquez

$\mathcal{M}$oby Dick. Think about it. What does it mean?" asked Julia.

"A big whale?" answered one of her students.

"Yes, yes, that's obvious. But why that name?"

"It's a penis!" blurted out a young female student.

"It's a whale of a penis!" shouted one of the boys in the back.

The whole class broke out in laughter.

"Sex does have a lot to do with it." Julia walked around the podium to approach the class. "Sex is what is behind it, but what does Ahab's obsession with Moby Dick represent? Anyone?"

"The male competitive drive?" answered one girl.

"Yes," said Julia, "the male urge to conquer, to take complete possession of another. In this case, to take possession of the feminine threat as represented by the whale, Moby Dick."

"But Professor Velásquez, Moby Dick is a male," said a student.

"Sure, but really a male in female disguise. Moby Dick is nature, Mother Earth, the thing that Captain Ahab and his whaling world live off of. Do you see?"

Several students shook their heads.

Julia continued. "The whale nurtures him; it is his reason for living. But he resents this. It controls him, and he cannot tolerate this power of the whale over him. So he has to dominate it, even to the point of destruction."

"A whale in drag!" shouted the same boy. Julia saw that it was Manuel.

"A whale dressed in white, for a whale of a wedding," said Julia, laughing. "But it doesn't matter if the whale is male or female. What matters is that the whale represents Nature, plus it is a white whale. This color usually symbolizes purity, peace, warmth—think of mother's milk—all characteristics associated with our feminine side."

"So Ahab hates all women and wants to kill them off," said another girl in the front row.

"Not exactly. He just wants to show who's the boss. Remember, Moby Dick took one of his legs. He is, literally, less of a man because of it. His masculinity has been mutilated."

"What does all this have to do with fishing? Isn't this just a great fish story?" asked Manuel from the back of the lecture hall.

This always happened in the course, thought Julia. Her feminist take on the Great American Classics made many of her male students nervous and defensive. She always had little Ahabs in the making, Julia thought as she looked at her watch. She had a few minutes to wrap this up before the end of class.

"Sure. It's a great fish story, like *The Old Man and the Sea*, but it's more than that," added Julia, sitting on the front edge of her desk. The beige ankle-length khaki skirt flowed over her crossed legs, stopping at her black leather clogs. She never wore stockings. They were too hot for Miami's climate. The loose cotton shirt was gathered at her waist by a thick black leather belt. She had the habit of rolling up her sleeves toward the end of the class. This exposed the few pieces of jewelry she wore. Julia enjoyed going to secondhand stores looking for Native American jewelry with unusual designs. She wore a wide solid bracelet of silver embedded with turquoise Aztec jaguar designs on her wrist, and framing her open face dangled a pair of matching earrings.

"That's what you're all going to write about for next week."

A wave of grunts circled the classroom.

"In a 600-word typed essay, write about the significance of the last scene, when the whale takes Ahab down with it. Who was the real hunter? Be specific. Also remember to start reading *The Scarlet Letter.* Pay particular attention to the way the men treat the women in this story. Any questions? No? Then see you next week."

Julia briskly got up from the desk and started to pick up her papers. She had wanted to leave early to meet Felipe for lunch. As she grabbed her briefcase, a student approached her. She noted it was Manuel from the back row, who had shouted out wisecracks during the class. She had noticed him before, a Mexican-American like herself, one of the few at the University of Miami, where she had been teaching for five years.

"Miss Velásquez, do you have a minute?"

Julia didn't like to turn students away, even when she was in a hurry. She put her briefcase down. "Sure, Manuel."

"The problem is, I don't know why you waste your time teaching this white man's garbage. We are Chicanos. We have to stick together. You are wasting your time and mine." As he spoke, Manuel got closer to Julia and she found herself pressed against the blackboard.

"I used to think like you, Manuel, but I have realized we need to know the insides del monstruo, whatever the monster might be, white, or male." Julia felt uncomfortable with his closeness. She could almost smell his breath.

He wasn't much taller than Julia, but he had a broad back and an intensity in his dark eyes that penetrated right through her. His eyes reminded her of the Mexican-American boys she had gone to school with back in San Antonio. They were hungry eyes. The Tex-Mex boys were always after her. She was a challenge to them. She preferred a long day with a girlfriend or a book to their sloppy kisses. Julia remembered her first kiss. It happened on an eighth-grade field trip to The Alamo. She and Marcelo, the other straight-A student besides herself, were sitting in back of the bus when he asked to kiss her. She agreed to the kiss, but what she felt was Marcelo's hands on her breasts. They had made her breasts feel cold.

"Plus, Manuel, as Mexican-Americans we can claim this heritage as well. We should expand our horizons, not limit ourselves."

"Sure, you say that because you've been bought off. You have been co-opted by the system." Manuel stepped even closer, trying to dominate her with his presence more than his words.

Julia began to lose her patience. "Listen, Manuel. It's not a matter of being co-opted. It's a matter of educating yourself. Plus Anglos don't have a monopoly on male domination." Julia squirmed her way around Manuel, not wanting to touch him.

"Is your boyfriend a gringo?"

"It's none of your business, Manuel."

"He isn't, is he? We have to stick together. We have to protect La Raza." Manuel's deep husky voice savored each word.

Julia found herself drawn by Manuel's passion. She reached for her copy of *Moby Dick* on the desk. He put his hand on it first, stopping her from picking it up.

"I'm proud of La Raza too, Manuel." Julia leaned over to pick up her briefcase. Manuel followed her movements. He watched her long black hair, straight and thick, drop over her shoulders as she reached down.

"Listen, Manuel. This is an important discussion, but not for now."

Her hair was parted on the side, partially covering one of her eyes, its loose strands caressing her high cheekbones. Julia felt like Manuel was stroking her hair with his eyes. She needed to cut loose.

"Come by the office next week," said Julia in a harsher tone than she would have liked.

"Sí, Profesora." Manuel looked like a wounded Ahab.

Julia looked at her watch and knew she was late for lunch with Felipe. He had sounded childish on the phone, repeating, "You'll see, you'll see," when she asked why such a nice place, why in the middle of the day, why all the mystery? Felipe was not the playful type.

"Hi, Felipe, sorry I'm late." Julia kissed his lips. She could taste the chardonnay he was drinking.

"This is my second glass. Another student?"

"I meant to end the class early, but I got carried away with *Moby Dick* and I was being hunted by a student." Julia smiled as she sat down. The waiter brought her a wineglass.

"I hope he survived. You know, Julia, the world needs men even if just to procreate."

"Well, I've needed you for three years, but not to procreate. Let's drink to that." They clinked their glasses. "So why are we here, Felipe?"

"Let's order first." He handed her the French menu.

Place St. Michel was not one of their regular eating places, especially for lunch. Julia had eaten there once before, when she first arrived in Miami. Her new colleagues at the university had taken her out for a welcome dinner. But Julia and Felipe usually met for lunch at more casual bistros on Miracle Mile near the Mexican Consulate. Felipe Juárez was the Consul for Mexico stationed in Miami.

As Julia read the appetizers at the top of the menu, she glanced over at Felipe. She liked his jet-black hair and the way it always fell over his forehead. That's what she had noticed when they first met. It was three and a half years ago at Books and Books, during a reading by Laura Esquivel, the Mexican author of *Like Water for Chocolate*. A mutual friend, Mitchell Kaplan, the owner of the bookstore, had invited Felipe to introduce the author. As he read from his prepared notes, Julia noticed his hair falling over his forehead. For a Consul with such a serious appearance, it made him look boyish.

But now, in the elegant French restaurant, he was acting boyish. He looked over at her and, smiling, said, "Ready?"

"Yes."

Julia chose an asparagus salad followed by a crepe filled with shrimp in a light buttery sauce; Felipe preferred tenderloin sautéed in a white mushroom sauce. He poured another glass of wine for her.

Julia waited as he poured the wine into his glass, then said, "Come on, Felipe, what's all the secrecy? It's not like you to keep me in the dark."

"Some things need to be said at the right time and place."

"Is something wrong?"

"No, the opposite. I have two items of good news to share with you." He broke a piece of his bread.

"Tell me," insisted Julia.

"The first thing is that I have been offered the position as director of the Pre-Columbian Archeological Museum in Guadalajara."

"Fantastic!" Julia said too enthusiastically. She settled her emotions and asked, "When did you find out?"

"Monday. I got a call from Cancio Domínguez."

Julia remembered Cancio from her stay in Guadalajara. He was the head of cultural affairs for the city. She was there last spring as a guest lecturer giving a talk on the future of Latinas in the United States. A pleasant man, she thought, but with loose hands. They were always on her for one reason or another, feeling like clinging lizards on her flesh.

"That was two days ago. Why wait to tell me now?"

"Well, I wanted to think about it, and I wanted to tell you in a special place."

"What's to think about? You've been hoping for this job all your life. You'll be going back"—Julia hesitated—"back to your hometown."

Felipe had grown up in Guadalajara, on the west coast of Mexico. He studied cultural anthropology at the University of Mexico and later at Arizona State. His research on the Chichimec tribe, ancestors of the Aztec civilization, earned him respect in his field but, as he told Julia, no money.

"Well, it's a big change. This is a job with a permanent place. The museum will become my world."

"You've always had your head in museums. I think you became a diplomat just to visit more museums," Julia reflected sadly, more to herself than to him, realizing the strain this would put on them.

"Felipe, it's a great opportunity, but this will create a problem for us, for our relationship."

"The job is not going to be a problem. I want the job."

"There's another problem?"

"Give me your hands."

Julia reached over and placed her hands in Felipe's. She felt his soft, supple hands in hers. They were a thinker's hands, she thought. He wrapped his thumbs over her knuckles and she felt the pressure increase.

"Marry me."

Three years, thought Julia. Three years with Felipe, comfortable, convenient, and compatible. How many nights spent at each other's apartment? That was the arrangement. It fell into place; the routine was to have no routine. He kept his apartment in the French Villas in Coral Gables; you kept your space in The Pathways, in South Miami. The names of the places even fit the script. Two different places, two separate but equal lives, each sovereign over itself. Your time with him felt like cultural encounters, a taste of each other's world. How many conversations about the world over restaurant dinners? How many trips to places married couples only dream about? Your work and his made it easy to travel: the summer trip spent driving, flying, hiking all over Mexico as he charmed his way through the state capitals; the time spent in the northeast, train hopping New England while you were on that book tour. You spent time and effort building the ideal relationship, you risked it all on one man. Felipe was your match. He was attractive enough, with his Spanish/Aztec looks and his worldly mind. You never met a guy who could read and talk about your books like him, who wasn't turned off by your ideas. He was polite, respectful. He always supported your space, your need to write, to be alone, to think. You went along with his life, his need to be unattached too. How many times had you met him at his endless cocktail parties, his diplomatic functions, the cultural affairs of Miami? Days went by and you never saw him. The phone was the marital bed; the pillow talk was like feathers, floating light, always interesting, always new, always pleasant. Sex was pleasant. Like an old jacket that always fit. You wore it on occasion. Sex was not central, not domineering, not messy. Felipe never pushed. A thinker's hands don't grope. He did not wear his machismo on his sleeve, nor under his pants. Three years. That's how long it took Ahab to get his whale. No, Felipe was not a hunter. But now, across the table, was there an Ahab wanting the harpoon to stick?

"Marry me. Come with me to Guadalajara. You've only been a part of my life, now be my whole life," Felipe said, still holding her hands. The waiter came to clear the table. Julia pulled her hands away.

"Your wife?"

"Yes. Say yes."

Yes to what, thought Julia. To marriage? And then what? Kids, neighbors, kitchens? Finding time to write between Pampers? A husband with an office? A routine of chores, domestic duties, spending fifty weeks waiting for two weeks to escape? Mexico? You spend three years shaping a relationship around your life, thinking this man understands you, wants you just the way you are, and now these two words. Were you wrong? Is the pact broken? You go your way, I go mine, and when we want to, we fall in love all over again. It worked for three years. Never stated, never written on paper, but just as legal and just as true. At thirty-nine, a professor, an author, a life made of experiences, a life of saying yes to changes, to accommodations, to yourself. Could she say yes this time, wondered Julia, watching Felipe rub his fingers on the stem of the empty wineglass.

Goya, her mother's maid, used to clean the glassware that way. She was hired to work twice a month cleaning the entire house.

It was a Victorian two-story house in the historic district of San Antonio. Her father bought it from an American couple who retired to Mexico. He lovingly restored it to its original condition. Goya lived on the outskirts of the city. She only cleaned four houses a week. Not enough to earn a decent living from. She made up the difference by being a Curandera, a soother of the soul. With her herbs and ointments, and her sacred statues, Goya would heal the troubled ladies who came to her for a consultation. Julia's mother used to tell her that a few of the neighbors visited Goya. Her mother never did. But Julia knew this already. Often she would walk Goya to the bus stop three blocks away. Sometimes Goya would stop at a neighbor's house and listen, then she would brew yerbabuena tea and give out her advice. Julia always listened to her words. The Curandera's words were clear as glass. She could use the Curandera now. What would she say to her? thought Julia.

"I can't answer you, Felipe. I need time to think."

Chapter 5

⸺ৎৡৡ⸺

Isabel

I got La Visita last night. That's what mami calls my period. Some visit. Like it was a good friend coming over for coffee. Well, this amiga comes over every month like clockwork. Coño, they can set Big Ben in London by my period in Miami. To me, PMS means Pretty Much Shitty. That's how I feel when I get my period. La Visita always comes on a full moon too. I feel like a werewolf. I want to tear everything to pieces. Howling at the moon is what David did during our last year of marriage. I went to counseling and he joined a men's group called The Night Howls. Once a month, during the full moon, he and his hombres would trek to some rural hilltop and howl at the moon. Idiotas. I would stay home and pray they all got La Visita. Then they'd have something to howl about. But last night I was doing the howling. I couldn't get any sleep. No matter how I turned the venetian blinds, the light kept flooding the bedroom. And ever since my parents moved in with me, mami has been brewing her nightly café cubano for me. I never drank the stuff until I moved to Miami. Now I drink it for breakfast, three times during work, after work, and finally before bed. "Cafecito makes the world go round," papi would say as mami filled his thermos with the thick, sweet, black fluid whenever he had to do the night shift at the foundry. Here in Miami, it's what keeps me going. If chocolate is the drink of the Gods, then Cuban coffee is the Devil's brew. Last night with the moon out, La Visita on my bed, and the coffee in my eyes, I could have used an exorcist or a silver bullet, probably both.

I got the alarm clock instead. It is supposed to sound like one of those birdcalls, Mother Nature cooing, but it reminded me of David's howling. In my house, by the time I get up, everything is set in motion. Already, David Jr. is pressed in his khaki pants, the white Oxford button-down shirt with the green tie and the school's monogram. Sam is dressed exactly like his older brother, except that he looks like he came out of the washer with his clothes on. With Sam, permanent press is an oxymoron. Mami is up at dawn, clanking in the kitchen, the cafecito aroma filling the house as she prepares breakfast. One of the benefits of live-in parents. Papi is still snoring, most likely because he stayed out late at the cockfights with Pepe, Mercy's uncle. And me? I get dressed in one of my usual pantsuits, grab an espresso, and haul the boys to school. This happens every morning, as precise as a Swiss Army watch. Timing is the virtue of single motherhood—or the curse. The boys have gotten used to my system. But that morning I was out of it, and David Jr. kept insisting on rehearsing his lines for the school play, *Romeo and Juliet*. I was in no mood to hear Romeo's love song to Juliet under a moonlit sky. The moon had kept me up all night.

Why is it that single men don't give up? The first thing I saw coming into my office was Dorothy with a letter in her hand and a bunch of flowers—more like a monument—on my desk. "Tropical Temptations" by FTD—gingers, birds of paradise, and anthuriums, nothing but flowers with protrusions? It looked like a monument to lust.

"Buenos días, Ms. Landon."

"Good morning, Dorothy. Who sent these? Don't tell me."

"They were here first thing this morning. The deliveryman just left. It came with this envelope."

"Is it dripping with sap?"

"What?"

"Never mind."

Encore Rubén

Querida Isabel,

    My heart breaks as a wave on a moonlit shore every time I read your note. A lover suffers, but like a lighthouse on the horizon, I want to guide you to safety. I know you have seen my love beam; you fleetingly acknowledged my floral signal. Your reply is all right with me, for prudence speaks well of a passionate woman. I treasure your words like a rare pearl in its oyster shell. My own passion rises with each full moon. You are my moon, Isabel, but I am not content with a monthly visit. Please accept my invitation to dinner this Friday. I will not sleep until I hear your voice.

                Your admirer,

                Rubén

Everywhere I turned, I got mooned. The curse of the were-woman?

"Dorothy! Get Jeff Miller on the line. Find out if he's still giving away those two tickets to the Heat's exhibition game this Sunday."

Jeff was my first Americano friend in Boxer. He saw me through the corporate-infested waters. He was the only man to treat me as an engineer from the start. It helped that his love interests are overseas. His current girlfriend is a Chinese tour guide he met on a Boxer Opportunity Trip to China. While pushing the virtues of Boxer's catheters to the Chinese Sub-Secretary of National Health on a tour of the Great Wall, Jeff was also pushing himself on the tour guide. And like he says, she pushed back. To Jeff, love is a three-letter word, fax. Now they fax each other nightly. Maybe I should fax Rubén to kingdom come. Carajo, these flowers are sticking out all over the place, like the viejo verde on the crowded bus when I was a teenager. This old guy kept pushing himself on me. I would feel something hard against my thigh. He always said it was a banana in his pocket. When I told mami, she blew her top. "Plátano?! Eso es un viejo verde enfermo!" The next day she came on the bus with me and, holding a pair of scissors, glared at the horny old man. He got the message, and so did I. I had to nip this Rubén in the bud, even if he was my own kind, like Mercy said.

What poison could I take to get this Romeo off my back? A dinner invitation? No way. Nunca. No. Unless it's business, with a colleague, in a large group, I don't do dates. Well, Rubén was a colleague, but only once a month, regular as La Visita except that he comes in the daytime. And then just as big a pain. But if I didn't meet with him, he'd keep sending those ridiculous flower arrangements. And to the office, no doubt. What next, the "Daisies Do Dallas Bouquet" by FTD? Never in a million years.

"Rubén García, please. Rubén, this is Isabel Landon from Boxer. I just received your flowers, thank you again. About the dinner invitation."

"Sí, I was thinking we could go to Place St. Michel in the Gables. The French food is poetry for the taste buds."

Place St. Michel! Too moonish for my taste buds.

"Actually, Rubén, I'm busy Friday. But I have two tickets to the Miami Heat game on Sunday?"

"A basketball game?"

"Sure, don't you like basketball? My father loves it."

"I had something else in mind. But if you want to go, it's fine with me."

"Perfecto. Then it's all set. It's an afternoon game starting at three. Can you be at my house by two?"

"An afternoon game? Pero, Isabel, I was thinking maybe something more intimate, just you and me."

"Rubén, these are luxury box seats. We won't be with the crowd."

"All right, Isabel, I'll be there at two."

So I hung up with Rubén and se acabó lo que se acabó. It was done. I could tell by the tone of his voice he was at half moon. Coño, this dating thing was turning out to be hard work. David and I dated for a year and that was almost twenty years ago. When was the last time I turned a guy down? Or turned a guy on for that matter? Place St. Michel, it's got one of those intimate little hotels on top, with little European rooms big enough for two, but not for me. I spent the rest of the week working on the design proposal for the Chinese catheters.

Exit Rubén

On Sunday, Rubén picked me up in his gray 1997 Saturn. He beeped the horn before knocking at the door. There he stood, with his gray pants, black shoes, and coatless white shirt, with flowers in his hands. I took the daisies and gave them to mami, who was standing behind me, giving Rubén the look-over. The boys were in the back playing basketball, so I didn't have to deal with that. On the way to the Miami Arena, Rubén played a Julio Iglesias CD. His greatest hits. As we neared the arena, Julio was moaning to all the girls he's had before. Viejo verde. I noticed that Rubén wore his thinning black hair just like Julio's, back and a bit plastered. I can count on my hands the words Rubén said in the car. Poetry on paper but not in motion.

We arrived five minutes into the game. The company luxury box was empty, so before Rubén got any intimacy ideas, I opened the big glass windows. Just then Alonzo Mourning blocked a slam dunk attempt by Allan Houston. Instantly I had 20,000 people sitting next to us. Papi would often tell mami, "For teenagers, the cure for sex is sports." He was right. Well, for Rubén the effect was like visiting the holy waters at Lourdes. Cured with a capital C. We ordered pizza and Cokes and I did all the talking. After attempting to engage him in various topics—the weather, the soccer finals in Buenos Aires, the movies, the latest International Quality Standards for Medical Products, my job, his job—and getting just nods and sí's—I was tempted to give him a pad and pen, but I remembered his two letters—I gave up and cut to the chase.

"Rubén, the flowers you sent brightened up the office."

"Qué bueno, Isabel."

"In all fairness, Rubén, I must tell you that I am not interested in a relationship. With work and the boys, I have no time left for anything else."

"You must think of yourself."

"I do. I am doing exactly what I want. Right now in my life I want to focus on my work and on my kids."

"But you are too young to deny yourself. You must take care of yourself. I can take good care of you, Isabel."

That's all I needed, a Head Nurse for my first date in two decades. I nursed David for years. Out of the two, I earned the higher grades. I got the first chemical engineering job fresh out of college, I made the contacts in Santo Domingo, and all the while I held David's hand. Look how I got taken care of. For my efforts, I was awarded the Purple Heart, except my medal was black and blue. And there I was, paying for everything and having to listen to this reluctant Romeo. Damn it, I'm no Juliet.

"Listen, Rubén. I appreciate your concern, but I am fine. I am doing exactly what I want, when I want to."

"You must be lonely."

"I'm not. The boys, my parents, my friends, they keep me busy. I have no shortage of love around me."

"It's lonely without a man to help you."

"Rubén, if your intentions with me are to pursue a relationship which I do not want, then we cannot continue our friendship as it has been. As a matter of fact, I'll be forced to ask for your resignation from the Chemical Engineers Association. I mean it. I can't go to the meetings thinking about where your head is at."

He kept coming back with one or two words; I kept pouring words on him.

By the time I finished talking, the Cokes were flat, the pizza was cold, and the Knicks were losing. Rubén sat like a limp daisy in a restaurant bud vase. I felt sorry for him. But I wasn't about to *English Patient* him. The sugar in that movie could take care of Miami's cafecito supply for the next 2,000 years. My nursing days were over.

Before Rubén could get a word in, Bill Travieso, the head of the Latin American Division at Boxer, walked in with Felipe Juárez. Felipe is the sweetest man I know. And charming enough to be the envy of every snake handler in India. He was there at Bill's invitation; Bill was trying to raise sales in Mexico. I know Felipe hates basketball, but he hates to say no even more. Just like a good diplomat. How long has he been going with Julia? Too long for my tastes. But Julia is a free Latina when it comes to relationships.

Julia and I met a few years ago at a get-together at Lucinda's house. Lucinda is the only friend I've kept from my Dominican days. I'm not the muchas amigas type. To me, friends are like a few good books, the more you re-read them, the more you get attached. Lucinda and Julia are two of my best-sellers. Julia is a best-selling writer. Writes about women and says the truth, I like that about her. What does she say? Better alone than in bad company. I can relate to that. But she's lucky. She has Felipe and they are a solid couple—in their own way. I could never live with a man. No matrimonio, no nada. I'm an old-fashioned Cubana in that way. But Julia is like a Mexican-American Murphy Brown, secure, successful, and single, yet without the acid tongue and the hard look that comes with it. I noticed Rubén giving me a look, so I introduced him to Felipe and Bill as an engineer colleague of mine—for safe measure. Bill has a big mouth when it comes to the company chitchat. Back at the office, Dorothy has him pegged as Billy the Lip. I let her get away with it because she's right. Julia says that when a man gossips, he's seen as being concerned about his fellow workers, but when a woman does it, she's being a bitch. Well, if I had a dime for every time I saw a gossip in a suit and tie, I'd buy these men the latest Herrera outfits and book them on a talk show. "Today on *Cristina:* Corporate America, from Drags to Riches!" Pero Dios, look at me, I'm thinking like Julia and sounding like Murphy Brown! I pray to God I don't get a hard look on my face. Felipe had a strange look on his face when I asked him about Julia. I hadn't seen her in a while and I asked what I thought would be an easy question. By the way Felipe answered, I could tell something was up. To my surprise, he gave me a straight explanation, something I thought was genetically impossible for a diplomat. When Rubén heard the story, especially the Place St. Michel part, he wilted some more, but the roar after the three-pointer that Tim Hardaway of the Heat made over Patrick Ewing was more than enough to drown his sorrow. Julia had hedged. I never took her for the diplomat, especially when it came to Felipe. He was leaving in a few weeks and he was confident he'd be a married man.

Diplomacy is the language of divorced married couples. David and I spent years talking in circles. And if you're a Latina, it's in your genes. Your mother, and her mother, and her mother all spoke in circular tongues. To this day, when papi gets home late, mami says, "Your food is cold," and then goes and heats it up for him. Eso es todo. It makes for a warm belly but, for many, a cold marriage. I could have told David that our marriage was getting cold, but in the tropics, cold is a relative thing. The sun makes everything seem warm and bright, even in a winter gale. But no amount of sun can melt the snow of a Kansas winter. I keep a picture of David, in a frozen cornfield with snow up to his nostrils, on my mental credenza. It keeps me warm.

The Knicks were sweating from all the Heat around them. The game was a rout. I asked my floral first date if he would mind taking me home early. Bill and Felipe stayed on. La verdad es que I don't like easy wins. It's not that I make things hard for myself. But if something comes too easy, it blunts you. And like mami used to say as she chopped her onions, "Isa, the best knife is a double-edged one."

I noticed Rubén took the long way home. I guess he wanted to prolong the date as much as he could. I didn't see how he could hope for anything more with me. This time he didn't say a word. I had one more thing to say and I said it.

"Rubén, por favor, no more letters and no more flowers."

"Está bien, Isabel."

As we neared my house, he put on one last song, from a Gloria Estefan CD. We said our good-byes to Gloria's "It Cuts Both Ways." I reminded him of the coming Association lunch. He said he couldn't make it; he said he was busy, and he didn't say gracias. Definitely my mother's scissors came in handy, and Gloria did a fine job with that tune.

Chapter 6

———❦———

Lucinda

When Carlos Colón came home from the bank, Lucinda was waiting for him, alone. She had Rosario take Brenda and Roberto, along with the González' kids, to dinner and the movies at The Falls shopping center, a favorite with the wealthy Latinos of Miami and far enough away from Cocoplum to give Lucinda time for the night she had in mind.

"Lucinda, where are the kids?"

"Everybody is out. We have the entire house to ourselves."

"Are we going out somewhere?" Carlos noticed her tight blue jeans, with the black suede high-heeled boots, the matching belt, and the white spandex top. Lucinda wore it with her shoulders exposed. Her hair was wrapped into a long French braid.

"I thought we would stay home alone for a change. Is that OK with you?"

Before Carlos could answer, Lucinda took the briefcase from his hand and walked to the den. She pressed the play button of the Bang and Olufsen CD player. The house was filled with the sensuous sounds of a bossa nova by Antonio Carlos Jobim. The bank decorator had had the idea of installing stereo speakers in every room of the house. Tonight was the first time these were ever used all at once.

"Why don't you go upstairs and get out of that uniform you are wearing?" Lucinda coyly asked Carlos, looking at his usual dark suit and wine-colored tie. "Get into something easier to take off."

"Lucinda, qué está pasando aquí?" Carlos asked as he headed for the stairs.

"Nothing is going on. Can't a married couple spend a romantic evening alone with each other without an agenda to consult?"

I remember when Carlos and I were always alone. I remember when we broke away from our parents, when we flew to New York and landed in each other's arms and that's all we had. We made a picture-perfect love affair. That's what he said to me the first night we made love. But what is he giving me now? A picture in a magazine that has grabbed my heart like a spider's web and I can't shake loose of it. Pero, is it in his heart?

"You're right." Carlos ascended the marble staircase loosening his tie, his throat still feeling tight. He looked down at his wife, wondering what was on her mind. Reaching the bedroom, he sat at the foot of the bed and began to undress.

He came down in a pair of khaki pants, an open beige short-sleeved shirt with a white T-shirt underneath, and brown leather sandals. When he walked into the dining room looking for Lucinda, he was taken by the mood she had set. Lucinda had dimmed the lights and lit the candles in the bronze sconces accenting the formal mirror. In the center of the table, she had filled the Baccarat crystal bowl with floating candles and gardenias. The flickering flames, the scent of gardenias, and the seductive melody caressed the room. Carlos hesitated in the doorway. They hadn't eaten alone in the formal dining room in years. Lucinda pretended not to notice his surprise and motioned for him to sit down.

She had asked Rosario to prepare Carlos' favorite dish, London broil, and she had bought a bottle of Gran Vin de Chateau Latour, his favorite red wine. They ate slowly and talked about the kids and the bank. The wine took its effect on Carlos. Lucinda noticed how much softer he looked. The candlelight rounded out his sharp banker's creases, and the music lifted the bank's weight off his shoulders. She could see more of him, she thought, more of his New York days.

"Espérame aquí. Don't go anywhere." Lucinda rose from the table and caressed Carlos from behind, giving him an open kiss on the side of his neck. She could feel his muscles instantly relax. As she headed toward the kitchen door, Lucinda glanced back; she caught Carlos imagining her naked backside. She smiled. He saluted her with a swig of the last of the red wine in his glass.

When Lucinda brought out the chocolate mousse, she saw that Carlos had taken off his shirt and was barefoot. He still showed the contours of a disciplined body. The white T-shirt clung to his skin with the vibrancy of a twenty-year-old. Carlos' body did not betray his age or his profession. For a banker in his early forties, he looked as sculptured as a competitive swimmer. His daily morning visits to the gym paid off handsomely, thought Lucinda, as she kicked off her boots and sat down. They ate the dessert to the waning light of the candles, hardly saying anything to each other. This is the way it used to be, thought Lucinda, looking into his eyes. Carlos, for the first time in the evening, looked into hers.

I can remember a thousand and one nights like this, when the crust of La Familia and the patina of success had not attached itself to our love. How many art galleries did Carlos and I visit? At a reception, in a crowded room, we'd hold tight to each other. And when one of my painter friends managed to separate us, we'd lock eyes from across the room. We had X-ray vision. We'd always keep an eye on each other, no matter how packed the place got and no matter who got between us. Has he forgotten that we could see right through to each other? What was it that Jean-Paul Sartre called it, transparency?

Carlos lowered his eyes and pushed his chair away from the table.

"Lucinda," whispered Carlos, "what's going on?"

"We need to spend more time together." Lucinda walked

around to him and, before he could get up, started to massage his shoulders.

Her hands worked their way over his chest; he could sense her warm breath cascading down his back. He reached over and with his arms brought her face down to his. They kissed slowly, as if exploring each other's lips for the first time.

"Let's go upstairs." Carlos nibbled her ear.

"Está bien," whispered Lucinda. They started up the stairs. She held tightly to his waist, pleased with the night and how it was turning out.

"It's freezing in here!" said Carlos as they entered the master bedroom.

"I know, I lowered the temperature. Remember those cold nights in the flat in New York?"

On cold nights, when the steam heater was not enough, Carlos used to come to me, both of us naked under the covers. He used to wrap himself around me, and after our love, he'd fall asleep. Then I was his only blanket for the night. Solamente yo.

Carlos playfully nudged her toward the bed. They tumbled into it. He began to undo Lucinda's French braid, gently, one strand at a time. With each loosened strand, Lucinda felt herself more weightless, floating in a sea of children's dreams. She kissed Carlos fully on the lips, a hard kiss, meant to leave an imprint. She wrapped her arms around his stone-smooth back, groping beneath the T-shirt. Carlos, sitting upright, took it off. Lucinda propped herself on her elbows and watched him in silence. He began to undo her jeans but she stopped him.

"Espéra, Carlos, wait."

"Where are you going?"

"I am going to change, just for you." She walked into her dressing room, closing the door behind her.

The darkly shaded violet brassiere and laced bikini brief lay arranged on top of the birchwood cabinet table in the center of the dressing room. She had purchased them earlier that day at an upscale lingerie boutique. Next to these lay her crumpled white silk robe, just as she had left it from its morning use. Lucinda took her time getting undressed. She watched herself in the full-length mirror, glad to see she had inherited her father's svelte physique. She prided herself in her youthful appearance, even though she was approaching forty.

"Todo para lucir encantadora," anything to look enchanting, Lucinda said to herself, glancing one last time at the mirror. The dark violet of the undergarments made her light-colored skin radiant. And the thin straps highlighted the curves of her hourglass figure. One more thing was needed to complete the picture, she thought. As Lucinda reached for her robe, a small piece of paper fell from its pocket.

"Lucinda! What are you doing in there?"

"One more minute, ya voy, I'm almost ready."

Lucinda lifted the picture off the floor. She stared at it as she had done a hundred times since she had found it. She could feel the threads of the spiderweb tightening their grip around her heart. Her hands began to shake as she folded the picture neatly in half and placed it in the cleavage of her brassiere. Lucinda stepped out into the bedroom.

"I'm glad you took your time," said Carlos, pleased with her image. He was lying on his back, already undressed. She could see that he desired her. Lucinda straddled him and gently began touching him. She could feel the blood flowing in his veins, feel his pulse beating in her hands. Carlos closed his eyes. Lucinda fixed her gaze on his face.

Coño, what am I doing? I'm so angry at Carlos. His is the only face I've known on a bed, like this. The only face I've trusted, the only one I've loved. And now I have this picture in my bosom and I want to know the truth, but I don't trust him. You see, I saw his face in the photo; I saw his eyes and they were open and I saw his soul through them and it was vulnerable. I haven't seen him like that in years, ever since we made the damned move to Miami, and now I see him with a younger version of myself and I see him with me now and I want to know if I'm crazy or if he's cheating us out of a marriage. This picture is either going to make a fool out of me or it's going to break my heart; either way I lose, but there is only one way to find the truth. La verdad es lo que importa aquí and I don't know any other way because we have spent the years like lovebirds in a golden cage, except that we stopped chirping a long time ago. I want him to open his eyes like he used to, to take me to a secret place, but now I have a secret for him, and it's his secret.

Carlos didn't open his eyes. He lay entranced by Lucinda's touch. Her hands slowly and deliberately traveled over his flesh— his chest, his arms, his hips, his thighs, smooth and firm, so enticing, she too lost herself in their feel. Then, she kissed her way back to his torso until she reached Carlos' lips. Kissing, they rolled over; Carlos preferred to sense himself squarely over Lucinda, in control. He opened his eyes and began to savor her neck. She could feel his hands groping, trying to remove her straps. "Wait. It will be easier if I'm on top," Lucinda whispered. Her heart was choking. She closed her eyes.

As he removed her brassiere, Carlos went to kiss her breasts. The folded image fell from Lucinda like a dry leaf in winter, briefly grazing his lips, and then falling onto his chest, where the coils of his hairs snared it.

Carlos stopped moving in her. Lucinda opened her eyes and silently watched him as he took the image from his chest. She saw as his pupils adjusted themselves to the dim light in the room. She noticed how his smile slowly set itself on his face. She saw as his eyes rose from the image in his hands to meet her eyes. At that instant, Lucinda felt the life force between her legs diffuse itself as Carlos slowly lowered his eyes back to the image of himself with Gabriela Sandoval.

"You did it, didn't you. Coño, you did it to us. To us! Shit!" screamed Lucinda, as she jerked herself away from Carlos.

"Qué carajo? What the hell is this, Lucinda?" Carlos said, sitting on the edge of the bed. Lucinda was now standing on the other side, her nakedness revealing the tense muscles of her soul.

"No! You're not playing that one with me. Pendejo . . . you tell me what you see . . . there in your hands." Lucinda pointed to the picture, tasting the tears as they mixed with the saliva of her rage.

Carlos stood up, the light from the nightstand lamp silhouetting his naked body. Lucinda could just make out his expression; it gave her the sensation of facing a cornered beast.

"What's the matter, Carlos? Háblame!"

"Why? You want me to believe the stupid story you're weaving in your head? What kind of a fool do you take me for, Lucinda? I should have known you were up to something all night," shouted Carlos as he threw the crumpled paper on the bed. "Tell me right now what the hell is going on?! I can't believe this!"

"You don't believe this? I don't believe you. The truth was right there in that photo, carajo, it was right between my legs! You son of a bitch, you bastard."

"Damn it, Lucinda. I never knew you for having that kind of a mouth!"

"And what does your mouth have for her? Eh? Tell me, how do you talk to her?" Lucinda grabbed the wrinkled image from the bed and held it in her fist, jabbing it in his direction. Carlos reached over the bed and grabbed it from her hands. He sat with his back to her and, hunched over, held the picture under the light.

"Qué está pasando aquí?" Carlos asked under his breath.

"Something going on? You've got some nerve. That's what I want to know, what is going on with you?!" Lucinda shouted back as she put on her robe. She turned her back to him and stared out the window. The shimmer of the moonlight's reflection off the moist lawn reminded her of the snow she once felt safe in.

"I don't know what you are talking about." His calmness infuriated Lucinda, and the heat welled up inside her throat, bursting in a torrent of anger.

"Quién es? Who is she? Who is this woman in the photo you can't talk about? Eh? If she is nothing, then you tell me everything about her."

"Lucinda, do you know how many people I meet every day? I can't tell you about every one."

"You're still giving me that shit! Don't sit there and talk to me like that, like a banker, like a banker calculating his next move. I'm not a client, Carlos. I'm your wife, Dios mío, your wife with two children, your wife who has put up with your banker's mierda and your family's shit for too long, and now this?"

"It's just a publicity shot like any other. I don't have to give you any explanations."

"I want to meet her."

"What? Are you crazy? What are you talking about? You can't meet her. She doesn't live here. She lives en la capital. End of subject."

"Carlos, you had better respect this marriage. If not for me, for the children. Tell me the truth."

"Lucinda, you see one photograph in the paper and you come to all sorts of conclusions. What is the matter with you? You were never like this before."

"I was never like this? No, I wasn't. I didn't need to be. You were never like this yourself, hiding things from me!"

"I'm not hiding anything."

"I know you, Carlos."

"And I'm telling you, Lucinda, this has nothing to do with you or the children."

"So there is something going on?"

"I didn't say that. I said this has nothing to do with you. I have never done anything to threaten the stability of this family and I never will."

"So, that's what we've become to you, this family, La Familia." Lucinda's voice cracked from anger and frustration. "La Familia, carajo, where have I heard that before? Remember the Portuondos back on the island? He had a little maid to help him with his Familia. And remember the Carreños, eh? How many years did she put up with his little Doñita? No, Carlos, I'm no perfumed mango while you go find yourself a little artist to screw around with. Remember! Carajo, remember I was the little artist you fell in love with. What is happening to us? I hardly recognize us anymore," screamed Lucinda, trying to stop the tears, feeling humiliated at having compared herself to Gabriela Sandoval.

Carlos walked around the bed to Lucinda. He stood in front of her, holding her shoulders as they trembled with her unconscious breaths of pain. Lucinda buried herself in his embrace but did not release her crossed arms over her breasts. She could sense Carlos' heart racing, his chest trying to hold back his emotions.

With the moonlight filtering through the laced draperies, their nude bodies framed by the arched window, Lucinda looked up at Carlos.

"Tell me. Tell me to my soul that Gabriela Sandoval means nothing."

Lucinda saw tears, like silver mercury, well up under his eyes and form glistening streaks down his smooth face. She felt his arms slide off her and stop at his sides; she saw his shoulders start to shake.

"Cobarde . . . a coward to the end . . . pendejo, hijo de puta . . . you goddamned son of a bitch!" Lucinda began to strike at his chest, slapping it and then fisting it, and then slapping his face, his ears, his bowed head, all the while choking on the pieces of her broken heart.

I know Carlos, I saw his face. Since I first met him, when we were children, I sensed he was for me, for us. I didn't know Carlos, but I waited for him. He came like a soul-mate through time; my heart knew him before my mind ever did. But now, esto es monstruoso. He's a monster, a chicken-shit, lying bastard. I'm getting out, away, no words, no heart, no soul. I'm running on empty as far as hate will get me, para el carajo, to hell if that's what it takes.

In a frenzy, without really seeing what she was doing, Lucinda grabbed what she could of her clothes strewn on the floor. She scooped the picture from the mahogany nightstand and, naked except for the open white silk robe, ran out of the room and down the stairs to the garage. She entered and closed the door behind her. Lucinda leaned against it, breathing rapidly. She was struck by the nauseating smell of her perfume mixing with the stale car exhaust still lingering in the air. She dressed desperately, fumbling into her clothes. She rushed into the topless Jaguar and turned the keys in its ignition, where she always left them.

Lucinda wrestled with the garage-door opener and managed to back out just as the door opened. She skidded down the driveway gunning the engine as she raced toward the gates. Lucinda wildly pressed another button on the garage-door opener, but it was too late. The midnight-blue XK8 smashed through the hand-wrought iron gates, leaving them grotesquely twisted in the shape of a gaping mouth.

Chapter 7

Amigas

*I*sa, teléfono!" mami yelled from her bedroom on the other side of the living room.

"Quién es?"

"No sé. I think it's Lucinda?"

I had to interrupt Mercy in midsentence. She had stopped by on her way home from Pan American Hospital, where her uncle Pepe just had his kidney stone vaporized. As usual, she stayed for dinner. Mercy has a knack for pegando la gorra, especially when mami cooks carne con papa, her special Cuban beef and potatoes stew. It's so potent that after a week, the aroma still lingers all over the house. It drives my American neighbors crazy. They love the stuff. A little bit of Cuba in Pinecrest Village is what mami likes to say, with a bit of a sting in her voice.

So I got to the phone in the kitchen with visions of Tío Pepe pinching the nurses left and right, according to Mercy, when Lucinda's voice stung my ears.

"Why are you yelling? Dónde estás? What do you mean you don't know? Lucinda, what's going on? I don't understand a word you're saying! Get yourself over here ahora mismo." Lucinda was running her words together, talking about how Carlos had flushed seventeen years of her investments down the toilet, about how she hated artists, about how she wanted to dye her hair blond or shave it off like Demi Moore, so no one could touch it. She was hysterical, like I've never heard her before. Lucinda has her moments like the rest of us, but she is basically easygoing, with an artist's sensibilities, always looking for other people's perspectives to understand them better. I've only seen her lose her calm exterior when she talks about Carlos' family. "La Familia" as she calls it. They've made her life impossible, even though you wouldn't think it seeing her live in the lap of luxury. But those things don't matter to Lucinda. She left Santo Domingo so she wouldn't have to put up with all that social status crap. She doesn't see herself as a Portes married to a Colón; she's just Lucinda. But they never let her forget. They must have been up to something again. Lucinda was out of it on the phone. So I told her to find US 1 and take it all the way to my house, pronto. US 1, Dixie Highway, nothing southern about it. In Miami, this is the Baskin-Robbins of roads: Thirty-seven cultures from the Mexicans in Homestead to the Jews in North Miami Beach and every Latin American culture in between, including Haitian and Jamaican for added flavor, can be tasted without getting out of your car. I yelled at Lucinda to get back in hers.

As soon as I hung up, I called Julia and asked her what was going on with Lucinda. She didn't know a thing. She had just walked in from an evening lecture at the university. She offered to come over. I felt relieved. Julia has a calming effect on a situation. It comes from all those years of dating a diplomat, or maybe from her Mexican-American background. She just doesn't lose it as easily as us Caribeños. Maybe it's the heat of the tropics or the brilliant reds of its sunsets. I don't know. But when we get mad, we see red, and we make sure everybody else sees it too. Composure is not a commonly used word where I come from. Not Julia, she can keep her cool in any circumstance. Even in the middle of one of her feminist lectures, when a guy kept winking and pursing his lips at her, she kept going to the end, not missing a single metaphor. After the talk, she walked straight up to him and said, "Not interested," all the while looking down at his crotch. Later, we had a good laugh remembering the guy's beet red face. But with me, if someone makes a sexist remark at my job, I let him have it on the spot.

Julia arrived before Lucinda. We decided it was best for Mercy to stay. I heard the Jaguar skid into the driveway, knocking over the recycling bin. We rushed out. I had never seen Lucinda in such a state. Her hair was loose and uncombed, her top was halfway off, and she was barefoot. She looked like a strung-out groupie at a Metallica concert. When she saw us, she burst into tears.

The three of us each grabbed a body part and practically carried her into the living room. Thank God it was only us women at home. Papi was at a Marlins game with Sam; David Jr. had taken off to a classmate's house to work on a school project. Mami was home, but she was discreet about these things. We sat Lucinda down on the couch and let her cry her heart out. My shoulder was soaked. My shirt felt like it came straight out of the bathroom sink after soaking all night in it. Lucinda finally lifted her head and looked around. Her delicate face was streaked with makeup, making her look like a Mardi Gras mask left out in the rain, her eyes shattered with pain. The three of us were stunned at this sight of Lucinda.

"I'm leaving him. I'm leaving Carlos" were her first words to us. I was sitting on the couch, with my arms wrapped around Lucinda's shoulders. Mercy and Julia were sitting in the big wicker end-chairs across from each other; we all gave one another a "What the hell is going on here" look. And that's just exactly what I said to her. She began to cry again like the Jibacoa waterfalls back in the Dominican Republic. Mercy went to the bathroom to get a box of tissues. She came back with a full roll of toilet paper instead. "Oye meng, believe me. This looks like a one thousand tissues night." Mercy has actually calculated the intensity of a broken heart by how long a roll of toilet paper lasts before the tears dry up. Julia gave Mercy an "I can't believe you" look, but before she could say anything, Lucinda grabbed the roll from the coffee table and unraveled a fistful of it. Mercy gave Julia an "I told you so" look, and I saw all this looking going on so I gave them both a "Shut the hell up" look. By the time Lucinda finished telling us what happened, she was halfway into the toilet paper. I can tell you that my house has not been that quiet since the day before we moved in, when it was empty.

Before any of us could think of what to say, mami entered from the kitchen. She was carrying a large pot of café cubano, along with four miniature cups, on the wooden tray. As she placed it on the low table in front of us, mami glanced at me; she knew this would be a hard night for me, for all of us. She quietly left us for the dark of the den, where she sat in her rocking chair. For a minute, that's all we could hear, her creaking rocker. Latina mothers have a way of knowing what to do when a heart is broken. They don't talk much, but they do a lot. It's a silent code of behaviors. A look, a touch, a low clearing of the throat, a well-timed tray of coffee; it's all subversive. It comes from years of experience with machismo. But nowadays with us Latinas, those macho days are shrinking. Like that old saying goes, "No somos machos pero somos muchas." Julia would translate that into something like "strength in numbers." What was the last count, women outnumber men two to one? There is nothing subtle about that, nor about my little cousin Mercy.

"You really put the picture between your tits? Coño!" Leave it to Mercy. She has the subtlety of an Osterizer blender. But it got Lucinda laughing along with the rest of us. We all had a good, solid laugh, like only women on the verge of a nervous breakdown can. Almodóvar must have been a woman in a past life.

"I wasn't planning to. It just happened. God put the picture there."

"God put the picture in your bra?" Mercy asked.

"It was fate. It was out of her hands. Destiny put it there," said Julia.

"Así pasó, it happened just the way I told you," Lucinda said to Mercy.

"I don't know about destiny, but I do know that mami makes the best cafecito in town." I served each of us the Cuban brew in the delicate porcelain tacitas with the mini handles, small enough to be lifted with the thumb and index finger only. After we gulped these down like a shot of whiskey, I served a second round. Everybody settled back and stared at the empty fireplace.

"What do I do now?" asked Lucinda.

"Lucinda, are you sure about Carlos and this Gabriela woman? A picture can say so many things."

"Isa, it's obvious by her reaction. This is about truth," said Julia.

"I've never met her. Pero esa mirada in the picture, I can tell she loves him. El pendejo!"

Mercy jumped right in. "Tremendo hijo de puta! After seventeen years, he starts up with this crap. No way, Lucinda. You don't deserve this mierda. None of us do. Look at you, so beautiful—he has to go and scratch his masculinity with some bimbo. I tell you, no va. Give me some more coffee!" Mercy chugged her third serving down like a sword swallower at a circus. "If you ask me . . ."

"Mercy!" I screamed. "This isn't helping Lucinda at all."

"Carajo que sí!" said Lucinda. "She's right. I'm not going to put up with this crap."

"Pero, Lucinda, all you saw was a photo. Maybe you should go back and talk it out," I continued.

"Talk it out! With that pendejo! I saw his face, Isa, I felt him. He might as well have confessed. I'm sure, as sure as I know I'm the mother of my children. Carajo, I can give birth to a thousand more kids and my guts wouldn't scream as loud as they're screaming now." Lucinda clutched her shirt in front of her stomach. "Y los niños? Los niños?" she began to cry in a whisper to no one.

How could I tell her that the kids survive this? That time and pain, the emotional equivalent of steroids if you can take them, bulk you up to where you're a superhero, and the kids go to you for life's weekday pains, and to their father for its weekend pleasures, and so you end up an unsung hero, but deep down you and the kids know who's the stronger one. I didn't say this to Lucinda; instead, I held her hands in a tight grip.

"You know what?" said Mercy. "I think Ramón is cheating on me. I know he is. After six months of dating, he doesn't ask me The Question. Y por qué no? I mean he calls me all kinds of sweet things—mi vida, mi cielo, mi corazón. I pay for everything and before you know it, we're in the sack making hoopy, or however Sinatra says it. And let me tell you, I'm no longer a virgin, well, to him I'm not. With a Latino, if you do it before you get married, then you're not decente enough for a wife, but if you don't do it, then you're a retrograda, an outdated date. Coño!" Mercy tore at least five squares of toilet paper from the thinning roll, wiped her tears, and blew her nose. "Men! I'm this close to giving up. If only I were attracted to women."

"Mercy, we aren't talking about you. And be careful, you might get what you wish for," barked Julia. Mercy, with a scolded puppy look, sat back down and began to play with her bracelets.

"Lucinda," continued Julia in a calmer voice. Julia has a perfect Lauren Bacall voice. Soothing and seductive. The people at National Public Radio go crazy with it whenever she does a piece for them. They've actually calculated that the male audience increases by 25 percent whenever her voice goes over the air. "I'm not going to say I can feel what you are feeling, because that's impossible. But I can see how much it's hurting you. Be careful, Lucinda, you don't want to be rash at a moment like this. It takes time to make a move."

I looked over at Julia wondering whether she was saying this to Lucinda or saying it to herself. I remembered Felipe telling me how he'd be a married man in no time, but Julia was obviously in another time zone.

"Ay Julia. And how much time did it take Carlos to make his move? Eh? How long has he been with her? Hell, I don't even know who she is!" Lucinda added the soggy tissue in her hands to the growing mound on the coffee tray.

Watching Lucinda get down to the last quarter of the toilet paper, Julia gently said, "That's just it. Right now you're not sure of anything. As I see it, you must be sure of what is going on between Carlos and that woman, and how involved it is. I know you love Carlos and I know he loves you. I don't believe seventeen years are worth nothing to him. Things happen. There must be reasons why, you must look for them." Lucinda kept shaking her head, not wanting to listen to Julia's advice.

"What Julia is saying makes sense, Lucinda. Just because he's acted like an imbécil doesn't mean you have to," I said.

"I can't go back to him. It's humiliating. We've always been so close, best friends; for him to do this now . . ." Lucinda's anger trailed off into a quiet pain.

We all got quiet again.

I noticed Julia began to roll up her shirtsleeves. She looked at me, waving her palm at her neck. With all the emotional talk and the hot coffee, the living room felt warm.

"I'll be right back. I'm going to lower the AC a bit." As I was getting up from the couch, Mercy waved me down.

"I'll handle it," she said.

Mercy bolted from her seat. She returned from the den, where mami was rocking all along, with an armful of newspapers. She stuffed these into the fireplace and threw four of those fake waxed logs we all go crazy for here in Miami because they smell like the real thing but don't give you any trouble and for a minute you're in Connecticut singing "White Christmas" with Bing as the tropical humidity hangs over the chimney. It was Mercy's idea to get me this house with the huge wall-to-wall, floor-to-ceiling limestone fireplace. She sold it to me as a safety feature. It would come in handy for the next big one, hurricane Andrew II, she said. But what we got now was Dante's Inferno, because before any of us could say anything, she had a bonfire going on in the living room, big enough for Tío Pepe to roast one of those huge hogs he raises on his ten acres down in Homestead.

"Qué estás haciendo?!" Lucinda asked Mercy as the wall of heat made its way past the coffee table and on toward the sofa.

"A Sioux Sweat Lodge."

"A Sue what?!" I think we all asked at the same time.

I got up to open some windows but Mercy yelled out to stop me. She wanted the house to sweat, that's exactly what she said.

"It works, let me tell you. I discovered this through a realtor friend of mine. She told me of her healing experience at a sweat lodge. There is one in the Everglades, up in Broward County. You go on a Friday, and you don't come out until Sunday, that's if you paid for the Deluxe Sweat."

"Qué carajo are you saying?" asked Lucinda, getting impatient with Mercy and wiping the sweat off her face with the toilet paper.

"No, wait, listen. It's a big tent, and there's a huge fire heating up the healing stones in the middle of it, and you sit in a circle with a blanket over you . . ."

"Who sits with you?" one of us asked.

"Gente con problemas, broken hearts. When you think of it, all problems end up a broken heart. I go to these whenever a boyfriend leaves me. I sweat out all of his toxins. It cleanses your spirit. And let me tell you, I sweat off at least five pounds over those hot rocks every time I go. I come out feeling like Rocky in that scene where he's bouncing up and down at the top of those steps, all sweaty and light."

"It must stink in there, all those broken-hearted people covered up in wool, breathing fire and wondering what brand of deodorant they're buying next because they're sweating up the Great Flood." I rolled my eyes toward the air conditioner vent on the ceiling.

"No, Mercy is right. I remember Felipe and me visiting something similar on the Pueblo reservation out west. They have chants, no?"

"Sí! We all repeat the chants of the healer, and before you know it, the chants sound like songs, everybody singing to the stones."

"Sioux Sing-Along Songs? Por favor, Mercy!" I said.

"Well, I don't know about you, but I'm taking off my clothes," said Mercy. "I forgot to tell you that we were all naked under the blankets." And with that she began to pull her blouse over her head.

"What are you doing? Estás más loca que . . ." But before I was finished Mercy was pointing at Lucinda.

"Look, she's already half naked!"

"Get some blankets, Isa. I'm taking off my clothes too," said Julia in her best radio voice.

"Mami!" I got my mother, who at times can look as stoic as one of those Navajo woman portraits in David Jr.'s history textbook, to look for every blanket in the house. I got up, fully dressed, and headed for the bar in the Florida Room. It was even hot in there. The whole house felt like a steamy locker room after a football game. Not that I was ever in one. I came back with a bottle of Cointreau, the sweet orangy liqueur Lucinda and I used to drink on the porch of her father's ranch back in the Dominican Republic, whenever life got too hot for Lucinda in Miami. We must have gone through a dozen bottles when I was divorcing David. We bared our souls on those nights.

And now, they were all naked. Mami was draping each one with a blanket. She left one for me on the sofa and went into the kitchen. I got the message. I poured everyone a brandy snifter of Cointreau and settled on the floor, wrapped in a blanket too. We stared at the monstrous flames; they looked like naked nymphs dancing a hot merengue at a Dominican nightclub.

"Do you remember any of the chants, Mercy?" I asked.

"Lucinda, what's your favorite song?" she asked instead.

"It's by Juan Luis Guerra and 4.40, 'Bachata Rosa,' you guys know it, don't you?" she answered.

We all knew it. His songs transcend nationalities. They sing to the soul, no matter where you are born. Julia started humming the tune and Lucinda started in with the lyrics. We all joined in.

Ay amor, eres la rosa que me da calor
eres el sueño de mi soledad . . .*

The melancholic song started us all crying again. I couldn't help but think of David and me back in Santo Domingo when we would play our 4.40 albums over and over again late in the night, as we embraced. Or when we would stroll down the Malecón arm in arm, along the seawall, stopping for a cold glass of Presidente beer. Those first years were good, before he became melancholic for English. It wasn't only David I missed, but also the flavor of life, the landscape of the island. Lucinda must have been thinking along the same lines. She took a mouthful of Cointreau and fixed her glistening eyes on the fire. I could see the fire reflected in her marble black eyes.

"I've decided. Ya sé. I know what I'm going to do. Me voy. Mañana mismo, me voy. I'm taking the kids and catching a plane for Santo Domingo."

"Holy shit!" whispered Mercy.

---

*Oh, my love, you are the rose that gives me warmth, / you are the dream in my loneliness . . .

Chapter 8

———∞∞———

Mercy

So why isn't she married?" Tía Clara asked.

"Cuántas veces have I asked myself that?" mamá answered. "It's not like she doesn't date men. Mercy has had many boyfriends, pero mi hermana, they never stick. Mira que I have tried!" I overheard mamá exclaim as she was frying the steaks.

"Perhaps Ramoncito will stick," said Tía Clara.

"Yo no sé. Sometimes I think Mercy is the Teflon Girlfriend. The men slide off her like the palomilla steaks in this pan."

"Mamá! I heard the whole thing." I was just on the other side of the kitchen swing door. In my family, there is no such thing as privacy. If you want to chismear, you've got to take your gossip out of town and out of Spanish range, somewhere in Kansas might work. Let me tell you, the days of Spanish gossip in public are gone. Between the outnumbered "English Only" Anglos who get mad at you if you say "sí" in public and everybody else who understands everything you say, the best thing to do is to learn sign language. Coño, I was in an elevator the other day, chismeando to a colleague in Spanish, when I noticed this Anglo giving us a Schoolteacher look and then this Latino putting his ear to every private word we said. Oye meng, as soon as the elevator doors opened I gave them both a sign that everybody understood. But mamá could never learn sign language; her hands are always into food. That's how she talks. "The way to a man's heart is through his stomach" is not just a little old saying to mamá, it's a Commandment. Let me tell you, in my love life, my boyfriends are Hansels to my mother. She likes to fatten them up for marriage.

"Mamá, I can't believe you are talking about my love life to Aunt Clara! I can't believe you are talking so loud about such a thing, with Ramón out there in the living room." I pointed to the swing door. "Qué pasa if he hears? Let me tell you, it's adiós vida mía! Men don't like to hear their girlfriend's mother talk that way. It clues them about the future mother-in-law!"

"So, am I going to be a mother-in-law soon?"

"No, mamá. Ramón has not popped the question. Pero I think this one is going to stick, if you don't jinx it." I glanced at Tía Clara.

"Perhaps these steaks will help!" said mamá as they smoothly slid off the frying pan into the flower-patterned serving dish. Flowers are my mother's design theme for her house. The good china, the furniture covers, and the wallpaper are all flowers. It helps her to forget the gray years in Cuba.

"I got these on special en la bodega. The butcher, Miguelito, said they were prime cuts, as tender as a baby's bottom."

When mamá went to the bodega for steaks, it meant business. To her, the buzzing of the meat-cutter's saw is like the sound of an Ave María sung at a wedding.

"Ay mamá, Ramón loves your food. If you keep feeding him, he won't fit into the stretch Levi's he wears to work. You know he has to stay limber so he can climb into the attics." I helped Tía Clara spoon the steaming white rice into the flowered bowl.

"Y eso?"

"You know, mamá, I've told you before. He works for Florida Power & Light checking for leaks in the air conditioning ducts."

"Ya sé, mijita. But he's a growing man. Ramoncito needs his energía."

If mamá only knew how right she was. Ramón's appetite was

insatiable, and I'm not speaking of palomilla steaks only. That's why I often invite him to the Kendall house. Mamá enjoys feeding him. He gets his fill, and let me tell you, I get a rest. Not that I'm shy for a good time with the man you love, but too much of a good thing is not such a good thing. The thing is that Ramón was in prison for five years in Cuba before he made it to Miami about two years ago. He's always reminding me how he still has three years left before he breaks even. Ramón measures celibacy in hours. But I'm saving some of myself for after we get married. There are other ways to get to a man's heart besides his lower extremities. Besides, in courtship, pacing is everything, except that to my cousin Isa, I'm always on fast-forward. But who can wait nowadays? Men are becoming extinct, especially the good ones. And let me tell you, to a realtor, extinct is a word you never want to hear. Who buys realty from a dinosaur? Oye meng, the competition is as fierce as those dinosaurs in the kitchen scene in *Jurassic Park*. Everywhere you go, there's another realty agent pushing her way into your territory. Some of them look like dinosaurs, too. That's why I had my picture put on my business cards. Cost me a bundle to do it. Pero Iko knows how to bring out the best in a little picture. It was his idea to put me in a little black-laced tulle blouse. Julia thinks my business motto should be "Cleavage is my leverage." Well, let me tell you, in realty, it's how you use your assets that makes the difference between ending up a dinosaur scratching at somebody else's listings or people calling you for the hottest properties. That's my goal, I want to be the hottest realtor in town. I want my picture to sizzle in everybody's hands, like mamá's steaks do in her frying pan.

In the morning I was making my rounds. That's why I was late to mamá's afternoon dinner. I take good care of my territory, like Sara, my miniature schnauzer, does in her walks, except that I leave my picture all over the place. I got Sara because she fits nicely into a one-bedroom apartment. And she barks like a German shepherd. No shedding hairs either, I can't stand loose hairs. I don't mind it on a body—Ramón is a walking area rug when it comes to that—but let me see hair in the bathtub and I freak out. I got this phobia from mamá back in our Cuba days. The one place she could really conquer all of the decay around her was in the bathroom. She would swoop down on loose hairs like a hawk on a poor field mouse in one of those *National Geographic* specials I use to go to sleep with. She always lit a candle to the Virgin Mary, in gratefulness for my father's early baldness. Less hairs to sweep up, she figured. I figure it's just a matter of time before a genetic quack doctor will discover the no-shedding gene. I'll get in line for that one.

I was waiting in line for my morning double cafecito at Los Atrevidos grocery store in Little Havana—I don't go for the designer coffee shops on Ocean Drive for my morning coffee, that caffe latte is just too limp-wristed for the hard work I have to do to get ahead in this Dino-eat-Dino world—when my cell phone vibrated. It was Ramón calling me from work.

"Ramón, you sound like you're in a bathroom." He was echoing his words.

"Estoy inside a giant air duct. Oye, tu mamá invited us for a big lunch this afternoon, around three. Dije que sí."

"She has your cell phone number? I thought it was just for me."

"Mi corazón, tu familia es mi familia."

"Ay please, Ramón. I'll meet you there, OK?"

"Bueno, I have to get back to tracing a leak somewhere in this monster duct. Oye, maybe tonight I can trace your perfume somewhere on your neck."

"Sounds good to me," I said as he hung up. You see what I mean? Now, when a man calls you from work, what does that say? He can't stop thinking about you. And what about that familia stuff? It was so sweet of him. Coño, Ramón's words caused goosebumps all up and down my neck. I wrapped my Versace scarf tighter hoping nobody noticed them. That's when Ricardo, my client and owner of Los Atrevidos grocery store, noticed me waiting in line.

"What is my número uno realtor doing in line?" He got me

straight to the counter and ordered his employee to be quick with my cafecito. After we drank our coffees, he told me what he wanted: to move his café-restaurant-grocery store out of Little Havana and into one of the hot sites in town: somewhere on Lincoln Road, South Beach, Coconut Grove, or even Coral Gables. He settled on Coral Gables. With its wealthy Cubans, who were the sons and daughters of the Little Havana viejitos but who wouldn't be caught dead setting foot in the old neighborhood now, and with the recent election of a Cuban mayor, Ricardo felt he had a good chance of making it as an upscale, to-be-seen-in eatery/gourmet market with a Cuban flavor but without the refugee-memories kind of place. It reminded me of something like the expensive, old-looking "distressed" furniture the relaxed rich are buying up in the Miami Design District—it might look like your mother's dresser, but it doesn't smell like it. We made our way to Miracle Mile, the little retail street with more lives than a Hindu cat. The place just won't go down even though it's got lousy parking and it's surrounded by regional malls. Us realtors call it the place where businesses come to rest, just like the elephants on the Ivory Coast back in Africa. But they keep coming, so we all make a nice commission while they're kicking. Who knows? Maybe this Latino thing will take off and I'll be eating and shopping at Ricardo's on the Mile. We spent all morning driving and walking from empty building to building, which made the prices attractive to "just on the edge of really making it" clients like Ricardo. Finally, he motioned for me to stop; a large corner property got his attention.

"This used to be a Woolworth." I pointed to the clean shadows left over the doors where the sign was supposed to be.

"Well, ahora it will be The Daring Ones Gourmet Café & Market. Can you picture it?" He beamed me a smile that made his black handlebar mustache stretch like Ramón's black Levi's. He was hooked on the place. He called his architect to meet him there, so I left him with the keys and his daring dreams.

The Daring Ones, carajo, there's a good title for the Latino success story in this country. It got me thinking about Lucinda. Coño, that was a wild night at Isa's. I looked at my Cartier watch, which I only wear with big-shot clients, and knew I'd be late by half an hour to my mother's place. Let me tell you, in America, el peso never takes a siesta. I'm never late for a client but I'm always late for my own affairs. So I got into my yellow Miata and broke every speed limit in my way. Along the way I called Isa. I couldn't get Lucinda out of my head. She was a daring one all right.

"Oye, Isa, it's me, Mercy. Are you going to mamá's big thing this afternoon?"

"The one you're late for? No, how could I be going if I'm still here at work?"

"Aren't you the big boss? Just close up and get over there."

"I'm in charge of inventory this week, Mercy. There's no way I can leave. Don't worry, tu mamá already knows. But tell Mr. Momento to leave me some of your mother's coco-flan! Where does Ramón pack it in? He's so skinny!"

"Listen, Mr. Momento might become Mr. Matrimonio by the time you eat breakfast tomorrow morning."

"Qué?! What gave you that idea? Don't tell me you read it in Walter Mercado's horoscope!"

"Oye, don't mess with Walter Mercado. I just got this feeling."

"I've heard that before."

"It's different this time. Ramón just says and does things. Eso es todo."

"Like what?"

"I can't get into it right now. I just know."

"Bueno, I'd better be the first to find out! Mercy, prepárate for anything, OK?"

"Está bien, don't worry. Speaking of worrying, qué me cuentas de Lucinda?"

"Nothing new since we last spoke. She calls me every couple of days to just talk. She's still at her parents' place."

"What's she going to do?"

"She's not sure. She has a lot to work out. Mercy, I've got to get back to work."

"Es que I feel so responsible. Like I put the idea in her head or something."

"Don't be silly."

"I would hate to see their marriage end."

"Me too. You can never tell with these things. Maybe she'll work it out."

"Maybe Ramón and I will work out."

"Listen to you! He hasn't even proposed and you're worrying about breaking up. I have to go now."

"Isa, Walter Mercado's horoscope told me to expect 'el hombre de mi vida' in the near future."

"Call me later, from the future."

"I'll be too busy celebrating!"

I could hear Isa's laughter as we hung up. I worry about Isa. Ever since her divorcio she hasn't given men a chance. I keep telling her it takes two to mambo. I give my men plenty of chances. I haven't taken any chances with Ramón, let me tell you. I treat him like I want to be treated. I like a man to spoil me from here to eternity. Money is no object. Ramón is not presently wealthy, but I'm taking good care of us in that department. I don't mind, hungry hearts can't be choosers. So why was mamá choosing to do this big food fest out of the blue?

I made it to the house just in time to serve the "food fit for a king and his court" as mamá put it to Ramón, who was seated at the head of the table at my mother's insistence. After I got the steaks from the kitchen and her gossip about my unmarried status, she sat me at the tail end of the table. I could tell the full-court press was on. In between Ramón and me sat my mother and Tía Clara with her husband, Tío Pepe, whose kidney was at peace, and on the other side of the table sat their three grown kids (the cousins I came with from Cuba) and one spouse. Running around the table were four little kids, belonging to two of my cousins. Three were within wedlock and one was out of wedlock. We call this one Fidelito. Little Fidel can't keep his mouth shut. This kid could out-talk Castro on his best U.N. speech days by forty-eight hours. We're used to it in the family, but I could tell it got on Ramón's nerves. He was sweating like an Arab in a Turkish bath. Ramón is not the kid type, but he puts up with all of my little cousins except for Fidelito. According to my uncle, Ramón suffers from Post-Castrotic Stress Syndrome—having heard too many bad speeches for too long. But we were at the dessert end of the meal and no one had given any speeches about Cuba tonight. Mamá must have read the riot act to everyone. The dinner talk was dominated by Tío Pepe's comparison of mamá's steaks to his kidneys. We all got a good laugh out of that one except for mamá. She was playing overtime making sure everything went smoothly for Ramón.

Tía Clara was bringing out the coco-flan when Ramón said, wiping the sweat from his forehead, "Mercy, is there a place I can make a call in private?"

"Sí, mijito. You can go to Mercy's room. No one will bother you in there," answered mamá before I could swallow the spoonful of flan in my mouth. "Mercy, show Ramón to your room." I could tell mamá was excited by the way she measured her words in order to not sound excited. She gave Tío Pepe a knowing glance, like those plump, sugary mothers in the 1940s romantic movies I like to watch. I took Ramón by the hand. It was all wet.

My room was in the back of the house. Mamá had insisted I take the master bedroom for myself since I was the one who bought the house for everybody.

I closed the door behind us and saw that Ramón was agitated. He was fidgeting for something in his pocket. I could see the drops of sweat gathering on his upper lip like clouds on a stormy day.

"Coño! Where is it? Shit!" He fumbled with some loose change in his hands. They were shaking so hard all the coins fell to the tile floor and scattered like roaches when you turn on the lights.

You could hear my heartbeat scattering all over the room as I watched him on all fours looking for something, and it wasn't his change.

"Ya! Aquí está!" And then he put it in his mouth and swallowed hard. I sat next to him on my ChiroComfort Ultra Supreme king-size bed. It was mamá's choice for me. She said it would make a great marital bed in the future. Ramón calmed down after a little while. He was drier and less jittery. I could hear his heart beat in slow motion. But his hands were on warp speed. Before I could say, "A pill, again?!" he had me on my back.

"Mi vida, mi vida. I need you ahora!"

"Pero, Ramón, we haven't had dessert yet!"

"Mercy, you are my dessert," he whispered as he began to lift up my skirt. Lucky for me I had on my Super Structure sheer pantyhose underneath. That, and the fact that he was also having a hard time getting out of his stretch Levi's because something else was stretched, gave me time to catch my breath.

"What do you want, Ramón?"

"I desire you, Mercy. Me haces falta en este momento."

"Why do you need me?" I managed to say between our wet kisses.

"I don't know." He kissed me on my neck. I licked his ear. "You just make me feel good." Then he made a bear noise and we rolled all over the length and breadth of the king-size bed. To anybody looking, we must have looked like logs rolling down the side of a hill in one of those logging camps in the Great Northwest.

I was feeling great, with Ramón trying to undo my silk blouse, when I noticed that the crucifix on the opposite wall was hanging crooked. I saw that mamá had lighted the big candle to the Virgin Mary statue sitting on the corner table. She lights it every time I sleep over. It's supposed to protect me from bad spirits or something. I saw the rosary on the night table and the family Bible on the dresser and the cheap oil painting of Jesus on the side wall and Ramón was getting to third base while the BIG UMPIRE in the GREAT BEYOND was obviously calling for a time-out. Let me tell you, I am not what you might call a devout Catholic, but how many signs can a girl miss before she gets kicked out of the game? Religion was never a game with mamá. I remembered how mamá used her religion to cocoon us back in Cuba. Coño, to mamá, religion was a tool of war. She used to say that Castro could beat the daylights out of the Devil but that he was no match for God. So she covered our walls with religious objects. Our Havana one-room efficiency looked like a wholesale warehouse for nuns. I went to first grade thinking I lived in a convent. That's what I answered when the teacher asked the kids where we lived. It almost got the entire family arrested. But mamá saved the day by holding up a crucifix to the neighbor in charge of interrogating us about our anti-revolutionary faith. He was also an officially certified Santero, a sort of Afro-Cuban Brian Weiss spiritualist. When he saw mamá standing guard at the door, the Santero got spooked and took off looking like a defeated ghost. But Ramón wasn't about to give up so easily.

"Ramón, espérate, wait. I can't."

"Huh? Qué pasa, you forgot the pill?"

"No. I can't do it in this room."

"Don't worry. Everybody is probably watching TV or something. I'll be quiet!" he whispered, diving into my cleavage.

"Ramón! Look around you."

"Jesus Christ!" he said while coming up for air. That's when he noticed the little metal plate with the etching of Saint Francis nailed on the headboard. I unfurled my skirt, pulled closed my blouse, and sat up, knees curled to my chest.

"He is my protector Saint. My confirmation name is Francesca, after him."

"Carajo, talk about a cold shower moment! How do you sleep in here?" Ramón flattened his hair while looking around the room.

"Muy bien. I never have nightmares in here. Ramón, those pills you take, why?"

"Nada, they just calm my nerves. Vamos, we can pretend we're a couple of horny teenagers in the back pew of a church!"

I opened my arms to embrace his head on my blouse. I ran my fingers through his hair and, looking directly at the portrait of Jesus, who was looking back at me, my lips moved.

"Ramón, mi querido, I can't make love in here. I love you too much. Maybe, when we are man and wife, my mother would be proud to have her son-in-law possess her married daughter in this room over and over again for as long as they both shall live." I don't know what came over me. Another voice was talking for me, like the big-nosed French guy in that *My Father the Hero* movie, except I knew it was probably my big-mouthed mother doing all the talking. Well, Mr. Momento lived up to his Isa-given nickname. He slowly lifted his head from my bosom, looked at his high-quality imitation Rolex, and asked for a moment.

"Sorry, Mercy, I have to make a quick call."

"It's OK, Ramón, take your time." I sat up on the edge of the bed. He called his "pharmacist" for another "prescription" while looking at me. He looked around the room shaking his head as if missing the mother of all sexual encounters. That's when I noticed he had an easy time zipping up his Levi's. He hung up the phone and then said, "Vamos." We walked out of the room, and now I was doing all the sweating. He held my hand as he said his gracias and good-byes to the family. Out in the front lawn, we kissed and talked about a date next Friday. As he got into his white Ford Bronco, he gave me the sweetest look a man has ever given me.

I went back into the house and joined the cousins in a furious game of dominoes. Dominoes is an endless game in my family. By the time all of the rounds and counter-rounds were played with all possible combinations of partners, it was time for me to go. The moon was rising over Miami by the time I made it back across the bridge to my penthouse in SoBe land, where "all fantasy is reality," as the city fathers like to advertise on the sides of buses. Miami shrank as I went up in the exterior glass elevator. By the time I got to the top, the city looked like a lit-up toy town. I heard my toy schnauzer shriek like she does every time my keys jingle at the door. Sara is like a Mexican jumping bean when it comes to greeting me. I made it to the kitchen, where I put away my mother's four Tupperware bowls of leftovers in the refrigerator, threw the keys in the empty fruit bowl on the dining room table, and opened the shutters to the beach balcony to let the moonlight in. Whenever there's a full moon, I like to keep the lights off; it makes me feel like I'm in another world where nothing can go wrong. I kicked off my pumps and stretched out on the smooth leather couch. That's when I saw the blinking red light on the phone. I had two new messages, so I pressed the play button.

"Mercy? Mercy, estás ahí? Did you remember to put the leftovers in the refrigerator like I told you? Listen, mijita, did you have a good time? I did, y la familia did too. Y Ramoncito? I think he liked the bistecs, no? He looked handsome. Both of you were perfect, a perfect couple! Pero he looked un poco nervioso, no? Did you guys talk about something important in the room? It must have been serious, he came out so formal and you looked so nervous. Mijita, let me know if I can be of any help. Tú sabes, men are not too good at these things; you might have to take the lead. Bueno, you know what I mean. Ramoncito es un buen muchacho. Remember, he's a Cuban Cuban, not one of those made-in-the-USA Cubanitos, es puro. Everything will come out fine in the end. Don't worry, lo que está para ti, no one can take it away. I think I'm taking too much space en la máquina de teléfono, no? Pero you didn't give me a chance to talk with all that domino playing. We'll talk in the morning. Que Dios te bendiga!"

Beeeeep!

I love mamá. Her mind is always planning the future. She doesn't like any surprises in her life. I guess the last surprise she got, the one about my father's death in Angola, almost killed her. Hell, to this day I get presents from her a week in advance of my birthday.

I myself don't mind surprises, they keep you on your toes. I slipped my toes underneath the couch pillow Sara was lying on and pressed for the other message to begin. Ramón's surprise almost killed me.

"Mercy, it's me, Ramón. Listen, mi vida—I was thinking—tu familia is great, tu mamá is a wonderful woman, tremenda cook!—you are an angel on earth, and a little devil in bed! Sorry—but you know it's true! Es que you are too good—too good for my own good, Mercy. What you said in your room— what a room! Tú y yo were meant for each other. The words came de tu corazón, yo sé, I know you meant them—the last thing I want is to break your heart—it's not you, Mercy, it's me—I'm like a clay pot and you are a brass pot—you are too good, too solid for me—I'll crack if I stay with you any longer!—what I'm saying is too important to wait, that's why I'm leaving it in your voice mail. I'm doing this for you, for us— yo sé que I'm making a big mistake letting you go—I'll be paying for this one all the rest of my entire future—es un sacrificio that I do for you—I'm killing myself—nunca te olvidaré—mi Voluptuosa—I'll never forget us!—I gotta go."

Beeeeep!

I had just enough strength to dial Isa.

"You have reached the Landon residence. We are not in. Please leave your name, time of call, and a short message after the cue."

Beeeeep!

"Isa, coño, it's me, Mercy. Pick up! Dónde carajo are you when I need you?! Shit! What is it with me and men? Ramón dumped me over the phone, over the phone! I deserve better than that, don't you think, mi prima? What an asshole, after everything I've done for him. I don't know what happened. One minute I am in his arms and he's calling me 'mi amor' and the next I'm a brass pot. He says I'm too good for him. He says he's a clay pot. Qué carajo, I'd like to dump his clay ass into the ocean. I've had it with men. I treated Ramón so well and for what? Mierda! Deja que mamá finds out. Let me tell you, *It's a Wonderful Life* is my favorite movie of all time, but broken-hearted women outnumber winged angels by a thousand to one. Every time you hear a wave crash, a woman's hope is dashed. How else can you explain the size of an ocean? Por favor, Isa, call me back. I won't be working anytime soon. Oye, mi big cousin, I'm calling you from the future, and let me tell you, there's a lot of water in it. Damn it, Isa, I'm drowning!"

Chapter 9

—⦿⦿⦿—

Amigas

*I*t was five o'clock in the morning and Julia was awakened by Ming Toy, one of her three cats, and not by her alarm clock set for seven-thirty. The cat was rubbing its back against Julia's face. She'd forgotten to close the bedroom door last night. Her three cats had free rein of the apartment except for her bedroom. She pet the cat and gently pushed it off the bed. Julia could just make out its shadow as the cat padded its way onto the high wingback chair by the window. It was her reading chair. Next to it, as high as the armrests, was a stack of her favorite books. Felipe loved to hear her voice. How many nights had she read him to sleep after they made love? Curled on her chair like one of her cats, with Felipe long asleep, Julia spent many nights reading into the early morning hours. It was her after-play routine. Making love left her restless, and reading aloud to Felipe and later silently to herself assuaged the restlessness. The book at the very top of the stack was Octavio Paz' *The Labyrinth of Solitude*. Her eyes drifted away from the book, and for a while she stayed staring at the cat on the empty velvet chair. She tried closing her eyes as if enticing the sleep back, but thinking of Felipe made her fully awake. She closed her eyes anyway and replayed the scene in her head.

Felipe held her hand. They walked through the entire mansion that Saturday afternoon. As always, Felipe knew more than the tour guides about the old Vizcaya palace. It was a leftover mansion from when American industrialists played at culture, buying Europe's architecture and shipping it piece by piece to the wild fringes of America. The colonization of Nature, Hollywood style, is what Felipe liked to call it. Julia and Felipe played at guessing the art periods of its furnishings. Finally, while strolling through its sculptured formal gardens, Felipe brought up the subject.

"Julia, what am I to do? You haven't given me an answer."

"I haven't given you the answer, Felipe."

"You don't say yes and you don't say no. What is a man supposed to do with that?"

"It's such a move for me, Felipe. Five years at the university, the remodeling of the apartment, I'm halfway into my next book. I don't know."

They reached the ornate gazebo at the water's edge before any more words were said. The wind had picked up. Julia held her hair back with one hand. Felipe still held the other.

"Everything you've listed can be taken care of. What does any of that have to do with us? With how we feel about each other? This is what really matters in the end, no, Julia?"

"Yes. Yes, it does. But you're asking a lot. If I give everything I have, then what's left of me?"

She shook her head and tried to speak some more, but he placed his finger to her lips.

"Don't say anything else. Let's just give it time."

Julia couldn't erase Felipe's expression from her mind. His eyes revealed a mix of fear with disappointment. At that moment of truth, her senses shut out everything but his finger on her lips. She could taste his whole being from this minuscule touch of their flesh. Sweet. Felipe was sweet. Standing behind her, he wrapped his arms around her waist. For a long time, they silently stared at the rising waves crashing on the coral rock base of the gazebo. It was time to go.

At the sound of the alarm, Julia realized she had dosed off staring at Ming Toy in the chair. She got up from the four-post bed and made it to the shower.

Later in the kitchen, with her hair still wet and wrapped in a towel, she brewed herself a cup of tea. She was thinking of her morning breakfast date with Isabel when the sound of the newspaper against the door caught her attention. She ignored it and fed the cats, who had been begging for their meal.

Wading through them, Julia walked into her writing office and sat at the French marble-top table. She grabbed her manuscript and slowly drank her tea, savoring its herbal scent while reading her own words. She was working on a book of essays entitled *Latinas on the Border*. Julia was interested in what she called the "Border Theme." She wanted to write about Latina women who found themselves on the edge of their culture, their roots, their loves, and even their sexuality. Her mother was going to love this book, thought Julia. She was always saying how Julia's father was driving her to the edge. Julia would have loved her mother's ideas on the book, but this was impossible. If she got her mother talking about these things, she'd never have the time to write. Mimi, as Julia called her, made up in words what her father lacked in patience. To Julia, Mimi was a walking run-on sentence. Yet the older Julia got, the more she realized how little she knew of her mother as a woman. Why is it that most people are content with knowing the image of a person and not the substance? Daughter, girlfriend, lover, mistress, wife, mother, grandmother, saint, or seductress, layer upon layer of images, but where was the true woman? Julia thought to herself as she took in her picture on the jacket of her last book, leaning on the windowsill. She finished the tea and got dressed for the morning brunch with Isabel. They had a few of these casual breakfasts a month. It was their way of keeping the friendship central to their busy professional lives. Julia wore a loose T-shirt with baggy cotton pants, raffia and canvas shoes, hand made in Mexico, and no socks.

Deli Lane Café on a side street in a little Jewish neighborhood was the perfect place to feel out of your usual place. The Miami morning sky was crystal blue like the bottom of a swimming pool in summer. The heat was tempered by a cool breeze from the east, a breeze coming from the ocean only a mile away. Julia arrived first, so she got first pick on where to sit. She looked up at the postcard climate, put on her sunglasses, and sat at a sidewalk table for two. Lucinda was still out of town and Mercy was not coming this time, so the table would do. A waiter offered to raise the wood and canvas sunbrella, but Julia liked the easy heat of the morning sun. She ordered an American coffee and waited for Isabel, who arrived just as the coffee was brought.

"I had to drop off David Jr. at Saint Anthony's. An all-day track meet regional something-or-other. What are you drinking? No, I'll take a café con leche. We'll order the food a bit later," said Isabel to the waiter. She was about to take off her sunglasses when she noticed the closed sunbrella.

"And Sam, what's he up to?" asked Julia.

"You see this?" Isabel pointed to the sunbrella. "Sam is sleeping, wrapped up in his sheets as tight as this thing is closed. Sometimes I think I've got a mummy for a son!"

Julia noticed how Isabel was dressed. She was wearing tan shorts with a white short-sleeved shirt and a safari-like vest. The brown leather loafers matched her thin belt.

"You look good, Isa."

"Hija, don't we all at our age, no?" Isabel answered. The waiter returned with more coffee for Julia.

"Let's order," said Isabel.

"Yes. I'm starved. We'll take the usual, the French toast with fruits for me, and she'll have the sausage and eggs, scrambled, with potatoes on the side. Thank you," Julia said, not bothering with the menus.

"And you, how's the book business coming along?" asked Isabel.

"Fine."

"Only fine? That doesn't sound too enthusiastic. Qué pasa, writer's block?"

"No, I never have trouble with words on paper. I can fill an entire library's worth of books with words. It's Felipe. The page is blank at this very moment with Felipe. I still haven't given him an answer. He's leaving next week."

"Julia, what is it? He seems to be perfect for you, and he's very much in love." Isabel quickly added, "Yo sé, commitment. It's a big move for you. It's a monster move for anybody." Isabel noticed her friend's worried look.

"I can understand his rush. He wants to start a new life with no loose threads. But Isa, I feel like mine would unravel if I go."

Isabel felt like telling Julia that dating a man for three years is not rushing into a marriage, but sensing something troubled in her friend's words, she tried to reassure her instead.

"So? Quién dice that you have to go? Who says you have to give an answer now? If he goes without your answer, then so what?"

"Yes, yes I know. What confuses me is why I can't give him an answer," Julia said, all the while over-stirring her coffee with the spoon making a loud noise. Isabel could see that Julia was uncomfortable with the conversation. Julia was as reluctant as a mule on break, Isabel thought, when it came to intimate conversation about herself.

"Well, you definitely have to wait until you're sure. Look what happened to Mercy."

"What now?" Julia placed the overheated coffee spoon on the used sugar packet. Julia hated messes. The waiter placed the food on the table and lingered over Julia's V-neck T-shirt, refilling her water glass. Isabel waved him away.

"Mercy is a mess," continued Isabel.

"What happened?" Julia asked, relieved at the shift in the conversation. She knew Isabel had done it on purpose.

"Guess."

"That Ramón?"

"Mr. Momento himself. He dumped her. And he did it over her voice mail. Tremendo comemierda."

"I can't believe it! I never liked that guy."

"Me neither. But you know Mercy, she hasn't gone to work in days. I want to get her out of the apartment."

"She hasn't even seen her mother? She must be in pretty bad shape."

"Not good," answered Isabel as she bit into her buttered toast. But then she began to cough from a piece of the bread stuck in her throat as she saw something unexpected behind Julia.

"Isa, take some water!"

Between the gulps of water and the coughs, Isabel managed to sign-language Julia into turning around without looking too obvious.

"This is not good . . ." Julia said under her breath as she took in the paparazzi moment.

"Coño! Can you believe it? You think he can see us?" Isabel finally said in a coarse voice.

They both noticed the row of areca palms lining the glass picture windows of the restaurant. By design or by luck, as Julia later put it, there was an opening in the thick foliage of the palm fronds. Because of the angle they were sitting at, Isabel calculated, they could see him sitting inside the restaurant, but he couldn't see them sitting outside.

Isabel could tell, from the look on his face, that Carlos Colón was engaged in an intense conversation with a woman. She had her back to the large windows, but Isabel could tell it was Gabriela Sandoval.

"How can you be sure?" asked Julia stiffly, staring at Isabel.

"I'm sure. Remember the picture Lucinda had? It's her."

"What are they doing?"

"Hablando something. He's holding her hand on top of the table. Their knees are touching."

"You can see that?!"

"I guess he feels confident since Lucinda is out of the picture."

"What are they talking about?"

"Por favor, Julia! You think I'm a lip reader? I can't tell what they're talking about, but he can't take his eyes off her."

"It must be about Lucinda."

"Who knows, who cares," said Isabel in a disgusted voice, dropping her toast, no longer hungry.

"Is she as pretty as in the picture we—"

"Ahora sí!" interrupted Isa. "They're getting up." Impulsively she added, "Now we separate the adults from the adulterers. Hold on to your glasses!"

Carlos was opening the door and gently guiding Gabriela out onto the sidewalk when he heard his name being called. It happened so fast, there was nothing Julia could do to temper Isabel's actions.

"Carlos! Carlos, over here!" Isabel motioned to him. Julia stared straight at her, impressed by her friend's gall, or as the Americans like to say in Spanish when it comes to a certain part of the male anatomy, huevos. Julia watched Carlos walking over to them as if he would give his left huevo to run the hell away from this scene. Isabel dominated the conversation.

"It's a small world after all! Imagine bumping into each other in a Jewish deli! Don't tell me you were having matzoh ball soup? Ah, I'm just kidding!"

"Isabel, Julia, good to see you both," Carlos barely got in. Julia detected a funeral director tone to his greeting.

"When is Lucinda coming back to Miami? I miss her—as a matter of fact, she'd be here right now if it wasn't for that emergency she had."

Gabriela went pale at the mention of it.

"What was it again?" asked Isabel, taking off her sunglasses, looking at Gabriela. She must be in her late twenties or maybe early thirties, thought Isabel. Nice complexion, olive skinned with a few freckles. She looked like a mix of Dominican with Argentinian, Isabel concluded.

"Her mother had some chest pains," answered Carlos, glancing at Gabriela. They were standing apart, businesslike, from each other. Julia noticed Gabriela's hands. They were smooth on the outside, but the flesh of her palms was callused and marked with many tiny scars. Julia wondered if this sculptress knew what her hands were shaping this marriage into. She was very attractive, thought Julia. She looked like the kind of woman a Picasso or a Neruda would have for a lover. But a banker, with two kids, an attractive wife, and a practical profession? What are they doing for each other, thought Julia as she heard Isabel make the introductions.

Carlos introduced Gabriela as a business client seeking financing for her own studio and art gallery.

"Sí! I remember seeing your picture in the *Vida Social* a little while back. You were together in that too." Isabel pointed at the two of them with her sunglasses like a judge points his gavel at the accused. Carlos looked at his antique Piaget watch and, as Isabel later said, scrambled his huevos out of there.

"Do you think he knows that we know?" asked Julia as she paid the tab.

"Qué carajo! I don't think so, pero Lucinda's going to know about this. Like mami likes to say, if a man makes his bed, then let him burn in it."

"It's lie in it. Or is it lay in it?" said Julia, as they left the restaurant wondering about Lucinda's marriage. Julia didn't give any more thought to Felipe.

They agreed to meet at Mercy's in the evening to take her out. Ever since Ramón's call, Mercy had secluded herself in the apartment, eating her mother's leftovers or food from any restaurant that delivered. The kitchen was overflowing with used food boxes. Her red Formica kitchen countertop was a "study in gastronomical multiculturalism," as Isabel later put it, having noticed the leftovers from a variety of countries. Mercy had agreed that her mourning period was over, and besides, she told her friends, the Sweat Lodge was booked for the weekend.

"Well, let me tell you, he's lying and laying in it!" Mercy said as Julia finished telling her the story. Mercy jumped up from the cherry wood vanity chair where she had sat attentively listening to Julia and adjusted her black skirt.

"How do I look?" Mercy turned to Isabel and Julia, both sitting on her queen-size cherry wood sleigh bed. Mercy's taste in bedroom furnishings leaned toward the Victorian Age, as she saw it in the movie *An Ideal Husband*. She had bought the video to get more decorating ideas.

"Like a widow!" said Isabel. But then they all saw their reflection in the big mirror on Mercy's matching armoire at the wall past the foot of the bed.

"We're all dressed in black," Julia said, looking at the image of themselves. They were all quiet for a second and then burst out laughing.

"Julia, what does the color black mean in literature?" asked Isabel, pulling her black bolero jacket tight to her waist.

Julia curved her hips to one side, leaned forward, and dropped the black-laced Spanish shawl just off her shoulders.

"Seduction! Sex! Salsa!"

"Coño, you sound like me, Julia!" said Mercy, still laughing.

"We could be executioners. Didn't the guillotine guy wear only black?" Isa asked.

"Cut out the negatividad, please!" said Mercy, but Isa continued.

"Doesn't 'lob it' rhyme with 'Bobbitt'? Remember the old news story about Lorena cutting her husband's"—Isabel hesitated—"you know, gene tube?" It took a moment for Julia and Mercy to figure out what Isabel meant.

"Gene tube?! Only an engineer would call it that." Mercy made a face at the thought of it.

"Well, when I think of Carlos y esa mujer, I get a clear image of my lab with its sharp objects."

"Isa, when was the last time you saw a live . . . gene tube?" Mercy asked, giving Julia an insider's look.

"Listen, when you've seen one, you've seen them all," Isabel answered.

"Sí, and you've seen only one, let me tell you!" Mercy kidded her cousin.

"The point is that Carlos is spreading his genes thin, if you know what I mean. When I think of what he's doing to Lucinda and his kids, it cuts right into me. I wish I could just cut back, eso es todo."

"You did a pretty good job of it this morning, Isa. Don't make Carlos the enemy. You know she still loves him. The hope is they'll get back together, no?" said Julia.

"Oye meng, I'm the one who got sliced and diced here, remember? You guys are supposed to cheer me up. I'm sick of men and of this apartment. I think I'm suffering from Cuban fever!" Mercy said.

"You mean cabin fever," said Julia. "Where are we going?" she asked Isabel.

"You'll see. Let's just go."

They each grabbed their black purses and were about to reach the door when Mercy remembered something.

"Wait! I forgot something. I'll be right back."

Mercy came back with a black rectangular jeweler's box in her hands. "I have to make one quick stop before we go."

They got in the elevator, getting off at the beach level. She led them to the pier jutting out into the black ocean. The moon was covered by clouds, making the night seem darker than it really was. Their image kept appearing and disappearing as they walked from lamppost to lamppost. Finally, at the pier's end, Mercy opened the box she was carrying.

Julia and Isabel had only a glimpse of the shiny gold-trimmed watch when suddenly Mercy ripped it from its velvet case and, yelling "Pa'l carajo!" lobbed it into the dark waters of the Atlantic Ocean.

"To hell with what?! What?!" Isabel asked, still staring into the waves below. "Was that a Rolex?" she whispered.

"One hundred percent legítimo. The real thing." Mercy turned her back to the ocean like an avenged lover does to her cheating man on a soap opera.

"Whose was it?" asked Julia.

"It was going to be Ramón's. I was going to give it to him for an engagement present."

"Couldn't you have taken it back? What's the matter with you?!" Isabel waved her hands in Mercy's face.

"Nothing. Starting tonight, I am a free woman. Let some shark choke on that for a while! And besides, I couldn't take it back."

"Why not?"

"Some client was low on cash for my commission, so I cut a deal for his Rolex."

"Pero, Mercy, all that money wasted and for what?"

"For her freedom, for herself. Don't you see, Isabel?" asked Julia.

"Eso mismo! Julia knows about these feelings. You writers are like Walter Mercado, except that you figure out the present instead of the future."

"Here we go again with Walter Mercado. Muchacha! Get your head out of the future. I think it's crazy to waste all that money. You could have given it to charity," said Isabel.

"Let me tell you, I gave God something worth more than all the money in the world. I made Him a promise to abstain from men, or at least from the wrong kind. Mamá willing!" Mercy exclaimed, crossing herself.

"It's a fresh change, a new direction for you, Mercy, starting tonight!" said Julia, excited by her friend's flair for the dramatic moment full of possibilities. Mercy was like that, always on the edge of the possible. Unlike herself, Julia thought, as she grabbed both of them by their arms. Felipe crossed her mind for an instant, but his image was puffed away by Isabel talking.

"Bueno, if that's the case, then a used Rolex was worth it," said Isabel. The three women walked back to the lobby.

"So, where are we going?" asked Mercy.

"Mercy, tonight your promise will be put to the test. I've planned an evening with no men in it!"

"There is a God, and She is smiling upon us!" laughed Julia as they reached Isabel's Ford Expedition parked in the covered garage.

Chapter 10

—◦◦◦—

Julia

*I*sabel drove them to a small Spanish restaurant off Eighth Street in the heart of Little Havana, Café Quixote. The building had the feel of a traditional Spanish city house with an interior central courtyard. Its various rooms opened to the garden found there. The garden was decorated with plants and flowers, a bench, a few tables, and a fountain. Black wrought-iron details were sprinkled throughout. Red clay planters accented the windowsills. A colorful collection of miniature clay Spanish dancers was displayed in a glass armoire; next to it, below a lantern, the wall was covered with photographs of famous Latin American personalities who had eaten there. Among the better known were the images of Julio Iglesias, Celia Cruz, Cristina, El Puma, and Ronald Reagan.

Isabel, Julia, and Mercy sat at a wooden table by a window in what used to be the living room. The thick, red, silk-embroidered leather of the seats cracked as they sat down on the wooden chairs. The waiter immediately brought them warm bread with olive oil and a carafe of sangría. The three women ate plentifully, especially Mercy, who ordered a Galician white bean soup and a sweet plantain omelet. Isabel and Julia shared a seafood paella. It was a time-consuming meal, allowing the women to talk a lot and drink three more carafes of sangría.

After they had finished the custard with caramel glaze desserts and while the coffee was being brought out, Isabel excused herself from the table. She made a call from the courtyard to check on her boys. They were home watching the *Star Wars* movies she had rented them. Isabel heard the sounds of a guitar and clapping wafting through the courtyard.

"Isabel, where are you going?" Julia asked, as she watched her friend return to the table and grab her purse instead of sitting back down. Isabel led her friends through the paths in the courtyard.

"You aren't thinking of going home already, are you, Julia?"

"Well, it's late."

"So? There's no work tomorrow; you can sleep in."

"But I wanted to get up early and do some writing," Julia protested.

"Un día es un día," said Mercy. "One day isn't going to kill you."

"I have a deadline."

"Julia, you always have a deadline," said Isabel.

"Vamos," added Mercy. "Do it for me. I've never been to a tablao before."

"All right, but I can't stay long." Julia tapped her watch.

"Bien. We'll stay for one set," Isabel answered.

They approached the darkened entrance of the small detached building which once served as a carriage house. Its exterior walls were covered with thick bougainvillea vines overflowing with fuchsia-colored blooms.

As they opened the thick wooden door, cigar smoke curled over them and the music stopped. They entered the small dark space, no larger than a modest living room. A freestanding bar took up the front of the room. The space behind the bar was cluttered with round tables large enough for two, but with four and six people elbowed around them instead. The women walked through the crowded bar searching for an empty table. The set was over and some people began to leave. Isabel spied a just-abandoned table tucked to the side but up front, right on the edge of the stage, really a small raised wooden platform. They had to lean back to look up at the performers. Isabel ordered Cointreau for everyone in honor of Lucinda.

After a while, a single guitarist, dressed in black, came out and sat on a wooden stool in the corner of the platform. His profile was hardly visible in the dim light, yet the guitar's smooth surface radiated in his arms. He strummed a couple of slow boleros on his Spanish guitar, then plunged into a rhythmic melody. A singer, an older man with deep lines in his face and a sonorous voice, joined him. He loosened his shirt collar and began to sing nostalgically for a love denied in a faraway landscape. The female dancer rushed the platform, quick and furious, like a sword thrust. She took up the song for a verse, her throaty notes carried by the smoke to the darkest slits of the room. Julia crossed her legs, the rise of the skirt exposing her smooth knees to the sudden spotlight. With a snap of her heels, the dancer threw the song back at the singer, who by now was accompanying her with his staccato clapping. Her long scarlet dress against the black background made her look ablaze. It hugged her trim torso until it exploded at the hips into a voluminous ruffled skirt. Long black tassels hung loosely from the V neck of the dress, accentuating her smooth bare back. She was a tall and slender woman, yet with a forceful presence. She lost no time getting started. Julia sat up in her seat riveted by the unfolding scenario.

Since the space was limited, the dancer used her footwork and body movements to show her emotions. With almost feline, sinuous movements, she turned her upper body in half and whole turns while adding subtle hip motions to the dance. Her long black hair, lightly held with a ribbon at the nape of her neck, accented her sensuous moves. It was pulled back away from her face, except for a single strand on each side, curled flat against her cheeks. With her thick-heeled shoes, she beat the floor, awakening it to the rhythms of the guitarist. As the dance continued, the dancer paused between *coplas,* as if to gather strength for the next verse, each successive one becoming faster, with more steps than the previous one. Julia felt herself transported onto the platform. It was hard keeping still. She wondered if Isabel and Mercy could sense her abandon as she clapped for the dancer. Julia ordered another round of drinks.

In the second set, the dancer clapped the wooden castanets in her hands. They had an even and soft mesmerizing sound to Julia's ear. But her heart was pounding in perfect timing with the dancer's steps, rapid and powerful against the wood of the floor, echoing through the room, through her soul. The singer kept the beat with his clapping hands. Raising them above his head, he encouraged the audience to join in. That's when Julia noticed the dancer's concentration suck itself down to her heels like a black hole in space, sucking in the entire room's energy. Everything stopped making noise but the Uzi-like bursts of the dancer's heels. The small room exploded with the pounding sounds. Julia felt her heart beating furiously, as furiously as she swayed her crossed legs.

Mercy and Isabel were carried away by the mood as well, clapping and yelling *Aii . . . aii . . . aii . . . !* Mercy beat the table with her hands, causing some of her drink to spill on the tottering table. Julia grabbed a napkin to sop up the mess. Isabel leaned over to whisper something in Julia's ear but couldn't get her attention. Julia was wiping and watching the dancer at the same time. The dancer's steps, though just as fast, were now whispering to the packed room. With the sudden kill of the lights, the dancer stopped and the crowd broke out in a stampede of applause. The set was over.

"Oye! Watch what you're doing!" Isabel's brandy snifter lay broken on the table. Julia had knocked it over while furiously wiping away. The sound of the breaking glass drew a waiter's attention.

"Muchachas, no se preocupen. Aquí estoy para servirles," he said as he swept up the broken glass with a small hand broom. He quickly had the stained tablecloth replaced and gave each a drink on the house.

"I'd like to take him to my house," said Mercy, watching the

Spanish waiter leave them. "Did you see that? He looks like a cross between Mel Gibson and Antonio Banderas. Talk about a clone made in Heaven!"

"Now there's the *only* reason in the world why I'd marry again. Imagínate, the best of the Anglos and the best of the Latinos all rolled up into one man." Isabel raised her glass and made a toast.

"Salud to Mega Man!"

"Looks more like Mega Gay Guy to me." Julia pointed her glass to the bar. Mega Man was kissing the bartender who was tenderly returning his change. For a moment, they touched hands as they parted.

Mercy squinted her eyes to get a better look, then shook her head in defeat.

"God works in mysterious ways," Isabel said, smiling at Mercy.

"So what is this, I can look but I can't touch?"

"That's lusting," said Julia, thinking of the dancer as the lights flickered to signal the start of the last dance.

The three women settled back on their chairs, the humming of the crowd ebbed into silence, and the house lights were dimmed even more. The spotlight was softer now, giving the dancer a diffused glow, like that of a romantic Old World painting.

Standing perfectly still, as if posing for a master painter, the dancer let the spotlight travel the length of her body. Julia was quiet, her concentration absorbed by the slow-moving circle of light. Curtains of dust and cigarette smoke swirled through it. The dancer's feet still, the dance movement was transferred to the wrists, undulating with her arms and hips. Each sway of her body was echoed by the strumming guitar. To Julia it seemed as if the dancer was pulling the strings. She lifted the ample skirt and swung it back and forth, hypnotically. Like a toreador in front of his prey, she aimed her movement in a set direction. She stood in front of Julia. Julia noticed the dancer's shapely legs. She could see the muscle's tense outline along the full length of her calves. Julia was sitting so close to the platform she could almost touch the bottom of the dancer's skirt. The circle of light widened, its arc illuminating Julia's upturned face. For a second, her eyes were drawn to the dancer's eyes. Julia knew they were as green and as deep as the ancient cenote pools found in Mexico, where the dark waters held the secret desires of its Mayan female victims.

In a swift motion, as if daring Julia to follow, the dancer turned her bare back to Julia, lowering herself on one knee while arching her back. She concentrated all of the motions in her arms and her neck. Suddenly the guitar began to scream in a frenzy of high notes. Julia's pulse was throbbing. She was a knot of feelings.

The music intensified with the dancer pounding her heels and snapping the castanets. Her movements traveled outside time and space, along with Julia's soul. In spite of her sensuality, the dancer's motions emitted an air of strength and virility and control. Everything appeared to be moving at once: the staccato beat of the feet, the sharp play of the castanets, the motions of her head, hands, body, arms, all in unison with the skirt, all escalating with a primitive fury. Her eyes fixed on Julia, enveloping her, stripping her, caressing her with a passion she had never felt before. Julia became conscious of her own breathing. She could see the dancer's sweat, veining its way past her eyebrows, down her elegant nose, and gathering at the corners of her partially opened lips. With a clean jerk of her head, but with her eyes never leaving Julia's, she shook the sweat off, the drops raining down on the stage floor and on Julia's face. Julia tilted back her chair against the table, finding balance on the two back legs. With both hands over her flushed cheeks, Julia traced her upper lip with the tip of her tongue. At its corner, she got a taste of the dancer mingling with her own warm sweat. The guitar gave one last gasp of a chord, exhausted by the dancer's demands. The music stopped. The dancer continued in a flurry of quick steps.

Julia leaned forward, but just as the dancer suddenly came to a complete and utter stop, she lost her balance. As the chair fell from under her, Julia lunged toward the stage. She broke the fall by landing on her knees, but her upper body was sprawled on the stage, her palms slapping hard on its floor. When she looked up, the dance was over; the performers had abandoned the stage.

"Dios mío! Julia, qué te pasó? Are you OK?" asked Isabel.

"Estás roja como un tomate! Your cheeks are burning!" Mercy helped Julia to her feet. Mega Man pulled the chair over, offering Julia a cold glass of ice water. Julia sat down, taking huge gulps.

"I'm OK. I slipped, that's all."

"You slipped! You can say that again. Coño, you practically rushed the stage. What were you trying to do, grab the dancer's skirt, o qué?" said Mercy. "Aren't you a little old for that?"

Julia felt herself flush like a schoolgirl. "Give me a break, Mercy, my chair slipped, that's all."

The waiter interrupted Mercy, asking if another round was in order, but Isabel asked for the check instead. Julia protested by ordering another round of Cointreau.

Isabel raised her eyebrows questioning Julia, who answered, "Well, a person can change her mind, can't she?"

"I haven't said a word." Isabel relaxed back into her chair.

Mercy got up to go to the bathroom, but first she exclaimed, "Now, that was dancing! Let me tell you, I love salsa and merengue, but this!"—she pointed to the stage, the bracelets clamoring for attention—"but this—"

"She danced like an angel," interrupted Isabel.

"Carajo, like an angel on drugs!" said Mercy as she left for the bathroom.

Isabel and Julia laughed, watching Mercy leave the table. When she passed Mega Man, his back to her, Mercy turned around with her hands in the prayer position, her eyes directed at Mega Man and then toward the ceiling. She gave a little wave to her friends as she was swallowed by the crowd.

"You think she'll ever find Mr. Right?" asked Julia.

"I don't know, but she always finds Mr. Right There."

"Chicas, mind if I sit right here?" the flamenco dancer asked, grabbing the chair next to Julia. "I noticed you liked the show," she said, sitting down looking at her.

"No, please, yes, it was very good, fantastic really, did you like it, Isabel?"

"Yes. My name is Isabel and this is Julia. Thank you for sitting with us." Isabel eyed the dancer.

"Es mi placer. Me llamo Beatriz Palol." She shook hands with Isabel and then with Julia. Julia saw that she was wearing a sleeveless black leotard with a red wraparound skirt. Shaking her hand, Julia could see the muscles of her arms, girlish yet well defined, like those of an Olympic gymnast.

"You stayed for the last three sets. I appreciate that. So what do you do?" Beatriz asked Julia.

"I'm a professor and a writer," was all Julia could answer.

"What do you profess?" asked Beatriz with a smile of her full lips.

Julia was taken off guard by the strange question. She was also distracted by the sharp contrast between Beatriz' long black hair and her emerald green eyes.

"What do you mean?" Julia sincerely asked.

Beatriz gave a quick side-glance to Isabel. "I teach too, flamenco dancing, part-time at a private school, Ransom Prep in Coconut Grove."

"My friend's kids go there. Have you heard of the Colón family?" asked Julia.

"Care to join us in a drink?" Isabel interrupted.

"Hey, everybody, look who I've got!" It was Mercy with Mega Man arm in arm. "This is Francisco. And I am his brand-new realtor! He and his roommate, Julián?"—Mercy looked at Francisco to see if she got the name right—"they're looking to buy on the Beach."

"Hola, Franco. Can you have Julián make us my special drink?" Beatriz asked while Isabel introduced her to Mercy.

"Excuse my Spanish," said Mercy, "but, coño! Can you dance. Let me tell you, you had Julia here sweating like Pavarotti's dogs!"

"It's Pavlov's dogs, and they were salivating," corrected Isabel.

"That too! Listen," asked Mercy in a conspiratorial whisper, "does Francisco have a twin brother, not identical in every way, if you know what I mean? Isabel, I'm just kidding!"

"We made a promise to not talk about men tonight," Isabel explained to Beatriz.

"Here are the drinks. Gracias, Franco. So let's talk about Julia."

"What's in these?" Julia raised the glass, looking through the empty half, noticing how it distorted Isabel's raised eyebrow.

"A blend of Carlos II brandy and condensed milk sprinkled with cinnamon. Like an Iberian eggnog. I drink it every night after my last performance. It soothes my passion." She raised her glass to Julia's, and as they clinked, Isabel and Mercy joined in on the silent toast.

After only a few sips of her drink, Beatriz rose to go. Julia, looking disappointed, said to her, "Before you leave, Beatriz, would you mind if I called you sometime? I'm writing a book on the life of Latinas in the United States and I'd like to have a Spaniard's perspective. Here's my card from the university." Julia pulled out her card and a pen. "I'll write my home phone number as well."

Beatriz took the pen from Julia's hand. She wrote on a napkin and, folding it, said, "If you want to talk, call me. I'm always home in the daytime." She then handed Julia the napkin and turned to Mercy and Isabel. "Adiós, chicas, gracias, come back again. Call me soon, Julia."

On the way home in the car, Julia sat quietly, still holding the napkin in her hand. She left it unfolded. She felt a strange sensation of mystery with familiarity whenever her mind allowed her fingertips to speak to her.

"Por Dios, Julia, are you listening?" Mercy asked, turning around in the front seat. "What was going on back there? That dancer was making a move on you like I've never been moved on by a guy. And let me tell you, I've had a U-Haul load of moves made on me."

"She's a dancer, she's supposed to move," Julia testily answered. "I really want to get her point of view on some things. She sounded very interesting," Julia added self-consciously.

Isabel and Mercy exchanged glances.

"I'm telling you, there was nothing going on," insisted Julia.

"Sure, anything you say, mi amiga," Mercy said, ignoring Julia's last comment. "You're quiet for a Cuban," she said, turning to Isabel.

"It's four in the morning, we drank too much, and my head is full of dancing. La verdad es que I had a good time. I hope you got over your widow's watch for Ramón," Isabel said to Mercy.

"Oye meng," Mercy said, staring out the window at the passing neon signs of Little Havana storefronts, "all I know is when cousin Isa says no men, watch out, she means it. She puts up a mile-thick shield without a minuscule crack for penetration, if you know what I mean. Let me tell you, at this rate, you won't need to go to confession for another four years!"

"Mercy, que boca!" Isabel said, both of them breaking into weary laughter.

Isabel could see Julia in the rearview mirror. She was looking down. Julia unfolded the napkin, and under the passing streetlights, she made out what Beatriz had written.

Para Julia,
    My phone number for your words,
    and a rose for a rose.
Beatriz Palol

Julia folded the napkin, making sure to follow the same crease. She closed her eyes, her mind wandering back to the dance, seeing the dancer's skirt, realizing how its folds resembled the blossoming petals of a red rose.

Chapter 11

———✦———

Lucinda

Dear Isabel,

Thanks for calling last night. It was good to hear your voice. You don't know how much it helps that you and Julia and Mercy are there for me. Everything helps: the letters, the calls, Julia even sent me a book on how Latinas can improve their self-esteem, *The María Paradox*, have you read it? It seems interesting. My self-esteem can use all the help it can get right now.

I just got back from my morning walk for fresh bread at the corner bakery. That's all I've been eating for breakfast since I've been here. It seems like I've been away forever. Bread and water. I feel like I'm either cleansing my bowels or doing time in a penitentiary. Why should I be the one doing penance? As I write this, you should hear what I'm playing on the CD— Gregorian chants but with a Dominican percussion accompaniment. Mamá hates it, but I say to hell with the European facade we've all bought into. Sabes qué? She had my father install a full-size fake Victorian fireplace in the ranch house! Mercy would love it! How is she? She sounded desesperada when she phoned me last week to see how I was doing. I'm glad she called. But you know Mercy, the conversation ended up being about her and Ramón. La pobre, she worked so hard on that relationship. Maybe that's our problem, Isa. We all work too hard.

I miss you all very much. But I can't go back, not yet. Julia offered to come down for a few days but I told her not to. I don't want to bother her. Además, I think it's good for me to be alone. You might think I'm crazy, but I'm enjoying my exile here back home. The kids are fine. They are enjoying being home tutored and I'm getting along—taking a lot of long walks. Remember El Malecón? It's still beautiful and rough around the edges. What did that sociologist friend of Julia's call it? The Ocean Drive of Third World countries? Bueno, give me the clamoring-for-space street vendors, the honking cars, the fuming buses, the crowing roosters, and the cool humidity of a tropical morning anytime over the disinfected isolation of my pent-up banker's neighborhood in Miami. Don't get me wrong, mi amiga, I love Miami. But those houses look like rows of large ornate mausoleums. I was dying in one. Y mi matrimonio? On its last breath? Thank God I'm down here. The gulps of home air my lungs are gasping for are keeping my heart from breaking apart any further. Somehow the more I lose myself in the nerve of daily life here, the more I calm my nerves.

So, here I am, still in the land of the merengues, where the men slip and slide in and out of beds, as much as my hips move when I dance to 4.40. Not that I've been doing any dancing lately. I am getting out more. It doesn't help (or does it?) that the few times I've gone out to dinner or to run an errand—mamá is always inventing something or other to get me out of the house—I've had more than a small share of "looks" and comments from the men. I'm not used to it anymore. I don't remember it bothering me so much when I was growing up, but now, all I see is Carlos lechering after that woman like these men after me.

But when your own husband is looking someplace else, you start to wonder what is wrong with you. I guess you went through all this too when David left you. I feel like I understand you better now, Isa. Qué sorpresa esta vida, mi amiga. I never thought I'd find myself on this side of a soap opera. It's true what you said last night. It's too easy for us women to meld ourselves to our husbands and our children. Before you know it, we have forgotten who we are. I have to learn to be alone again. To be honest, I can't remember the last time I went somewhere or did something simply because I felt like it.

The other day I went to one of papá's business dinners at El Lina restaurant. Mamá asked me to come, as a distraction from my "melancolía." This is her word for any female problem under the sun. I told her no, but you know how persistent mamá can be, so I went. (See what I mean?) Well, a man, some supplier for one of my father's friends, decided to supply me with a chunk of his leg. He sat next to me during the dinner, and during the entire meal he kept opening his legs so wide, I had no choice but to feel his thigh rub against mine. And if that wasn't bad enough, he dropped his napkin on my side during dessert. As he bent down to retrieve it, he "accidently" raised my skirt under the table and stroked his hand on my sandaled toes. I gave him the dirtiest look; he just smiled. And he talked, more like pontificated, about the latest stock upturn on fertilizer. Then he passed me his business card under a sugar packet while preparing my coffee. And that's when it hit me, Isa. I hit him right across his successful face! Julia would have been proud. Pero, for a second, he looked like Carlos in another few years, all puffed up and full of shit. You know the kind I'm talking about. My father guessed what had gone on. We know each other. You can imagine his reaction. Papi might be a successful businessman and highly educated, but when it comes to honor, he's still a guajiro, and you don't mess with a country boy. He was on that little cock as quick as one of those champion roosters your father is always betting on! Mamá was cackling like a hen in a fox's den. She didn't know whether to hit my father, hit the guy, or hit me, she was so embarrassed. The worst part was that while all this was going on, the guy's wife sat on the other side. She didn't say a word or lift a finger. That could have been me, Isa. Me and Carlos putting up with each other's revenge.

The manager of the place took my father's side immediately and escorted the escoria out, his wife leading the way with her head held high.

I got up and took a taxi home, alone. I'm sure mamá made up the most appropriate excuse for my behavior. Tremenda distracción! The episode just reminded me more of Carlos. I get disgusted thinking of him and what he is doing to me. I always saw him differently from these "I deserve you" guys. But now I don't know anymore. Did Carlos slip his phone number to that woman too? Maybe I was even there, oblivious to the whole thing. Is this his first time? Isa, how could I have been so stupid not to know. It seems so pathetic to me. I hope our sons show more respect for their wives and themselves. My father never went back on his vows. I know, I asked him.

Papá wants me to join him again in la finca por unos días. He has to inspect some new cattle he's having shipped from Ocala. Mamá wants me to leave the kids with her in the city. She thinks it's unhealthy for them to see their mother "en mi condición." In my condition, as if I had some ailment. She completely disapproves of my coming home, and I found out she called Carlos in Miami the minute I walked in the door. He refused to come get me as mamá requested and told her he respected my decision. Can you believe that! Respected my decision! He has some nerve using the word respect. Some kind of respect, a buena hora. Pendejo.

Mamá, of course, doesn't see it that way. She thinks I should go home. "Una señora never packs her bags unless she means to never return. Una familia no es un juego," she declares in her preacher voice. I tell her my family is not a game to me, but she doesn't listen. She wants me to return and apologize to him for abandoning my home. Can you believe her? Sí, and she keeps asking me what I did wrong. "A man never looks outside unless he's unhappy inside," she repeats over and over. So that means in her world I was making Carlos unhappy; I drove him to another woman's arms. The way she sees it, yo soy la culpable y él la víctima. I have to tell you, Isa, mamá is not the easiest person to live with, especially at a time like this. I think she's more worried about Carlos than me. And the publicity a divorce will bring to Las Familias. She fears the newspapers and the magazines as much as she loves to read about her friends in them.

By the way, have you seen this month's *People en Español?* There was a big sign for it at the supermercado. You would have loved it: Luis Miguel and Leonardo DiCaprio both on the cover. If you squint your eyes, you can blend (or morph, as Brenda says it) both into one and the same. A sign of the future, don't you think? That's what I need Isa, a sign. A sign from God to help me figure out what to do.

I can't figure out what to do about that woman. I can't bring myself to write or even say her name. I've been going crazy trying to "run into" her all over town. I have gone by the gallery where she exhibits her so-called art, by her studio where she works; I even drove by her house near the Botanical Gardens. It's as if she disappeared from the face of the earth. La hija de la gran puta, excuse my French; while I'm going crazy looking for her here, ella con mi esposo arm in arm in some Jewish deli in Miami. Thanks for telling me. It must have been hard for you to do so, but believe me, I needed to know. I must be insane to be here when she is there. Carlos probably told her I was gone. But you know what? In a way it's good I don't run into her. If I saw her right now I would use her face as modeling clay and mold myself a spittoon for the vaqueros in the ranch.

I've been going to the gym almost every day since I've gotten here. Two hours daily. Mercy calls me G.I. Juana! I don't know what I'm preparing myself for, but I know it's stronger than any Navy SEAL make-believe exercise. I haven't seen my in-laws yet. I don't know if Carlos has said anything.

Isa, I'm so angry at Carlos for putting me through all this. A part of me wants to annihilate him, desintegrarlo, so I never have to see him again. But the problem is, another part of me is frozen with fear of that very thing. I want to stop being so angry and afraid all the time. I don't know how but I'm trying. Did I tell you that last Sunday I fainted in church? I was praying so hard, asking God for a sign. When I came to I was in the arms of a very old priest who was fanning me with the Mass song sheet. He kept saying "re-vivir, re-vivir" or something like that. Te confieso que I felt different, almost re-nacida, born again as the Americans say. But then I think of my children, Roberto and Brenda, and I'm dead again. I have to think for all of us or we'll lose everything we've worked so hard to build. And I don't mean material things. Can a marriage be born again?

Well, this letter is way too long already. Sorry for the descarga. You are a good friend, Isa. I'm sure Mercy will get back on her realtor's feet soon. She's much better at finding properties anyway! As for Julia, I wish I could have seen her sprawled on that stage! Don't worry about the dancer too much. Julia has always handled unwanted advances well. It's too bad she said no to Felipe, but it doesn't surprise me. From our conversations, I can tell she's searching. Felipe was convenient; I think she wants more than that. Please say hola to mis amigas, tell them I miss them very much. Take care, Isa, of yourself and your boys—this may be as good as it gets. Por ahora, anyway.

Cariños, Lucinda

Chapter 12

—∽∽∽—

Lucinda

Lucinda mailed the letter the next morning while leaving the gym after a tough workout. Just a few minutes before, while showering in her private stall, she had noticed her reflection in the full-length mirror. Before it steamed up, the effects of her training were evident. Curves yes, always curves, but now she noticed firmness and definition to her body. Her muscles stood out, her posture was sure of itself, her femaleness had an edge to it. The mirror began to steam up, and Lucinda saw her old reflection haze itself into existence. Soft curves, she thought, like a catcher's mitt, always absorbing the blows. With her left hand she slowly wiped away the fuzzy image. She looked straight into her eyes; they too had an edge to them, like a pitcher's eyes, knowing exactly where to throw the ball next: to the Colóns.

She decided she had avoided seeing her in-laws long enough. She felt strong enough to face them. After stopping at the post office, Lucinda impulsively called Don Carlos on the cellular. To her surprise he was home. She declined his mid-day lunch invitation and agreed to meet at two in the afternoon. This delay gave her time to prepare. Lucinda feared what Don Carlos would do with his. But she knew, deep inside, he was always prepared. After the phone conversation, Lucinda stopped at a small chapel. She made an offering to St. Jude, the saint of hopeless causes, by lighting a candle and making a silent promise.

St. Jude, show me the way to save this marriage. I can't do it alone. I promise to fight for my family. I took vows. I intend to keep them, but will Carlos? Help us, help me, give me a sign, please. Amen.

As she was walking down the steps of the church, the whirl of a helicopter overhead abruptly broke her inner silence. She traced its path over the city's skyline. Then, she rushed into the car and made her way through the mid-day traffic.

Lucinda arrived at her parents' apartment just as her children were finishing their private lessons. The apartment was spacious, occupying the entire fifteenth floor of the luxury building. Its marble floors reflected her mother's collection of Andújar and Bidó paintings. But her prize painting occupied the central wall facing the elevator doors in the large foyer. Her mother had bought the Wyeth with the first profits from the cattle ranch many years ago. Now it was worth millions. She stopped in front of it, just as she always did when she was a schoolgirl coming home for lunch.

Because of you I studied painting. I wanted to paint. Mamá never let me touch you, but I know you touched me. It was our secret. I thrived with the knowledge you gave me. I grew old before my time, seeing your brush strokes for what they were doing, shaping life into a possibility that no one else could imagine. But can any brush paint what I am imagining? I want to touch you, finally, like a touchstone, like the little girl that once imagined, no, saw her destiny in your texture and knew what she had to do.

"Mami! You're here!" Brenda said, rushing out of the den.

Her brother, Roberto, followed. "Wait till you see what we got!" he added.

Lucinda allowed herself to be pulled away from the painting. The kids took her to the large family terrace overlooking the city.

"See? Brand new bicycles!" the children exclaimed almost in unison.

They could see her hesitation. "Don Abuelo gave them to us! The black one is mine and the red one is hers," Roberto declared. "Don Abuelo" is what Don Carlos liked his grandchildren to call him.

"When did these get here?" Lucinda asked the young tutor, who had just come out of the den.

"Around an hour ago. I put them out here because they were a major distraction, as you can imagine."

Lucinda kissed her children and sent them back to the den to finish their lessons before lunch. She dismissed the cook and prepared their lunches herself. She made the kids extra-thick sandwiches and let them have their fill of potato chips, even allowing them to have as much Coke as they pleased. A good old American lunch, Lucinda said to herself as she thought of Don Carlos' bicycles. For dessert, she dismissed the tutor early. The kids were happy, but Lucinda was disappointed with herself.

She left them watching TV as she prepared for the meeting with Don Carlos at two o'clock. She chose to wear a navy blue double-breasted pantsuit accented with gold buttons. Isabel's business mantra kept repeating itself in her mind. "When going into a lion's den, dress like a lion." She grabbed the keys to the only car she'd been using since arriving in Santo Domingo, her father's beat-up Hummer. He was proud of the fact that it had the dents to show for its ranch workhorse status. Lucinda got comfort from the irony of driving in a military vehicle to her in-laws'.

The armed guard let her through the gates of their eight-foot white stucco wall. As she approached the large circular drive in the distance, she thought of Don Carlos' first words to her at her wedding. "En esta familia no hay divorcio."

—nn—

Don Carlos was tall and slender like his son. Only his unruly gray hair and slightly hunched shoulders revealed his age. He was wearing his usual hand-washed and starched linen guayabera with charcoal gray pants. Don Carlos slowly rose from his lavish horsehair-upholstered couch, deliberately taking his time. For a few minutes, he didn't speak. He paced the large room, finally motioning for Lucinda to sit. Lucinda looked around her and for the first time saw the house for how she felt inside it, a gilded trap. These are the trappings of Carlos' childhood, she thought, as she felt the crushed blue velvet of the Queen Anne chair rub against her pant legs. She was sitting in the grand living room surrounded by eighteenth- and nineteenth-century English and Continental furnishings under a high cathedral ceiling. The centerpiece was a magnificent mahogany breakfront secretaire bookcase with a swan-neck pediment adorning the top, above a carved fretwork cornice. The top section had glazed doors protecting Don Carlos' rare book collection, and the bottom had numerous small drawers. It was overpowering the room, much like Don Carlos, who finally spoke up, looking straight at her.

"Problems like this," he said, "can damage La Familia, and the Bank."

Lucinda felt her stomach clench. She didn't expect the knockout punch so soon. Her heart was trembling as she crossed her legs and squared her shoulders.

"With all due respect, this has nothing to do with the bank. This is a personal matter."

"Nothing is strictly personal, Lucinda. People will think, if the Presidente can't keep his house in order, how can he manage the Bank."

"It's no one's business," said Lucinda, noting the rococo chandelier in gilt bronze and cut lead crystal towering above the dining table in the adjoining room. Suddenly it looked dangerous.

"Business is everyone's proposition. In our world, these things get around, Lucinda. Sometimes the wife is the last to know," said Don Carlos.

Ever so slightly, her shoulders hunched at the realization that he knew of his son's infidelity before she ever did. He sat in the matching chair next to her and, reaching over the antique wine table, grabbed her hand.

"Remember, Lucinda, without the Bank, you and Carlos, well, let's put it this way, you would have a much different life in Miami."

His words placed a picture in her mind of the life he threatened her with, the very life she desired, the very life she had before his bank proposition snatched it away. Lucinda felt like snatching her hand back, but instead she held on to his, slightly tightening her grip, to her surprise and his.

"I'm well aware, Don Carlos, of the bank's role in our lives." Lucinda released his hand, standing up. Looking down at him she said, "But if you are worried about the reputation of the bank, why not talk to your son. He's the one creating the problem."

"Sit down, Lucinda." Don Carlos poured himself a glass of vermouth from the decanter on the maple wine table. She sat back down but declined his offer of a glass. "You love him. Don't be naive. It's all in your hands. It's up to you to handle this discreetly."

"Handle what? Your son's, no, my husband's betrayal is not a Bank deal, Don Carlos; this is my marriage, and there is nothing discreet about Carlos' behavior," Lucinda said, raising her voice to him.

"Por Dios, Lucinda. He is your husband and the president of the Bank. And he is my son. Or have you forgotten? What is important here is to remember La Familia comes first!" He walked around the chair and gripped its back with one hand, the other still holding his vermouth. Lucinda could see the whites of his fingertips against the blue velvet.

"My family comes first," Lucinda answered, turning to face him.

"I don't know about that. After all, Lucinda, you are the one who abandoned her home and dragged her children out of school." Don Carlos calmly eyed her.

"Cómo se atreve, how dare you say such a thing to me? You don't know a thing about—"

He interrupted her with the wave of a hand. "Listen to me, Lucinda." Don Carlos very carefully placed his glass down on the table. "I don't know why you came here. What goes on between a husband and wife should stay between them. I think you need to accept that these things happen and go on with your life. Besides, hasn't Carlos provided well for you and the children? That's all that matters. Now stop this foolishness, pack your bags, and go home to your husband, where you belong."

"I know exactly where I belong. I have sacrificed too much."

"Sí, te has sacrificado. Isn't love a sacrifice after all? You have been a good woman, why throw that away?"

"Una buena Señora? What good did that get me, eh?"

"Lucinda, you are taking this too personally. Trust me, I know about these things, and this has nothing to do with you. Buy yourself a new dress, Lucinda, some jewelry, and you'll see how much better you'll feel. I'll send a chauffeur to take you to the airport first thing tomorrow."

Lucinda raised herself from the chair. There was nothing more to say.

"That won't be necessary. I can arrange my own things, Don Carlos."

"As you wish, Lucinda. Just remember before you make any more reckless decisions that Carlos has finally found his way and is very successful at it. We all need to support his efforts. Nothing should interfere now."

"I won't stay in a relationship without trust."

"In this family there are no divorces."

"I take my marriage seriously."

"Ay Lucinda, you haven't heard a word I've said." Don Carlos raised his arms, signaling her to follow him. He led her through the grand French doors, to the back terrace overlooking a large walled-in garden edged in statuesque royal palms. Brick paths rambled through rows of red, pink, and white hibiscus bushes alternating with clusters of birds of paradise and red and yellow heliconias. The paths all led to a French-style gazebo in the middle. "You see this land, Lucinda, this house, the banks, it'll be your children's one day, all of it, but now we need Carlos to continue his work. He can't be distracted with personal problems. Focus on what is important, Lucinda, and don't let the details divert your attention. These things pass. Go home. You have more to lose than you imagine."

"Lucinda!" It was her mother-in-law, Doña Ofelia, approaching from the family quarters. "I am sorry I took so long. But I know Carlos treated you as he should." Doña Ofelia was dressed in a light green button-down silk dress, with her trademark scarf loosely wrapped around her neck, diverting attention from her age. The tight dress accentuated her plump figure.

"Let's get some coffee and sweets. Then we can have a good chat."

"No, Ofelia, Lucinda has to go now. We are finished here, no?" Don Carlos patted his wife's plump arm.

"We're finished here, Don Carlos."

They accompanied her back through the house, its fine furnishings suffocating Lucinda as she walked to the pace of Doña Ofelia's heels crisply striking the slate floor. Outside, while waiting for the attendant to bring the Hummer, Lucinda felt her legs buckling under her; she strained to return the good-bye kisses offered. They left her as she waited. Lucinda held herself up on one of the two Parisiene iron streetlights dressing the portal. She remembered kissing Carlos under these lights. More than once, she had been impressed by the fancy European furniture, the rococo chandelier, the delicately brocaded upholstery; it all seemed out of place now. Then she had been impressed by such an atmosphere of Old World posturing. But outside, in the blinding sunlight, she saw the brush strokes of such a life for what they were. Now this place seemed like a hotel painting, with its images too large, its brush strokes too obvious, and its oil paint too thick. With the Hummer having arrived, the attendant by its open door, Lucinda shook the dust off her shoes. Taking slow, long breaths of fresh air, she looked up at the brilliant tropical sky, at the riot of green trees reaching toward it, and at its cookie cut-out clouds. She knew that this unadulterated canvas would be her fresh start.

As the gate closed behind her, she knew she wouldn't be at the airport the next morning. She would join her father in the finca instead.

———

Lucinda felt the weight of her heavy mood begin to float away as she and Don Leonardo left behind the gray landscape of city buildings and the clattering noises of car horns. She rolled down the Hummer's window and imagined huge pieces of armor being lifted and blown off her body by the rushing wind. She pictured them banging and clanking off the road, finally coming to a rest by some clump of weeds. When she was growing up, the countryside was always her escape route, her salvation, when city life got so hectic that she couldn't take it anymore. She got this feel of the country from her father. Looking over at him, his grayish black hair dancing with the wind, she remembered how happy he always looked.

"Qué bella es la tierra, eh Lucinda? Let's turn off the air and breathe it all in." He smiled at her. After a while on the road, he said, "Look, the city has stopped." Don Leonardo pointed to the passing place where the last city block could still be made out.

Living in Miami for so long, where one city merges into another in every direction, Lucinda had forgotten how Santo Domingo sharply comes to an end. She saw this herself from the air on the few occasions she accompanied her father in his helicopter on the way to the ranch, usually when the roads had flooded or were under repair. After driving by a few vendors in their palm-thatched stands, selling literally the fruits of their labor, they stopped at one. Don Leonardo always bought coco frío for the two of them. He never haggled, always paying the asking price. "Imagine the luxury of having someone stand out here all day long so that you and I can drink this cool, fresh coconut milk! It's priceless," he would say to her when she was younger.

"Don Manuel," her father addressed the old parched-skinned vendor, "muchas gracias. Y su familia, todos bien? Let us pray for a really hot day, eh?!" The campesino laughed at her father's sly way of wishing him good fortune. With his overly used but still sharp machete, he whacked the coconuts just so and placed straws into the slits. Lucinda swallowed hers in gulps, feeling the cool, heavy water glide down her throat as her father drove on. The coolness of the coconut milk inside her, along with the warmth of the rushing wind, made her sleepy. She closed her eyes for a while. A jolt of the Hummer awakened her. She suddenly felt herself swallowed up by the clean, green coolness surrounding her. The lush foliage lined the highway, occasionally crossing over the curb, as if trying to consume the asphalt and her. Here, nature, not man, was still in control, thought Lucinda. As they drove up into the now hilly countryside, she took in a deep breath, as if trying to inhale an antidote.

The road narrowed as they deepened their journey into the hills. Lucinda could smell the soil and almost touch the branches of the bamboo and banana leaves along the roadside welcoming her back. The ranch was only three hours north of the capital, but with its palm-filled hillsides, its sugarcane fields, its pastures, and its small pueblo, it seemed like a million miles away.

Lucinda took it all in as if seeing it for the first time. They passed a wooden shack along the road and slowed down at the approach to the little country bodega painted yellow. Lucinda noticed it was the only painted structure around. Two boys came rushing out of it and running barefoot across the river-stone path, waved at Don Leonardo. He pulled over beside a cluster of coconut palms and called out to one of the boys.

"Mario, está tu padre?"

"No, Don Leonardo. Fue a la capital."

"Tell him to come by la finca tomorrow. I have a job for him."

"Sí, Don Leonardo."

Don Leonardo took out ten pesos from his pocket and handed them to the boy. The boy hesitated but finally took them with a wide grin.

"Gracias, Don Leonardo. Gracias!"

Don Leonardo continued to drive into the interior. "Money is like a seed, eh? Plant it in a fertile soul, and watch the miracles grow," he said to himself.

"It's too bad some people treat money like manure."

"Give it a rest, Lucinda. Mira, we're almost home." For as long as she could remember, her father had called the ranch home while he referred to the city apartment as the office.

Finally, before dusk, Lucinda made out the approach to the finca. The neighbor's house at the top of a hill was an easy give-away. Like a watchtower, it loomed over the countryside. She had never met the couple but was told a pair of Americanos had built the house back in the seventies. They had passed away since then, and their children and grandchildren occasionally came to visit in the summertime. Her father had been trying to buy it for years.

Don Leonardo pulled up to the immense wooden gates; she rushed out to open them. He didn't wait for her to get back in the Hummer. Since she was a little girl, she had always insisted they drop her off at the gate so she could slowly make her way in. She meandered down the long dirt path. She picked a few wildflowers. With a whisper of air, she watched the down-like dandelions in her hand flitter away, each one carrying a bit of her anger. She reached the edge of the forest in front of her. Don Leonardo left the large tract of forest as a buffer between the pasture fields and the ranch house. A small creek ran through it, perpendicular to the road. Rather than divert the road or the creek which ran over it, he dammed the creek, creating a natural swimming pool to one side of the road. The spillover gave the effect of a miniature waterfall, and the sound of the running water always put Lucinda at ease.

She took off her shoes and sat on the ledge dangling her feet into the water. The sun hid behind the hills, taking with it all traces of air. After looking around at the empty fields beyond the house, Lucinda removed her dress. In her bra and underwear, she slowly slid into the black waters. The cold of the water penetrated her skin, feeling like a razor blade cutting right at her pain. She floated on her back staring long into the night sky, still tinted a purplish hue. This felt right, thought Lucinda.

After a long while, Don Leonardo came looking for her, prepared with a towel and a robe. She quietly held his arm as they walked up to the house. He went ahead to bed. Lucinda, too awake for sleep, changed clothes and sat on the wooden chair on the front porch, her legs resting on the hammock hanging between two posts. She poured herself a glass of Cointreau. As she sipped the orangy liqueur, she felt every muscle in her body relax, all the way to her extremities. After the first glass, Lucinda lay in the hammock. She was feeling like a sky diver who never had to land. Her last thoughts were of Isabel. She would be proud of her, she thought, not one tear the entire day.

But for the next five days, Lucinda could not stop crying. Her mother called her twice daily, in the morning and in the evening, offering platitudes of advice Lucinda could not stomach. Her father spent the days working the ranch and quietly serving her plates of home-cooked meals he made himself. Don Leonardo did not believe in having servants at the ranch house. It was by watching him that Lucinda had learned to cook. But she barely ate, and the only information she processed was the goings-on about her children. Her father barely spoke to her except to comment on the rain of the last three days.

"Did you know two thirds of the world is still under water? Perhaps Noah's Flood isn't over yet."

"Perhaps we're all drowning in God's toilet."

"Lucinda, you've been locked up for five days. You know, if you were a tree out there in one of my acres you'd be soaked and happy, and the next day you'd be the better for it."

"Toilet paper is made from trees."

"Mi hija, eat what you can. I have a long day tomorrow." Don Leonardo went into the master bedroom, leaving Lucinda sitting at the large wooden kitchen table. She slowly began to eat the cassava and pumpkin soup he had made for her. He had left the window over the sink open. Lucinda could smell the aroma of the soup mixing with the smell of the wet vegetation coming through the window. The sensation put a picture in her head of when, as a ten-year-old, she would play in the rain and her father would call her to dinner from the same window.

The next morning, Lucinda woke up early with the sunlight pouring through her open bedroom window. Her father had laid out her old pair of ripped blue jeans, a short-sleeved ivory cotton blouse, boots, and her rabbit-skin leather-brimmed hat on the old trunk at the foot of her bed. Lucinda dressed slowly, feeling at ease in this attire. She made her way to the kitchen, which was filled with the aroma of fresh-brewed coffee. On the table was a backpack with a note from her father next to it. Lucinda read it as she poured the coffee into her mug.

Good morning! Qué día para ti. I have to go to the far field and help Don Mario with the fencing for the new cattle. I had him saddle up Sonora for you. That horse is still wild! There is enough food in the backpack for a good long ride. Expect me past sunset. Tu padre

Sonora was Lucinda's horse, a strong thoroughbred mare her father had bought from the American neighbors on the hill. For a few hours, Lucinda rode through the grazing fields, up and down the hills and between the coffee trees. Her depression was passing like last night's front that brought out the sun. As the sun grew stronger, every living thing around her seemed greener. If life were a color it would have to be green, thought Lucinda as she galloped with Sonora, who, like herself, was full of an energy she couldn't hold back. Lucinda touched the muscular neck of the animal beneath her and felt its warm sweat. She trotted down a woody slope to a riverbank and got down. After tying the horse to a tree trunk, she pulled off her boots and soaked her feet in the stream. She flipped her long hair over her forehead and let the current comb it for a while. Then she took off her red bandana and soaked it in the stream. She wiped its cool wetness across her brow before tying it around her neck again. The dripping water drenched her blouse. Lucinda sat on a large sunny stone in a clearing and undressed to her jeans. Laying the blouse and bra over the stone to dry, she peeked in the backpack and began to eat the cheese and bread her father had prepared earlier. He'd put in a full bottle of red wine and a large plastic cup. Lucinda had already made up her mind to stay out all day, so she ate exactly half of everything she had. The half bottle of wine she drank, along with the warmth of the stone, aroused all her senses. She lay back on its round, smooth surface with her arms beneath her head. She felt the warm breeze on her bare breasts and caught herself wishing Carlos were with her.

She remembered one morning in particular when they had come to la finca to spend a week away from the New York chaos. Like today, they had risen early to go riding. They rode to the south end of the property up a high hill. Once at the top, they got off to give the horses and themselves a rest. Sitting at the peak they took in the view. Carlos sat up erect and looked around quietly; Lucinda lay on the ground and placed her head on his lap, content in his presence. The sun beat down upon them. Lucinda felt the sweat cover her face. Carlos fingered her hair, drawing it away from her brow; he reached down and kissed her on the lips. Carlos' hands began searching her body. When he started to fumble with her shirt buttons, she sat up and teased him to stop, mentioning the ranch hands off in the distance.

Her remembrance was interrupted by the din of a helicopter somewhere in the distance. Lucinda opened her eyes as the sound drew closer. Suddenly over the treetops, she saw a shiny black helicopter rush by, disappearing over the ridge of a nearby hill. The sound returned as the helicopter circled once, high over the clearing, and continued toward the direction of the main house. Probably some business from the capital. Papi must have finished his field work earlier than he had planned, thought Lucinda. It wasn't his helicopter, though; his was white. Don Carlos' was black. But in all her married years, she recalled, he had only used it to get to his banks across the Caribbean. Lucinda pushed the black image from her mind and settled back on the stone. Slowly its warmth mellowed her resistance to the memory of Carlos naked in the field.

Carlos insisted the ranch hands couldn't see a thing, but Lucinda, now laughing, got on her knees trying to scramble away from his touch. He pulled her back by the legs and they both fell, letting themselves roll down the hill to where the grasses were so high, their bodies flat on the ground were hidden from sight. She caught the scent of the grass, of the rich and dark soil, and of his cologne blending with her own perfume. Carlos untangled the tall blades of grass mingling with Lucinda's hair. They undressed each other, taking turns with each article of clothing. Finally completely naked and on their knees, they embraced. Carlos leaned toward her gently. She lay back, feeling the stems crushing beneath her. Lucinda looked up past Carlos' eyes at the sky, to where the wind blew in the tops of the highest palm trees, and back to him. He too seemed entangled among the stalks. They moved together in perfect rhythm, without a word, like figures made of the earth. She felt Carlos release his energy into her, and she, through him, had released hers to the sky.

With the wish for this memory, Lucinda dozed off by the river. When she awakened, the sky was overcast; she breathed in the impending rain. She got dressed and untied the horse. Back on the trail, she let the animal lead her back home. On the way, she pulled up to a small clump of guava trees. With her pocketknife, she cut the fruit open and bit into the pink juicy pulp. She was about to reach for a second one, when large droplets began to fall. Suddenly, the rain burst upon her, surprising the horse. Sonora charged ahead, galloping through the rain and the trees. Lucinda had to lean into the horse to avoid being knocked down by the oncoming branches. She screamed at the dark skies and let the reins slip from her tight grip. Lucinda squeezed her thighs against the mare, trying not to fall. As the horse jumped over a fence and onto the dirt road, Lucinda gripped its mane. To her surprise, the freed horse slowed down, maintaining a steady trot under the rain all the way back to the stalls. Like the horse returning home, Lucinda was returning to her life, through the thick of its cloudbursts, to her children, to her wish, to her promise to St. Jude. As the horse neared the main house, Lucinda felt at peace with herself, until she made out a tall figure standing on the porch. It was Carlos.

Chapter 13

—∞∞∞—

Isabel

A mazing Amazon Woman Found Deep in the Brazilian Jungle! Anthropologists Astounded by Nature's She-Man! and below the red bold headlines is a picture of a woman's head on Arnold Schwarzenegger's body. This is what I have to see on the checkout line at the Grand Dixie, where shopping is always stressful and you can never find an empty check-out line. I always check out the tabloids while I am waiting for the cashier to scan the day's hunt. I never buy them, but this one I bought on the spot. I'm sending it to Lucinda for encouragement. Why do women have to look like men to be considered fighters? Mira Lucinda, in the fight of her life. Hell, in the fights of her life. La pobre, all alone like one of those gallos finos thrown into a cockfighting pit, except that she has to peck and claw at a fistful of family. I have to claw my way out of the supermarket. It's a good thing Lucinda is getting in shape. I don't get to a gym very often. My workout comes from having to carry $200 worth of groceries every week. I don't have a maid to carry my bags for me, nor a man. Both would soften me up too much. I have my boys, but they're always into a "structured" activity. So I'm left with the bags in this family. Mami carries her own bags. She insists on still going to the bodega for all of her Cuban goods. I tell her the grocery store down the block has an "ethnic foods" aisle, but she doesn't buy it. "The minute that store spreads the Cuban foods around the aisles, like Cubans are spread around Miami, I'll give it my money!" mami says. It's a cultural food fight out there. No amount of money can make Lucinda's lucha any easier. But if her fight were a rooster's match, I'd put my money on her.

Lucinda hates cockfighting. Not me. I come from a long line of cock-fighters. My grandfather started the family on this. He was a little cocky rooster himself. After he retired from selling tools to hardware stores at the age of fifty-three, he got into breeding fighting cocks, gallos finos. He said that's where the money was: you own the fighter, you own the fight. That is until La Revolución put an end to it; Fidel wanted to be Cock of the Hill and take a huge percentage of the winnings. Abuelo knew everything there is to know about fighting cocks: which breed to pick, what food to use, how to exercise the cocks, and even how to cut their feathers and crest in a special way. I wish I knew that much about men. Pero qué cosa, even knowing that much my grandfather lost a few big fights. Some cocks have a knack for blindsiding their way out of a fight.

Never go on a blind date with your eyes open. It really wasn't a date, more like a blind get-together. My high-powered American neighbors, Helen and Jared (she's a judge and he's a lawyer), whose kids happen to be friends with mine, whose legal services I've used, and whom my mother sends extra helpings of her Cuban cuisine to, invited us over. I couldn't say no. Helen mentioned her recently divorced cousin would be there. Jared said he was a wine connoisseur. He didn't say he was a cigar smoker. He was good-looking, until the smoke cleared, then he looked like everybody's bachelor cousin looks like: a rental car, shiny on the outside, pero full of cigarette burns on the inside. I spent the whole night tasting wine and fanning Edmund's cigar smoke out of my face. We sat alone by the far end of the pool. In spite of myself, I was flattered by his attention. Then he began to talk about the seduction of the palate and how, in wine tasting, the tongue is everything. Pretending to drink wine, he said in a low husky voice, "Look. You let the wine fall into your mouth, like this. Never suck! You let it roll off your tongue. Then you massage the wine with the tongue, like this. You've got to make sure every taste bud is drenched, but smoothly, not like a flood! If not, you miss the finer bouquets of the wine, and the seduction fails completely." As Edmund demonstrated his technique, he edged closer to me, wanting me to practice it along with him. His voice was as smooth as a Rothchild '88. I have to admit that all that wine got to my head, and Edmund got real close to my mouth, until I had an *Ally McBeal* moment. All I saw was a huge snout with its tongue extended, its tip curled, like a finger calling me over. Coño! Right before my eyes, he turned into an aardvark. That's why I don't drink too much and don't do blind dates. Edmund was blind to my body language. I was getting up when he began to talk again, this time about cigars and how the best are rolled on the thighs of women rollers. David Jr. came rollerblading by just in the nick of time. I thought Edmund was going to roll his cigar on me at any moment. I excused myself between his puffs and my coughs and let my son tow me from another stalled engine of a date.

My Expedition's big engine never stalls. It was hauling me and my bags back to the house, where mami was preparing the night's dinner and papi was getting ready for his visit to the cock-fights.

"No me esperen for dinner. Tonight is the big event. I want to stay until the last match. El Turco Negro against El Cid Canario, the two top gallos south of Hialeah! I have a lot of money riding on El Turco," papi said while buttoning his checkered short-sleeve shirt.

"Is David Jr. ready?" he asked.

"You're taking David Jr. with you?"

Mami just looked at her pot on the stove. She poured in the beer as she stirred the chicken and yellow rice. This was papi's favorite dish.

"He is almost a man. It is time for him to see a cockfight. La lucha de gallo is good training for life's luchas." I kissed them both as they closed the front door behind them.

Papi never took me to a cockfight while I was a kid even though I begged him constantly. But I got to know all about cockfights from my abuelo. Whenever he could, my grandfather got into the habit of taking me to his little finca, where he bred his roosters. He appreciated the fact that I enjoyed a good fair fight. But my real first time at an actual cockfight was in Santo Domingo, when David wanted to experience "authentic" Latino life. Jesus, I should have taken that for a clue, but I was clueless then.

Never fall in love with your eyes closed. Gallos rarely close their eyes when fighting. They fight instinctively too, whether you train them or not. We sat real close to la gallera, the small twenty-foot-diameter arena. It was surrounded by a two-foot-high wall. A fighting cock is never supposed to jump the wall. If it ever does, the fight is lost and its owner loses face. I lost the battle for my marriage when David jumped, but I still have my face on. Mercy calls it my game face, always ready for a fight. So in that first fight, all I could see was scattered feathers, sharp spurs, and splattered blood. The two cocks pecked and clawed at each other, their spurs tearing at the flesh beneath their colorful feathers. It was a boxing match at the speed of lightning, but I didn't miss a swipe. The gallera was as loud as a soccer match with the yells of the men who were sitting on the comfortable upholstered benches. The really big gamblers had their own sections with tables and chairs for their gambling comfort. Coño, how a fool and his money are soon rewarded. I never gambled except when it came to David. And I'll never gamble in that arena again. I can't risk another low blow like that, especially not after clawing my way back to where I can provide my boys with a decent living and a sane mother. How did he put it in the divorce papers? It was an "intolerable situation"; that's how he saw his years with me. I almost went insane that first official court-sealed lawyer-brokered bank-busting anti–authentic Latino life of a divorced year. The truth is that culture has nothing to do with why I don't let men into my life. La verdad es que I'm scared, scared that a man otra vez will trample over my life and leave me with the "intolerable situation" of having to start all over again with no heart left in me. On the scale of recovering divorced women, from a low one to a high ten, I'm hovering around a seven. Each year I nudge up a bit, each year I'm alone, and each year I'm higher than when I started. Life's luchas get easier. I'm content to leave it at that.

Once David and I invited some higher-ups from Texaco to see the cockfights at la gallera. David thought it would be a change from taking these business types to the casinos on the beach where they usually went whenever a visit to Santo Domingo was scheduled. On this one and only occasion, we invited Lucinda and Carlos along. The first fight was an especially fierce and bloody one. Both roosters were barely able to ruffle a feather let alone lift a spur after the half-hour match. The referee called it a draw. The crowd of mostly men applauded the two owners as they retrieved their exhausted fighters from the arena. Our two executives from Boston were busy wiping away the sweat from their faces.

"I hope no one takes umbrage at what I'm about to say, but I do not understand why Dominicans like such a primitive sport," said one of them.

David nodded his head in agreement. I was taken aback by the insensitive comment, as if semantic gloves are supposed to soften the blow, but Lucinda got into the arena on this one. She turned to the Bostonian and said,

"Cockfighting is an ancient sport, originating more than thirty centuries ago in Southern Asia. The illustrious Romans took it up. Indeed, it was they who began the custom of using artificial spurs on the cocks' legs. And it was they who introduced it to the tribal English, where eventually it flourished under the various monarchies. So much so that it was classified as a Royal Sport. The backward colonies, as the English used to call America, adopted this sport. A sport patronized, by the way, by none other than Washington and Jefferson. I would hardly call them primitive."

The Bostonian replied, "I guess I should be quiet," and he was for the rest of the fights.

That was the only time Lucinda ever went to a cockfight. She really showed her spurs that night though. I hope she's kept them sharp. In Miami, papi doesn't breed cocks. Mami would never let him. She ate too many dead cocks in Cuba, especially after the chicken rations ran out. To soften up their lean muscles, she had to boil them for hours. And as she often says, like so many men, they aren't worth the trouble.

I was having no trouble eating mami's arroz con pollo. Since it was only Sam, mami, and me, we ate at the kitchen counter watching the evening news on one of those little TVs you hang from the bottom of the cabinet. It was a gift from Mercy, who thinks I'm electronically challenged for a woman of the millennium. We were watching the Spanish news on channel 23. Sam puts up with it. It helps him with his school Spanish. Mami hasn't picked up on her English yet. I bought her a fifteen-videocassette English language study program hosted by Ricardo Montalban bound in real Corinthian leather. All she does is dust it off once a week.

"Mami, cuándo vas a learn English?"

"Cuando me haga falta."

When she needed to, I couldn't argue with that. Some subjects are just off limits with the older generation. I noticed that my younger generation was watching the Spanish newscast too intently. They were showing a piece on Jennifer Lopez and Daisy Fuentes. It was more like a certain piece of them. With Sam in full complaining mode, I changed to channel 7, the English news station with a Spanish scream of a delivery. Suddenly, we were all screaming like locos watching the local late-breaking news unfolding before our eyes.

"This just in! Undercover police have just now busted a huge cockfighting ring on the border of the Everglades National Park. Our cameras were the first on the scene! More than a dozen arrests have been made! But as you can see, many of the cockfighting patrons are scattering into the dark night."

As the camera panned the pandemonium, Sam yelled.

"Mami, mami! Look, it's abuelo and David Jr!" We could see them both right behind the reporter's head. For a second they froze looking at the camera's light. They looked like two cats about to spring from a just-raided bird's nest. I could almost see feathers peeking out of their mouths.

"They're running!" Sam screamed.

"More on the ten p.m. report. Seven News, always on the lookout for you!"

We saw them in the small screen disappearing into the black of the Everglades night. We stayed silent, stunned by what we saw. Mami crossed herself and began to pray, then cry, then cuss. Sam began to run around the house like a cat with hunting fever, yelling something about his brother going to jail. I began to calculate. I figured that if they were arrested, I'd get a call in about two hours from the county jail. We passed the time channel-surfing to get the latest news anywhere in town. The phone rang three hours later.

"Hello?"

"Yes?" I answered.

"It's me, David."

"David?! What do you know about papi?" I blurted out, not realizing who I was talking to.

"Your father? Is something wrong?"

"No, never mind! David, where are you?" It was my ex calling. I insist on calling it the way I feel it.

"In Miami on my way to an oil refining conference in Saudi Arabia."

"David, I can't talk now. I'm expecting a very important call sometime soon."

"At ten at night? No matter." I hated that phrase. It's his "I'm OK, you're OK no harm done no feelings hurt everything's all right by me so why are you crying" phrase. Coño, how many KOs did I feel like delivering to his OKs. I could feel my fists clenching. He continued, "Listen, I'd like to have the boys next weekend. I'll be back by Friday. We can stay in the corporate apartment on the beach. Is that OK with you?"

I'm not one to get a lumpy throat, but the one I felt at that moment was about the size of Montana. I hesitated by clearing my throat too many times. David pushed his point by inviting me to come along. It was just like David to get the signals crossed. If it were up to him, we'd be the best of friends, one big happy family three times a year, as the conferences fly. Not me. I don't believe in those post-marriage buddy relationships. Mija, you might as well stay married, lumps and all. My throat cleared up real quick. I said no for me but yes for the boys, crossing my fingers that I wouldn't have to post bail to get David his son back for the weekend.

Around midnight, I began to call everybody I knew my father knew. No one had seen him. When I called Mercy's house, Tío Pepe answered. He knew all about it, being an aficionado of the rooster fight himself.

"Not to worry. Tu padre is a wise old cock. He'll get himself out of it, especially for David Jr.'s sake. Get to sleep, no news is good news, like they say in America!"

No news means no sleep for me. Between her prayers and her cusses, mami brewed some strong coffee, which helped pile on the anxiety. Sam was showing signs of worry as well. By three in the morning, I was crawling up the walls. At three-thirty the back door flew open and in crawled my son with his abuelo by his side. They were covered in wet dirt from head to toe. They had bug bites on every exposed body part. And they were hungry as hell. Mami thanked God and gave them huge servings of yellow rice with pieces of chicken. I gave them both a Montana-size piece of my mind. I'm not one to yell often, but I yelled like it was the last chance I'd have on earth. I yelled so much that even Sam, the professional yeller in our house when it comes to getting his way, covered his ears with his hands. Papi was too exhausted from his brush with the law to say anything. When I was all yelled out, I finally settled down into a silent glare, waiting for a reaction. Between his swallowing and his scratching, David Jr. reacted.

"It was awesome, Mom! The place was packed, especially for the last fight. Then this guy, he looked like a regular country cowboy, stood on a table and showed this badge. He was a cop! But the cockfight was incredible! El Turco Negro and El Cid Canario kept fighting all through the raid! Abuelo's friend, the owner of the joint, right abuelo? He led us out a back door. Man, there were cops all over the place! Everybody scrammed out of there. El Turco was winning, right abuelo? But the lights caught us by surprise. We froze in our tracks! Then we heard the sirens and ran. You should have seen abuelo run! I didn't know old people could run so fast. Sorry abuelo! We ran and ran and ran right into the Everglades. Bam! We dove into a ditch and stayed there all night, until the last cop car left. It was pitch black. I couldn't see anything but we could see the lights of the cop cars. Abuelo was mad because he had a thousand bucks riding on El Turco. But at least we weren't riding in a cop car, right abuelo?! Then when the coast was clear, we made our way to the car which abuelo parked about a block away in this all-night mini-mart. That was smart, abuelo! Man, those roosters are brave. Not one gave up. Just like us, right abuelo? Bro, you would have loved it!"

After that story, what more could I say? David Jr. and his grandfather looked at each other and I saw their secret friendship grow tighter. I made David Jr. thank God for their deliverance from danger and for the lesson taught. I don't know which lesson was more effective, God's or abuelo's, but my eldest son became a little older after that. We all got to bed at about five-thirty in the morning. I told the boys about their father's plan for the next weekend and then I sank into bed. A mother's lucha is never finished.

Mami was up early as always. I could hear papi snoring down the hall, and my boys' rooms were too quiet, which meant they'd probably stay in bed until one. On Sundays, I stay in bed until noon. It's a rule around here that on Sunday mornings, I'm not just a single mom, I'm single. I need time to myself. After all, who can make a week's worth of miracles without taking a break? Thank God for Sundays. Isn't He a single parent? I go to the evening Mass on Sundays. Even though Monsignor leads it, it's more relaxed, unlike the morning ones where the top guns of worshippers fill the pews. Like I do every Sunday, I was relaxing in bed with the paper and a cortadito mami brought to my room. The headlines were screaming scandal in the White House, but this was too close to el escándalo in my house last night, so I skipped to the Travel section. It was all about islands in the Gulf Stream. There was a list of the top ten tropical paradises to run away to. I added these to my mental list of the places I'd like to escape to. So far in the last four years I've made it to Disney World twice. And it's not even on my list. But after a night like last night, carajo, I'd settle for eight hours in The Tikki Tikki Tikki Tikki Tikki Room. I'm not complaining, my three Sunday hours of splendid solitude in my bedroom are just enough to get me going for the week. But for now I was indulging in Great Escape fantasies when the phone rang.

It was Julia. She asked me how I was doing so I told her about last night.

"But isn't gambling allowed on the Miccosukee reservation?" asked Julia.

"It turns out that the land is owned by a Miccosukee but it's not part of the reservation. He leases it to El Dominicano, papi's friend. It's complicated. Pero mi amiga, I feel like my life is just one continuous complication. How are you doing?"

"Are you reading the paper?"

"Sí, por qué?"

"Pull out *Parade* magazine. What do you see?" said Julia.

"Hey, congratulations! You're on the cover. Who are the other people? What's this about?"

"It's a profile they did on Latino writers from around the country. About six months ago, they got us together in L.A. for the photo shoot."

"You look great," I answered. "Who is the guy standing behind you? No, the good-looking one?"

"The good-looking one! Since when have you been looking at men?"

"Since they've become two-dimensionally flat!" I laughed, drinking my coffee.

"You're definitely relaxing, Isa."

"There's no sin in looking."

"That's not what you tell Mercy."

"I'm just curious."

"His name is Orlando Adams. He's a screenwriter from Hollywood, a professional friend of mine. He's been living in Miami for the last two months, on a boat."

"A professional bum? You see, I've lost my touch." I flipped to the article.

"He's more like a bohemian professional."

"Cual es la diferencia? Nice quote about how writing is the common thread for cultural understanding, you said that?"

"Yes, and much more, but you can read the article later. I called you for another reason. Listen, Isa, I'm going down to Key West next weekend. It's part of 'Just Us Writers,' a writers' colony I'm a member of. Do you want to come along?"

I told her there was no way I could take a three-day weekend off. Mami made plans to clean the whole house, papi wanted to flush out the garage, and I needed to get ahead with the computer systems switchover in my department.

"Isa, you're going to make me go alone?"

Lately that word has been following me like an abandoned dog in a lonely alley. After a while it gets attached to you. The Scarlet Word, mami calls it. So what if a woman is alone? Why should I be ashamed of my successful status in my post-marriage singledom?

"Writing is a lonely profession, Julia. You'll be fine."

"I know, but I want us to spend some time together. Face it, Isa; even you need a break."

"Not right now. I have too much piled up."

"Well, you can't say I didn't try. I'll call you as soon as I get back."

"Bien." I hung up the phone.

Then I remembered David. Whenever David is in town I get PMS sympathy pains. I remembered he'd have the kids for the weekend and I remembered the lousy night of a family get-together I just went through.

So I called Julia back and on Friday morning I found myself skipping work, making my way down to Key West in Julia's white Discovery Land Rover listening to Janet Jackson's "Escapade" on the oldies station. I could use a Key West weekend getaway—runaway—escapade escape. Another thing I remembered from the visits to my grandfather's rooster ranch: even the champion rooster has to take a break from all the fighting.

"How long is it to Key West?" I asked.

"Around four hours."

"On this skinny road?"

"Isa, quit calculating."

The only other place I've seen so many keys together is on my key chain. For the first two hours I saw nothing but flat land, flat ocean, and flat strip malls lining the road. Even the music got flat. Barry Manilow's "Copacabana" was playing on the radio. Julia put on a ballad from Luis Miguel's *Romances* CD as we hit the Seven Mile Bridge. His remake of "Bésame" worked. For the next seven miles all I saw was crystal clear water to the tune of kissing. My body melded with the Land Rover's La-Z-Boy of a seat. I absorbed the leather's coolness while my mind took in the view of approaching paradise.

"What kind of a name is Orlando?" I asked.

"It's Spanish, but I don't know from where."

"Es Latino? With Adams for a last name?"

"I don't know where he's from. He doesn't have an accent."

"In which language?"

"English."

"Ha, neither did David."

I noticed Julia giving me a side look.

"What?"

"You're thinking of a guy you saw in a magazine?"

"No. I'm thinking of men in general. David used to be everything for me. Now"—I looked at my ring—"he's only the father of my children, a small piece of my life."

"The boys must be happy, having their father come to town by surprise like that."

"Sí, David is a full-time surprise father. Sometimes when I see the three of them together, I can't tell who is the adult. I want my boys to grow up. There are too many boys in men's bodies out there. Julia, te lo digo, I haven't met a truly grown man yet."

"You went out with Rubén and what's his name, the cigar man?"

"Edmund? Wine and cigars are his Mortal Kombat! Y Rubén, a flower child in disguise. I might as well wait until David Jr. is in college to date his roommates!"

"So, are you going to give up on love?"

"It's lonely at the top, mi amiga." I was thinking of Mercy and all the effort she puts into finding love. She doesn't give up. All that energy for a slim chance at paradise. "So where are we staying again in this paradise you're taking us to?"

"It's a surprise. Listen, I have to get gas at the first place we find. Maybe we can eat something?"

"Sounds good to me," I said as Julia pointed to a roadside gas bar & grill joint down the road named Havana Joe's Keg. After filling up the car, we walked to the "thatched roofed and driftwood planked open air and on the water bar & grill." That's exactly how the sign on the roof read. We sat down on the dust-covered oversized picnic table and ordered two Havana Hot Dog Specials with black beans on the side. The Havana side of the hot dogs came from marinating, then frying them in Mojo, the A-1 sauce for

Cubans. I noticed the rack of sauce bottles next to the liquor bottles on the bar shelf. This guy had a contingency sauce for every possible nationality. The sour orange and garlic combination of the Mojo made us thirsty, so we asked for two very cold Presidente beers. As the overhead fans stirred up the flies, Havana Joe put a tape in the portable cassette player on the bar. The list of the top ten island getaways I had read about came to mind as the Beach Boys' "Kokomo" played over and over again. Why does paradise always look better in pictures?

"I hope Key West looks better than this," I whispered to Julia.

"Don't worry, I made reservations at a quaint bed-and-breakfast right on Duval Street. You'll like it." She turned to Havana Joe, who was restocking beer cans behind the bar, and said, pointing to a pile of old inner tubes stacked up in the parking lot, "Hey, what's all that junk piled up outside?" Some of the inner tubes were held together with frayed ropes, others with wooden planks.

"Cuban rafters' leftovers. It drifts ashore from time to time; people bring it over, I collect it." Havana Joe opened himself a Budweiser.

"What are you going to do with all of it?" I asked.

"Don't know. Maybe I'll build a monument to them or something. Did you ladies know that for every rafter that makes it, three don't? That's pretty scary, don't you think?"

"That's the truth." Julia finished the last bite of her made-in-the-USA Cuban hot dog. "At least Mexicans don't die trying to cross the Rio Grande, unless they get shot at. Florida gets rafters and Texas gets wetbacks. It's just plain people, trying to save themselves," Julia added. "In water there is unity!" she said as we clinked the beer bottles in a toast to water. And salvation, I thought.

"Where are you both from?" asked Havana Joe.

"My friend Isa is Cuban by way of Miami and I was born in San Antonio, Texas," answered Julia.

"Maybe you all can build a monument made out of wet T-shirts back in San Antonio." Havana Joe laughed at his own cleverness, exposing his crooked, yellow teeth.

Julia smiled politely and dropped a twenty on the table. I followed her lead and got up after gulping down the last of my beer. No point in wasting it, especially the way paradise was turning out.

Back on the road, we hardly spoke to each other. Finally, we arrived at the inn. We found a shaded parking space in a narrow back street behind the bed-and-breakfast, not an easy task on Key West. We checked in. As I carried the small suitcase up the stairs, it felt like a ton of rocks, one for every day of the previous year. In the room, I collapsed on the king-size bed under the oversized fan. Julia walked to the Bahama shutter doors across the bed and opened them.

"Isa, get a look at this!"

I dragged myself up and joined her. The doors opened onto a large wooden terrace. It overlooked a medium-sized kidney-shaped pool nestled amid a tropical garden of traveler palms, bamboos, torch gingers, and birds of paradise. I was surprised by this lush garden, a haven hidden from the front of the building, which rested on the very edge of busy Duval Street. The peace was palpable. I began to feel lighter. I could almost float.

Then I saw Julia wave at someone swimming in the pool. She signaled we would go down.

"Julia, what are you doing?"

"It's Orlando, let's go down."

"Qué va! I'm staying right here. I came with you to escape, not to work a crowd." I plopped down on the canvas hammock swinging on the terrace.

"You call one guy a crowd? Fine, stay here. I'll see you later."

"Perfecto."

After twenty minutes I changed my mind. I kept hearing Julia's and Orlando's voices floating up to the room. I felt bad for leaving Julia on her own. A thought kept floating in my head: what's the point of being alone in a room in paradise? But to be alone, with no kids, no parents, and no co-workers, that's a rarity for me. I heard Julia laughing.

Reluctantly, I brushed my hair and changed my clothes. I looked at myself in the bamboo-framed mirror. In blue jeans, a yellow sleeveless tank top, and sneakers, I didn't look so bad for the mother of two teenage boys. I grabbed my beige cap and headed down.

By the time I got down to the pool, Julia and Orlando had come out of the water. He was putting on shorts over his blue bathing suit. His skin still glistened with wetness. I have to say that in his case, the photo and the reality were the same thing. He wasn't particularly tall, maybe 5'9", and he was well built in a husky way. His short black hair was sprinkled with gray on the sides. There was no gray on his well-defined eyebrows. These, along with his broad cheekbones, drew me to his eyes. They were deep-set eyes with a longing look. He saw me first, and I caught him looking at me. He didn't divert his eyes. Julia got up from the deck chair.

"This is Isa, Isabel, a friend of mine."

"Isabel, great you made it down," said Orlando, looking at my eyes.

"Even a fighting rooster needs time off." I gave him a firm handshake and returned the look. I find that a firm handshake puts men on notice. Orlando's hearty laughter did not soften his own firm handshake.

"When did you get here?" I asked.

"Early, I left Miami before dawn," he answered, still looking at me.

"Do you like the inn?"

"Yes." He turned to Julia. "Thanks for making all the plans."

"Anyone else from your group here yet?" I asked.

"I don't think so. At least I haven't seen anybody."

"It's still early," said Julia.

"Have you all eaten? I'm starved. I was just going to eat something. Want to come?"

"We just ate, sorry," said Julia. "We can get together when you get back."

"Actually, I made plans for after lunch. I figured I'd take an afternoon sail before the others arrive," he answered.

"That's a good idea," I said. I began to wonder how much small talk I had left in me.

"Isa is into planning," said Julia, out of the blue.

"Would you like to come?" Orlando said to me, smiling. A picture of the Seven Mile Bridge spanning the blue water crossed my mind.

"No, I didn't mean to invite myself."

"I'm the one that's inviting. Come along—you too, Julia."

"I would love to but I can't. I should be here when the others start to arrive. But Isa, you go. No point in both of us staying."

I was about to decline again when Orlando said, "It's set then. I'll be back to get you in an hour. Wear a bathing suit just in case." He turned and walked off.

I followed him with my eyes. I'm not used to being dismissed, especially without giving an answer, and especially by a man. I couldn't tell whether he was a boy in men's clothing or a man taking a break. He rounded the poolside cabana and was gone.

"Isa, take a break. When was the last time you had permission to just have fun? Listen, even the Aztec rulers drank pulque when ruling got to be too much! Go, I'll busy myself with setting up the talks."

So why not? I hadn't done anything fun in years, and if Orlando wanted to play with a boat and have me along, no gran cosa. I figured an easy sail with a pleasant companion would be adventure enough.

⸺

I found myself on a sixteen-foot Hobie Cat wearing my black tankini covered by my tunic-length, off-white mesh shirt, sailing at hurricane speeds over a clear aquarium of an ocean thigh to thigh with Orlando Adams. The speed of the catamaran and the fear of capsizing kept us close on the high side of the boat. Every time I tried to put some distance between us, Orlando slid me over with his arm around my waist.

"I need your body, if not we'll go over for sure!" he exclaimed as I slid over and felt his warm wet leg constantly rubbing mine. He kept one hand on the tiller and the other one on the mainsail rope, or as he called it, sheet. My hands were trying to grab on to anything.

"Here, hold on with your left hand to the bar like this. Put your right arm around mine," he instructed me.

I tried hard not to lose my balance, but for a minute I felt like I was in one of those watercolor pictures that little kids draw; all feeling and no form. The sun was yellow, the sky was blue, the water was green, Orlando was tan, and my heart was humming like the hulls of the Hobie Cat over the sea. He didn't say much, but I noticed him looking at me more than a few times.

"You want to go flying?" He was like a teenager showing off his prowess. He didn't give me a chance to answer. As the boat gained more speed, I just held on tighter to his arm.

"Hold on. Don't move!" And before I could say OK, the hull we were sitting on was up in the air and everything became still. In slow motion, we glided silently over the waves. I didn't dare move. I got the sensation of being in a gently swaying hammock. Orlando's arm felt familiar. The old feelings of being physical with a man made a mad rush to my head. My whole body became instantly warm, like it used to after making love to David. Suddenly a gust caught the sails and I lost my balance. We capsized with a capital C. Like a pair of newly hatched chicks, we tumbled into the sinking mainsail. Before I realized what had happened, I found myself on top of Orlando, who was laughing and yelling for me to grab hold of something before I slipped off the sail. I grabbed on to his leg—more like hugged it—as he untangled the lines. I could feel my heart untangling too.

We tried to right the boat but nothing worked. It turned out the hulls were too full of water, making the Hobie Cat too heavy to straighten out.

"We'll have to let the waves carry it to that sandbar ahead. We'll float there and empty her out. Isabel, I'm sorry. I just like to ride to the edge on a boat like this."

He gave me a hand and we both sat on the exposed hull.

"It's OK. I—"

"You enjoyed the ride."

"Yes, yes I did. But don't you ever let someone put in their two cents' worth?" I asked, smiling.

"What do you mean?"

"You asked me if I wanted to sail with you and you asked me if I wanted to fly this thing with you, but you answered the questions yourself. Now you just finished a sentence for me."

"True," he answered, smiling back, "but in all three instances I could tell what you were thinking."

"So, you're a mind reader?"

"Only of certain minds."

"Which are those?"

"The ones that want to be read." He looked straight into my eyes. I looked back into his. This was not a boy talking.

"Oh, I see, so you think I want to be read?"

"I think you want to tell your story. Watch out!"

I lost my balance again, a wave caught me by surprise. Orlando caught me by the waist.

"Stay next to me, Isabel, and you won't fall again." He didn't let go.

"Julia mentioned you are a screenwriter." I had no place to put my arm except around his back.

"I was a screenwriter."

Before I could ask any questions, he pointed to the approaching sandbar. We hit the shallow water and jumped off. I helped him drag the boat out of the water. When he opened the drain plugs, two running faucets of water began to gush out of the hulls. We sat on the warm sand. The waves kept trying to reach us but failed. Mami's Son-of-a-Bitch-Ometer failed to buzz when he got closer.

I leaned back on my arms, shaking the water from my hair. I opened my eyes to the blinding sun, and then, like an eclipse, Orlando's face blocked the light and all I saw was him.

"What do you do now?" I asked. Orlando was getting closer to my face.

"Nothing. I'm free from obligations. What about you, Isabel?"

I felt his arm reach over and graze my left shoulder. I sensed his body weight shifting. Something came over me because before I knew it, we kissed. For as long as the kiss lasted, I was blind to everything. I don't know if it lasted a second or una eternidad. I closed my eyes. I felt my own obligations fluttering off me like a thousand butterflies. Sensations came in at the speed of light but I absorbed them in slow motion. I felt his hard thighs against my own soft ones. I felt his wet chest press against my suited breasts. I felt the grains of sand rubbing up and down our legs. I felt his burning back with my cool arms. I breathed in his smell. I tasted his burning kiss. It was like kissing the sun.

We pulled away from each other. The sun's light hurt my eyes as Orlando sat back next to me.

"Where did that come from?" he said, more to himself than to me.

For the first time in my life, I didn't know what to say. Was this what he read in my mind? Was this what my mind was thinking? We quietly watched the waves.

"Isabel," Orlando finally said, turning his face to mine—I liked the way he said my full name—"tell me all about you."

I waited to see if the Bitch-Ometer was malfunctioning, then I looked into his dark eyes and saw tiny reflections of myself. As the water poured out of the hulls, I poured out my life to Orlando.

I kept talking while he got the boat straightened out. We sailed back to the main island and I kept talking. We walked into the inn and I kept talking. When I was all talked out, I asked him the same question.

"That's for another sail," he answered instead. "I better get ready for this writer's thing." Then he added, "Isabel, un nombre bello como el día de hoy." And then he walked off, toweling his hair and smiling. I floated to my room with Luis Miguel's tune in my head—bésame, bésame mucho—and Luis crooning—kiss me as if for the very last time—bésame, bésame—like I haven't been kissed in four years. Later that night, I told Julia I liked him instantly.

And then I hardly saw him for the rest of the weekend. I don't know qué carajo pasó. I left myself wide open with a total stranger who got to my heart because of a bad couple of days and because of too many years saying no to any kiss and because of too many Sundays spent alone and because the Key West sun was like a floodlight to my alma and because Orlando asked me for my life like no one else had ever asked. Qué cosa! I spilled the frijoles of it to a damned stranger when I have never spilled anything in my life, not even my milk when I was a little girl. Now, I felt like I spilled my heart and I was hoping that this Orlando didn't turn out to be a trapo of a man and sop it up and wring it out like Mr. Clean now living in Kansas did.

Chapter 14

—⟨∂∅∂⟩—

Julia

*I*sa, it's me, Julia. Thanks for coming to the Keys with me the other weekend. Guess what? I think I'm gay," Julia was thinking of saying over the phone to Isa. She was sitting in her office at the university trying to do some grading but thoughts of Beatriz kept interrupting her concentration. She kept her hand on the phone but did not make the call. How could she tell Isa something she wasn't sure of herself? She looked at the student paper on her desk and tried to focus on it, but her mind was focusing on something else.

How do you tell your friend that at the age of thirty-nine you think you're gay, she thought to herself; or you think you think that; or you think that that explains your answer to Felipe; or you think that your thinking is all screwed up? The fallout with Felipe—how elegant you tried to make it, like one of those *Masterpiece Theatre* English programs where no one yells while they're screwing up each other's lives. The breakup had been as cool as ice. But now, what are you considering plunging into, you ask yourself, remembering that hot rush of emotion felt when you first saw Beatriz on that stage. It was so hot that Moby Dick would be nothing but boiling blubber in such an ocean. But the water of Beatriz' sweat made you thirsty for something you never even thought about—and you make your living from thinking. You turned Felipe down for some very good reasons, so you think. And just because you're attracted to Beatriz doesn't mean you're gay. Or does it? What does it mean to be gay, anyway?

Julia picked up the receiver and dialed Isa. She could hear the ringing. "Isa, I'm gay—I think," she thought of saying to her. Instead she hung up.

It's all this work you're doing on your book, Julia thought to herself. Always pondering and writing about women. Maybe you shouldn't see Beatriz; maybe you shouldn't see her for a while; maybe you should just let things settle, Julia thought. She settled into her chair and took a deep silent breath to clear her mind. Her eyes were drawn to the wrinkled napkin pinned to the corkboard on the wall. It was almost buried under all the other urgent Post-it messages from her students.

Julia quickly dialed Beatriz' number. It was eleven-thirty and Julia knew Beatriz would be home from her morning dance class at Ransom Prep.

"Beatriz, it's me, Julia." She hoped that Beatriz would not feel the nervousness in her voice. They had already met on previous occasions to talk about the book, and those sessions had been relaxed, though they had taken place only at her office.

"Do you have plans for lunch? I wanted to talk to you some more about our conversation last week. I reviewed my notes last night and I have a few more questions. Of course, if this isn't a good time, we can meet later in the week."

"No, está bien, chica. Today is good. But I've had it with fluorescent lighting! It interferes with my brainwaves and I can't think straight after a while. Instead of your office, why don't we meet somewhere else?"

"That's fine. I could use some fresh air too." Julia noticed for the first time how the reflection of the fluorescent lights in her office interfered with the view from the large window overlooking the Student Plaza.

"How about someplace outside?" inquired Julia.

"Sí, el día está bello, reminds me of Barcelona on a clear day," added Beatriz.

"Have you ever gone to Fairchild Tropical Garden?" asked Julia. "I have a yearly pass and I volunteer there once in a while when I have time. They have a little outdoor place, the Garden Café, where we could eat."

"Is it far?"

"No. It's close to my apartment. We can meet there and drive over together. You would like it."

After she gave Beatriz driving directions to her place, they agreed to meet in half an hour.

"Great," said Julia, letting go of the receiver long after Beatriz had hung up. She straightened out the papers on her desk, selected the file of essays she needed to grade for the next day, and placed these in her briefcase. She would finish them at home, Julia efficiently thought. She did not think of calling Isa and instead hurried home to change into something more casual.

Julia was glad she had changed into a T-shirt and khaki shorts. It was warm at the Garden, but the breeze from the bay nearby created a pleasant atmosphere for the shaded picnic tables where Julia and Beatriz sat to eat. Beatriz was dressed in a tropical floral rayon skirt with a green Danskin top.

"It's beautiful here." Beatriz took in the expanse of the Garden with its many individual smaller gardens, lakes, and exotic trees and shrubs. "What do you do when you volunteer?"

"Different things. Sometimes I assist in the nursery potting plants for research. Other times I lead walking tours. My favorite is helping in the fern and orchid conservatory."

"Can you show it to me after we're finished?" Beatriz took a bite from her key lime honey turkey sandwich. Julia had ordered the same.

"Yes. I think you'd like it," replied Julia, slightly choking on the tea she had swallowed too quickly. "You're practically wearing the garden! Your skirt is beautiful."

"Gracias, chica." Beatriz laughed as she lightly touched Julia's arm with her hand. Julia became conscious of her touch, vaguely remembering that Spaniards are known for their physical intimacy in socializing.

"I found it in a little store in Coconut Grove. I think it's called Coquette's. They have the most unusual things."

"I've been there! I love their Mexican silver." Julia looked at the etched silver ring on her finger.

"So, you like to write, you like to garden, and you like unique little stores. What else do you like? I mean when you're alone, with few responsibilities to keep you company," Beatriz pressed on.

Julia looked at her sandwich before answering. Her favorite alone activity was to read. And then a picture of Felipe sleeping in her bed while she read came to mind. Julia brought the sandwich to her lips answering, "I like to snuggle up in bed with a *New Yorker* by my side."

"Is this New Yorker male or female?" Beatriz asked in a serious tone. But Julia sensed that she was being coquettish by the devilish look in her green eyes.

"It's the magazine I'm talking about!" Julia laughed a bit too heartily.

They made their way to the conservatory through the Rain Forest section of the garden. A path of wet leaves snaked them through the wall of green enveloping them as they slowly walked side by side. Julia was proud of the fact that she could answer Beatriz' questions about the plants. Julia asked her if such a garden existed back in Barcelona.

"Sí. El Parc de la Ciutadella. We have a northern Mediterranean climate, though. It tends to be cooler." Beatriz pulled her hair back away from her face, looking up at the canopy of trees holding in the humid air.

"Were you born there, in Barcelona?" asked Julia, noting a change in Beatriz' voice. It sounded like a blend of excitement with sadness. This made Julia more curious about her. She put aside any questions about the chapter she was supposed to be working on with Beatriz and instead added, "Do you miss it?"

"Sí, muchísimo." Beatriz then began to tell Julia how she ended up in Miami. After graduating at the top of her dancing class, she took a position with the Ballet Folklórico de España traveling throughout Europe honing her flamenco style. She then stayed in Paris for two years.

"What made you stay in Paris, a dance offer?" asked Julia as they approached the entrance to the conservatory.

"No, me enamoré. For two years we were inseparable, but then she left me. Nothing came of it except that my flamenco got better. After the breakup, I decided I needed a change of scenery, so I left Paris for Miami," replied Beatriz with a prideful jerk of her head as Julia opened the door and let her pass. Julia was flustered by her directness, something she was not good at. The part about "she left me" kept dancing around in Julia's head.

Julia watched as Beatriz stopped on the oolitic limestone overhang. Julia caught herself studying Beatriz. She could see how someone could be attracted to her. From the back, Julia noticed her dancer's posture. Beatriz seemed tall and sure of herself. The muted colors of her clothing blended with the subdued tropical scene.

"I can see why you like to come here. It's tempting." Beatriz turned to Julia.

Julia took her down the carved curving stairs into the fern gully. Its cave-like walls were covered in giant staghorns and ferns of all types. Julia pointed down to her favorite ferns along the footpath.

"Look, see those? These come from the Maidenhair fern family. There are over 200 varieties."

Beatriz knelt down and stroked the spray of roundish leaves. The small stems trembled in her hand.

"They are so delicate. They do feel like a little girl's hair." Beatriz looked up at Julia. "Give me a hand."

Julia helped her, wondering why a dancer in such obvious good

shape would need any help getting up. She was aware of Beatriz'
hand in hers. There was a firm grip to it, yet her skin was soft and
smooth like a little girl's.

"Are there any flowers?"

"Follow me."

Julia led Beatriz through a natural wood archway into an enormous glass-roofed orchid house. As they walked into the moist,
warm room, Julia singled out the colors and began to talk about
particular orchids. Beatriz walked on as Julia talked, giving her the
impression that she was alone. Julia saw her stop under a clump
of white and yellow Cattaleya orchids. Beatriz looked back at Julia
and began to speak. As Julia got closer, she realized Beatriz was
reciting a poem.

> La flor delicada, que apenas existe una aurora,
> tal vez largo tiempo al ambiente le deja su olor . . .
> Mas, ay!, que del alma las flores, que un día atesora,
> muriendo marchitas no dejan perfume en redor.

Julia knew the poem and as Beatriz spoke, she found herself
translating the words in her head. This was an old habit from her
early years as a translator back in San Antonio.

> The delicate flower that barely outlives the dawn,
> may leave its fragrance for an eternity . . .
> But, O!, the poor soul that hoards flowers for an entire day,
> that die wilting without a trace of a scent.

"That's part of a poem by Gertrudis Gómez de Avellaneda," said
Julia.

"Yes. I love this poem. That's the only part I can remember by
heart."

"It's a sad poem, no?" said Julia.

"Yes." Beatriz walked on past the orchids to a small pond
coated with a green veil of duckweed. There was a rip in the veil
where the water cascaded down from a stone waterfall covered

by ferns the size of trees. Beatriz sat down on a bench nearby and said, " 'Soledad del alma' is the title, loneliness of the soul, the deepest kind of loneliness, don't you think?" Beatriz looked straight into Julia's eyes. Her eyes matched the green of the pond, thought Julia, as she sat next to her.

"I never thought of distinguishing different types of loneliness," said Julia, listening to the water rolling over the stones.

"You can be lonely because you miss someone. But when you feel a hollowness inside that permeates your very essence, that's loneliness of the soul. It's a place I only reach when I dance. It's the fuel of flamenco," said Beatriz passionately.

"You love the dance, don't you?"

"Es mi vida."

Julia enjoyed her work, was dedicated to it, but she could not see herself speaking about it with the emotion Beatriz revealed. What makes a person surrender their entire life to one thing, thought Julia, or one person, as Beatriz was obviously capable of doing. You want to ask her what it feels like to abandon oneself completely, but you don't, you remain quiet. You think instead. You think about her, and the story you've pieced together from the little information you've gathered. You think about yourself, about Felipe, about Lucinda and what she was going through. At least Lucinda had a vague notion of where she was headed. Felipe always knew what he wanted too. He felt it in his heart when he asked for yours. You think about your life and how for the first time you're out of touch with your own heart. Then you feel a touch.

"Julia, let's go." Beatriz was standing over Julia nudging her shoulder. "The water!" said Beatriz, looking up. A mist was descending from the top of the entire conservatory.

Julia suddenly realized the sprinkler system must have gone off. The conservatory had a schedule set up for daily misting to keep the humidity high. "I don't know what happened. The sprinklers don't usually go off during visitor hours!" As Julia rushed to get up, she slipped on a moss-covered stone and fell. Beatriz turned back to help her and slipped herself. They looked at each other, Julia flat on her bottom and Beatriz on her knees, their hair clinging to their faces, and broke out in laughter. Beatriz reached out her hand to Julia and they pulled each other up. Laughing still, they ran hand in hand through the different plant rooms, making their way out of the mist. By the time they found the exit to the conservatory, they were both drenched.

"Let's get out of here! We look like two possessed joggers!" said Julia, noticing how the clothes clung to their bodies as if they had run the Miami Marathon in mid-August.

Back at the apartment, Julia let Beatriz walk through her front door first. By the time she had closed the door and turned the lock, Beatriz stood on the Chiapas area rug in the center of the living room completely naked with her clothes hanging off her right arm.

"Chica, get me a towel I can use," said Beatriz standing on her toes trying to keep any water from dripping on the rug. But she could not avoid noticing the look on Julia's face.

"Perdóname. It is a dancer's habit. Undressing is like breathing for us. But I can see you're uncomfortable. I can also see you're dripping all over your nice wooden floor!"

Julia rushed to the hall closet and grabbed a white terry cloth robe. She gave it to Beatriz and then ran into the bathroom to undress herself. As she toweled her body, she saw her face in the mirror; she couldn't tell whether it was flushed from the running or from what she had just seen. Her whole naked body felt flushed as though it had just gone through an incredible workout. She sat on the toilet top, her towel absorbing the water and her mind absorbing Beatriz' naked image. She is a dancer and dancers do that, thought Julia, like sometimes professors talk to themselves more than to the students without realizing it. A professional habit, a quirk from years of familiarity with a job, thought Julia, while slipping into her blue sweat suit. She forgot to put on her undergarments.

When she came out of the bathroom, Beatriz was in the

kitchen pouring herself a glass of water. Julia took Beatriz' wet top and undergarments and threw them with hers into the clothes dryer. She hung the rayon skirt off the shower rod by the open window. Julia hadn't said much since they arrived. They both sat down in the living room.

"It shouldn't take long to dry, but the skirt, I don't know," said Julia.

"Don't worry, if not, I'll borrow something from you." Beatriz smiled and added, "Bueno, chica, why don't we talk about the book while we wait."

Julia asked, "Do you want to put on some of my clothes?"

"I'm OK in this."

And so they spent the rest of the afternoon in deep discussion about Latinas on the border. Though the clothes were long dry, Beatriz did not bother to change and Julia didn't bother to ask her. Julia found Beatriz' views on Latinas provocative.

"Latinas are still playing a tug of war with the womb," said Beatriz.

"What do you mean?"

"Women can be mothers, lovers, sexual creatures, and still be on their own, independent and self-sufficient, passionate and professional, both and all of it. Why not have all of it?" asked Beatriz, drinking the tea Julia had made.

"But you can't do it all well, or get it all right."

"Why not? Why is it that Latinas feel they have to either choose their minds or their hearts?"

"What about being gay?"

"What about it?"

"Doesn't that complicate your choices? The consequences?"

"It does if you don't know yourself."

"But doesn't being Latina add another dimension, another obstacle to the whole thing?"

"Mira, chica, I'm way past that." Beatriz looked at Julia adding, "Aren't you?"

Julia did not answer Beatriz, but she knew she'd have to answer this very question in her book. Her thoughts were racing as fast as the clock on the wall was ticking. She saw that it was getting late and that Beatriz was in no hurry to go. She sat on the loosely upholstered white cotton couch, her legs crossed beneath the robe. And as Julia saw that Beatriz was comfortably ensconced, looking like an angel on a cloud, dinner came to mind and she suddenly wanted Beatriz to stay longer.

"I think that in Europe, we are a bit more culturally loose. So I may see a bit more through the conventional veil constantly in front of women. You know who my hero is? Queen Isabella, now there's a woman who saw clearly what she wanted!"

And she got everything she wanted, even love, thought Julia, rising from the matching chaise lounge diagonally placed in the corner.

"Would you like to stay for dinner?" asked Julia.

"Is it that late? I'll stay on one condition," smiled Beatriz, getting up from the couch. "I'd like to do the cooking."

After acknowledging Julia's protests, Beatriz took inventory of what was in the kitchen. She settled into preparing a cool gazpacho soup and a dish of fish sautéed in olive oil and chives. She didn't feel like getting dressed yet so she cooked in an apron tied around the robe. She refused Julia's offer to help, gently pushing her out of the kitchen. To Julia, looking at her from the living room, it looked as if Beatriz had lived in this apartment all her life. Julia thought of grading a few papers, but the thought of Beatriz in her kitchen drew her away from the task. She settled on writing down Beatriz' thoughts at her writing table. Soon the aroma from the kitchen began to fill the studio and Julia began to feel its scent enticing her thoughts.

These were interrupted by the mailman out in the common foyer. Julia went out to gather her mail. She was standing by the open door, looking it over, when Beatriz announced that dinner was ready. She dropped the bundle of mail on the demi-lune table against the wall and forgot about it. Beatriz' skirt wasn't yet dry, so Julia lent her a pair of old white jeans she wore when hanging around the house. Julia opened a bottle of chilled B&G Chablis and they both sat down to eat the well-prepared meal.

Beatriz had Julia laughing at her Spanish jokes. Beatriz laughed uninhibitedly, with her mouth open as her head tilted back. Julia could see the musical notes of her laughter floating out of her mouth like the bubbles in a glass of sparkling wine. The conversation took a subdued tone when Beatriz began to talk of her troubled youth with her father. He had misunderstood her sullen expression for that of a spoiled brat, but in fact, she was really furious at seeing her brother get away with so much unquestioned independence. So she took up flamenco and flew the chicken coop of a life her father had planned for her.

After dinner and with the bottle of wine still two thirds full, they sat on the couch to eat dessert. The evening was warm and breezy and in no hurry, just like Julia felt.

"I'm afraid that Oreos is not a very elegant finish for your stupendous meal. It's all I have by way of a sweet." Julia offered the cookie package to Beatriz.

"White wine and Oreos, that's like imagining Elizabeth II drinking a Budweiser!"

"Have you ever heard of the Grupo Límite?" asked Julia.

"No."

"It's a fantastic group of tejano musicians; they have a unique sound. They're very popular and were the first Mexican group to play at the San Antonio Rodeo."

Julia played their latest CD and Beatriz noticed a subtle German polka beat to it. She swept the area rug aside and began to improvise dance steps. Julia laughed as she watched Beatriz mix flamenco, the Texas Two Step, and salsa all together. She pulled Julia off the couch and got her to dance along. Julia let herself go. Beatriz spun her around, got her to bang her heels on the floor, and even got her doing some flamenco moves combined with line dancing. For twenty minutes they did this until Julia collapsed on the couch, holding her side in protest. Beatriz served the last of the wine on the table and threw herself beside Julia. They offered a toast to each other's dancing, and as they drank the wine, the phone rang.

Julia got up and answered it in the bedroom. It was Isabel. She wanted to talk about Lucinda and her decision to come back to Miami. This took Julia by surprise; she listened intently as Isabel filled her in on the details. By the time she hung up, half an hour had passed. She came out of the room excusing herself but found Beatriz asleep on the couch. One cat was on the windowsill, another by her feet, and the third was making itself comfortable on the floor by the couch. Julia placed the terry cloth robe over Beatriz' legs. She picked up the day's mail from the little half-moon table and, stepping lightly, returned to her room.

As she sifted through the mail, Julia thought about the day she had had with Beatriz, how much at ease she felt around her, how Beatriz just seemed to fit into her world, how casually intimate they were with each other. She was also aware of a thought hovering somewhere in the back of her mind: how aflame she felt with Beatriz near her.

Her thoughts were interrupted by the postcard in her hand. It showed a wide-angle view of the central plaza of Guadalajara. She turned it over and read the familiar handwriting.

Querida Julia,

It is still a mystery to me.

Love, Felipe

Julia mulled over the mystery in her hand and in her heart and on her couch as she fell asleep with the light on. She woke up with the morning light and with the thought that she hadn't told Isabel about Beatriz in last night's phone conversation. She walked into the kitchen to find Beatriz already up and dressed with a hot mug of coffee in her hand and the Mr. Coffee pot half full on the tiled counter.

"I have to get an early start today," said Beatriz, filling up a mug for Julia.

"Won't you stay for breakfast?" Julia took the hot mug in her hands.

"I can't. In two weeks I have to find a place to live. The owner of Café Quixote is turning my little studio into a private dining room. He needs the space for more business. So, chica, as he grows, I go."

Julia found herself following Beatriz to the front door. She found herself hearing Beatriz say what a great time she'd had, and as she found herself closing the door, she opened it again. Beatriz was halfway down the steps and somehow Julia found herself saying, "I have an extra room."

"Is it for rent?" Beatriz asked, looking up at Julia.

"Yes."

Chapter 15

—⁓⁂⁓—

Mercy

Y ou mean she invited her to lunch, to dinner, and then to move in all in one day? Coñ-ñó!" I yelled into my cell phone as a head of full dreadlocks flew by me on a bike. I had the white top down and was enjoying Miami's open-air tanning salon when the biker looked in my direction and almost hit an oncoming delivery truck. Mamá always says my voice can raise the dead; I didn't want to be responsible for any living casualties, so I tried to get the top up. I couldn't from the front seat, so I rolled up the windows to the Miata and turned on the air conditioning instead. I needed privacy for this conversation. I wasn't getting any stuck in traffic on Ocean Drive. Oye meng, the roller bladers on the sidewalk were making better time. Grabbing a quick lunch on South Beach is impossible, like me going to the opera without thinking of how to get out of it before it's done. I never think of leaving when I go to the teatro bufo with mamá. Those operettas on Eighth Street are the only time I see mamá really laughing. Her favorite one is about a ninety-eight-year-old Castro giving up his life as a dictator to run away with a titanium-hipped Hillary who is recuperating in Cuba while Bill is caught, Depends down, with an orderly named Lowlipski in the presidential library in Little Rock. It's called, "The Lips Won, Fidel Is Done!" Los viejos can't get enough of it. It's been running for two years. But let me tell you, I wasn't running anywhere sitting in a convertible on Ocean Crawl listening to Isa fill me in.

"Primero, she dumps Felipe, and now she asks this Flamenco Flame to move into her house? Qué le pasa a Julia?" I said.

"I don't know. She says something came over her and before she knew it she had blurted it out and couldn't take it back."

"Y qué dijo Beatriz?"

"She said yes."

"Y what did Julia say?"

"She said yes."

"Oye, Isa, don't you think that Beatriz is un poco feliz?"

"Feliz? Where does that come from?"

"Feliz, you know, gay." I shuddered like Lucy in that Vitameatavegamin episode of *I Love Lucy*. Don't get me wrong, some of my best clients are gay, but Julia? There was a long pause from Isa's side.

"Julia says she lived once with a woman," Isa finally said.

"Didn't I tell you! I knew it." I was about to hit the horn out of excitement and to get traffic moving. Then I remembered no one blasts their horn on Ocean Drive because everybody wants the attention but they can't look like they want it. It's the chivalry code of chic on the Drive. And let me tell you, with me being a night citizen of this slice of paradise, I wasn't about to draw wanted attention to myself. So I put my hand on the wheel instead.

"That doesn't mean anything," Isa was saying.

"Sure, and Fidel is going to elope with Hillary in the future!"

"Bueno, at least she won't be alone, and Julia is as straight as they come and . . ."

"Isa, you think they did it?" There was another long pause on the line. "You know, IT?" I clarified.

"Mercy! What are you saying? You better control that mouth of yours. Anyway, enough sobre Julia and Beatriz. It's none of our business."

"But knowing that Beatriz is gay, Julia still asked her to move in?" I thought out loud, but then I could feel Isa's hard stare and I said, "Sorry, not one more word about it!"

"Why did you call me?" Isa asked.

Carajo, this thing about Julia detoured the good news I had. But what Isa told me was more interesting than an episode of *La Usurpadora,* which I only watch when I happen to stay at mamá's and she's glued to her favorite soap reruns. Let me tell you, the only time she tears herself from that Fernando Colunga is when I bring up the topic of boyfriends. "Bring *him* home and I'll never have to find one for you again!" she says. I have to admit Fernando es un tronco, but he's on TV. Why do I need him when there's a tronco crossing the street right in front of my car. I lowered the window to wave at Osvaldo, a lifeguard and ex-water polo player I dated a couple of times. He had an oak tree of a body with full pecs on top and a Speedo waist below, and to complete the ensemble he had a shaving cream commercial of a face. And that was his problem, he was too much into himself. Oye meng, let's face it, I love to look at men, I don't care what Isa says about me being too obvious. Pero Isa is not obvious enough.

"Sorry, Isa, I got distracted by Mr. Mennen."

"Mr. who? Olvídate, so what's the good news?"

"Remember that penthouse Arab I told you about? Well, he wants me to be his only realtor for this condo building he just had renovated on Collins and Fifty-third. It's called Aladdin's Palace and he's got Disney in on it. This guy could be my ticket to realtor Magic Kingdom!"

My phone started crackling so I said my adiós to Isa's last words, which came across the line sounding like "mouse trap cheese." Isa is too cautious for this world. If mamá hadn't taken a chance on that Splash Mountain of a ride across the Gulf Stream, where would I be today? Let me tell you, I wouldn't be sitting in traffic in the hottest spot in the continental U. S. of A. with a realtor's exclusive clause over my name. I'd probably be sitting in the hottest tobacco factory in Cuba rolling cigars on my thighs all day long for some horny tourist to brag about in the land of the free and the brave.

Mamá was headed for the homeland at the end of the week. Ever since the Pope went to Cuba, she's been more excited than ever about her yearly visits. After lunch I was taking her on preparation rounds all over town. Mamá prepares for these trips like Eisenhower for the D-Day invasion. That's the only fact I remember from my tenth grade American History class at Miami High. Coño, for that entire year I slept through class—I used to have weird dreams of Ike and me rolling on the river and Tina, who turned into Celia Cruz, singing, while proud Mary kept on praying for all of us. I could relate to crossing water, let me tell you. Mamá always wants me to cross back to Cuba with her. Pero who's got the time? I was barely getting across to Lario's restaurant after traffic got moving again. When I finally arrived, I handed my keys and the ten bucks to the Nicaraguan valet and entered Emilio and Gloria Estefan's slice of Cuba on the beach. Lario's is my favorite place for lunch. Where else can you get the chic South Beach ambience with the Cuban decibels that remind you of home? The food tastes homemade too, let me tell you. But I never tell my mother this.

I sat at my regular table next to the men's bathroom just in case a rich and famous Latino with Luis Miguel eyes gets an urge to mingle. I ordered a Media Noche sandwich with a side of yuca, and for the sizzling traffic heat still on my skin, I asked for a Mojito. The sweet rum and lime mix on ice with yerbabuena leaves wipes out any thirst and evil spirit still lingering around you. My thoughts were lingering on my new Arab partner while I munched on a warm bread roll. I thought for sure I'd never hear from him after that mess of a penthouse sale. I started planning for my own realty company the minute he made me the offer. Now with this genie in my hand, I knew I'd have to handle the sales like a bomb expert, very carefully. All I needed was to have this "once in a lifetime opportunity" blow up in my face. I was dreaming up a name for my very own company, eating to the sounds of "Let It Be" with a salsa beat sung by Willie Chirino. I like him a lot, let me tell you. His songs get my hips moving every time I hear them. Thinking of hips got me thinking of Ramón. I missed him. I was thinking about what happened in my room that night when my phone rang.

"Mercy, dónde estás?" It was mamá. "The school had early dismissal so we didn't serve lunch to the kids. Me vas a pick up en la casa?"

"What do you think of Magic Genie Realty Services?"

"Qué, un nombre? It sounds like a cleaner we use in the school cafetería."

"Mamá, I'm almost done with lunch."

"No dessert."

"I'll be right over."

She was anxious to get started on her trip. I paid the waiter and left Lario's for my car. I noticed the valet running from around the corner with the keys in his hands and no car.

"You have a flat tire."

"Can't you fix it?"

"No, señorita, it's not part of my duties as a valet."

Qué carajo, the guy was worrying more about his white shirt and his clean shorts than the bills I waved in his face. Helping a dama in distress is a thing of the past, let me tell you. And now there were two of us in distress, me and mamá, after I called her with the news. I noticed time passing so I called Triple A as I made my way to the car lot a block away. I had about an hour to kill so I bought myself a *Vanidades* magazine at the News Café.

I reached my Miata, which was slumping to one side like abuela used to after her hip surgery back in Cuba. The starched-shirt valet had left the top down and the sun bounced off the white leather interior like a tennis ball aced by Venus Williams at the Lipton courts on Key Biscayne.

I hopped in and took a seat while I was waiting. I was leaning back reading Walter Mercado's full-page ad for his astrological phone club in *Vanidades* with my Versace sunglasses when this

Jupiter-sized tow truck pulled up. It was orange too with wall to wall chrome. I adjusted my red skirt as I swung my high-heeled legs out. My shaded eyes adjusted to the glare coming off the cleanest tow truck I'd ever seen. The sign on the door read HUNKS "R" US TOWING SERVICE. My heart took a second beat at the name, but I couldn't see past the super-tinted windows. The door opened and out came a not so hunky guy. I scrolled my mental Rolodex of stars when a taller and younger Paul Reiser from *Mad About You* hit my mind. I used to like that show. Two people loving each other in spite of everybody else. Let me tell you, I get so mad when people get in love's way. I was getting out of the way when I noticed there was nothing about this guy to go mad over except maybe his full head of black curly hair. He asked me for my keys in a foreign accent, I think from New York, and got right to work on the rear left tire without saying another thing. I sat in the air-conditioned truck listening to the classical music that was playing and dialing Walter's club to get the latest on my future. The horoscope didn't mention any men in it but it did say wealth would be coming my way soon. I imagined Walter Mercado dressed like an Arab sheik. It also said the number two would "play a dominant role in the coming days." The voice advised me to "visualize" it.

"Ahora, Mercy, practica seeing the two in your head. Close your eyes and say to yourself two, two, two. Lo ves? Very good!"

I closed my eyes and was imagining selling two condos at a time when the voice told me my introductory twenty minutes was up and to expect the twenty-dollar discounted fee on my next phone bill, and did I want to continue at the normal rate of two dollars a minute? I had never seen so many twos in my life.

"Lady, are you all right?" The tow trucker opened the door. I opened my eyes. "Your car is in as good a shape as you are," he added, not smiling.

I gave Mr. Hunkette a twenty-dollar bill for a tip because I was down to three twenties and I hate not tipping. He turned it down. Instead of haggling I gave him a card and offered him my realtor services. The cellular rang. It was mamá. I left him looking at the picture on my card. I was taking in the fact that he wasn't that bad looking himself—no tronco, but he wasn't a twig either. Este mental walk in the woods was interrupted by mamá's pleadings.

My first stop with mamá was at the Wild Hair Beauty Salon on Giralda Avenue. We drove into the parking garage across the street. Let me tell you, only in Coral Gables do you find a parking garage with exterior porches, tile facades, and landscaped trimmings that looks more elegant than the Hyatt Hotel next to it. Mamá thinks it's a waste of money, not me. Oye meng, at least in the City Beautiful you can see your tax dollars growing as you pump the quarters into the parking meters beneath the oak and ficus trees. Better in the dirt than in some politician's bank account, I say to mamá. We walked into the salon and Aida, the owner, was already waiting with two plastic thimble-sized cups of coffee. Aida's is the only salon in Coral Gables where Café Bustelo out-smells the zillion hair products she uses. She likes the cafecitos to stimulate her clients. One day I was minding my own business under the drier, when I heard Aida scream. A forty-something-year-old guy got so relaxed under Aida's hands, he nodded off in the middle of his haircut. Aida's razor took a roller-coaster dip into the sleeping client. He wasn't too happy with the crew cut she gave him to fix the lawnmower accident on his head, let me tell you. Ever since, every December I buy Aida fifteen packages of Café Bustelo for a Christmas present.

Mamá has been going to Wild Hair for at least fifteen years. Oye meng, it's like visiting family. Aida even looks like mamá, short and strong, but with red hair instead of mamá's brownish tint. While mamá gets her hair done, I do my nails with Teresita the Manicurist. That's what everybody calls her. To this day I don't know her last name. But we were born on the same day so we're like sisters. She was filing down my nails, I was going for a French Tip, when we heard mamá tell Aida she was leaving for Cuba.

"I don't know why you bother to go. To give your money a ese loco!" said Aida in her high-pitched laugh. She was washing mamá's hair.

"Qué voy a hacer? Blood is thicker than water. I still have family over there," answered mamá, wrapping her wet hair in a towel as she moved to the styling chair. "I do what I have to do."

"After you leave, they'll be back to making café out of garbanzo beans and steaks out of grapefruit peels, that's if they're lucky," yelled out Teresita the Manicurist while she started to put a primer on my nails.

"I know," said mamá. I could tell the comment got to her.

"La familia is very important. It's all you have left when everything is gone. And who are we to judge? Castro will get his day in court, allá 'bajo." Aida pointed with her clippers to Hell.

"You're right, Aida, but mientras tanto, I have to do something," said mamá. "You know what they ask me for the most?"

"What?"

"Bras, underwear, T-shirts, and socks; ropa interior. I'm also taking my sister her blood pressure pills, her son's potassium pills for la depresión, primo Julio a pair of shoes, baby clothes for Ester's newborn, and for everyone, soap and shampoo."

"They need everything we have here in Miami, including libertad," said Teresita the Manicurist.

"Sí, pero you can't put all of Miami in one suitcase." Aida laughed as she set mamá's hair in curlers.

"That's nothing," answered mamá. "Once I even took an electric rice cooker. But with the apagones, the rice was always hard. Now I bring the necessities of life and American cash."

"Ha! Castro hates the Yankee but he loves the Yankee dollar. Now as long as you have dollars, you can get anything, even meats and candies. It's like going to a Sedano supermarket," said Teresita the Manicurist while she taped my nails.

"You see?" said Aida. "That's exactly what I mean. Where do you think those dollars end up? Buying carrazos and fancy houses for all the fidelitos."

"I know, but I'm not going to let my family starve. Things are changing, Aida, I feel it since the Pope's visit. El Papa made a difference. I'm sure of it. I have faith." Mamá sounded like Charlton Heston in *The Ten Commandments,* like a rock speaking.

I don't speak much about Cuba. In my social circles nobody wants to hear bad news. And who wants to hang on to bad memories, anyway? Let me tell you, the day I go to Cuba I want to go like my "non-Hispanic white" classified friends go when they visit their own motherland, to see the sights the old ones talk about, to explore my roots, and to make peace with my history. And as for Castro, well like he says, "history will absorb him," or something like that. But just in case, I always write mamá a check for a thousand bucks to take to Cuba. Oye meng, one thing I've learned in my crash course on capitalism is to cover all bets.

Aida did a pretty good job of covering mamá's roots and Teresita the Manicurist was done French tipping me, so we gathered our things and started to leave, but not before Aida asked mamá for a favor.

"Si puedo, I'll smuggle back a few of the tamales you like so much. And for Mercy, I'll bring back a fresh Cubano!" said mamá as I was holding the glass door open.

"Es que, there's nothing like the real thing, baby!" Aida laughed, sweeping the cut hair off the white tile floor. I couldn't tell if she was talking about Cuban food or men.

We store-hopped the rest of the afternoon. When mamá finally bought enough of Miami for all of the relatives, she asked to make one last stop.

"Take me to St. Michael the Archangel's Church on Flagler Street. I have to get some crosses."

The fighting angel's church was a new stop for us. None of the relatives, as far as I knew, had strong religious inclinations, not like mamá's anyway. As I was getting down from the car, she asked me to stay. "I'll only take a minute," she said, getting down in a rush. My feet felt heavier than an elephant's, so I didn't argue. She came back a few minutes later with a paper bag as plump as a newly filled water balloon.

"Now I'm finished. You can take me home," she said satisfied with herself. When I asked to see what she had bought, she simply answered, "Unas cruzes for the family in Cuba," tightly holding the bag to her heart.

Mamá left the next morning. I waved her off as she got in line for her boarding pass. She was up to her fresh hairdo in suitcases and boxes. She looked like the lady in *A Passage to India*. A couple of elephants would have come in handy.

Whenever any of us travels, we agree to call each other after two days have passed. I spent the next two days setting up my company. Overnight I had a lawyer, an accountant, a secretary, and a partner. Setting up a business in America is as fast as getting take-out food at Canton's Chinese Restaurant. That's what I was eating when mamá called me on the third day telling me everything was all right. And, of course, she mentioned that everybody loved the stuff she brought over and that cousin Julio had a really guapo friend with a medical degree who worked in a turista hotel as a successful cook and was trying to leave the country. Let me tell you, men were the last thing on my mind. Giving birth to my company was taking all the energy I had, so my male drive was on neutral. Isa was proud that two weekends had passed and I hadn't gone clubbing. I was holed up in my apartment with corporate papers up to my cleavage. I couldn't help but notice that I was turning into my big cousin Isa. The only thing that kept me going was that I knew my male-less condition was temporary and by choice.

I was so busy I hadn't noticed that mamá's next scheduled call was late by two days. But then three more days passed and no phone call. Finally, I put in a call to my cousin Julio's house where she was staying, but I couldn't get through. After two more days of trying, I got a call at four in the morning in the middle of the week.

"Es la operadora, tengo una llamada para María Mercedes Virtudes, acepta?"

"Sí, sí, acepto," I said to the operator.

"Mercedes, es tu primo Julio, de Cuba."

"Sí, yo sé. I tried calling for days. How's mamá, está bien?"

"Mercedes, tu madre fue detenida!" he yelled out.

"Qué! What are you talking about?"

"Detenida! Arrestada, tu madre—!"

Click. The line went dead. I went berserk.

I started calling Cuba. Let me tell you, I called every relative from Pinar del Río to Guantánamo. And nada. No one knew where Julio was. No one could tell me anything about mamá. Either they didn't know or were afraid to talk. Mamá arrested! It was impossible. She was a U.S. citizen. They couldn't do that to Americans. I woke up the U.S. Interest Section in Havana. The secretary didn't know a thing about it. She told me to call back in a few days. A few days! Quién carajo has a few days to spare when your mother is in a hellhole of a country? Coño, I lost my father to the revolución and now this.

"Mamá arrested in Cuba, Isa. In Cuba! I can't lose her now. Coño, what if I never see her again?" I yelled into the phone.

Chapter 16

—⟨∞⟩—

Lucinda

The clouds were heavy. They hung low over the land, as if God himself wanted to press the misericordia out of the earth once and for all. Their black-gray color reminded Lucinda of what a bruised heart must look like. The slap of thunder overhead cleared her dark thoughts at the sight of Carlos. She took in a deep breath of the green life around her and continued riding past the porch. She ignored him. Sonora maintained a slow and easy gait approaching the twenty stalls. The horse reminded Lucinda that she was on familiar ground. Her father's trainer had done a good job with this horse, thought Lucinda, as she jumped off and began to unbuckle the saddle. She threw it over the hitching rail under the overhang in one swift motion. The skies grew darker still and the rain began to fall again, sparsely, in big loose drops. Lucinda unbridled her horse. She heard the thunder echoing in the distant hills along the horizon. She stood for a few minutes caressing Sonora's head, breathing in the scent of the animal. Suddenly the wind rushed through the long row of stalls. It was cooler and cleaner than the stale air of the city. The air stirred up the hay in the stalls. Sonora breathed noisily at the wind. Lucinda smelled what the horse was smelling, a mix of hay with soil, and rain. She could not contain Sonora any longer. With one last look into the horse's eyes, Lucinda slapped its hindquarter. It took off into the hills, galloping as if between the raindrops.

To the trainer's frustration, Lucinda was pleased that he could not break Sonora into staying at the stalls. Once, Lucinda had tracked the horse all day long to see its secret place. After that, Lucinda asked her father to order the trainer to stop his efforts to corral her. Her horse was the only one that demanded a compromise for itself. Lucinda sensed a lump in her throat, the thought of Carlos clouding her mind. With a sigh as heavy as the rainfall making its way toward the ranch house, Lucinda sat down on the wooden bench her father had built. Slowly, she removed her spurs and began to wipe the mud off her boots. Then she started to wipe down the saddle. Lucinda enjoyed doing this herself. After a few minutes, she gathered the various pieces of her horse gear and carried them into the tack room. Having returned every piece to its proper place, she returned to the main entrance of the stalls. By now the rain was falling like a solid sheet of lead, thick and heavy and unforgiving. As she brushed her hair, avoiding the line of sight to the ranch house, Lucinda heard footsteps, wet and heavy and slow, making their way toward the stalls.

"Hola, Lucinda," said Carlos. Lucinda noticed the dark shadows under his eyes and how they matched his wet, dark suit. He removed the soaked jacket, draping it over the wood rail. Lucinda recognized the Armani label. It didn't go well with the sturdy piece of log, she thought.

"What are you doing here?" she said after a long silence.

"I had some Bank business en la capital," Carlos answered, "and I had to see the children," he added, placing his hands in his pant pockets.

"Did you see them?"

"Sí. They look well."

"They're confused," said Lucinda.

"It's understandable. Por qué no?"

"Why did you come here, a la finca?" she said, for the first time noticing the black helicopter in the field to the left of the stalls.

"Yes. That was my helicopter that flew over the clearing," answered Carlos. He stood behind Lucinda, looking over her shoulder at the helicopter. Lucinda stepped away, turning to face him. She returned the hairbrush to the backpack still on the bench.

"Did mami send you?"

"No, Lucinda. I've hardly spoken to her. I was worried about you."

"Bueno, you don't have to worry. Estoy bien." Lucinda felt the strength of all the nature surrounding her. "You can return to your business," she added, swinging the backpack over her shoulder. One of its straps got tangled with some of her long hair.

"You look fine," said Carlos looking at her neck, still flushed from her long ride. As he reached out to the backpack, he glanced at her toned body, accentuated by her tight jeans and her damp shirt.

"Let me do this for you," he said in a low voice. Lucinda did not move.

Gently, he began to untangle the strap from her hair. The rustling sound of the rain could not drown out the gentle rhythm of his breathing. Lucinda closed her eyes and remembered the last time they made love. Her breathing got deeper as he pushed aside the strand of hair now loose from the strap.

"I miss you, Lucinda," whispered Carlos as his lips brushed her exposed neck. She opened her eyes to see Sonora in the distance, standing silent under the wide canopy of a tree. She could just make out the wisps of steam coming off her back. Then the horse disappeared into the wall of woods. Startled at feeling Carlos' hands around her waist, she shook off his touch and said in an angry voice, "No, Carlos. Esos tiempos se acabaron. The old days are over for you and me."

"Lucinda, this has to stop. You have to come home. We can't go on like this." He reached for her arm as she was leaving the stalls. The rain clung to her shirt like a million teardrops. She could feel his grip on her.

"Is that why you came here?!" she yelled as she tried to free herself, but Carlos would not let go. "To bully me into going home? I am home, coño! I am home! Tú te fuistes, you left me, you, you!" she screamed as the rain smothered the two of them. "Let go, animal!"

"No, Lucinda. Come home. I'm asking you to come home!"

"There is nothing there for me." She freed herself from Carlos in a clean motion of her arm. She was surprised at her easy strength.

"Did you sleep with her in our bed? Did you sit naked together on our couch? Were you wet like this, like this together in our bathtub, eh? Eso ya no es mi casa, Carlos. Es una casa de miseria!" Lucinda instantly regretted using such words to describe her children's home.

"Lucinda, how can you talk like that?" Carlos raised his wet shirted arms toward her.

Lucinda grabbed the backpack from Carlos and started walking toward the house through the pouring rain.

"Wait, Lucinda!" Carlos hurried behind her trying to keep up. "At least we can still talk. You haven't answered any of my calls. I want to talk to you," said Carlos almost pleading as he ran in front of her to block her way.

Lucinda pushed him aside using both of her arms. She took the steps in firm strides to the raised porch. By now there was a muddy pool at the foot of the steps leading to it. Lucinda stood in the doorway watching Carlos for a few seconds. He was standing in the black mud. She noticed the stained leather of his soggy Florsheim Imperial shoes. "What do you want, Carlos, eh? You want to hear that I forgive you? No puedo! I can't forgive what you have done to me, to us," she said, looking down at him with piercing eyes.

"Forgiveness has nothing to do with it!" Carlos raised his voice in anger for the first time. He stood on the steps, waiting for Lucinda to move, but she did not.

"How can you say that? It has everything to do with us. You

brought a stranger into our lives. I trusted you. I loved you in spite of everything!"

"It just happened," Carlos said, staring past Lucinda, as if outside of himself.

"I don't believe that! People let things happen. You let it happen. Shit, Carlos, abre los ojos!" Lucinda ran to the far corner of the porch to where she could see the winding road leading up to the house. Carlos followed her, coming in out of the rain.

"How could you do this to us, after so many years, how could you do this?" Lucinda turned away from Carlos.

"What do you want, a divorce? In my family there are no divorces!" Carlos yelled. The sound of her father-in-law's words caught Lucinda by surprise. She turned around to face Carlos. As the rains subsided and the clouds allowed the sun's last rays to crawl on the earth, she saw Carlos for what he had become, a younger version of his father. For an instant, which seemed a lifetime to her, they were silent. She remembered her promise to St. Jude, and at that moment, with Carlos' mimicry of defiance staring her in the face, she felt the weight of her hope back itself into the pit of her stomach. A picture of a rooster in the pit of a gallera flashed through her mind. And as quickly as a pinned rooster on its last hope, Lucinda struck out at Carlos.

"Nothing is yours, nothing is mine, nothing! You are nothing!" Lucinda said, her eyes flashing, full of defiance and calculation, making Carlos hesitate at their searing honesty.

"What are you talking about, Lucinda?"

"Nothing is yours, Carlos! Don't you get it? You depend on the bank for everything. Look at that suit you're wearing." Lucinda's contempt gushed off each sentence like the accumulated rainwater gushing off the tin roof. "How did you pay for it?" she poured on.

"Qué sé yo?! What is the point, Lucinda?"

"The point is you don't want to see how things are paid for."

"I have to go." Carlos backed away from Lucinda, but she continued getting right in his face.

"And that stereo you're so much in love with? And the paintings? Do you really think they all have those little bronze plaques labeling them Banco Dominicano for tax purposes? And those shoes," she said, pointing to the ruined Imperials, "who do you think will pay for the replacements? And that watch I gave you, who do you think paid for that too? And the cellulars, and the children's school, shit, even your silk boxers, who pays for all of it, Carlos, quién carajo pays for your life? Eh? Dime, I want to hear it from your own mouth."

"Lucinda, stop this! I have worked very hard to get to where I am."

"Sí, para tu padre. You've come full circle. Don't you see it, Carlos? You have fallen into your father's footsteps. And now a querida too! I'm not putting up with another woman. If you walk that way, you walk without me."

"Why are you doing this now? I came to talk things out, not to fight."

"Talk then!" yelled Lucinda. She walked around Carlos, encircling him. "Tell me what it's like to feel up a lover in a dark place hidden away." She continued moving in closer. "Is it the danger that excites you, Carlos, tell me, the unexpected? Or is it the softer skin of youth? The tighter grip? Do you find more pleasure in her touch, in her wet kisses? Go ahead and talk, carajo. Tell me why my lips don't satisfy you anymore!"

"Stop! Don't do this, Lucinda, don't humiliate us like this!" said Carlos moving away from her.

"It's too late for that, Carlos. There really isn't anything to talk about. You've chosen your way. I can't follow you anymore." She turned her back to him, grabbing the railing with both hands to brace herself for what she was about to say.

"I'm leaving you."

"Lucinda, are you mad? I won't accept that! I don't believe that."

"Believe it, because I'm not going back to you. I don't know who you are anymore. I look at you and I don't recognize you."

"Lucinda, don't do this. Think of the children."

"A buena hora, eh? Don't you dare talk to me about them! I'm going back, but not to you nor to that house. Not for now, maybe not forever. I just don't know." Lucinda looked out to the hills to where Sonora must be.

"Lucinda, what do you want from me?"

"I want you to choose, to choose between Firstborn and First Wife."

Carlos thought of his parents. "It's not that simple."

"It should be."

Carlos didn't answer. Instead, he paced back and forth across the porch. To Lucinda, he looked like a caged rooster. She had the key to release him but couldn't. He had to find his own way out, thought Lucinda. She continued to watch him without speaking. He leaned against the porch post. He looked out over the countryside, its immensity overwhelming him, much like what she was asking him to do. He buried his head in his hands, exhausted.

"I have to go," he said.

"Vete. Do what you have to do."

She watched Carlos disappear behind the stalls, making his way to the helicopter. The machine slowly ascended past the roof. She didn't take her eyes off it until it became a minuscule black dot on the horizon. Lucinda wondered if Carlos had the strength to save the marriage. She wondered the same thing about herself.

The rain finally stopped for good. She heard the sound of an engine.

"Who was that?" asked Don Leonardo coming up the path after parking the Hummer by the stalls.

"Carlos. He came to talk. Papá, I'm leaving for the capital tomorrow. I'm going home soon."

Don Leonardo didn't ask any questions. He only smiled and wrapped his arm around Lucinda's shoulder. Lucinda let his strength fill her. They stood quietly on the porch steps watching the sun set over the treetops.

"Bueno. Then you'll need to take this back with you." It was Carlos' jacket.

—⁓—

In spite of Mercy's own troubles with her mother's arrest, she still took time to help Lucinda out. She found Lucinda the right property to buy: a townhouse on Edgewater Drive by the canal. By what Lucinda had described, Mercy realized what she wanted, and as soon as she showed her the place, Lucinda fell in love with it. There was something about its two white wooden porches, its metal roof, and its large corner garden that gave Lucinda a sense of peace. As she looked up at its gray-blue walls, its tan wooden window shutters, the thick posts elevating the whole building, she got an image of a sturdy ship. The canal in the back, opening to Biscayne Bay just around the bend, had given her a sense of excitement, like when she used to sit in front of a blank canvas, her eye imagining all of the possibilities. Across the canal stood Cocoplum; she had wondered why she had stopped painting there. Looking over the watery boundary, she had been reminded of a trip to Washington, D.C., where she had seen Arlington National Cemetery across a highway. To Lucinda, her old home took the image of the neatly kept cemetery. That is why she had rushed to call Mercy from Santo Domingo. She didn't want to fall back into the familiar and safe routine of her petrified Miami life.

While packing up her things in the Cocoplum house, it was difficult for Lucinda to hear Carlos going about his business and the children acting natural while their eyes betrayed their hearts every morning. Carlos went to work and she stayed packing all day. Rosario helped by silently handing over the wrapped artifacts of Lucinda's life.

"Y esta estatua del Quixote?" asked Rosario.

Lucinda stared at the wooden likeness of her hope. A crazy thought lodged itself in her soul. She did not wrap her father's Don Quixote statue.

"No, Rosario. He will stay here." Lucinda returned it to the bare white shelf on the studio wall. The brown of its wood stood out like a stain on a white carpet. Lucinda noticed it was the only color and the only thing of hers left in the artist's studio. She looked at Rosario.

"I cannot take you with me, Rosario," she said in a whisper, as if to the room itself.

The old nanny cried when Lucinda informed her she would not be with her or the children. Seeing her old, thick tears almost broke Lucinda's will, but she helped Rosario by giving her the opportunity to return to Santo Domingo or to stay with Carlos. She agreed to stay because Carlos had asked her to.

Carlos and Lucinda barely spoke to each other. There was silence in the house, the kind of silence that comes from knowing too much. But to Lucinda, this silence was a respite from the anger and the sadness that had come between them. They were like passengers on a crowded subway, strangers forced to look into each other's eyes, to feel each other's bodies, to smell each other's breaths, to ignore each other. They maintained this routine for the children's sake. Lucinda saw they needed a steady hand to hold on to.

She also saw that she needed money for her plans. Mercy had set a date for the closing and found a lawyer who was preparing the legal matters. All Lucinda had to do was show up with the deposit money. Mercy made the move perfectly trouble-free, but Lucinda realized Mercy was not free of her own troubles. Throughout their dealings, Lucinda found Mercy unusually quiet. When she asked about her mother's plight, Mercy broke down crying. Lucinda realized the effort Mercy was making to help her. She vowed to repay her somehow, but Mercy just shrugged it off, saying that amigas should be "duty-free" with each other.

The next morning Lucinda put on her tan sleeveless C-neck dress. Its simple line on top along with the single string of pearls she wore around her neck made her look elegant and commanded respect. But the knee-length skirt gently flowing open around her thighs satisfied her artist's inclination. She felt more fluid with this length. It was a perfect compromise for what she had to do, thought Lucinda, as she pulled up to the bank parking garage in her blue Jaguar. She parked at the space reserved for her, next to Carlos' Mercedes 500. Lucinda glanced at the stack of mail Rosario had given her on the way out the door. She had absentmindedly thrown it on the passenger seat next to her. All that packing had gotten her behind with the mail.

Giving one more look at the cars as she walked to the private elevator that would take her to the private banking floor, Lucinda laughed in her mind. The sight of the two cars side by side reminded Lucinda of what her relationship with Carlos had become, polished and refined for a seamless highway, but utterly useless when the road got rough. She declined the company car washer's offer to wipe the dust off the Jaguar.

"Dust gives it character," she said, sounding like her father. The attendant looked on as the elevator doors closed.

When she entered the floor to the Banco Dominicano Private Currency branch, Lucinda was greeted by most of the bank officers sitting in their offices as she passed by the open doors. Through the years, she had met them at bank functions and special events. Now Lucinda wondered how many knew about her troubles with El Presidente. Lucinda walked straight to the last office to find Harry, the person she always dealt with on matters concerning family finance. He was on the phone. Lucinda sat down to wait as he finished with a client.

"Hello, Mrs. Colón. How are you? And your mother, I hope all is well with her back on the island?"

Lucinda looked at him for a moment. He was wearing a brown pinstripe suit. She looked at his gold-rimmed glasses and noticed how his blond thinning hair went well with the suit. Harry was a pleaser, even down to avoiding fashion contrasts. He was a coordinated man, thought Lucinda, pleasant enough for handling other people's money.

"I'm fine, Harry, but there is nothing the matter with my

mother." Lucinda's heart raced as she realized that the cover story for her absence had made the rounds with the bank employees and that she had forgotten about it. "That is to say, she is much better now. Thank you for asking."

Harry silently looked at her. Lucinda could not stand his pleasant expression. He was too coordinated, she thought.

"Yes. How can I help you? Please sit down."

Lucinda was already seated. She smiled at his slipup. It didn't suit him at all, she thought, getting down to the business at hand.

"I need a cashier's check for $50,000, made out in my name."

Harry turned to the PowerBook on his desk. "We just received these laptops, all of us in the branch. They are much more appropriate for this type of banking. Very elegant, and more discreet, wouldn't you agree?"

Elegant and discreet, just like the cars parked below and just like her marriage for the past ten years, and just like you, Harry, thought Lucinda, visibly losing her patience with his coordinated motions.

"We can't do it," he declared looking up from his screen.

"What do you mean? I know there's plenty in my account."

Harry excused himself with a raised finger and swiveled his leather chair to the discreet phone behind him.

"Let me make a call."

Lucinda leaned toward the edge of the desk wondering why he didn't use the phone on it.

"I'm sorry, Mrs. Colón," said Harry as he hung up and swiveled back to face her. "There's a cap on that account. You need a countersignature."

"What are you talking about, Harry? I've never had to do that before."

"It's a high cap, $10,000; you probably have never gone above it."

"I've never heard of such a thing!"

Harry punched a few keys on the laptop and swiveled it to Lucinda. On the screen was a scrolling record of every check she had written for the last year. He even went skipping back a few more years. No number ever passed the cap of $10,000.

"It's a special type of account. The line between private and corporate finances can get fuzzy," he said, turning the computer around. "It's a safety trigger," added Harry, after seeing Lucinda's face redden.

"What do you need then?"

"I need the cosigner."

"My husband? He's upstairs, I'll be right back, Harry." Lucinda reached for her purse on the desk.

"No, Mrs. Colón. You have misunderstood. Your cosigner, the one who has to approve the withdrawal, is Mr. Colón Senior."

"What?!" yelled out Lucinda, pushing the chair back as she rushed to get up. The sound of the fallen leather and walnut chair echoed throughout the hallway.

"You need him," said Harry, elegantly placing the chair where it always was.

"We'll see about that, Harry," she said, storming out the door. Lucinda tried to keep her composure as she made her way through the long hall, but she could feel the sting on her neck from all the eyes following her out. No one said good-bye.

The elevator doors shut as if for good. Lucinda leaned on a corner trying to control her sudden urge to get sick. She looked around, attempting to grab hold of something for her eyes to focus on, but the steel walls suddenly looked like a coffin at a morgue. She closed her eyes tightly, forcing a thought of la finca with its green hills and rain-soaked air into her mind's eye. She pushed the penthouse button.

Carlos' office had a commanding view of Miami's banking district. Brickell Avenue by the bay is what Wall Street would look like on vacation, colorful, laid back on its wide streets, and fashionable. As the elevator doors opened, Lucinda exited, her eyes seeking Carlos.

Carlos was sitting behind his big Camilo-designed peninsula desk. Its dark cherry wood surface gave an aura of big deal making. How many deals had Lucinda witnessed on that surface while she waited discreetly on the burgundy leather couch for Carlos to keep his lunch promise, she thought. Now she was not about to wait. Carlos was on the phone.

"Carlos! What the hell is going on, eh? Carlos!" yelled Lucinda lunging at the phone by his ear. She slammed the receiver down as Carlos stood up, a pained expression on his face. He wasn't expecting to see her at the office.

"What's wrong, Lucinda? Did something happen to the kids?"

"The kids?! This has nothing to do with the kids. It has to do with your precious father!"

"Did he call you? I told him not to get involved."

Lucinda vaguely took note of his last comment. It was not part of his script. She slightly backed away from the desk.

"Since when does he have to sign off on my account?" Lucinda asked.

"He doesn't, Lucinda."

"No, eh? Well, I just tried to withdraw money and Harry said he did."

"How much?"

"That's my business. It shouldn't matter."

"It does matter, Lucinda. How much?"

"Fifty thousand."

"Fifty thousand! Why do you need that kind of money?"

"You know I'm buying a place, Carlos, I told you!"

"You're rushing into this, Lucinda. Why don't you rent?"

"We've been through this, Carlos. I want the children to have permanence. I want it. I need it, damn it!"

"You can stay at the house. I'll leave."

"Como siempre, acomodándote. No, the decision is mine and I already made it."

"Wouldn't it be best for the children, for us?"

"Carlos, I'm not here to talk about us. I need that money. It has to be our money after ten years of so much work and sacrifice. Is it?"

"Of course it is."

"Then, qué carajo does your father have to do with it?"

"He signs off on all accounts, Lucinda. It's always been that way."

"You knew about this?"

"It's not a big deal, Lucinda. It's a business decision, a procedural matter."

Carlos said this in a voice lacking conviction. He walked over to the large glass wall and stared into the distance. Lucinda looked at his back, once firm and sure of itself, now rounded.

"And you? Do you need his signature too?"

"Sí."

"Then we have nothing? Nothing is in our name?"

"Lucinda, don't leave. I've done my best!" Carlos said as he watched Lucinda's reflection in the big glass. She was backing away from him. He turned to face her.

"I don't believe this," she was saying more to herself than to him. "All these years and nothing, nothing to show for it, nada me queda. Nothing is my own? The car! I'll sell the Jaguar."

By the look on his face, Lucinda knew not even that was hers.

"Lucinda, I never realized . . ." But Lucinda left without hearing him.

She drove stunned. She drove without seeing the street signs, any of the people on the sidewalks, the buildings passing by. As the car came to a stop, Lucinda found herself parked next to a sidewalk by a seawall. It was a familiar place, not far from the bank.

Lucinda pushed the button on the door armrest. The windows lowered simultaneously. The hot breeze invaded the interior. Lucinda gave up. Her face collapsed into her arms over the steering wheel.

"No lo creo, no lo creo, no lo creo," she kept saying. The words of disbelief came out wrapped in all the pain of a long and difficult birth, pushing themselves out, like an unwanted child demanding to be given a chance at life. Her eyes were closed tightly trying to squeeze out every tear left to her.

She could feel her tears snailing down her wrists, down along her forearms. The air in the car lacked life. Suddenly Lucinda gasped, as if coming up for air after a long descent into a still ocean. She wiped her eyes with the ball of her palms. She took a deep breath and slapped her shoulders onto the seat back, her arms extended straight out, her hands gripping the top of the steering wheel. Just as suddenly, her whole body relaxed, allowing the heat to melt her. Nothing crossed her mind except for an unbearable thought. She couldn't afford the plan for her marriage's future, a future free of queridas, free of Don Carlos' grasp, free of the damned Bank, free of their own triteness. Nothing else was left.

Then she noticed the mail on the seat next to her and grabbed the stack. She looked through it, not looking for anything in particular, but to feel the comfort that comes from a routine. She sifted through the stack twice. On the third go-round, her glazed attention was pierced by a familiar wax seal. She dropped all the envelopes on her lap. Her slender finger knifed through the seal. She wiped her eyes one last time and read.

Querida hija,

Your mother and I miss you very much. We have been praying for you since you left. I have been thinking about you. Como pasa el tiempo, mi Lucinda. Do you still have the statue of Don Quixote I gave you all those years ago? To me, el loco was not that crazy. He just saw past others, much like you and me. I know you are suffering a lot and are going through a very difficult time in your life. Pero, if it is worth anything in this world, I want you to know a few things that are in my heart. You are my daughter, and I am grateful to God for allowing that. But you are much more. Ever since you were born, I have seen your independent soul. You always insisted on doing everything for yourself. Your shoulders are strong, they have carried you well. My grandchildren are un reflejo de tu fuerza y amor. The love you have given your mother and me has been generous, with no strings attached. Let all this love support you now. You have it in you, Lucinda, you are strong, you can make it through this.

I saw how your heart suffered. I also saw how your mind was working. Mi querida Lucinda, I am not one to meterme en tus asuntos. Your life is your life, but I do know that in this world, for good or bad, money has become part of the equation. It cannot solve all the problems, but it helps. For this reason, your mother and I have transferred $150,000 into an account under your name. This is really your money, Lucinda. Remember college? All those academic scholarships you earned paid for it. Bueno, that did not stop us from keeping the college fund we had planned for you. Este dinero is yours, you earned it in more ways than one. Use it now as seeds, mi querida Lucinda. I know wonderful things will grow, like God has made you grow into a wonderful human being.

Tus padres

P.S. See Evan Costa at Banco del Pichincha on Brickell. He is the son of a good friend and knows what to do for you.

Lucinda was still crying. She turned the rearview mirror and caught the closeup of her face in it. She saw her father's eyes reflected in her own and was grateful. Her other hand pressed the button that closed the windows. She straightened the mirror and started the engine, the coolness of the air conditioner drying her face. She knew that bank; it was around the corner, right next to St. Jude's Catholic Church.

Chapter 17

———

Amigas

This is a beautiful spot. What's it called?" asked Isa.

"It's called Coquina Cove," answered Julia as they both made their way from the parking lot to the piano bar.

Coquina Cove didn't have much of a beach. Through the years, water had inched its way in from the bay through a narrow depression, forming a lake-size lagoon; an inland beach had been created around it with white sand and hearty coconut trees, making the whole thing look like a small South Pacific atoll. There was a bike path laid over the atoll, and benches were spaced throughout it. The benches faced the open bay waters. La Luna Bar was built facing the lagoon, across from its mouth. Julia and Isa checked with the doorman to see if Lucinda had arrived.

"She's not here yet. Let's take the bike path," Julia suggested. They walked past the outdoor tables and began to follow the path circling the cove. When they reached the small bridge spanning the mouth of the lagoon, Isa noticed a wide canal snaking its way around the right side of the atoll.

"Where does that end up?"

"The channel? It goes to the marina, right behind the bar. See the masts popping up over the roof?" Julia pointed.

The masts were dancing in the air. The breeze was causing

small waves which gently rocked the boats. The sound of the ropes slapping the aluminum masts gave off a windchime singsong effect enveloping the entire scene.

"How did you discover this place?"

"To be honest, Mercy told me about it. Felipe and I came here a few times. You should see it when there's a full moon out."

"That's why it's called La Luna Bar?"

"Yes. And on every full moon they throw a wild party. The bike path becomes one heck of a dance floor!"

"No wonder Mercy knows about it. I can just see her leading a conga line around the cove! Pero you and Felipe, I thought you were into a more quiet scene."

"On the other nights there's only a duet. They play classic Latino songs with a little of Sinatra and Ella thrown in. They are really good."

"That's Lucinda waving to us," said Isa.

Lucinda hadn't been out much since the return to Miami. Setting up a new life took much of her time. The children, their school needs, and especially trying to make a living drained all of her energies. But Isa was right, Lucinda had thought. It couldn't hurt if she went out one night while Brenda and Roberto spent the weekend with Carlos. She missed him but didn't want to think about him tonight. Lucinda waited for her friends. She was glad she had recognized them in the distance. She didn't want to enter the bar alone.

The sun was just about to set; the three of them stood quietly watching the horizon as if participating in a silent ritual. After the sun melted into the sea and the sunset breeze picked up, they looked at each other and began to laugh as good friends do when they realize they're together again. They greeted each other with kisses all around.

"Lucinda, it's good to see you," said Julia.

"I've been so busy. I'm sorry."

"Don't worry," said Isa. "We know what you're going through.

We've been there." Then she added, looking over to Julia, "Well, I've been there. We just want to help."

"You are, believe me, you are. And Mercy too. She's helped me a lot with the house. Where is she?" asked Lucinda.

"She had a closing rescheduled for late in the day. And she's still waiting for word from Cuba," said Isa.

"Qué lástima," said Lucinda. "I wish there was something we could do."

"She's desperate. I don't know how she can keep going like she does," Julia said.

"Qué remedio le queda? She has no choice. I've got well-connected neighbors who I think can help," Isa said.

"I hope so," said Lucinda as the three of them stood quietly at the entrance to La Luna Bar.

"Let's go inside." Julia asked for a table with a view. The night sky was deeply orange with the sun's rays still arching back over the horizon.

The glass top of the table, the chairs, and even the sand radiated with an orange hue as dusk settled into night. The duet played a slow "Girl from Ipanema" as Julia ordered a bottle of merlot and tapas with cheeses, ham, sausages, olives, and bread.

Lucinda took a deep breath and settled into her chair. She looked around the room, then back at her two friends, and taking another breath, as if from life itself, said, "You both look great." Julia was dressed in a loose dark brown pant and blouse cotton outfit. Isa wore a crocheted orange cardigan-sleeved tee with khaki pants. Lucinda noticed Isa's slightly exposed midriff.

"What is this? Desde cuándo?"

"Since Key West she's been exposing herself all over town!" said Julia.

"You mean since Orlando, and I'm not talking about the city, as Mercy would say!" Lucinda laughed.

"Look who's talking," said Isa. "You're the one who looks like Jane of the Jungle. Además, I never dress like this when I'm at work."

"G.I. Juana, that's what Mercy calls me, remember? What can I say? I work out every day at the gym. It helps me release stress, but believe me, it won't last long."

"Keep doing it," said Julia noticing how the long fitted polo teal dress hugged Lucinda's contoured body. "It's good for you. You look splendid!"

"Well, my gym days are about over. No hay tiempo for those kinds of things now," said Lucinda, looking at the reflected evening sky on the lagoon.

"It is hard, what you are doing," said Julia.

"It's almost impossible," added Isa. She knew how much she had tried to save her own marriage. In the end, David didn't want it, she thought to herself. What was it that the counselor had told her in the very first session? Most marriages can't survive adultery, whether of the bodily kind or of the cultural kind. One partner's interest was elsewhere, and the other's pain was unrelenting and unforgiving. But she could see that Lucinda still had a vision of their love. And Carlos, like an undecided helicopter, was still hovering around her.

The waitress brought the wine and tapas to the table. The women silently watched as she poured the merlot into each glass. Isa saw a shadow of fear flit across Lucinda's fine forehead. For an instant, tears made an attempt to spill from her eyes. Isa grabbed her wineglass and said,

"A mis amigas; salud, dinero, y amor!"

"How about love first, then health, then money, in that order? I can dump the last two, but that love one, that one is hard to grab a hold of once it leaves you." Lucinda blinked back the tears.

"If you think about it—" Julia was saying.

"And you're always thinking!" Isa interrupted.

"No, I mean this," continued Julia. "When you really think about it, every human being is just in pursuit of a little love."

"Bueno then, to a little love, and to a whole lot of dinero and salud!" answered Isabel.

She noticed more people arriving. "Is it my imagination or are there a lot of single people in here? They look old."

"Oye, my old friend, if you haven't noticed, these 'old' singles are around our age," said Lucinda.

"Felipe once commented on that," said Julia. "Especially forty-something women."

"Like you, eh?" joked Lucinda, surveying the crowd.

The Luna Bar was getting crowded with many single men and many more women. Their clothing and jewelry spoke of people who have made it, but their eyes spoke louder for a soul-mate missed or desired. As Isa said, everybody was looking at everybody else a bit too intensely.

"I've never been part of the divorce scene," said Isa watching a nearby table fill with women dressed to kill in tight work suits and high heels. They joked and laughed in a conspicuously loud way.

"I don't know, when I was single, I never did the 'looking for the love of my life' cosa in some bar. Why should I do it now? It seems so desesperado to me," continued Isa.

"Looking for love in all the wrong places seems to be Mercy's expertise," said Julia to Isa.

"Well, she hasn't been up to no good in that department lately. Can you blame her? Between setting up her new company and figuring out what to do about her mother, she hasn't had a minute for any men."

"Cómo están tus varones?" asked Lucinda, not wanting to talk about love. "I haven't seen them in a while."

"The boys, bastante bien. Sam is turning out to be some mad scientist. I think mami is going to kick him out of the house if he ruins another of her treasured pots with one of his experiments. Sometimes I can't tell whether I'm eating off a dessert dish or a petri dish! David Jr. is running like mad with the cross-country team. He's going to some celebration party tonight at one of the runner's homes." Isa looked at her watch. "I was supposed to drop him off but he got one of the seniors to drive him. Y los tuyos, how are they holding up?"

"They've adapted well, considering. I'm keeping watch over Roberto. He shows a lot of anger toward his father. Brenda is still very much a small child. Ransom School has been wonderful. Its counselor, Linda, has really taken them under her wing."

"Sometimes it's good for them to have an outsider to lean on," said Isa, remembering what her boys went through after the divorce.

"Do they know anything?" asked Julia.

Lucinda really didn't know what they knew about their separation but she knew they felt the anger, the sadness, and the tension.

"No, I haven't told them why we've separated. I just told them that papi and I are having problems with our relationship, and we're figuring out how to fix it while we're apart."

"Y tú, Lucinda, cómo estás tú?" Julia asked, gently touching her arm.

Lucinda took a second to answer. "Me, I won't lie, it's the hardest thing I've had to go through in my life. Every day I wake up knowing I'm walking on a minefield. There are days when I can't get up without wanting to explode at Carlos, but I don't want the kids to think they have to take sides. And then there are his parents, constantly there, still blaming me. Y esa mujer, you know, I refuse to talk about her. He never brings her up. But I think he's more alone than ever since I moved out." This last comment changed Lucinda's mood and she added, "I'm much better than I was a month ago."

"That's what counts," said Julia.

"How about you? Isa tells me you have a roommate now? Y eso?"

Julia could see Isa tense up.

"Yes, yes, I do," she answered, looking at Isa. "Beatriz Palol, the dancer we met at the tablao."

"She's helping her with the new book," Isa added.

"I bet she's helping you forget about Felipe leaving," Lucinda said smiling.

Julia laughed nervously at Lucinda's directness. She realized her amigas were probing.

"She's helping me with one chapter and she's an interesting person. We talk about many things."

"Which chapter is she helping you write?" Isa asked looking down at the napkin on the table. It reminded her of the one Beatriz had given Julia.

"The one on relationships."

"And?" Isa insisted.

"And sexuality," Julia answered, not wanting to go where the conversation was heading. "But here's to you, Lucinda—to your new-found life."

"And may you find yours," Lucinda added.

The three clinked their glasses. The musical duet began to play "Love Is Here to Stay."

As the middle-aged couple performed, Isa whispered, rolling her eyes, "Can you believe this? They're playing our song." Instantly Julia thought of Beatriz, Lucinda had Carlos in her mind, and Isabel tried to forget Orlando. When they realized what Isa meant, they laughed loudly and conspicuously. The pianist looked over at their table. He nodded at Julia.

Julia explained to her friends that Andrés was an Argentinian who played the piano like a hybrid of Erroll Garner and Armando Manzanero. Vivian was an Afro-Cuban who sang her heart out like Celia Cruz and Ella Fitzgerald rolled up into one. They met in Miami while he was on tour with a band. She only sang in church and at family gatherings at the time. Andrés fell in love with her voice and then with her. He stayed, they married, and soon he talked her into performing with him at small clubs. Julia had befriended them.

"She's a great singer, no?"

"Wonderful," said Lucinda. "They make a striking couple."

The women sat still for the performance. They watched as people began to tentatively ask each other to dance. By now the sunset was complete and the night sky glowed with an aura of lights. Miami's skyline was off in the distance across the bay, radiating its night pulse into the sky like a distant searchlight that never gives up.

"I'm glad I never gave up on this city," commented Lucinda. "It's such a beautiful place."

Isa and Julia nodded in agreement. Julia washed down a finger roll of serrano ham and cheese with the last of the merlot in her glass. The waitress refilled each glass for another round of wine.

"Speaking of beautiful places, how's the nascent art gallery coming along?" asked Julia.

"How are plans?" Isa also asked, taking her gaze off the distant lights.

"Mercy and I found a perfect place in Coconut Grove. It's just off a side street, around the corner from the Grove Playhouse. Mercy said this would be good for business. It's not large. The front of the store has plenty of room for exhibiting artworks. In the back, there's a huge porch with a big canvas overhang. I want to make that an outdoor children's craft studio."

"What about for you, where will you paint?"

"There's room for me in the studio, but I want to use it to give classes for kids after school. I'll paint at home, in the garage."

"Te la comiste! I love that idea," said Isa. "So it's all set?"

"Almost, this week I'm going to sign the lease. I'm excited about it and nervous too of course."

"You'll do fine," said Julia in her reassuring voice.

"I hope so, I know so, but I couldn't have done it without you both. It was so good of you to help me out. Thank you, de veras, gracias."

"You've thanked us enough already," said Julia. "Just make us a good profit on our investment; and that's you."

"Seguro, and if you have any ideas, let me know."

"No, no," said Isa. "We're silent partners. You've got the artist's eye and you've got Mercy, the Queen Midas of Real Estate!"

Just then Andrés and Vivian began to play Sinatra's version of "Witchcraft" with a little Latin swing beat on the piano à la Garner. A tall man approached the women's table. Isa had spotted him coming from the bar where he had been standing.

"Buenas noches, muchachas." He smiled at the three of them. Isa got an image of the Big Bad Wolf in her head. He asked her to dance. She declined. He then asked Lucinda. She politely said no. Still smiling and still trying to huff and puff his way to a dance, as Isa later put it to Mercy, he asked Julia. She said yes. Julia gave her friends a "you put me on the spot" look as she followed the fifty-something man to a spot on the floor.

"He's not that bad looking, bald spot and all," said Lucinda. "When does it happen to a woman that bald spots don't matter in a man?" she wondered aloud, making a hole in a slice of ham on her plate with a toothpick.

"Julia is going to cut a hole on the floor with her dancing. She's not that bad," said Isa, looking at Julia swinging and salsa-ing away to the music.

"Where did she learn to do that?"

"From Beatriz I guess; she dances, remember?"

"Sí, verdad."

"They dance a lot," answered Isabel without taking her eyes off Julia.

"What's that supposed to mean?"

"Nada. It's just that ever since Beatriz moved in, we haven't heard much about Felipe."

"What's bugging you about that?"

"I'm worried about her. Mercy is convinced Beatriz is gay. I'm not so sure she's wrong."

"So what?"

"What if Julia . . . ?"

"Well, all I see is that since Beatriz moved in, a weight has been lifted off her shoulders. Look at her." Lucinda pointed toward the dance floor. "I wouldn't worry about Julia if I were you."

Isabel thought about this. It was true. Everybody always

thought it was her book deadlines that made Julia seem so burdened. But even her apartment looked lighter with all of Beatriz' things arranged throughout it.

Looking at Julia dancing away, something kept dancing in the back of Isa's mind. It was a conversation she had had with Mercy after Beatriz moved in with Julia.

"It starts that way," Mercy had said, "let me tell you! And before you can say 'hot tortillas,' Julia has flipped. Está vulnerable with the Felipe thing and this Beatriz has her dancing on a Crisco'd frying pan, just waiting for her to flip. Yo lo sé, I've seen it happen! Oye, mi cousin, wake up and smell the lesbians. Qué palabra! Watch out if we don't start seeing her in boots and nose rings, let me tell you!"

"Mercy! You go too far," Isa had said to her. "Julia felt alone. Beatriz came at the right time for her. A little companionship goes a long way."

Watching Julia now, Isa wondered if her friend was dancing her way to more than just a roommate. She wanted to ask Lucinda how she would feel knowing a friend turned out to be gay, but she couldn't ask such a question in a bar. To Isa, the question felt like asking to take a short stroll into a deep and cavernous place. It would take a lifetime to emerge from it, Isabel thought. She needed time.

"What a great time I had!" It was Julia returning from her dancing. She introduced the tall man as Benny, who proceeded to tell his divorced life's journey without sitting down. By the time he got to the part where his mother still warms his bedsheets with her hair blower, the duet had done four songs and Isa had had enough.

"Benny, it was great hearing your story. How long did you say you've been with that divorce group?" Isabel asked, pointing to a large mixed group taking up three tables.

"Ten years." He said this as if he were saying ten minutes.

"It was nice talking with you, but we have to get going," Isa declared. The large group was beckoning to Benny, who said his good-byes and left to join the group.

"What happened?" they both asked Isa.

"I don't want to see myself like that in ten years. Benny isn't divorced, he's married to that group. Eventually, you have to be out on your own, no matter how hard, or lonely, or frightening the whole damned thing gets."

No one made a move to leave. Andrés the pianist began to play a long, solo rendition of "Sabor a Mí," giving his singing wife a vocal rest. The waitress noticed the empty wine bottle and offered another. Lucinda asked for three liqueur glasses of Cointreau.

"Have you heard from Orlando?" asked Lucinda.

"He's called a couple of times. We've talked."

"Really? The last I heard was that he ignored you in Key West."

"I told you, he called once to apologize for being so busy that weekend with Julia's writing thing. Since then he's called again, just to talk."

"You haven't seen each other."

"I gave him my beeper number."

"How romantic."

"Mercy thinks Isa believes in the 'obstacle course' way to love," Julia interjected.

The Cointreau arrived with a small tray of ladyfinger cookies.

"He hasn't asked you out yet?" asked Lucinda.

"He wanted to go out tonight," Isa said, making sure that her tone left no doubt about her decision for the evening, but she still felt a small tightness in her throat as she said it.

The large tightly knit group of divorcees suddenly rose from their tables like a flock of startled birds and flew onto the dance floor. The noise of the sliding chairs got Isa's attention. She looked at their just abandoned tables and noticed Orlando sitting behind them. He saw her. He began to walk toward her. And she saw that he was alone.

Julia turned around to find Orlando standing behind her. Isa noticed how stunning he looked in a charcoal polo shirt, black jeans, and shiny black shoes. He carried a camel-colored blazer over his shoulder.

"Orlando!" said Julia.

"We were just talking about you," Isa said to him.

"And I was thinking about you. What a coincidence seeing you here. I was just coming to have a beer," he answered, looking down at her.

Julia introduced him to Lucinda, who right away saw the possibilities for Isabel.

"Mucho gusto," he said reaching out for a handshake while still standing. "I don't want to intrude."

"Come on, sit down. You can't leave after just saying hello," insisted Julia.

"No, of course not," he said, smiling at Isa.

Orlando's beer came; Isa noticed it was a Presidente, her favorite. The four of them chatted for a little while about the weather and the arts.

"That's a nice tune," Orlando said turning to Isa. "Dance with me?"

They left Julia and Lucinda sipping their liqueurs and wondering what made Isa hesitate toward this man.

Orlando put his right arm around her lower back. He took her hand in his. They began to dance. Isabel liked his understated confidence. His whole body moved that way.

"Here, watch this," he said to Isabel.

Orlando twirled her around twice and then made a move that ended with him behind her and Isa wrapped in his arms, both gently swaying to the music.

"I copied that move from Fred Astaire. I have every movie of his. I got that from his 'dancing cheek to cheek' routine," Orlando said. She could feel his breath on her cheek. "So, we're finally on a date—sort of."

Isa tensed at the idea. Orlando let her go and they faced each other again. He slowly pulled her toward him.

"I'm a perfect gentleman. Don't let my Hollywood past give you a bad impression of me." He smiled at her. Isa remembered that smile from the inn on Key West, when she first saw him in the semi-flesh, she thought to herself. She felt her body tense a bit more; so did Orlando's.

"And besides, your two chaperones are keeping a close eye on me."

Lucinda and Julia waved at them. Isa smiled back, and for the first time in a long time, she wasn't conscious of her smile's muscles.

"She kissed him, right?" asked Lucinda, returning the smile.

"It was out of character, she said. I even think she went to confession over it. But she liked the kiss. They look good together, don't they."

"Like equals," Lucinda said. "Mira, they're dancing another song."

Lucinda noticed how Isa let Orlando's arm hold her by the waist. The musicians began to play a slow tune.

"I feel like I've danced with you before. That's not a line, Isabel."

Isa, smiling, answered, "I love to dance."

"I can tell," he said as they sailed across the wooden floor.

"Do you go dancing often?"

"Sometimes, but I haven't found a good dance partner in Miami," he said, not looking at her.

"And tonight?" she asked, not looking at him.

Orlando did not answer. He looked straight into her eyes as he pulled her closer to him.

"Tonight, after you turned me down," he reminded her while stepping away but still holding her hands, "I went out to dinner—alone. Then, because you are going to ask me, I stopped off at Diego's, in the Gables, but it was too crowded. My heart wasn't in it, so I left," Orlando said, not taking his eyes off hers.

"And here? Do you come here often?"

"Here? Yes, all the time. I practically live here," Orlando said playfully.

Isa looked at him perplexed.

"My boat, remember? It's here in the marina."

"Sí, verdad, you told me about the boat." Isabel remembered the channel going to the marina behind the restaurant. "I didn't make the connection."

"We can walk over there later," he said as the music stopped.

Isa pulled away and, turning toward the duet, began to clap. They both lingered for a few minutes on the dance floor watching Andrés and Vivian prepare for a new song. Isa felt herself leaning against Orlando's arm. He affectionately wrapped it around her shoulders. It felt like his arm belonged on her shoulder, like she had a physical memory of it always being there. It was a feeling that pleased her. She looked sideways at him and instantly knew she could trust this man. The thought of it frightened her.

Andrés and Vivian burst into a song. Orlando grabbed Isabel, pulling her by the waist.

"Un merengue," he said excitedly, as he took Isa's hand with a firm grip in his own.

"Sí, an original Johnny Ventura," Isa added, remembering her Dominican days with mixed emotions. Orlando's small steps showed only a hint of a limp-like motion to the right. They were fast and close steps. Isa was able to match him step to step. They turned, their hips barely touching, as Orlando curled his body into hers.

"You dance like a Dominican!" Isa said.

"I like the smooth, more controlled short steps," he said. "You don't like it?" he added in a full, low voice, almost whispering in her ear.

"Al contrario," Isabel whispered to herself, wondering if he had heard it. The easy movement of their dancing, as well as the tone of his voice and the feel of his body, engulfed Isabel's senses. In her mind's eye, she felt herself naked, stepping into a steamy whirlpool. Isabel forgot to think of her friends, her boys, her work, and even herself.

"Good," he added as he lifted Isabel's arms up in the air along with his. They continued moving in short, quick steps, Isabel letting her hips swing just slightly. She could feel the cool air swirl along her exposed midriff. She closed her eyes. Then, still holding her hands, Orlando brought their arms wide and began lowering them until they rested along the sides of their bodies. He slowly pulled her in, so close she could feel the muscles in his chest and arms against hers. Quickly he grabbed her waist firmly and twirled her as he too rotated his body, both meeting face to face again as the music's tempo accelerated. For an instant they touched foreheads. Isabel kept her eyes lowered, but she could feel his eyes taking in every detail of her face. Orlando turned his cheek, brushing it against hers. She opened her eyes just in time to catch a glimpse of his earlobe and she found herself wishing she could caress it with her lips. Isabel's eyes also caught her friends looking at her, and she became worried that her face showed the pleasure and abandon she was feeling.

"Isa is having so much fun!" said Lucinda.

"Yes," answered Julia. "I hope she's letting herself go. I'm sure God gave her the go-ahead a long while back, but you know Isa."

"Siempre poniendo los frenos. She's been so . . . ," Lucinda wanted to say *guarded* but continued saying, "cautious after what she went through."

"True, but Orlando is different somehow. He's hecho y derecho—a man who suffers no fool. Plus, he seems taken by her," Julia was saying, thinking of how similar Isa was in that way.

"She should give him a chance," declared Lucinda. Carlos came into her mind just then. Julia looked at her quietly, thinking the same thing.

"Maybe she will," said Lucinda as she looked over at Isabel.

"From what I see, she's not riding her brakes tonight." Julia watched Isa and Orlando laughing as they circled the dance floor.

When they passed near Lucinda and Julia, Isabel motioned for them to come to the dance floor. They shook their heads no, but Orlando, noticing Isabel's intention, worked his way to their table. After exchanging glances with Isabel, Orlando grabbed Julia's hand and pulled her to the dance floor. Isabel did the same for Lucinda. Soon the four of them were gyrating all over the crowded floor. Isabel bumped into Benny while they were dancing. He gave her a wide toothy smile, which quickly turned into a frown when Orlando ignored it. Benny moved back toward his divorce group when Julia declined his dance offer.

The paired-off divorcees formed a line creating a tunnel with their arms high in the air. Their smiles and nods urged the dancers to merengue their way down its length. Orlando and Isa joined in, dancing beneath the arched arms, as did Julia and Lucinda. Each couple took its turn holding the archway, as well as dancing along its length. After the merengue, the duet rapidly continued with a guaguanco and then a mambo. Julia and Lucinda, carried away by the infectious tempo, kept on dancing alongside Orlando and Isa, occasionally alternating partners.

When the duet announced a break, the dancers all agreed. The four of them returned to the table. Orlando said something to Isabel, which her friends could not hear. He excused himself saying he'd be right back.

"Qué calor! Is it only me, or are you both hot too?" Isa asked, dipping a napkin in the water glass and wiping her neck with it.

"I can see the steam coming off your neck!" Julia teased her.

"He's a nice guy, Isa. What are you going to do about it?" said Lucinda.

The direct question and its implication took Isabel by surprise. Her friend had really changed, a lot, she thought to herself.

"I know what I'm going to do. Let's get going or we 'old' singles are going to pay for this night with heavy bags under our eyes and aching bones tomorrow morning." Julia gathered her purse.

"Here comes Orlando. Let's say our good-byes," added Lucinda.

Orlando accompanied them to the entrance.

"I really enjoyed myself tonight, thanks to you," he said, looking at Julia and Lucinda. He gave each a light kiss on the cheek. Lucinda noticed he didn't kiss Isabel or say good-night to her. He didn't accompany them to the cars.

They stayed quiet as the three women approached Isa's car. Isa hesitated unlocking it. Julia saw her glance back toward La Luna Bar's entrance.

"Would you mind if I stayed a little longer, Julia?"

"Don't worry," said Lucinda. "I'll give Julia a ride home."

Julia and Lucinda left the parking lot slowly. They were trying to see what Isabel was up to. They saw her meet Orlando as he was coming out of the bar.

Orlando and Isa made their way slowly around the lagoon. The bike path was lit by lamps low on the ground. It was a dark night. There was still a light breeze coming off the water.

"It's your turn now, Orlando."

"My turn? For what?"

"Remember? To tell me all about your life."

"Ah yes, that's true." He looked out to the sea. Isa saw his eyes squint just slightly.

He took her hand in his and began to talk in an even, gentle tone.

"I was born in Cuba, and because you are going to ask, I am forty-four years old, but left the island as a teenager."

"You're older than me."

"By a lot, right?"

"Why Adams?"

"My great-grandfather was an American. He stayed in Havana after the Spanish American War, seeking a piece of paradise. He was part of Teddy's Rough Riders. He met my great-grandmother while traveling the countryside looking for land to buy. Well, he bought the land and fell madly in love with the seller's daughter. He never left the island again in spite of having a fiancée back in the States."

Orlando and Isabel sat on one of the benches. By now many other couples had left the bar and were strolling or sitting along the lagoon.

"So, those are my American roots. My Cuban roots come straight from my parents. My grandfather and my father both married Cubans. By the time I was born, my parents were 99 percent Cuban in their daily life, but they weren't communists. We became exiles by returning to the States."

"And Los Angeles? How did you end up in L.A.?"

"You've been asking Julia about me?"

"No. She's been telling me about you. There's a difference."

"Did she tell you I went to college in Stanford, decided I wanted to write screenplays, and moved to L.A. to make it happen?"

"What happened?"

"You could say I made it."

"Why did you leave, then?"

Orlando remained silent, drawing Isabel's attention. She saw in his eyes that he was debating whether or not to answer her.

"I got tired, I guess." Orlando got up from the bench. He grabbed her hand and guided her toward the marina.

"You never got married?"

"Not really."

"That's like being half pregnant."

"I never got married. I had a few serious relationships. Not many."

They made their way past a few docks. Orlando stopped in front of the luxury catamaran motorboat.

"This is it." He pointed down at it. "This is where I live now."

"It's beautiful," said Isa. "It doesn't look like anything I've seen."

"It's different. It has twin hulls to give it more stability."

"It's big."

"Sure, it has a large cabin. Do you want to see the inside?"

Isabel hesitated. She was quiet, it seemed to her, for too long. She looked at Orlando. They made eye contact. She looked at her watch. "I'd better not. It's late and the boys should be home by now. You don't mind, do you?"

Orlando gave her a sweet smile. "No, qué va, it gives me an excuse to invite you again."

"You won't need an excuse," Isa said as they started to walk back.

"Good." He took Isa's hand in his once again.

Isa took in the familiar feel of his palm against hers. He didn't grasp her hand. There was no weight to his grip, but there was substance. She held his exactly the same way.

When they reached Isa's car, Orlando said, "Now you know all about me."

"I doubt it."

"Don't doubt so much, Isabel," Orlando said in a low, romantic voice. Isabel heard the sincerity in his words. To her they almost sounded like a gentle pleading.

"May I kiss you again?" he asked in that same tone.

"You didn't ask the first time," Isabel answered, surprised by her own voice.

"You're right. That was not a proper kiss. May I make it up to you?"

Isabel dropped the hand with the car keys to her side. Orlando placed an arm on top of Isa's car as he leaned in toward her. Her body relaxed against the door. Their lips, already parted, met. It was a slow and searching kiss.

"Good-night, Isabel," he said as she opened her eyes.

She got inside the car and closed the door. She turned the keys in the ignition. The window silently slid down.

"What is the name of your boat?"

"*The SeaLove.*"

"Me gusta ese nombre."

"I knew you would."

Orlando stayed standing in the darkened parking lot until Isa's car disappeared into the mangrove-lined road leading out to the main street. He walked once more around the lagoon before heading back to his boat.

Chapter 18

Isabel

The kiss. After four years of puckering up in front of the mirror, along comes Orlando and his lips stick to mine more than any smudge-proof lipstick Revlon could invent. After four years of being in a love-dry desert, after four years of belly-crawling my way out of the scorching heat of a broken marriage, after four years of fearing any man for another mirage, along comes este Orlando in the flesh and blood. My lips were still warm and pulsating. He was right. That first kiss was not a proper one. This time I kissed him back. I kissed him searching for yo qué sé and I found qué sé yo. I know nothing. Can a woman know a man by a kiss? Especially a woman who hasn't kissed a man in a long time and who might just be aching for it? I know one thing. I felt different.

With Orlando I didn't have to mold myself to him. I could be myself. I was myself. That day in Key West when I talked, he listened. He listened and I could tell he was registering every word. His eyes told me that. And when he talked, his eyes wanted me to listen. I did. I heard every word and my soul knew every meaning. They say people go crazy on a full moon, that it pulls at your blood like it pulls at an entire ocean. Bueno, that night La Luna Bar pulled the ocean flowing through my veins all the way to my lips.

And when we kissed, I could feel the fullness of the high tide in his.

I was getting too poetic with myself so I turned on the radio. I played with the seek button. I watched the digital numbers dance back and forth. The multilingual sound of Miami blended into one sweet hum as I searched for a sound that would bring me back to my reality.

But reality was staring at me as my face reflected off the windshield. I looked at myself, there floating in glass, and saw someone I had forgotten. I saw someone who was open again, abierta otra vez a una posibilidad. The possibility of Orlando and me danced in my mind like a pesky fairy with a tale to weave.

I found myself weaving past a stopped car in front of me. I got lucky no one was coming in the opposite lane. That's all I needed, to tell my family that their executive provider was off in La-La Land with a fairy for a co-driver and that's why she smashed the car on her way home from a happily-ever-after feeling of a surprise date.

I caught myself laughing out loud at the cuadro painting itself in my head. I looked at the radio once more and released the seek button at the count of three. I arrived at my house listening to an old Gershwin song, "Let's Call the Whole Thing Off," which I thought was a good way to off the giddiness I was feeling. I drove into the open garage and noticed my father's car missing. I looked at my watch and by the late hour, I knew something was off.

Before I turned off the engine, mami was running out the connecting kitchen door.

"Isa, Isa, Isa! You're home! Al fin, Dios mío!" she screamed as I closed the door behind me. "Dónde has estado mijita? We've been calling you on the cellular all night. We couldn't find you. I didn't know what to do. I called David. Your father said it was lo mejor. He's flying down in the morning."

David only flies down for two reasons, when he's feeling fatherly or when something's wrong, really wrong.

"Tu padre, he left two hours ago with Sam. I wanted to wait for you. We have to go. Vamos, hurry."

Mami's hands were trembling as she pushed me against the door of the car. I could hardly make out her words through the sobs. I felt the heaviness of her weight against my chest as she broke down weeping. An old scar of a memory flashed in my mind. I remembered feeling this heaviness from mami the time her mother died back in Havana after twenty-five years of not being able to see her. The weight of that loss almost crushed mami. I held her up by the shoulders, trying to hold back my own sinking feeling.

"Qué pasó, mami? Tell me slowly."

"I couldn't reach you, I'm sorry, perdóname," she kept repeating.

"Está bien, mami. I forgot the cellular in the glove compartment." I was trying to reassure her, but my eyes were burning a hole through the glove compartment to the damned phone, snug in its leather case. It was off for the night. Just like I had been. I looked over at mami and saw her red face, puffed from the crying and worrying. "It's not your fault. Qué pasó?" I whispered.

"Tuvo un accidente."

"Por Dios, mami! Who had an accident? Tell me."

She buried her face in my neck. I could feel her lips moving against my throat. My body shivered as it registered what she was saying.

"David Jr.—intensive care—a car accident."

I looked up to the garage's ceiling burning a hole through it looking for God. All I saw was a starry night suddenly blacking out completely. I felt a weight shifting under me and I realized mami was doing the holding up now.

"Where is he?"

"En Mercy Hospital. Tu padre is there with Sam."

"Let's go."

As I raced through the dark empty streets, mami kept crying and explaining, "I didn't know what to do. We kept dialing you."

"Está bien, mami. I understand."

I grabbed the cellular from the glove compartment. My mind was racing, trying to negotiate every possible turn. I called my third cousin Francisco. He was the Director of Pediatrics at Dade Memorial Hospital. I woke him up and made him promise to meet me immediately at the hospital.

"Mami, do you know anything about his condition?"

"Está inconsciente," she answered, looking at me like I used to look at her when I was a little girl and she knew all the answers. All I had was questions. The more I asked myself, the more I pushed away the thought that while my first son was dancing with death for all I knew, his mother, his only protector when it really mattered, was out dancing with a head full of fairies. A thought of David Jr.'s head full of bandages crushed my heart.

"How long was he unconscious? Why was he unconscious? Where was the crash? Who was driving? Mami, dime everything you know!"

"Hija, no sé más, no sé más nada. No sé . . . ," she said, her body shrinking into the car seat.

"This can't be happening," I repeated over and over to myself. Mami pulled out her rosary from her dress pocket and began to fumble with its wooden beads.

"Dios te salve, María, llena eres de gracia. . . . Dios te salve, María, llena eres de gracia. . . . Hail, Mary, full of Grace. . . . Hail, Mary, full of Grace . . . ," her chanting drifted around the interior of the car. "Holy Mary, Mother of God," she continued, and I found myself talking to the Virgin, woman to woman. Why, why my son? I kept asking her. Tú sabes what it feels like to see a son suffer. Help me! Tell me! Tell me I can have my David Jr.! But all I heard were her prayers. The sweet humming of mami's Hail Marys kept me from losing my mind, especially at the sight of Mercy Hospital looming large in the night. I circled its main driveway. That's when I noticed the larger-than-life statue of the Virgin Mary in the center of it. I know we eyed each other; her kind, passive, and lov-ing rock-solid eyes met with my questioning, fearful, and tear-soaked ones. I have to confess that as we slowly circled each other, I wondered whether this woman and I would end up loving each other more than ever, or end up the worst of enemies.

We finally entered the lobby to the emergency room. Sam rushed to us and wrapped himself around me.

"David's hurt, mami, David's hurt, David's hurt."

"I know, sweetie." I caressed his hair, trying to calm him down. Running my fingers through my boys' hair has been a ritual of mine since the very first wisps appeared on their baby scalps. I buried my face in his scalp and took in the deep scent of my youngest son.

"Where is he?"

"Inside, with abuelo." He pointed at two large metal doors.

I walked, still hugging Sam, to a couch by the windows and sat us both down. Mami followed, quietly mouthing her supplications. The waiting room had two couches and several chairs. The smell of stale coffee permeated the brightly lit room. It was too bright for me, for the middle of the night, and for what the hell was going on. Why in God's name do these rooms make you feel like you're trapped in some over-lit two-bit night carnival? There was not a dark spot in the place where I could hide. I took in the sight of the people around me. An elderly woman slept across two chairs. A young man watched TV in the back of the room. A middle-aged man paced back and forth across the entrance, chain-smoking his way through whatever brought him there. We all seemed to be serving time, as if in Purgatory. I felt a chill wrap itself around my spine.

"Mami, stay with Sam, por favor."

Sam didn't protest. Kids have a way of knowing when not to get in the way.

I walked through the two heavy gray doors, their black rubber seals smacking apart like hungry lips. I felt like I was being swallowed up by a vile, gaping mouth. If the waiting room was Purgatory, then this was the mouth of El Infierno. This hell was dark and sterile, but cold, freezing cold. Nurse types kept whisking by me as I walked deeper into it. The only signs of life besides the monk-like nurses were the endless blinking lights and the gurgling, bubbling noises coming from the endless stall-like rooms I kept passing. I could hardly make out the patients in their beds.

The last room was David Jr.'s. It was dark, but the white bandages on his head reflected the light of the monitors he was hooked up to. My mind surveyed my son's appearance. His face was puffed up, almost all black and blue. My heart registered his pain as precisely as any of the machines measuring his vital signs. I almost couldn't recognize him. The tears in my eyes blurred my focus to where the machines became just blobs of gray, and then I saw through all of the digital numbers straight to David Jr.'s face. I saw that he was sleeping peacefully, his angelic face out of place in such a dark infernal room.

"David, mi vida, es mami," I whispered. No answer. I got a sudden urge to lift him right up and hold him forever.

"Ten cuidado, Isa. He can't be moved," my father whispered in a tired, coarse voice.

I hadn't seen papi sitting on a stool behind me. I turned to look at him. He was in a dark corner, holding his glasses in one hand and his wrinkled linen handkerchief in the other. All I could see was that white crumpled ball of cloth bobbing up and down from his knees to his eyes, and back again. It reminded me of mami praying.

"I won't move him. I just want to touch him, papi."

I touched his hand, his wrist, his arm. I delicately stroked his thigh through the sheets that covered him. There was no reaction. I bent over him. He smelled like the hospital, a combination of medicine and disinfectant and life held by machines instead of a mother's arms. I couldn't recognize his scent. That's when the panic really hit me. Not the loud, emotional, in-your-face kind that screams to the world for help, but the kind that is still and sharp, that stabs at your heart with a silent scream that makes its way to God.

I made my way to his bandaged head. I saw a sliver of exposed hair. I lingered over it. For a fleeting instant, I recognized David Jr., the fifteen-year-old boy/man who still kissed me good-bye even in the school parking lot, and at the scent of him, I burst into tears. David Jr. was there and I couldn't pick him up in my arms. I wasn't there to pick him up after the party, I wasn't there in the ambulance, I wasn't there.

"Isa, Francisco is here." I hadn't realized my father was holding me up. He gave me his handkerchief with its Guerlain smell that has been imprinted in my senses since I was a little girl sobbing at my ya-ya of a finger cut and his pañuelo would heal all wounds faster than any Band-Aid ever could. We walked out into the hallway. I gathered whatever composure I had left in me at the sight of the doctor my cousin was pointing to.

"Isa, this is Doctor Harris, he's the attending doctor."

I looked him over. He was an old doctor, what I call a World War II Americano, the kind that saved the world with steady hands and knew the difference between real shit and bullshit.

"Doctor García tells me he's your cousin. He was the best resident doctor I've had." He smiled at me.

"Isa, David Jr. is in the best hands possible."

The old doctor took my hand in both of his. He dropped his smile but his blue eyes remained friendly.

"We are doing everything to make sure your son will be all right."

"What is wrong with my son?"

He answered in a slow, clear voice, measuring each word. "He's suffering brain trauma caused by the impact with the windshield of the car."

"Brain trauma?" I whispered, holding the handkerchief to my mouth.

"It's a swelling of the brain due to the heavy blow. To be exact, it's a swelling that takes place in the space between the brain and the skull."

"Why hasn't he woken up?"

The doctor looked over at my cousin.

"We are optimistic. His blood pressure is within acceptable norms considering the extent of the injury."

"That means he's OK?" I asked, grabbing at a crumb of hope.

"He passed the neuro-check with flying colors. His pupils were equally dilated and reacted to light. Mrs. Landon, he reacted just as well to painful stimuli. These are good signs, but we need to wait."

"How long?"

"Isa," Francisco answered, "the X-rays show no fractures and the CAT scan confirmed this. But . . ."

"Qué? But qué? Tell me, Francisco."

"There is some activity, small seizures that the monitors pick up."

Small seizures? How can seizures of the brain be small? My fears seized up on this news and I felt the cold air of the hallway settle into my lungs. I felt the blood drain from my face and leave it stone cold.

"Will he wake up?"

The doctors hesitated. I've been in business long enough to know what that means, that slight no-one-noticed taken-aback too-clear-of-a-question hesitation. It means no one the hell knows.

"We have to see the seizures diminishing in frequency," Doctor Harris was saying.

"When will David Jr. wake up? I want no bullshit!" I almost lost it but Doctor Harris seized my hands firmly. He looked me in the eye, took in the full measure of who I was, and took a chance. He was a good soldier in the trenches of the war going on in my head.

"I can't say. It could be hours, days . . ."

"Months?"

"Could be minutes."

"In other words, you don't know. He could be in a coma permanently, couldn't he?" I felt the blood rush back into my head, like a mad midnight tide. "You just don't know. Nobody knows. Dios mío!" I said looking up at the fluorescent lighted ceiling.

"Isa, cálmate, I know this is hard," said Francisco, "but remember what Doctor Harris said: be optimistic."

"Yes, but you can't tell me if he has a concussion or is in a coma? What now?" I said composing myself and looking straight at the doctor.

"We'll keep an eye on him here. He'll stay on an I.V. and we'll keep administering the medication to help reduce the swelling."

I couldn't hear any more of this. I didn't let him go on. I let myself go.

"Listen to me, both of you. I understand what you're saying and I appreciate your efforts, but this is my son! I want him well taken care of. I don't want any HMO bureaucrat pinstriped doctor has-been telling you what is cost-effective for my son. I want you calling the shots on this! I want to be told of everything, and I mean everything! Estoy clara?"

One thing I am clear on is that corporate culprit of a bean counter that measures out a boy's life not in heartbeats, but in how many pennies above or below the bottom line those heartbeats cost. A heartbeat could make the difference between a brain and a vegetable.

I was desperate and I sounded that way, but in a desperate situation you throw everything you've got into the battle for your son's life. To their credit, the good doctor and my cousin took it on the chin well enough.

"Mrs. Landon, when his brain shows regular activity, he'll be transferred to a private room. He'll be kept under observation until he regains consciousness. Up there they'll assign a specialist. I know what you want, Mrs. Landon, I know what you want. Please feel free to call me. Here." He wrote his home phone on his card.

"Thank you, Doctor, thank you for everything," I said, firmly shaking his hand. Dr. Harris' words and his tranquil demeanor somehow got to my fears, if just a bit. He quietly left. I went in to see David Jr. I would have crawled into his bed, into his bandages, not to have to leave him, but I remembered my mother and Sam. I left Francisco talking to papi.

Back in the waiting room, I told mami and Sam what Doctor Harris had explained. I kept out the "nobody knows" part. My mother's prayers intensified. She asked Sam to take her to David Jr. The waiting room air was stale. I could hear an ambulance driver joking with the receptionist. Laughter usually picks me up, but in that room it sounded like a taunt from the Devil himself.

I went outside to get fresh air, but the earlier breeze of the night was gone. It was replaced by an oppressive heat. Off in the distance, I watched sudden flashes of light fan across the darkness of the night. The heat lightning turned the clouds into grotesque images.

I wanted to call Lucinda, Mercy, Julia. I wanted to wake up the whole world and let them know that there was a mother suffering like only her son could suffer. To lose a child, your own child, I had no clue what that meant. The possibility began to twist itself around my guts. I needed someone to talk to, to scream to, but I knew I would wait until morning to call las amigas. Orlando crossed my mind. My heart wanted to call him, but my mind couldn't take the thought of it. There was nothing to do but wait for Purgatory to change into Heaven or Hell.

Back inside I tried to convince mami y papi to go home. They refused. I wasn't surprised. We each took turns sitting with David Jr. He was never alone. That's the way it has always been with the family. We stick by each other like chicle to a shoe. In the waiting room, we waited.

Around dawn I dozed off in one of the couches. I woke up to the smell of fresh coffee, a shift in nurses, and mami's voice calling me,

"Isa, wake up."

"Qué pasó?"

"Nada. You've been sleeping for a couple of hours. They finally moved David Jr. to a private room."

"Why didn't you wake me up?"

"No importa. You needed to rest."

"Do you have the room number?"

I went looking for it. Papi was standing outside the new room. "Y Sam?" I asked.

"Inside—with his father."

As I slowly walked in, I saw Sam sitting in the vinyl butaca next to his brother. His father was leaning on it. Sam's head was resting on his father's arm. They were holding hands, watching David Jr. asleep, his chest rising with his every breath. I felt my heart rising in my throat as his father looked up.

"Hello, Isa."

I sensed Sam's eyes burning a hole through me expecting qué sé yo from me when I greeted his father. He walked out with some excuse about going to the bathroom.

David and I stood on opposite sides of the bed. By the look in his eyes, I could tell he was just as devastated as I was.

"When did you get here?"

"Just now. I took the earliest flight I could."

"Sam needs you."

"He needs us, OK?"

"I'm so sorry this happened."

"Sam told me what happened. It was an accident. There's nothing you could have done."

"I should have driven him. I should have been there."

"Isa, you're always there." He said this like he was letting me know that he wasn't. "Don't go blaming yourself."

We both stood quietly watching him, the metal railings of the bed keeping us apart from David Jr. and from each other.

"He's so much like you inside," David said in the tender voice I had forgotten about because he had stopped using it with me long ago.

"He'll come out of this, Isa, you'll see. He's got fishermen's blood in him. He won't give up."

I smiled back at David, unable to speak. It was true. David Jr. loved to go fishing with his dad as much as he liked to track fighting cocks with his abuelo. Two worlds flowed in his blood. He was the better for it, unlike his parents, whose worlds clashed like catsup and salsa on the same sesame seed bun. I laughed inside because that's David Jr.'s favorite combination on his hamburgers. I looked at him, at his father across from me, and at my image in the mirror behind David. And then I saw that my son embodied the best of both worlds, the best of both of us. I was praying that in his world, our mixed blood would be strong enough to carry him through.

I was standing there, thinking about all this and about how natural I was feeling standing across from David, when the old feelings began vibrating in the back of my memories. For an instant I didn't feel divorced from David. And then I felt the beeper vibrating in my pocket. I looked at the number. I hesitated. A part of me wanted to end the vibration in my head and in my pocket and to erase the number. Another part of me wanted to hold on to that number with a life-saving grip. It was Orlando calling.

"David, I'm glad you're here," I said, putting the beeper back in my pocket. David followed it with his eyes and then looked at me.

"You know that when it counts, I'm always here."

I was so grateful to see him and so worn down with fear that I forgot to be angry at David for hardly ever really being there when it counted. Sam returned and sat down on the butaca. His father stayed on one side of it; I was on the other. Sam held our hands. I knew that when it counted, I could be a family again. The beeper vibrated again.

"Someone is calling."

I kissed David Jr. on the cheek. Sam didn't want to let go of my hand. We lingered there, the three of us holding hands. I would have lingered longer, but the image of Sam's hope in the mirror brought me back. We weren't a family any longer, no matter what a little boy wished. It took me a long time to break through Sam's glass hope. For over a year after the divorce, he insisted on renting *The Parent Trap* every weekend. It's the only Disney movie I refuse to own. Too much fantasy for our own good. Pero I wanted some fantasy to take me out of what was happening. I could have grabbed at the make-believe reflection in the mirror; instead I grabbed at the beeper in my pocket.

I kissed Sam and purposely touched his father's hand while looking at him. I went looking for a private place to call Orlando. I stood at the end of an empty hallway facing a large windowpane dialing his number, watching the pouring rain dripping over the condensation on the glass.

"Orlando," I said to him.

"Yes, Isabel."

"I'm at the hospital."

"I know where you are. You're crying."

I didn't ask him how he knew. I just wanted to know that he knew.

"It happened while we were dancing," I blurted out. The line was silent for a few seconds.

"Orlando, are you there?"

"Yes, yes, I'm here, Isabel. How is he?"

"The same as last night. He won't wake up."

"Do you want me to come over, Isabel?"

"No, no, don't come."

"Are you sure? You don't sound well."

"Yes, I'm sure. I'm just tired. Don't worry, I can handle it."

"I just want you to know I'm here for you. For whatever. If you need to talk or you just want me to bring you something, let me know."

"Gracias, Orlando."

"I'll call you later?"

"Está bien."

"Isabel?"

"Sí?"

There was a long pause on the line. I imagined him on his boat sitting inside its darkened cabin, the rain tapping on the portholes and our hands trying to touch through the glass.

"I'm here for you, Isabel."

When I hung up, I realized every muscle in my body was aching. I slowly slid down the windowpane and crouched in the corner. I sat there, letting fear, desire, hope, and pain run like a pack of bulls through the narrow streets of my ordered four years into a divorced heart. I realized that Orlando's words were meant, and meant for me.

"Are you all right, honey?" a nurse asked, looking down at me.

"Yes, yes I am," I answered her, looking at the cellular in my hands. I walked back to the room. Mami and papi were inside with David Jr.

"Sam went down with his father to eat breakfast. Why don't you go, we already had coffee." Mami y papi could survive on cafecitos. I wasn't hungry, but I knew I should get something in my stomach. I called Dorothy at her home to tell her why I'd be out, indefinitely. She took the news hard. But I knew I wouldn't leave this hospital unless David Jr. walked out with me or I lay down beside him. As I was getting out of the elevator, I ran into Lucinda.

"Isa."

We embraced. I felt her hands stroking my back.

"Lucinda, es horrible. He still hasn't regained consciousness."

"Don't lose faith, Isa. He's strong."

"I don't know what I would do . . ."

"Don't even think about it."

"Basta! Estoy volviéndome loca," I said, wiping my face with papi's handkerchief. What was left of my eye makeup and my lipstick was smudged all over it. I cleared my thoughts and asked, "How did you find out?"

"Mercy called me after your mother called her. She should be here any minute. Julia is coming too."

"Gracias por venir."

"You should have called us last night, Isa."

"I wanted to, believe me, but there was no point. There was nothing to do but wait. We're still waiting."

"Here," Lucinda said handing me a cup of café con leche. "I brought you some zucchini muffins too."

"Sí, thanks."

We sat down on a couch in the lobby. The warm liquid flowed down my throat and for the first time since I'd been in the hospital, I felt civilized.

"David flew in this morning. I'm glad. He'll be a big help to Sam."

"And to you?"

"I don't know. I suppose so. I'll worry less about Sam."

"How are you holding up?"

"Good," I said in my best executive voice. Lucinda's look saw right through me. "Not so well," I added. The café con leche was acting like a truth serum. "I feel like a broken arrow, una flecha inútil."

I guess Lucinda saw me sinking deeper into the couch.

"Isa, pray for the best. Even the strong need someone to lean on in times like these." Lucinda's hand brushed back the mess of my hair from my face.

"Listen, Isa. Let's walk over to La Ermita. We can get some fresh air."

"I don't want to leave."

"You have the cellular, no? Entonces? I'll tell your mom to beep us if there is any change. I want to go up to see David Jr.; I'll tell her."

Lucinda took out a hairbrush from her purse and gave it to me, pointing at the bathrooms.

"It's a five-minute walk to the chapel, nada más."

I gave her a long blank stare. I closed my eyes and let out a long sigh.

"Está bien. I'll be ready."

After Lucinda returned, we walked along the seawall behind the hospital to the chapel. I had forgotten about this little chapel by the sea. It was built by the Miami Cubans to honor the Virgin of Charity, the patron of Cuban Catholics. She appeared to three lost fishermen off a stormy Cuban coast. The cone shape of the chapel is supposed to look like the wide skirt of the copper statue still found in Cuba. I grew up with a miniature statue of her. Mami also has one—hers has survived a number of storms. Mami has literally carried it with her from home to home, country to country, for over forty-five years. It still stands almost new on her bedroom dresser.

I entered La Ermita de la Caridad like I was going under her skirts. I have to admit it felt safe there. Lucinda and I knelt in the middle of the empty chapel. I looked up at the tall painting of the Virgin on the wall behind the altar. It was surrounded by other images, images of an exile's culture. That giant mural spiraling up the Virgin's skirt reflected the hopes of every Miami Cuban. I wanted to take my lipstick and paint David Jr.'s face up there, next to José Martí's goatee and George Washington's white wig. Instead I desperately prayed for my son's life. I asked this Virgin of Charity to pull my son out of the storm he was drifting in. I don't normally ask for charity, but this time I was begging for it.

"Isa," Lucinda whispered, tugging at my arm. "Julia told Orlando about David Jr. I hope you don't mind."

How did Orlando get in the picture? I let his face take over my prayers.

"We talked this morning. He offered to come."

"You said no, eh?"

"It's not appropriate."

"You're right."

But I could tell from Lucinda's face that she saw what I was feeling.

"My head tells me that but not my heart," I confessed to her.

"You feel guilty because you were enjoying yourself for the first time in a long time, right?"

"I . . . ," but I couldn't say it.

"Isa, you're an excellent mom. You've raised a pair of wonderful boys. No te eches esto encima. You aren't responsible. It was an accident."

"Yo sé, I know, I know." But I didn't believe myself.

Mercy, who made such a big deal of the fact that the doctor had David Jr. moved and how that was a sign from the Virgin, came by later that day. So did Julia. David Jr. stayed the same. My parents took turns going and coming from the house. After the second day, I sent Sam back to school with the promise that his father would pull him out the minute David Jr. woke up. Life has a way of creeping back into its routine even in the middle of the war. I now know what a soldier survives on in the middle of Hell. Little things become lifesavers. I stayed put. The only fresh air I got was when Orlando called. He called every morning and evening and late at night. His voice kept me going. I still didn't want him to come to the hospital. I never called him. He said he understood.

⟶

"What are you doing here?" It was Orlando. I found him by the entrance to the cafeteria. I said those words in whispered disbelief as the weight of the hospital began to lift itself off my shoulders. I looked a mess, but I didn't care.

"You see that table? There's a full breakfast on it, for two. What are we going to do about it?"

"Put it in the microwave?" I wearily smiled at him.

"Julia told me about your morning routine. The café con leche is still hot."

"So now you're asking her about me?"

"Always."

We sat down, and I have to admit that I enjoyed every forkful of Orlando's surprise. I hadn't eaten a full anything since I arrived at the hospital. Between mouthfuls I calculated the chances that my family or that my ex would bump into us. They were pretty nil considering the hour. So I relaxed a bit.

"You know, desde que te conocí, I've pretty much stopped cussing in my head."

"So now you're only going to be foul-mouthed out loud?"

"No, really. Yesterday I became aware of it."

"Isabel, if there's a person in this world right now who's got the right to cuss as she pleases, then that person is you. How's your son?" He asked like he meant it.

"Gracias a Dios, the seizures stopped."

"When?" he asked, leaning over the table.

"Last night. Actually, early morning."

"It's great news! What do the doctors say?"

"They're optimistic. But I want the hell for him to wake up! Why won't he wake up?"

We stayed quiet for the rest of the meal. I actually felt comfortable in our silence. I let the clanking of our forks and plates, the humming noise of the crowd, the droning paging over the speakers take over my senses to the point where the only sense working was my sight. We looked over at each other in the middle of the noisy silence. Now I know how tunnel vision works.

We said our good-byes. I walked him to the glass doors, where he turned and kissed me on the cheek, holding my hands. I kissed him back when, over his shoulder, I saw David walking right at us.

They bumped into each other as Orlando was turning around. David accepted his pardon. He looked him over while Orlando walked away. Then he looked me over.

"Who was that?"

"Un amigo."

"How long has he been 'a friend'?"

Without blinking an eye, I answered, "Not long."

He stumbled on the glass door he was holding open for me. I heard him mumbling under his breath something about a friendly friend. Together, we went up to David Jr.'s room. Doctor Harris was already there.

"Good morning, Mr. and Mrs. Landon." Saying our names like that sounded out of place to me. "Your son is showing the best signs possible for an eventual recovery."

"But you don't know, you can't be sure, you can't pin it down. Doctor Harris, what am I supposed to do with that?"

"Isa, let the doctor talk."

"Mrs. Landon, look at what has happened. The monitors all tell us what we want to hear. The last thing was for these seizures to stop. They have. Now we want to make sure they don't return. Your son is, at this moment, healing himself."

That got to me. David Jr. was not a quitter. He runs his heart out in those cross-country races just to stay in the top ten spots. I saw an image of my son running alone through the remains of a battlefield with no weapons but his legs and his big heart to get himself out of it.

"Cuban and American hearts are huge!" Mercy was telling me in the waiting room, which now looked like my Florida Room.

We each had our own blankets thrown over the chairs we claimed. Mami had moved her cafetera and a few of her dishes to the nurses' station. They appreciated her cantina cooking so much, they let her claim the microwave as her own. Papi made a deal with the ambulance driver to bring him the daily paper. And Mercy? She was compensating for her own troubles by being overly optimistic about mine.

"There's nothing but good news for David Jr.'s condition. Olvídate, he has a big Latino heart with an American beat. He'll beat this thing!" Mercy said.

I wanted to offer her encouraging words as well. Her mother was still trapped in Cuba, and I could tell it was taking a toll on her. But Mercy was already on her way out the door, going to her office in Aladdin's Palace. Mercy always reminds me of a plump exclamation point on high heels. That's what I needed, a big exclamation point to end this miseria of a hospital visit. But David Jr. was still asleep.

I couldn't sleep for the next few days. My hopes were riding high but my fears were dragging me down. I called the office a couple of times. Dorothy was keeping the fires burning. She told me about Rubén's flowers for me and David Jr. Even Edmund sent a box of California wine to the office. Everybody was being real nice, but I couldn't celebrate anything. I told the Virgin Mary that I had to have David Jr. back. I wasn't going to accept a compromise.

And then he woke up. One night, around eleven, he woke up.

He opened those brown eyes of his as if waking up from an afternoon nap. He asked for me, me, his madre for life. When the nurses told me I flew to his arms. They held me like they used to. God, what an abrazo! I called everybody. I had David wake up Sam and drive him over just like I promised him. The doctor came all the way from his house on Key Biscayne. Everything checked out until Doctor Harris asked him a few simple questions.

"What is your name?"

"I don't know."

"Who are these people here with you?" Doctor Harris pointed to David and Sam.

"I don't know."

"Who's this woman?"

"My mom. Listen, when can I go home?"

The doctor assured me that this was typical short-term memory loss. Probably in about a week he'd regain his full memory. I will never forget that he remembered me.

I went to La Ermita the last day at the hospital. The Virgin came through like the good Mother she was. I promised her in return, I'd be the best mother en el mundo entero for as long as my heart beats, and then some. As I looked into her ever-smiling face, a thought kept knocking around in my head. At first I dismissed it. It sounded too self-serving, but it wouldn't go away. Mothers are called, called to be little gods on earth. My God, the things we see and do and put up with and forgive and forget and go on doing for everybody else. I swear I smelled sweet roses in that empty chapel.

I did one thing for myself. For the first time, I called Orlando—first.

"I'm very happy for you."

"Thank you, Orlando. There were times when your calls kept me, kept me . . ."

"They kept me too, Isabel."

There was a long pause on the line. By now I knew that silence for what it was, our own language.

Chapter 19

Julia

Julia was sitting at her desk making last-minute changes to her finished manuscript. She weighed its pages in her hands. The manuscript felt light yet solid. The bulky feel told her she was done. All of her thoughts were expressed on each page, each wanting to spring on a reader's mind and curl there, like one of her cats. She got ready to plop the manuscript on the table. This was her best-seller test. The resonance of the thud would determine the popularity of the book. Mercy thought she was crazy, but it had never failed. She squared her body on the chair, closed her eyes and dropped the manuscript. It was the loudest thud she had ever heard. It even continued after the pages lay on the table. Julia opened her eyes and that's when she realized someone was knocking on the door. She got up and went downstairs to answer it. She found Beatriz in the hallway grinning, standing next to two shiny green bicycles, her arms carrying helmets, gloves, and water bottles.

"Surprise!" exclaimed Beatriz. "Mira, bicicletas!"

"Where did you get these?"

"Do you like them? I saved some money from the security deposit you didn't accept and the low rent you are charging me, so I took it and bought these!"

"They're beautiful," Julia answered, looking at the two dark green Specialized city bikes.

"Look, they have shock absorbers on the handlebars and on the seats." Beatriz pressed down on these to show Julia.

"They must have been expensive. You didn't have to do that."

"I know. Come on, let's try them."

"Now?" protested Julia.

"You're always talking about how you used to love bike riding all over San Antonio."

"I haven't ridden a bike in years."

"You never forget. Look, I got us helmets and water bottles and these," said Beatriz excited as a kid on Christmas morning. Julia hesitated as Beatriz handed the gloves over.

"Vamos, Julia. It'll be fun."

"I'm working." Julia felt the leather and nylon gloves with her fingers. They were as crisp and smooth as her pages. Looking at Beatriz, she knew the gloves were full of thoughts too, waiting to curl themselves somewhere as well.

"You're always working, Julia, at school, at home, in your head. Vamos, chica. It's good exercise."

Beatriz looked at her for a moment without saying anything more. She lifted a bike with one arm and with the other opened the door.

"I'll change," answered Julia more to herself than to Beatriz.

She came back out in a pair of jean shorts, a T-shirt, and sneakers. Beatriz was waiting for her outside with both bikes. She had on a dark blue sports bra and matching jogging shorts, her black helmet with a built-in visor, and sunglasses.

"Wow, you look like a professional."

Beatriz laughed. "Follow me."

They headed out through the neighborhood streets toward Old Cutler Road, where a bike path extended for miles. The five-minute ride took twenty because of Julia's rusty biking skills which Beatriz got a few laughs out of.

"Cars won't bother us on here. Now, let me see you ride like you say you did in your San Antonio days of thunder!"

Julia felt unsteady on the bike. She swerved along the path and floundered on its curves. She had a hard time getting the bike started after each stop.

"Chica! You ride a bike like Charlie Chaplin walks down a street!"

Beatriz pulled up next to her. She got off her bike and began to instruct Julia.

"Mira, sit down firmly, like you mean to lay some eggs! You move your legs, not your rear," said Beatriz, playfully slapping Julia's buttocks with her gloved hand. "And what's with that straight-as-an-arrow back? Ride with your upper body leaning toward the handlebar." Beatriz straddled the front wheel of Julia's bike and guided Julia's shoulders to the proper position. Julia found herself leaning forward toward Beatriz.

"Like that. Keep your hands on the grips," she concluded, wrapping her hands tightly over Julia's. Julia quickly looked at her hands, not wanting Beatriz to notice her noticing. Beatriz made her do a couple of solo practices and then pronounced her ready to take off. Julia quietly rode behind Beatriz. She watched Beatriz' lean and agile body stretched out over the bicycle. She admired the way Beatriz maneuvered the bike with the same elegance she had on the dance floor. Her long dark braid hung below the helmet and swung from side to side with a rhythm like a mesmerizer's watch. Julia gradually gained confidence with her own movements. She let her instincts, long familiar with the feel, take charge. She raced past Beatriz.

It was a brilliant ninety-degree day, but the bike path, shaded by large ficus and oak trees, made the air feel cool against Julia's exposed arms and legs. Every time Beatriz tried to pass her, she would block the way. The fast ride, and the idea of Beatriz behind her looking, made her heart race. They rode past canals, along the perimeter of the Fairchild Tropical Garden, and through parks and lushly planted neighborhoods. Julia gripped her handlebars firmly and pedaled hard to keep ahead of Beatriz. For the first time since her youth, she absorbed the life around her without scrutinizing it: the sweet scent of jasmine, the purple bougainvilleas cascading down the coral rock fences, the barking springer spaniel, the squawk of the orange and green parrots high up in the trees, even the honk of cars, all surprised her with the sheer pleasure of their experience. On the bike, Julia felt weightless and swift. She felt like Beatriz looked.

She looked back at her and pointed toward the bridge ahead. It was a low bridge, just spanning a canal cut fifteen feet into the limestone. But the bike path led down under it where it hugged the banks of the canal for a short distance until it found its way back up to the street level. Beatriz nodded in the downward direction. The wind whistled past Julia's face as she let gravity rush her toward the water's edge. They stopped to look out over the water. A few sailboats and yachts lined the coral limestone banks of the wide canal winding out to the sea. They caught sight of a large manatee just below the surface of the water. Beatriz had never seen one before.

"What is it?" she asked. Julia told her and mentioned their possible extinction in Florida. Julia was always moved by the sight of these large mammals gently gliding along, like solitary mermaids. Looking at Beatriz, she realized she wasn't lonely anymore.

"I and a bunch of other writers wrote a book titled *Naked Came the Manatee*. It's a crazy detective thriller," Julia told Beatriz. "It even made the best-seller list for a short while. We donated all of the royalties to the Save the Manatee Fund."

"Who would want to eliminate such tender creatures?" asked Beatriz.

Julia looked over at her. Beatriz had removed her helmet and loosened her braid. Her black wavy hair buoyed tenderly like a mermaid's. Watching her, Julia thought of a line from a T. S. Eliot poem and said in answer to Beatriz, "I have heard the mermaids singing, each to each. I do not think that they will sing to me."

Beatriz looked long and hard at Julia. Julia sensed that she was making up her mind. Finally Beatriz spoke.

"Men don't know how to listen to the sounds a tender creature makes. Women do. Women talk; men walk. They walk to their loud games, to their noisy machines, to their wars; they walk over their wives and lovers." Beatriz picked up some loose grass and placed it in the water. The manatee slowly rolled toward it. Julia thought of Felipe and said, "Not all men trample, Beatriz."

"Yo sé. You say that sailors thought these to be mermaids? Your Eliot's line says it best. The mermaids sing each to each because he would not listen, Julia. Most men don't." Julia sensed she said this from a deep and painful place within her. At that moment all Julia wanted was to take Beatriz in her arms and caress her tenderly. She wanted nothing else but to kiss the scars that made her think such thoughts. Julia wanted to listen to Beatriz' song, but instead she was hearing the faint sounds of her own murmuring heart. She forgot all about the get-together at Isa's house.

—⁂—

"Do you hear that? It's David Jr. playing Nintendo. I never thought that sound would be music to my ears in this house!" said Isabel.

"Give the kid a break. Every day he remembers more and more. It's too bad his father had to get back to Kansas before he was remembered," Mercy said, realizing it came out sounding funny.

"Don't worry, his brother can fill him in on it. Pass me the apples."

Mercy was cutting up apples for Isa's tuna salad dish. They had agreed to meet at Isa's house for a late lunch get-together. Mercy had gotten there early, for breakfast. They were both waiting for Lucinda and Julia to arrive.

"Remember the last time all of us were together? Aquí en tu casa. What a night, all of us naked like that, like in a Sioux Sweat Lodge!"

Isa noticed Mercy fidgeting with the tiny croquetas on the plastic tray. She kept rearranging them like they were Lincoln Logs.

"What are you doing? You're going to mess these up. Quita la mano de aquí!"

"Mira, it's just that you either go this way or that way," Mercy was saying, making a point by twirling a croqueta in two directions on the tray, "but you can't flip back and forth. You'll become a Sloppy Joe." She squished the finger food with her fingers on the tray.

"There goes a perfectly good croqueta," Isa said while sliding the tray away from Mercy. "What are you talking about?"

"That's just my point. There goes a perfectly good Julia. Coño, you think she was looking at me that night, when we were all naked?"

"Don't go there, Mercy," said Isa, turning away from Mercy to stir the boiling asparagus soup on the stove.

"You think she'll come?" asked Mercy.

—⅏—

"Julia, let's go," Beatriz said, interrupting Julia's thoughts. She was thinking how lonely she had felt with Felipe, even after three years of more or less being together.

And yet, after such a short time with Beatriz, thought Julia, loneliness had left the picture like a small mole on your neck you've had all your life and one day you notice it gone. Felipe was gone, though he still kept in touch with his postcards and a few calls. You've answered these, almost out of nostalgia, like to a distant relative not seen in a long while. You kept the communication from Beatriz. Hoping for what? Fearing what? Hope and fear are two sides of the same coin. You want to twirl the coin, flip it, watch it dance in the air, but you hope (or fear?) as it drops, that it may land on a certain side. What does it mean to be gay, anyway, Julia thought, looking at Beatriz.

"Which way?" Beatriz asked as she took the lead. Julia pointed in a direction under the bridge and up to Edgewater Park on the other side.

Beyond the bridge, they followed the bike path through the small park bordering the canal. Julia noticed a woman sitting on the grass. She was doing stretching exercises.

"Wait! Beatriz," Julia yelled out to Beatriz riding ahead. "I think that's Lucinda."

They rode across to where Lucinda sat. Recognizing Julia, she stood up.

"Julia! Qué sorpresa," said Lucinda exchanging kisses. She looked at her friend. "I didn't know you rode bikes."

"Neither did I, Beatriz just got these for us."

"Beatriz, I finally get to meet you! I'm Lucinda."

"I'm sorry, I forgot you hadn't met."

Lucinda and Beatriz exchanged handshakes.

"So you got Julia bike riding!" said Lucinda. "It's a beautiful day for it."

"It's my first ride in years," Julia responded as Beatriz nodded.

"How do you like it?"

"You know what? I love it," Julia said smiling at Beatriz. "I like it more than jogging," she added, her attention now back on Lucinda.

Lucinda had obviously been jogging, her T-shirt drenched in sweat. "I know what you mean," she said.

"Do you live around here?" Beatriz asked.

"Sí. I recently bought a townhouse down that street. Do you want to come by for a drink?"

"I don't know," Beatriz answered, looking at Julia, who said, "I don't think so, Lucinda. We'd better get back. But how's Isa? Have you talked to her this morning?"

"I just talked to her. David Jr. is getting better by the minute and she's getting ready for—"

"Good," interrupted Julia. "What a scare! I want to go by and see him."

"It was hard for a while but gracias a Dios the worst is over," said Lucinda. "Mercy is already at Isa's." There was an awkward silence between Lucinda and Julia. Beatriz pretended not to notice. "I'd better get back," added Lucinda. "I left the kids alone. Nice to meet you, Beatriz. Come visit one day; we can talk."

"Seguro," Beatriz said with a wide smile.

"Bye, Lucinda," said Julia, knowing she wasn't going to be at Isa's later.

"I'll call you."

Lucinda jogged off in the direction of her street while Beatriz and Julia turned around to ride back underneath the bridge. When they reached one of the quiet neighborhood streets, they slowed down and rode side by side.

"Are you happy, Julia?" Beatriz asked.

"You mean right now?"

"Right now."

"I'm very happy. My book is finished, my friend's son is OK, and I'm on a bike ride"—she wanted to say "with you," but she didn't. "Thank you, Beatriz. Thank you for the bikes."

"Por nada, chica. I can just picture you in San Antonio beating out all the boys with their low-rider Schwinns, while you glided by on your Barbie Bike Deluxe!"

"That was my mother's idea of a proper American bike for her girl. But you know what? That bike got me to places my mother will never know."

As they rode on, Julia looked up at the trees thinking to herself.

You haven't felt such exhilaration, such a bearable lightness of being, just being and not analyzing, in such a long time. Look at the breeze swirling through the treetops making them bend in directions they hadn't intended to go. You felt the same way as those branches, and you knew it had everything to do with Beatriz.

Nearing the apartment, Julia spotted a Sun Juice Bar. They parked the bikes and ordered one mango and passion fruit smoothie. Sitting outside, on a bench overlooking the street, they savored the thick cold drink, taking turns at the straw.

"This is huge. I don't think I could have finished this all by myself," said Beatriz.

Julia watched as Beatriz pulled at the smoothie with her lips.

"Am I making a face? Do I look like a loca, chica?"

"No. No." Julia was caught off guard. "How about you?" she asked, delighted with the embarrassment from the exposed staring.

"Qué? Happy with the bikes?"

"Are you glad you moved in?"

"Very glad." Beatriz placed the plastic glass between them on the bench and gave Julia a long look.

"So am I," Julia said. Their hands touched around the wet, cold glass; neither one hurried to pull away.

"Are you working tonight?" Julia broke the silence, which was not awkward to either of them.

"Hoy? No, por qué?"

"Why don't we rent a movie on our way home?"

"On the bikes? The video place is pretty far."

"So?"

"You're getting very ambitious on your first ride," said Beatriz smiling the way she did when she meant more than what she was saying. Julia remembered that smile from the Café Quixote night. She smiled back.

For forty-five minutes they roamed the aisles at Oscar Night Videos. Each was trying to please the other.

"Do you like adventure films?"

"No. How about a drama?"

"Too heavy. I feel light and airy, to use a gastada image."

"Well, we certainly are wasting time. Here, a comedy?"

"*Tootsie*? Too old! *Mrs. Doubtfire*? Too cute. *To Wong Fu, Thanks for Everything*? Too macho! Julia, what's with the crossdressing comedias?" Julia shrugged her shoulders. Beatriz laughed in her uninhibited way.

They kept going back and forth to where the head clerk became nervous and had another clerk shadow them around the store. They stood in front of the foreign film section, each scanning the shelves. Julia plucked one out and waved it at Beatriz. They finally agreed on renting *Ay Carmela!*, a tragicomedy set in Spain during its Civil War. It centered around two performers madly in love and madly making love among the ruins and the fascists. Julia could not believe Beatriz had never seen it before. It was past one in the afternoon when they finally pedaled to the front door of the apartment.

Beatriz prepared a meal of pasta in pesto sauce while Julia showered. Julia made an avocado salad and whipped up a dessert of guava shells with cottage cheese just as Beatriz was finished with her shower. Julia could hear Beatriz' bathroom noises as she set the table. The shape of the dessert spoon in her hand reminded her of Beatriz' naked shape, remembering it from that time in the middle of the living room. She pictured how Beatriz would be drying herself, padding her long limbs gently, while her wet hair sprawled itself on her back. Julia dropped the spoon just as Beatriz reached the dining room.

"Qué hambre! I'm starving."

"Me too."

They ate, savoring every bite and talking about Julia's book and what that could mean for her. Beatriz talked about the time she spent listening to her grandfather's tales of his Spanish Civil War underground days. She told Julia of how she missed those big family almuerzos at her grandfather's country house. And just at the mention of this, the thought quickly crystallized in Julia's mind that she had ignored the get-together at Isa's house. And just as quickly, she put it out of her mind.

At the finish of the meal, they went into the den. It was really a third bedroom Julia had turned into a guest room with a sofa bed, the TV, and more bookshelves. Both had not bothered to change out of their bathrobes before the meal, and now they sat on the sofa, each with a small bowl of the guava and cottage cheese dessert, as the movie started.

They watched the film, focusing on the couple struggling to perform their song and dance routines for the underground rebels, without getting caught. In another scene, their fascist guard drunk asleep, they find a glorious bed among the ruins of an abandoned apartment and make love to each other in the middle of the afternoon, in the middle of enemy territory. Julia and Beatriz quietly watched.

After the scene, Julia walked to the kitchen with the empty dessert bowls. The phone rang. It was Lucinda asking her why she wasn't at Isa's. Julia told her how biking took longer than she thought and how they had just finished eating and were now resting, watching a movie. No, she wasn't going to be able to make it.

When she got back to the den, Beatriz had stretched out on the couch, her head on a pillow. She started to sit up, but Julia motioned for her to stay. Julia sat down sliding her lap under the pillow with Beatriz' head on it. Beatriz settled herself with ease and continued watching the movie. Her hair, loose and still slightly wet from the shower, overlapped the pillow and covered Julia's lap. Its coolness contrasted sharply with the warmth of her thighs. Julia began lifting it with her right hand, feeling the long strands glide through her palm, smooth like silk, as they fell back down on the pillow. She repeated the motion over and over again, each time lifting the hair higher so she could feel it flow down through her fingers like water. Once she grazed Beatriz' cheek, soft and supple like a baby's. Julia touched it again, this time with the fullness of her palm, as if to confirm her initial impression.

"That feels nice," Beatriz whispered, turning over and lazily smiling up at Julia. Julia bent over. She slowly kissed the top of Beatriz' moist head, breathing in deeply the fresh scent of her hair. Beatriz raised her face to Julia's and kissed her softly on the lips. Julia froze.

She could not hear the movie nor see Beatriz' face. She could not remember where she was in the house, what time of day it was, or what she was doing. All she could remember was the immediate sensation of being totally free of all her other senses.

Beatriz had a look of doubt on her face at Julia's stillness. The doubt was quickly assuaged by Julia's face, eyes closed, slowly moving toward her, searching for her lips. Julia found Beatriz' fully open lips meeting hers, the tenderness of her love exposing itself in the hungry kiss.

Julia was not concerned with what her amigas were doing.

—⌁—

Mercy opened the refrigerator for some of Isa's mother's dulce de leche dessert. "I'm still hungry."

"Did you call Julia?" Isa asked, wondering if Julia would at least make it for dessert.

"Sí, she's not coming. She's staying in, watching a movie with Beatriz," answered Lucinda.

"Watching a movie? Julia?!" exclaimed Mercy. "Coño! That's a first."

"The cooking was great, Isa. Let me make the coffee," offered Lucinda.

"Como ha cambiado," added Mercy. "It's that Beatriz woman."

"I saw them this morning, bike riding."

"On a bicycle built for two?" said Mercy.

"What's wrong with bike riding?" asked Isa, handing Lucinda the bag of Café Bustelo.

"She looked very relaxed," said Lucinda. "Julia needs to loosen up."

"Let me tell you, soon enough, she'll be as loose as a—"

"Don't go there, Mercy," said Isa.

"Why not? Isn't it obvious?"

"Isn't what obvious?" said Lucinda.

"It's Julia. You know she's sad and confused about Felipe."

"She didn't look sad and confused to me today," interrupted Lucinda.

"She's all alone," continued Mercy, "then comes this Beatriz woman."

"Why do you keep calling her 'this Beatriz woman'? She seemed very nice to me."

"Puedo continuar? Then along comes—this Beatriz woman,"

said Mercy looking at Lucinda, "this passion flamenco fruta, and," she paused, raising her index finger, "don't forget, gay, woman— oh sí! let's sweep it out from under the closet! And what happens?" Mercy asked, leaning over the counter like a prosecutor in a packed courtroom. "Let me tell you, primero, she moves in, segundo, they're bike riding all over Miami, tercero, they're watching movies together, y cuarto," Mercy hesitated for dramatic effect, "I leave that to your own bedroom machinations."

"It was Julia who asked her to move in," added Isa.

"You know what? I don't care," continued Lucinda. "I haven't seen Julia this happy in a long time."

"Do we have to talk about this?" asked Isabel. The coffee was brewing on the stove. Lucinda removed it just as it was boiling over.

"Why not?" Mercy asked.

"This is Julia we're talking about. These things make me feel incómoda."

"Uncomfortable? This is just the tip of the ice shelf!" said Mercy.

"I don't know why you're making such a big deal," said Lucinda. "As long as she's decente and Julia is happy, it's none of our business."

"None of our business? Oye meng, Julia is our best friend!" Mercy said. "Isa, you're telling me you wouldn't care if tomorrow Julia came to you and told you she was gay."

"She hasn't."

"What if she did?"

"I don't know."

"Well, it wouldn't matter to me," Lucinda said, aggravated. "And you know what? It wouldn't surprise me either."

"I wouldn't like it, not one little tit—I mean bit!" said Mercy.

"And since when are you the righteous one? Why are you so defensiva, anyway?" asked Lucinda.

"I have nothing against gays. Pero, our Julia?"

"Why not?"

"She's one of us."

"What does that mean?"

"You know what I mean."

"No I don't."

"Things wouldn't be the same."

"She would be the same person she's always been."

"No she wouldn't. Not to me she wouldn't," said Mercy. "Give me a break. Think of all the things we do together. Y qué me dices when it comes to talking about men?"

"You don't just talk about men. . . ."

"My little cousin, you're Mother Nature's answer to Viagra!"

"That's beside the point. El punto es que, think about it, with women?" Mercy's whole body trembled as if shaking off an evil spirit.

"I couldn't," she continued. "And what if she wants us to start going to gay bars with her? Qué va! Yo sí que no bailo ese tango. I have enough trouble shaking men off at the clubs, I don't need any sensitive truckers, if you know what I mean, eyeing me up and down."

"You're being ridiculous, Mercy. Julia doesn't even go to bars. Why would she go to gay ones? You have a one-track mind and it always leads to the bedroom," said Lucinda. "There's more to relationships than sex."

"So I've been told! Y tú, my big cousin?" said Mercy turning to Isa. "What do you think?"

Isa sat intently listening to her friends, wondering about Julia and about her own clouded feelings.

"I don't know. I don't understand it yet, if it's true," answered Isa, quickly adding, "How is your mother?"

Lucinda served the hot coffee while they listened to Mercy's woes, but Isa's mind was on Julia and Beatriz.

———

Neither Julia nor Beatriz listened to the end of the movie. They didn't hear the crackling buzz of the blank tape as it played itself out. They heard nothing but their own intermingled breathing after the kiss expired. Julia opened her eyes first. A wave of panic stirred itself in her mind as she realized what had just happened. Then Beatriz opened her eyes and the infinitely deep green of their color absorbed Julia's shock wave. She saw it dissipate itself in those eyes, which had the look of someone deeply in love.

"This changes everything," said Beatriz.

"I know."

Beatriz sat up and held both of Julia's hands. She stroked them, taking turns with each one, saying nothing. Julia focused her attention on their hands together. They felt like hands long ago separated and now reunited after a lost journey.

Beatriz stood up, still holding Julia's hands, still silent. She looked at the hands and then at Julia's upturned face.

"I'm going to my room, mi chica," Beatriz tenderly said.

"I know, I know," Julia whispered back. Alone in the den, she turned off the VCR and the side lamp. She sat for a while in the darkened room letting her thoughts sift through her mind.

This does change everything, everything as you knew it, as you had lived it, as you had forgotten about it when you spent all that time reading to yourself after Felipe's love; when you felt like an incomplete idea, a half-written book, a puzzle with 999 pieces making up life's choices but the one thousandth one, the central piece to the entire picture, still missing, but now, after tonight, you're alive and complete. The picture of your life with its zigzagging grooves reflected a love like it never had, never could, before—a love at peace with itself. A love big enough to allow for a passion long denied. With Felipe you had existed on thought, your mind negotiating the passion, thinking it through until it was comfortable and safe, tamed. With Beatriz, that minute you saw her on the dance floor, you went on instinct, your heart pounding your thoughts out of existence and wanting to break out of your fear-imposed exile. Beatriz brought you out, not from a closet, but out of a coffin a dozen nails away from being sealed shut. It wasn't that you were denying anything or anyone, it was simply that you had not crossed paths with that final missing piece of your life's puzzle, so familiar now, so undeniably Beatriz.

Julia walked past Beatriz' shut bedroom door. She noticed the light coming from under it. She didn't stop but quietly made her way to her own bedroom. After finishing with her nightly routine, she lay under the covers wide awake. Her eyes kept looking at the phone on the night table. She had to make the phone call.

"Isa?"

"Julia?"

"Yes."

"Díme, what is it?"

Julia answered, "I think I'm in love."

There was silence.

"You've never said that before."

"I know. I know," Julia whispered.

There was another pause.

"You don't have to say anything, Isa."

"Yo sé."

"I'll see you soon?"

"Sí."

That night she went to sleep without having read a word. Her miniature pillar of books remained slanted by the reading chair. Julia finally let go of the receiver, her mind empty of all the words, which had obscured her feelings until now.

Chapter 20

Mercy

The night I found out about mamá's arrest Isa put me to rest. And I needed it, let me tell you, because it was a night from here to maternity. What I mean is that so many things happened that night que I felt like I was going through a multiple birthing; one new thing kept popping out after another. I like kids, don't get me wrong, so long as I don't have to raise them. Oye meng, I don't need to add going around mopping up noses all day long with all that I do. That's my image of a kid, a big runny nose on two scrawny legs and me chasing after it with my Magic Mop high in the air. Isa says that if I keep thinking that way, I'll have my own kid to answer to. I keep telling her I need my own man to answer to first. That Magic Man seems to be mopping my big cousin Isa off her feet. Let me tell you, ya era hora! She's been guarding her divorced virginity like if she was wearing a full-bodied chastity belt and for too long too. I read in *Latina* magazine that keeping your sexual drive in neutral for too long can cause early menopause. Maybe that's what's driving Julia into the arms of another woman. Coño! Isa better hurry up and let this Orlando work his magic on her before another Beatriz type gets in there first, if you know what I mean.

I was taking a backroads shortcut—which in Miami really

means going through the suburbs—to Isa's house when I noticed my Miata pulling at the wheel like Sara pulls at her leash when she wants to sprinkle the curb. All of a sudden I heard a loud shot. As I went to step on the brakes, I accidentally pressed the gas pedal instead and the Miata tore through the empty night street like a Batmobile—except that I could feel the crunching of the tire wheel all the way up my spine as it finally pulled me up to a freshly minted sidewalk curb and came to an emergency train-stopping stop. That's when I noticed the brand new and unfinished houses lined up in a row for as far as the eye could see, and I couldn't see much because the lampposts were not all on. I also saw the dented rim with its minced tire smoking into the night as I walked around the front of the car. Now, let me tell you, getting stuck at night in a never-been-deserted-because-it's-never-been-occupied development out in the suburbs is like reading a Stephen King novel naked, alone in the house, with the lights out, the doors open, and the phone not working. I creeped my way back to the car seat and lunged for the cellular. Its battery was dead.

Oye meng, I don't scare easily but when I went for the spare and realized it was the flat tire, from when Mr. Hunkette changed it back on the Beach, I froze. Who's got time to get a flat fixed? My mind started to replay TV scenes to me. I began to see weirdo construction guys coming out of every half-finished and dark-holed house in the graveyard of a neighborhood I was in. I started thinking of every horror movie scene ever made cuando I saw this pair of lights bouncing toward me way down the street. Let me tell you, I have seen too many slice-the-chick flicks to wave down an approaching car so I got into mine, turned off its lights, buzzed up the windows, and lay real low across the seats. I felt the stick shift stabbing at me like the knife the driver would stab into my stomach as soon as he realized his prey was trapped. It was so quiet all I could hear was my breathing in rhythm with the crunching tire noises of the approaching car. As I heard it pass me, I took a peek over the dashboard. That's when it stopped.

Carajo, my heart stopped too at the sight of the car backing up. All of a sudden the idea of being locked up in a Cuban jail appealed to me and I wished I was next to my mother in her roach-infested cell. I dove into the seats as deep as I could go and grabbed hold of the cellular like a caveman holds a rock. I was ready to at least bash the pervert's face in before the knife came ripping through the convertible top.

"Lady, you need any help? You, in there"—he tapped at the window—"you all right?"

"Go away! Lárgate! Nyet!" Russians were now coming to Miami so I figured I'd try to get rid of this guy in any language I could, but he didn't move. In a fit I raised my head off the passenger seat and with my hair all crazy, began to bang the cellular rock on the window. My last hope was that he'd think twice before committing himself to murdering a crazed woman. The guy backed away and then came in for a closer look. I got a good look at him, too.

"Aren't you that realty lady from the Beach a while back?"

He looked over the Miata.

"Yeah, I remember this yellow bird. It's all right to come out now. Look, no tools in my hands, see?" he said, smiling like he could read my horror-infested mind.

I stopped ranting and bashing long enough to remember Mr. Hunkette.

"Hunks 'R' Us Towing, right? Where's your truck?" I asked coming out of my imagined coffin with my cellular weapon.

"What are you doing way out here at this hour? Let me guess, you didn't fix the flat in the trunk, right?"

I was imagining the odds of meeting the same tow-truck driver twice for two messed-up tires in two very different parts of town on two different occasions, when Walter Mercado came into my mind with his twos. I looked at Mr. Hunkette twice before talking. He didn't look deranged. As a matter of fact, he looked good out of the jumpsuit I last saw him in. Right before my eyes Paul Reiser was morphing into John Leguizamo. He was dressed all in black, black T-shirt, black pants, black shoes, and probably black underwear—probably one of those little jockey briefs. I took a brief mental inventory of my own looks. I was wearing jeans and a hugging long-sleeved pullover. My curves were showing.

"No, I forgot to fix it," I answered truthfully, trying to comb my hair with the cellular in my hand.

"Well, lady, you're not alone. Towing statistics say most don't until they get stuck again. You look stuck again."

"Can you help me?"

I got inside his fully restored 1974 black T-topped, tan-rawhide-seated Camaro Z-28. He introduced me to the car like it was a close friend. Hanging from the rearview mirror were two little flags, one of Puerto Rico and the other of Italy. Some classical geezer, Bach, he said, was playing on the radio. As my eyes raced across the dashboard to his hands on the leather wheel, they made a pit stop on a business card pressed against the speedometer glass. It was my business card with my picture looking back up at him.

"It's the card you tipped me with. Best tip I ever got."

Let me tell you, I have never seen my picture in any man's place, not even his wallet. Mr. Hunkette must have been driving my picture around because it looked a bit toasted, like when it's been sitting in a hot car for a while. Then I noticed his gloved hands. He was wearing black leather racing car gloves and it wasn't cold outside. Carajo, Miami was a million miles away from any winter at the moment.

"You don't find it strange that we met again in the same way?" I asked, looking at my picture and his gloves wondering if he'd been stalking me and that's why he just "happened" to be there in an empty development with me and my flat.

"Two times. No such thing as coincidencia."

"You speak Spanish?"

"Neoyorrican and a little Italian. Just the 'colorful' words. In my business, Italian does wonders with a ticked-off road jerk."

I looked at the gloves and my mental TV began to play the scene where the killer leaves no fingerprints around, not even on the victim's neck.

"You like my gloves?" he asked not even turning around to face me.

"Why do you wear gloves in ninety-degree weather?"

"Oil—either skin or mechanical—ruins the leather on the wheel. And these leave no marks," he said, this time with a toothy grin and lo juro, with his eyes flirting at me. I got a thrill in the pit of my stomach from hearing his accent.

Puerto Rican-Italian with a dash of New York-American, talk about an exotic foreign dish. I could hear faint grumbling noises in the pit of my heart. I made a mental note to check Walter's horoscope tomorrow. The thought of tomorrow made me get back to mamá and her disappearance. I got real quiet trying to hold the tears in. I didn't want to burden Mr. Hunkette with more of my troubles. I tried to distract myself by looking out the window and for a couple of more deserted blocks of "dream come true with your very own bidet in the master bedroom suite" houses I stayed that way. Oye meng, bidets used to be a thing for old or sick ladies in America. But let me tell you, nothing sells a house to a Latina woman—and they run the house—like a bidet. They're mushrooming all over the suburban Latino landscape wherever a developer, Americano and otherwise, gets a whiff of an easy cash flow. Mamá loves the bidets I had put in at the Kendall house.

The messages the passing billboards were throwing at me weren't enough to stop the thinking of what a hard time mamá must be having and qué carajo was I going to do? Tears began to flow from my face as I tried to stop them from dropping on the leather seat with the hanky from my purse. I looked like I was trying to stop a leaky roof from ruining a masterpiece. I noticed him looking at me.

"What's wrong? Tell me."

I've never been asked by a man to tell him what's wrong. So I poured out my mother's story like Mariah Carey pours out a song with all of its low and high notes and some medium ones thrown in to catch my breath.

"That's a tough break. Listen, I'm sure your cousin will help you figure something out." He put his hand on my shoulder. "It's all right to cry." So I did all the way to Isa's driveway.

He walked around and opened the door for me. He practically lifted me out of the car saying, "You're going to be all right."

"What's your name?" is all I could say to him.

He pulled a card from his wallet.

"Here. Tony, Tony Coppola. Listen"—I noticed his eyes lighting up—"don't worry about your car. I'll take care of it. You get your mother out."

"Gracias, Tony."

I started to walk away when he called.

"Lady! Mercy." He pushed the seat back forward and pulled a package out.

"These are for you."

Let me tell you, I couldn't believe my eyes. He handed me a bunch of red roses wrapped in green tissue paper.

"My date doesn't need them like you do."

—⁓—

I kept Isa up and for the rest of the night until the sun interrupted us I drilled her for advice. We just couldn't figure out why mamá would get arrested on a family visit, especially since she's had a few of these throughout the years and nothing, not even a parking ticket, is on her travel visa.

Isa gave me good advice, let me tell you. First thing in the morning she woke up her high-powered neighbors who were taking a break in their vacation condo on Sanibel Island. I made plans to rent a car and take the three-hour drive to get face-to-face advice from the lawyer and judge couple. I called my Arab partner to fill him in on the news and told him where I'd be if anything came up at the office. I was wondering where my good luck had gone. First my big cousin Isa with David Jr.'s accident, then me with my jailbird mother, and what about Lucinda with her roaming bird of a husband? What next? Beatriz dumps Julia? I don't know if that would be bad news, necessarily. Let me tell you, I think a woman can be very beautiful, heck, I think that every time I look in the mirror. Now one thing is looking and another thing is touching. Es que I prefer to leave the touching to the men. Pero, what if you're all alone, where the broken hearts roam, and the mender turns out to be gay? Yo no sé.

I was about to roam my way out west to Sanibel when the sight of my Miata parked outside Isa's house put Tony in my head. I grabbed the roses and took Tamiami Trail road heading west across Miccosukee American Indian territory to Sanibel Island on the Gulf side like a Pony Express rider except that I wasn't riding a Mustang. Pero knowing that my trusty Miata had been in Tony's hands gave me comfort.

He had fixed the car and towed it through the night mist all the way back to Isa's house. I could just picture his big breathing dragon of a tow truck pulling my little Tweety Bird of a car to safety in the wee hours of the morning. Oye meng, qué román-tico! The thought of Tony doing this made my face tingle like an avocado facial at Aida's Wild Hair Salon does. Her facials erase all worries as they do the wrinkles. Not that I have any wrinkles worth doing anything about yet, but I like to get a head start on worrying.

"You've got to get a head start on this matter," Judge Helen was saying as she poured a cup of tea for me. They insisted I stay for lunch. Oye meng, I've never had a Jewish lunch before but I fig-ured these were Isa's friends. Ahora when I saw the plate of Moros con Cristianos rice and beans along with the bowl of mat-zoh ball soup in front of me, I relaxed. The smoked salmon and the fried sweet plátanos maduros didn't clash either. I always thought Isa's neighbors were Anglos, not Jewish. Qué carajo, only in Miami is a Jew an Anglo. Why am I so picky with these labels? Let me tell you, I sell to anybody in Miami and I better know where they're coming from. All I know is that in realty, with a big commission on the line, knowledge of the cultural kind gets you the sale. Pero I was totalmente ignorant of what to do for my mother. Isa's Jewish-Anglo-American friends—qué cosa, our slogan should be Miami: City of Hyphens—were more than willing to help. They were also being generous with their portions too. So somewhere between mouthfuls of matzoh and maduros, I got their generous advice.

"I've got some contacts in Washington, D.C., with the State Department. I'm sure we can get through using official channels," Judge Helen said.

"The first thing is to find out why she was arrested. Does she have a history of anti-Castro activism in Miami? Is your mother a known subversive in Cuban circles?" Lawyer Jared, her husband, asked.

"No." But I didn't tell him she was a celebrity subversive in my dating circles.

Jared the lawyer walked over to the terrace and looked at the beach. The Australian pines were swaying just like he was. Finally he turned back to the table, sat down, and jabbed at a maduro with his fork. I scooped up a matzoh ball.

"I was thinking, what you need is somebody down there, someone who goes with the Cuban legal circles. Helen, how do my Miami-Cuban clients put it?"

"Palanca?" I interrupted.

"Yes, something like that, leverage, pull, with the system in Cuba itself," Judge Helen got in.

"We'll take a two-track approach. Helen, you take the official diplomatic track. I'll use my contacts to open a back-door channel. Let's see which way gets us our man in Havana."

"And money?" I asked not too discreetly.

"You need your mother. They need American dollars. Let's hope they blink first."

"I'm sorry my husband is being so blunt, but you are family to our friend Isa. We feel we can speak to the point and not waste time."

I can appreciate bluntness. I showed my appreciation for their concern and their food by leaving my plate clean. After some small talk and a promise to get back to me, I left. I drove back east across the Everglades on a wing and a prayer, crossing myself for mamá's sake that Isa's friends could get her out.

"Crosses! Quién carajo gets arrested for carrying crosses?!"

I was yelling at Isa in the middle of the third car dealership we'd been to that day. It took three days for the judge and the lawyer to find me a man in Havana who could help us. That's two days longer than it takes my mother to find me a man in Miami. But at least Havana Man—that was his code name—knew where she was. Using his real name could have jeopardized his high-placed position in the Cuban government. I placed the cellular back in my purse after Judge Helen finished dándome la información. Havana Man found out she was being detained not in a jail, but in one of the old mansions in Miramar Row. That's the neighborhood where the rich capitalists used to live, but now only rich communists live. It turns out the only reason why she wasn't dumped in a real jail was because her jailer thought she was connected to the Vatican. She showed him the certificate, with the picture of the Pope blessing her and signed by him authenticating her visit to the Vatican. She had called her Italy trip a call to arms, a crusade. I remembered it because I paid for it. Well, it paid off because the jailer bought her story. I was telling all this to Isa while the car salesman was telling me all about the Infiniti in front of us. I showed my displeasure with its color by talking to Isa and ignoring him.

"Resulta que mamá decided to express her religion more publicly!"

"How?"

"She went one morning to La Plaza de la Revolución and just started handing out those little silver crosses to everyone walking by."

"So? What's the big deal?"

"Crosses engraved with 'Cristo sí, Castro no!'?" I slapped the rear of the Infiniti. "Can you believe it! To go to Cuba y hacer eso!"

"And choosing the Tiananmen Square of Cuba to do it in? Only your mother could think of such a thing! Why didn't you stop her from taking them?"

"How was I supposed to know what she was thinking?! Millennium mania? I don't know!" The salesman thought I was talking to him.

"Mercy, this can only happen to you," Isa was saying as she gave me a cousinly abrazo. I noticed the salesman giving his colleagues a "Gays Alert" look. This made me picture Julia and Beatriz and made me feel bad. I didn't like his look and I didn't like what my words on the matter must have looked like to las amigas.

"Yo no sé!" I yelled at him.

"So what is this Havana Man doing?" Isa asked while the salesman showed me another rounded sedan, this time a gray one. I turned him down. Gray was too serious. I was going for something more respectful but less corporate. At the Mercedes and the Lexus dealerships, we also narrowed it down to a gray number that day. It's not that I was trying to forget about mamá or anything like that, but my life as a newly minted entrepreneur had a beat of its own and I couldn't stop it. I had to keep busy with something, especially since I couldn't do anything about her situation.

"He's doing what can only be done down there. He's looking for palanca with the jailer."

As we left the dealership, Isa asked, "Why are you looking for another car? Didn't you buy the Miata last year?" I gave the salesman a dirty look because he gave me one first.

"I don't know. I need a change I guess. But I've had enough for one day. Thanks for coming with me. I feel better."

"Está bien. Let's hope this Havana Man comes through. Y Mercy, remember, in Cuba, todo va a paso de tortuga. Don't get desperate, yet. Let me know as soon as you know anything. And stay out of any líos!"

I didn't mention Tony to her at all. Oye meng, no sense in fighting on two fronts. And with my family, when it comes to love wars—batalla avisada, guerra perdida.

I drove her back to work, even though it was already four in the afternoon. Isa is that way. The only thing that made me feel better, especially in the rush-hour traffic, was seeing Tony's business card on my dashboard.

That night I got an urge for Italian so I heated up a frozen lasagna and served myself a glass of red wine. I even sprinkled parmesan cheese on Sara's dry food. I got something else too that night, a direct call from Havana Man.

"Your mother is safe. They are treating her well. I have worked on the Vatican angle but I do not know how long I can keep that up," Havana Man said in very proper English. I could tell it was book learned.

I didn't ask who he was or how he got my number or why he had to speak in English. I just wanted to know, "How do I get her back?"

"Official channels are closed. The Cuban Government's tolerance for Miami-Cubans is very low this season. There is nothing that can be done for her, officially."

Havana Man was sounding more like a car salesman by the ever charging telephone minute. I know when the options are being reduced to just one. I let the minutes click by until he said, "I know her jailer."

Palanca! Jared the lawyer was right. Even in a coffined-up government like Cuba's, there's always someone with a crowbar who, for the right price, is willing to lift the lid even just a crack.

"How much money? I don't care!" I yelled blinking first.

"He does not want money."

"What does he want?"

"It is what he wants that matters most because it is the only way he will release her."

Dios mío! I got the feeling I was talking to Darth Vader in the Evil Empire. What did the jailer want, my soul? I almost fainted when he told me his terms.

"Marrone! What does a Cuban jailer want with parts for a 1954 Starchief Pontiac convertible?"

Hunks "R" Us was the only place I knew, besides a car dealership, having to do with cars. Además, Tony was more than willing to help, again. I had made plans to meet him at his office the next day. I was surprised at how nicely kept the office was. The plants, the dustless desk, and the paper organizer all pointed to a woman's touch but there were no pictures of the female kind anywhere I looked. Heck, not even one of those calendars with the nearly naked bombshells posing over spotless cars you see in every garage was hanging around. Then I saw the small knitted tapestry hanging on the wall behind him. Inside the knitted antique car, in red knitted letters, I read "Mother Knows Best."

"I thought you might know best where I could get such parts? They're my mother's ticket out of Cuba."

"What's in it for the guy?"

"Es un loco! Havana Man says the jailer wants to get the hell out of Cuba but he wants to land in Miami with lots of money in his refugee-lined pockets."

"So?"

"So, he's been rebuilding Hemingway's old car from the ground up and now he just needs a few more parts to finish the job."

"As in Hemingway the writer's car? What does he want to do, sell it to the highest bidder?"

"Exactly! He's had the car hidden somewhere on the southern coast of Cuba ever since Hemingway died."

"Why didn't he just ask you for the money?"

"He thinks he can get more for the car than for mamá."

"Unbelievable," Tony said, shaking his black curly head from side to side. "How is he going to get it out of Cuba? Never mind! Let's just concentrate on getting your mother out of there starting now."

He grabbed my hand and led me out the side door. We walked across the parking lot weaving between his fleet of wreckers. I noticed every truck was a different color. It felt like I was walking around in a bowl-full of Lifesavers candy. We crossed the dusty street weaving between the big-wheeled rigs speeding by. I was praying one of my high heels wouldn't get a flat. Finally I saw the sign of the place he was taking me to. I looked up past the dust clouds to read FIRST CLASS JUNK PARTS.

"Hey, Tony!" said the Junkman from behind the counter. "Who's the classy lady?" he asked eyeing me up and down. I noticed he lingered on the down look.

Tony looked at me and said, "She's the one I'm gonna marry." I didn't see him wink or anything. He said it like it was a done deal. Let me tell you, I was almost a done deal, a crispy fried well-done toasted deal at the mention of marriage coming from a guy first and not mamá. This was a first ever in my marriage-seeking life. And for the first time ever, I ignored the comment. Tony was being nice, but I was there to make a deal with Junkman, so my ever-wishing-for-a-true-loved-marriage heart had to beat its way back to reality.

"Qué?! Don't be so fresco!"

I slapped his arm. By the way he flinched, I guess I slapped it un poquito too hard. Tony took the list from my hand. We got down to business with Junkman, who reminded me of Steve Martin.

"Give me a minute. No, I don't have these particular parts. Man, this guy knows what he wants. Let me bring up something on the Net."

Junkman clicked the keyboard some more with his fingers.

"We got something. Let's see, there's a guy in Iowa, another in Vermont, one in New Mexico, and three out in Texas all saying they've got parts for such a car. Man, a car like that—in restored condition? with its history?—can bring in a bundle. What do you want to do?" Mamá was in Junkman's hands.

It took three more weeks to get the parts to Cuba from all over the States. Havana Man had me box them as medicines and mail them to a State orphanage a relative of his runs in Cuba.

Tony made it a game to deliver a part in a different restaurant each time Junkman got his hands on one. I can vouch for Federal Express, let me tell you. I never knew so many dead car parts could be delivered so fast. Oye meng, Tony and I were moving just as fast as FedEx. I think I finally fell in love when he handed over the ignition switch while we ate lobster thermidor at The Fish Shack next to the canal on Okeechobee Road. It was his favorite fish joint. Only out-of-town truckers or adventurous Miamians ate there. In those three weeks while the car parts were flying all over the States, I was flying with Tony to the best little restaurants around Miami. I could tell he was a man who was into food, and a man in a hurry. Bueno, I matched him fork to fork and flirt to flirt. We also exchanged each other's histories.

At the Palacio del Pollo he told me all about his younger sister.

"She got married too early. Now the ex-guy wants to keep the kid. I pay for her lawyer. Shit, you know what it feels like to have a lawyer on retainer so that I can retain my nephew? I'd like to retain the ex-jerk's face in the Miami River for a couple of minutes. I slip my parents a couple of bucks here and there to help pay for her stay at their house. She doesn't know it."

"Your whole family is in Miami?"

"Yep. My little brother works with me. He's my ace wrecker. Here's the hubcap Havana Man wanted." Tony reached over the lemon and garlic roasted chicken in the middle of our table. I told him a little about mamá.

At the Thigh Thai, over some peanut sauce fish and rice plates, and with miniskirted waitresses skirting around, whom Tony ignored the whole time, he told me why he likes his work. I liked the fact that he was concentrating on me.

"Ever since I was a skinny mojón, I liked helping people. I got this from my Puerto Rican mother."

"What did you get from your father?"

"Italian cuss words and a love for cars—and for Spanish dishes."

"We're in a Thai restaurant."

"Who said I was talking about food?" he flirted with me, narrowing his slow smile and sly eyes. We left the restaurant holding between us the steering wheel Havana Man had asked for. I talked some more about mamá.

Another night, at El Colmadito, as we ordered gandules with pasteles, his favorite Puerto Rican dish, which they didn't cook as good as his mother, we got down to business rápido.

"Junkman almost gave up on this one, but the guy in Vermont came through with it," Tony was saying as we sat in the booth. He gave me the near perfect driver's-side armrest in one of those long Cuban bread bags.

"Did you know your mother is a celebrity prisoner on the Net? Junkman has every parts guy in the country looking out for her. They comb the junkyards knowing that your mother is one part closer to freedom with each discovery they make. One guy in Utah wants to start E-mail dating her as soon as she's out."

"Tony, no one should know about this. Havana Man made it clear."

"Don't worry, Brett dressed up the truth a bit. As far as the parts heart's club is concerned, they're rescuing your mother from some government conspiracy."

"Brett—that's his name?—sounds like an *X-Files* fan."

"That is my mother's favorite show. I never really told you about my mother, uh?"

"No, except that she's Puerto Rican," I said, getting nervous. When a man tells you about his mother, without you asking, that can only mean una de dos cosas; either he's serious about you, or he's a mama's comemierda. Well, I found out his mother is a killer cook and was dying to meet me. I also found out she had a frying pan temper. Mamá would love to meet her, I said to Tony. And I told him everything about mamá, except the "Made in Cuba" love-union label she insisted every hombre have if they wanted to tag me.

Yo no sé, I always thought falling in love was about exchanging glances, but we fell in love over used car parts. Esa noche, when he gave me the ignition switch, we twitched.

"Did you feel that?" I asked him, jerking my hand away from his and dropping the switch on the table.

"You're a turn-on, Mercy, what can I say." He touched my arm and I felt the same shocking jolt.

"We make electricity together." He smiled at me in his devilish little-boy way. Then he began to tease and threaten me with his index finger. Those static bolts he was throwing at me made my entire body jiggle. Let me tell you, I've never jiggled so much for a man the way I jiggled for Tony that night.

In all that time, with all that parts gathering, restaurant hopping, and intimate talking, we didn't sit close, we didn't even kiss. All we did was chat, eat, flirt, and fall in love. And, along the way, he was helping me get mamá out of Cuba. Still, the thought of falling in love with a man you've never touched, bueno, I'd be lying if I didn't say it felt foreign to me, and if I didn't admit to a little nerviosismo at the thought of falling for a man that could not receive mamá's Cuban stamp of approval no matter which way you looked at him. I knew mamá was going to be microscoping him down to his tiny underwear, which I hadn't even gotten a glimpse of in all that time. Let me tell you, lust is a terrible thing to waste. The only parts of Tony I was handling were the mechanical ones, and besides, mamá's jailing gave me no choice. I can only handle pain and pleasure one at a time.

Everything went without a hitch, but the last item, the fully chromed rear bumper, was a real rhymes-with-hitch to box. Tony had the idea to label it a stretcher, and that's how it flew straight to Havana. True to the jailer's and Havana Man's word, mamá flew back all in one piece gracias to Jesús, María, y José—and Tony.

I didn't waste any time in throwing mamá's coming-out party. She didn't waste any time in letting me have it.

"So, aquí tú estabas, looking for un hombre, while I suffered down en Cuba!" she whispered yelling at me. We were sitting next to each other at the round table. Tony was sitting across from us.

His family hadn't arrived yet. I had booked the banquet hall of The Daring Ones Café & Gourmet Market in Coral Gables for her liberation party.

"No, I was looking for car parts. And you? Buscándote lío with those crosses."

"I don't like him," she glared.

"He saved your life."

"No es cubano."

"Habla español, Italian, and Neoyorrican."

"What country speaks that?"

Just then, Tony decided to speak.

"Señora Virtudes, I am so glad you are safe. You must have suffered so much. Tell me about your experience, if it's not too much to ask."

I could tell that Tony's sly smile got to mamá because she hesitated, but then she saw her oportunidad. Let me tell you, the Man in the Iron Mask was nothing but a guest at a masquerade ball in the king's palace feeding his face with stuffed quail compared to mamá's version of her Cuban jailing.

"Y así fue. Un poco de bread, water, and for dinner, una papa hervida en agua de churre. A potato boiled to a certain degree of hardness which, as you can see"—and here she opened her mouth—"left me with this. This!" she emphasized, showing us the missing parts of her dentures. I was showing my pena by rolling my eyes at Tony. He knew the real version. According to Havana Man, they had put her up in the master bedroom of an old mansion feeding her the best Cuban food available, which sounded like what you can get in any second-rate Miami Cuban restaurant.

"It was an act of God, my freedom!" mamá declared.

"Señora, you're safe now, but Brett over there"—Tony pointed across the room toward the band, which was playing "Cuando Salí de Cuba," to the Junkman in his best pressed overalls swaying to the guitar—"him, he was your deliverer."

Mamá didn't have a clue what it took to get her out. And I had no clue as to what happened next. As soon as the music stopped,

I stood up to toast mamá's safe return. I grabbed the plastic champagne glass full of El Botero cider and I thanked Isa, her kind neighbors, Tony, and the Junkman. I thanked this country for the head start it gave all of us, I thanked my Arab partner for making my sugary Americano dream come true, and let me tell you, I even thanked Castro for mamá's freedom.

She, claro, immediately stood up and said, "I thank the Pope."

We all drank to that. Then Tony stood up with a cidra glass in his hand. "Ladies and gentlemen, I want to take this occasion, while Mercy is surrounded by her loved ones and is with her mother again, to tell all of yous something. Ever since I first saw her, she's been the fiancée of my heart. And with every car part I gave her, along went a piece of my heart too. It's in your hands, Mercy, all of it. Now it's your turn to give me some."

I saw that flirty twinkle in his eyes. That's all I saw because my nerves were numb. All I could feel were his hands holding mine and it felt like when you are on Novocain and you're just beginning to get some feeling. His next words hit me like a lightning bolt.

"Mercy, will you marry me?"

THE question, his question, the $64,000 pregunta floored me like no man could ever floor me, even on those few occasions when I really did do it on the floor. Bueno, it floored my mother because when I turned to give her a hug, she was bent over, still sitting on her chair, out like a broken cocuyo.

"Don't nobody move! Tony, what did you do? Eddy, go and get me some wet paper towels. Don't worry, honey, your mom is OK, Carmen is here."

Carmen and Eddy were Tony's parents. Eddy was tall and light skinned for an American-Italian. I thought they all had that bronzed Tony Bennett look. I noticed he was balding but he still looked handsome. This was a good sign when it came to Tony's future. Carmen was short, tanned, and as tight as a shock of electricity. Eddy handed the Corningware dishes he was carrying to

Tony and took off to the bathroom. Isa and Lucinda came over from their table.

"We should call 911," Lucinda was saying.

"Maybe there's a doctor here, Mercy?" Isa asked.

By then Julia and Beatriz—qué cosa, I couldn't invite one without inviting the other, no? yo no sé, but Beatriz was being real helpful—they were helping Carmen stretch mamá out on the floor as Eddy came back with the paper towels.

"We don't need no doctor. Tony, get me a spoon and that bowl." Carmen pointed to the table. She had mamá's head cradled in her arms.

"There, honey, you're coming out of it. Here, take a few spoonfuls of Carmen's sancocho. There's nothing like a good Puerto Rican soup to drown out those bad Cuban jail memories, right, honey?"

Mamá snapped out of it. I could see her looking around until her eyes and Carmen's locked. She still had the spoon in her mouth.

"Look everybody, she's OK. It's gonna be all right, honey. Carmen will take care of you. Hey, everybody, we're almost suegras!" Everybody applauded as Carmen spoon-fed my mother. Las amigas looked at me shell-shocked, but I could tell they survived the bomb shelling. I looked at mamá wrapped in Carmen's arms and realized she was in my deliverer's hands.

Tony and I spent the rest of the party slow-dancing every song, even the mambo. Let me tell you, I never knew what being tight with a man meant until that party with Tony. We danced so tight. Carajo! If we'd get any closer, we'd be behind each other, that's how tight we were. Coño! We were so tight we could feel each other up from head to toe and not lift a finger. Oye meng! We danced so apretado not even a fireman crew with one of those Jaws of Life aparatos could separate us.

I looked over Tony's shoulder and saw Eddy walking from table to table serving everybody a cupful of Carmen's sancocho. I looked over at my table and saw Carmen giving mamá an earful.

I looked and saw Isa and Lucinda looking back at me. I saw Julia and Beatriz watching the really good dancers. I moved my face just enough to see Tony's eyes. They were closed. I closed my eyes también and that's when I felt his hands on my back. They were gliding down toward the lower curves but—like a good caballero—stopped just at the spot, if you know what I mean. Just then the music stopped and we headed back to the table.

"Mercy, you a good dancer, just like my Tony. I taught him everything he knows!" Carmen was saying as mamá was flaring.

She grabbed Tony's arm and said, "Come, let's show them."

I could hear Carmen's laughter as Tony spun her around the dance floor. I could also hear mamá's snarl.

"Qué espectáculo!" she said watching them.

"You know what, mamá?" I said in a voice so calm I could hardly recognize myself. "I think it's sweet. Y ese hombre is going to be the father of my children." And this time I could tell it was me putting those words in my mouth.

Let me tell you, when I saw mamá flare her nostrils at me—and when mamá flares her nostrils it means she's getting ready for algo grande—all I could think of doing was offering her some more sancocho. She drank the entire bowl, as if she were drinking her enemy's blood.

Chapter 21

━◈◈◈━

Isabel

I have to go. It's the third time mamá has beeped me," Mercy said, throwing the beeper back in her large leather purse. "I told her I'd go by this morning. She probably wants to talk about Tony. That's all she talks about since returning from Cuba. She's obsessed with Tony!" Mercy continued saying as she kissed us good-bye. "Worried sin razón, I tell her. But you know mamá. Cuando lo coge con algo, she's more persistent than a two-year-old at somebody else's birthday party."

We all laughed. Ever since the rescue from Cuba, Mercy's mother has been relentless in her pursuit of a suitable love for Mercy. So what if Tony happens to be Puerto Rican–Italian by way of New York? He seems to be a decent guy. Definitely he's a cut above Mercy's usual collection of men. According to Mercy, Walter Mercado's horoscope predicted him. It said something about meeting a foreigner. I keep telling her he's an American, but she just loves his accent. Her mother doesn't love the fact that he's not a Cuban. The way Mercy tells it, "no tendrá nada de cubano, pero tiene todo de hombre!" explains why she's for the first time giving her mother such a hard time in the mating department. This, combined with the fact that Tony had a big part, or I should say, a lot of parts, in getting Mercy's mother out of a Cuban jail, explains Mercy's resistance toward her mother.

We watched Mercy get into her brand new car parked by the curb next to our table.

"Now that I'm a company president, I need a more serious image. What do you think?"

We all nodded and waved as she took off in the red BMW Z3 roadster.

"I'm leaving too," said Lucinda. "I have my first art class this morning." Lucinda started to walk off toward her studio when she added, "I'll be calling Beatriz soon, thanks, Julia."

I had forgotten Julia's offer to Lucinda of Beatriz' teaching expertise.

"Call me later. I want to know how it went with all those kids," Julia said.

The studio was not far from Greenstreet Café, where we had met for our monthly breakfast. It felt good to start the tradition all over again. I was about to ask Julia something when we heard a loud horn beeping around the corner. It was Mercy again.

"Isa! I can't find my appointment book! Look inside!" she pleaded pointing at the restaurant. The waiter was running out with the mini palm computer in his hand before I took another step.

"I'll take that, thank you." Mercy's is the only one I've seen with its plastic shell worn down from so much overuse.

"You're working too much," I said, giving it to her.

"You're saying that to me? My, my! What a spell Magic Man has on you!"

"'Magic Man' is what she calls Orlando," I said to Julia as Mercy rushed off in a big red blur.

"Are you in a rush, Julia?"

"Not really. We made plans to go bike riding later on. Why?"

"Let's walk a little."

I didn't say anything about Beatriz even though Lucinda and Julia kept bringing her up during breakfast. They didn't talk about love or anything like that. It was all about her talents, but I swear I thought Mercy would choke on one of her forkfuls of eggs Benedict every time Beatriz was mentioned. But to her maturing credit, she kept the eggs down along with her thoughts on the matter. I was contemplating whether it was any of my business who Julia falls in love with anyway. They didn't ask me about Orlando but they told me what a great guy he was. The expression on my face probably gave me away.

"Did you notice Mercy's face turn red every time we talked about Beatriz?" Julia asked as we walked down Bayshore Drive. "I definitely sensed some anger toward me. Has she said anything to you?"

Now it was my face turning red. Lucky for me a gang of middle-aged, designer-leather-clad, Harley puff-riders blared past us just in the nick of time. The noise would have been enough to raise the roof off the zoning board's chamber from the complaints made, if it had been a gang of Chicano low-riders blaring its way through these guys' designer neighborhoods. By the time the bikes, sounding like a bunch of honking geese with a bad case of bronchitis, settled on the curb in front of the restaurant, I was off the hook.

I pointed toward the entrance of the Barnacle House and we walked into Miami's past, where the noiseless woods made us whisper our conversation. We took the old buggy trail winding through the hardwood hammock. The lush property is the last patch of Miami's original look. Now the old pioneer place is strangled between mansions and high-end townhouses. When I visit, I get a sense that in the old days, nature could blunt the hard edge of a tough day or a tough conversation. With every step we took down toward the water's edge, the frontier landscape beckoned me to whisper what I was feeling about Julia and Beatriz. Then the old Barnacle home saved me. Julia and I absentmindedly followed the tour already in progress.

". . . a tropical pioneer Victorian home with large wooden porches and high windows opening to the sea. That was before air conditioning and highways and arenas and malls, before Harleys and karaoke bars and—"

"Illegal aliens, right? Ha-ha . . ." interrupted a tourist, I think from Kansas by way of her accent.

The young tour guide looked at her with his crystal clear ranger's eyes and said, "Ma'am," in a clear Latino accent, "it was not before the Tequesta Native Americans. To them, we're all aliens."

"I thought he was from France!" whispered the woman to her beet-red-faced husband.

"Now, the old seven-bedroom cottage built in 1891 by Ralph Munroe, a ship designer, stands as a museum in the face of all that progress. Please feel free to go about the property."

The handsome ranger made it a point to smile at us. Actually, he smiled a lot at Julia. Men were always smiling at Julia. I remembered that from the days when we were first becoming friends. Julia has always attracted men. And now she's attracted Beatriz. I looked over and saw how attractive she really was.

"Probably a former student," she whispered to me. I smiled back.

The rocky dirt path led us to the open grassy field below from where the cottage sits on a small rise overlooking the sea.

We took our time walking down to the boathouse. At the water's edge, there was no other place to go.

"Something is on your mind, Isa."

A mystery was on my mind. Now I like good detective stories, something like Carolina García-Aguilera's page-turners; her Lupe Solano private eye always figures out what's going on. But I can't take suspense in my own life—I've had one too many twists and turns. And unlike Lupe, I need to know what's going on ahora. So I turned the page and asked my friend, "What's going on with you?"

"I wish I knew."

I stayed quiet.

"All I know is that I am attracted to Beatriz. I can't believe I'm saying such a thing—"

"Pero she is a woman—"

"I know, I know! But I like her, I like being with her, I like her looks, I like that she lives in my house! Isa, I like the way I am when she's with me. Does all this make any sense?"

I wanted to say that all this was very confusing and very different and very scary, but all I could say was, "No, it doesn't make sense. I saw you so perfect with Felipe."

"With Felipe my life was perfect, yes, it was too perfect. It was so perfect that I couldn't see myself anymore. Isa, I was disappearing."

I felt like disappearing from this conversation, but then I saw Julia's face. We've been friends through thick and thin, and even though what she was asking of me was as thick as that Berlin Wall, her tears felt like the sledgehammers those desperate Germans used to beat the fear out of their past. Maybe her tears could beat the fear out of me.

"Isa, please try to understand. I can't explain it and I'm scared of it. For the first time, I'm letting go, Isa, I'm letting go," she said, sobbing between her smile.

I saw my friend standing there, at the edge, trying to let go and sail off to a place I can't even imagine. I wanted to say that I was petrified but instead I said, "I'm scared for you." Hearing myself say this, I reached over and hugged Julia. We hugged until I began to cry too and for a while we both cried in each other's arms. I was never so scared of letting go.

"Julia, you told me you think you're in love. Bueno, that's more than most of us can say."

"Life feels like a jacket that doesn't fit anymore," Julia said. "I think Beatriz is meant for me. I really do."

"Lo que está para ti, nadie te lo quita," I said, taking refuge in an old Spanish saying my mother used to repeat when there was no other place left to go.

"And Mercy?"

"Mercy? Qué cosa, you know Mercy, she'll come around as soon as you and Beatriz need a bigger place, one with a dance studio for a living room!"

Julia laughed through the tears and said, "You're right. We've been practicing the tango, you know." She offered me some tissue paper for my tear-streaked face.

"Be patient with us, Julia."

"I don't want to lose our friendship over this."

"You won't," I said, composing myself. We kissed and then Julia left to go on her bike trek with Beatriz. That was it.

I saw her walking, nervous but a little less scared, up the gentle slope of the land until the woods took her in. I stayed a while longer, letting nature absorb some of the fear still in me. The echo of what had just happened was still bouncing around inside.

I sat down on the floor of the wooden porch and rested my back on one of the railing posts. I looked out to the bay and watched a regatta of small sailboats make its way around an obstacle course of buoys. With the wind's changing directions, some of the boats were struggling. I was struggling to make sense of Julia's change in direction. She was not one to make reckless decisions. But to change directions in mid-course? Especially when the winds seemed so fair? Felipe seemed so perfect for her. What did she mean they were too perfect? Isn't love supposed to be perfect? Ay! Talk about a relapsed thought, I could just hear my old marriage counselor. Why is it that you don't get a refund from a marriage counselor who doesn't deliver? There's no complaint department for broken marriages. I've learned the hard way about perfection and love. It comes at a high price with no guarantees, no returns, and no refunds. When I married David I expected everything, and look what I got. Love doesn't blind you, perfection does.

Signs of the emotional kind always throw me off-course. Give me a chemical formula and I'll figure out the final product in a second, but if I can't weigh, measure, and calculate the physical properties, I might as well be blind. Pero to see Julia with another mujer? No amount of calculating could get me to see that.

But what's the whole point of calculating? To get to what you can't see: that's what I do for a living and I'm good at it. And, that's how I've been running my heart since the wind changed on me four years ago. But who am I to counsel Julia against following her heart? Look how they discovered Pluto, by sheer calculation. They knew that planet existed before anyone could see it. I can tell Julia is in mid-calculation. She probably sees something in Beatriz I can't, or don't want to, or am scared to. But sitting on that porch by the sea, picturing Julia's face as I watched the little sailboats struggling to reach their mark, I could tell she needed me.

I feel better when I'm needed. It's a habit I've developed since single motherhood sailed my way. I slouched back on the post and let the morning sun toast my face. A picture of Julia and Beatriz, along with the question "What is love anyway?" floated in my mind. A laundry list of silly answers fluttered in the breezes of my thoughts like a worn-out flag; un feliz encuentro, a happy miscalculation, an unexpected return? A loud ring interrupted my silly thoughts on the matter. My cellular phone was screaming. Someone, probably Sam, had raised the ringer to a decibel only Arturo Sandoval could reach on his trumpet. It was Orlando reaching.

"Hola, Isabel."

"Hola."

"Tell me, where are you right now?"

"I'm by the ocean, sitting on an old porch. And you?"

"In the marina, sitting in my boat, drinking champagne."

"Oh?"

"I heard from PBS."

"What did they say?"

"They want it."

"They took to your 'getting along multicultural hotspots in America' idea?" I said. I think I got it right.

"And, they're offering me a two-year contract to develop more shows for them."

"That's great."

"Are you free later?"

"Christie's restaurant for dinner?"

"I had something else in mind."

"Like what?"

"Just be at the marina at five p.m. It's not too early?"

"I'll be there. Me tienes intrigada."

"Good. And, because you're going to ask, dress casual."

Another mystery in my life. But with Orlando turning the pages, it wasn't so bad.

I got back to the house feeling a little like my pre-marriage self, when the center of the universe was me.

David Jr. was back to his old self again. It took him longer to get better, more than what the doctors had told me. Once in a while, he'll forget something, like his homework assignments or calling his father. Mercy thinks he's faking it. I just want to make sure nothing ever happens to him again. So I keep a mother hen's watch on him. He had negotiated with me all week long to let him go out to the movies in his best friend's car. I finally agreed as long as he got home before nine and took along his brother and my cell phone. It took a lot out of me letting him go out again at night. Pero, with a growing boy, I had no remedio. Un hombre was coming into my life and there was nothing I could do about that.

The boys knew about Orlando but had never met him. I preferred it that way. It was enough for one heart in the family to take a risk again. The boys didn't need to risk theirs, not yet anyway.

What is it with mothers? We never really rest. As I was getting myself ready for Orlando's surprise, my mother threw one at me.

"Así que vas a go out with this Orlando again." I never knew her to comment on my affairs. I turned from the mirror ready to get into it.

"Está bien," she said with a woman's insider look. Actually, she looked like the Cheshire Cat in *Alice in Wonderland*. "It is good to see you going out." She smiled at me. "Cuídate, mijita," she added leaving the room as quietly as she entered it.

Take care of yourself? I looked at myself in the mirror wondering what I was getting into that made my mother take notice. What did she mean? A Wonderland from where I'll be spit back to this side of reality? How much did I really know about Orlando? He was attentive, and after four years, it felt good to be paid attention to and not just because I'm a boss or some valuable possession à la Rubén or Edmund, my two post-divorce attempts at dating liftoff. Orlando and I love to take off and dance, to eat out, to talk. That's what we usually did on our dates, though I can't get used to the word. We've had a few since David Jr.'s accident. He was there. I thank the Virgin for that too. "Cuídate," she said. My mother, who only speaks when she's not sure she's been heard in the body language department, was telling me to take care. Of what? Coño, I am always taking care.

I feel Orlando taking care of me. That's all I know, and it feels good for a change. So he's a writer. So he lives on a boat. So he doesn't have a real job. Bueno, perfection has its limits. The truth is, he's good-looking, he cares for me, he isn't pushy, and he's an extraordinary kisser. "Cuídate," she had told me. By my calculations, I told her I'd be back by nine.

I was busy making a list of all the things I didn't know about Orlando when I arrived at the marina. I saw him standing by the pier waiting in his jeans and his untucked navy blue polo shirt. He was barefoot. We greeted each other with a kiss. He took my hand and led me down to his slip.

"Did you forget something?" I said looking at the small boat where his big one used to be.

"No. It's out there." He pointed to the horizon.

"And dinner?" is all I could think of saying. "I haven't eaten anything since breakfast."

"On the water. It's all taken care of."

"In that little thing?"

"No! That's a dinghy."

It was dinky all right. But his mischievous voice made me reach for his hand as he guided me into the little boat.

"My boat is anchored about thirty minutes away."

I had been postponing going out on the *SeaLove* alone with
Orlando since our one and only sea adventure in Key West. But I
was hungry, and I have to admit, I was intrigued by his little mystery plan, so long as I trusted his page-turning abilities.

"Do beepers work out in the water?" I asked, pressing the
power button on my little lifesaver.

"You won't be in the water this time, Isabel. I promise."

"I promised my mother I'd be back by nine."

"I have a meeting with my agent in La Luna Bar at nine-thirty.
We're just a pair of consenting curfewed adults, Isabel!" he said,
making us both laugh at our teenage situation.

As soon as the marina was in the distance, he increased speed.
I felt the wind against my face as I watched the little bow tear
through the bay. Orlando had picked a perfect day to celebrate; a
few white clouds bobbed in the sky. The palm-lined coast shrank
to where it became a thin green line on top of a thick blue one. I
turned around to face our destination and a lonely green spot way
out in front began to turn into a small island with a few boats anchored around it. The loud rumble of the engine, the vibration
under my seat, and the undulating motion of the boat persuaded
me to relax. Orlando's voice took my attention from the setting
sun.

"Finally, you left the city life behind you. I can tell."

"Can you tell me what's up?"

"Welcome to my very own waterfront restaurant. What do you
think?"

"I hope the food lives up to the view," I teased him.

"It does," he countered, looking at me. I looked at my watch.

He slowed down as we approached the *SeaLove*. We hopped
onto the boat. He had taken her out earlier to claim an anchorage
spot because the small island was a favorite with boaters. There
must have been twenty boats around us. After he checked the anchor line, he disappeared into the cabin and came out with a bottle of wine and two glasses. Anticipating my protest of drinking
on an empty stomach, he handed me the glasses and went back

into the cabin. He returned with a block of Gouda cheese, napkins, and a knife.

"You're always prepared."

"For any emergency and any contingency, such as you finally being on my boat—I should say, my home. Thanks for coming, Isabel. It means a lot."

We toasted to his successful deal with PBS and then I listened as he told me all about his Benchmark Catamaran. I never knew a man who knew so much about his home.

"Why live on a boat? It seems so temporary," I said as we sat watching the sunset. He took a sip of his wine, bit into the cheese, and asked about David Jr. Orlando had a keen interest in my son's recovery, and he was always asking me about Sam as well. I always bragged about them.

As dusk settled on the water, a cool breeze swept through making gooseflesh out of my arms and legs. I was wearing my light cotton pants and camisole outfit, which was not doing a good job of protecting me from the elements. Orlando went below and brought out a folded dark green blanket with white thick socks on top.

"Here, let me put these on your feet." He took off my sandals and slipped a sock on each foot.

"It's funny how cool an evening on the water can become," he said while crossing his legs and placing socks on his own feet. Then he spread the blanket over our laps. I didn't know whether it was the coolness or his proximity that caused me to shiver.

"Are you all right?" he asked.

"I wasn't expecting this chill."

He put his arm around my shoulders and asked, "Better?"

I nodded. "Why a boat?" I had to know.

"I'll tell you," he said, letting go to serve himself another glass of wine, "because you will understand it, I think."

He told me how his life was on shaky ground at that moment, how everything he had had was not what he wanted and how everything he wanted he hadn't gotten yet, except for the *SeaLove*, which was his first step on his new journey.

"Living on a boat, Isabel, is like taking a journey on a train. Everything moves around you, and you yourself are moving; you can feel the earth rumble underneath you, but your soul is as still as a stone in a Japanese garden."

I knew what he was saying because I haven't stopped moving since David moved away. As for my soul, well, Orlando's *SeaLove* was gently rocking it to a standstill. But deep down, I knew what he was saying. It was what I wanted for myself, that feeling that while the entire world swings by, your soul is as still and as solid as Mount Everest.

Orlando told me how the deal with PBS was his second step and how he was doing things for himself from then on.

"What do you mean?" I asked.

"I was successful professionally, but I didn't control it. It was taking me to where I hadn't thought of going: to other people's places, other people's ideas, and other people's control."

He paused, pointing to the night sky where the stars marked their turf with a vengeance against Miami's city lights.

"Out here, Isabel, the stars are fixed. They're what helps a sailor find his way."

"Maybe stars are reflections of our souls then."

"Yes, we just have to find and follow them . . ."

We said this to each other while looking up.

". . . no matter where they lead us." And as he said this, our lips met. We kissed under the stars and under that blanket and my mind went blank as I tasted his soul.

I felt the thick layers of ice melt from me as if spring had come to Mount Everest and melted all the locked-up eons of frozen water in the peak of the world, always alone.

"Are you lonely, Orlando?"

"No. I was—once."

The boat was dark except for the green and red lights at its ends. The breeze had stopped blowing for a while and the sea was shiny and flat. Little streams of lights, from the other anchored boats, reflected on the dark water's surface. They all seemed to be pointing at us. Orlando pointed at his watch and suggested dinner.

"Don't go anywhere. I'll call you." He disappeared into the darkened cabin. A light went on below and the *SeaLove* radiated its own light into the night. I snuggled the blanket up to my neck, leaned against the cockpit, and tried to look for my soul among the stars.

"You may enter!" he said, ringing a big brass bell attached to the other side of the doorway, or as he called it, companionway. I walked below, and to my astonishment, Orlando had set up a dining table with a huge spread of fresh peeled shrimp, pâté, grapes, French bread, and a steaming pot of plantain soup. There was only one light on in the cabin. It was a small table lamp with a pleated shade and one of those wood and brass ship's wheels for a base. It matched the life-sized one in the front of the cabin. I stood motionless in the gentle light. As my eyes adjusted to it, I noticed the glow of the wood all around me. It was deep and rich and solid.

"It's beautiful, all this wood."

"Little by little I've been replacing the factory stuff with the real thing. It's a labor of love."

Orlando took off the blanket I was wrapped in and led me to my seat in the corner settee. Reaching into a cabinet behind his head, he put on a CD.

"Do you like Lecuona?"

"Ernesto Lecuona? Sí."

I loved the Cuban composer's classics but hardly found anyone among my peers who knew of him. I told Orlando that when the boys were babies, I would play an old LP I had of his and hum them each to sleep. Once, Sam came home crying because his Spanish teacher had crossed out Cuban and written Spanish in red ink over the composer's nationality on his report. I immediately called her and set her straight. I was sitting up straight now watching Orlando pour more wine into my glass and hand me a bowl of the hot plantain soup. Ernesto was playing "Noche Azul."

"Sopa de plátanos? This is a surprise. Did you make it?"

I was surprised by his answer. Part of his new journey included digging up his Cuban roots. So he had made the soup from scratch, following a classic Nitza Villapol Cuban recipe. He showed me an old first edition of her cookbook as we started on the shrimp.

"What did you survive on in L.A.?"

"Boutique restaurants. There are hundreds of them, all stylishly contrived to give you an authentic culinary experience. In L.A. it's called an epiphany."

"Food for the gods?" I asked laughing.

"Food for the god wanna-bes!"

"So how deep were your roots buried?" We stopped laughing.

As he put some pâté on a piece of bread, I felt his foot rubbing against mine and I suddenly realized he had been using it as a scratching post for a while. I didn't bring it to his attention.

"Isabel," he said, still rubbing, which, for some reason, seemed romantic to me, "they were too deep, almost too deep to dig them up again."

"What made you want to start digging?"

He stopped eating and remained quiet. He stopped scratching too, but kept his foot on mine. I don't think he noticed.

"We're talking too much about me."

By the way he said this I could tell my question was too close to his truth, but I had already spilled my truths and now he had to trust me like I trusted him, so far.

"I missed my café con leche y pan cubano," he said looking into my eyes.

"I'm sure you can find those in L.A." I reached for his hand.

"It's not like Miami."

"I know."

"And it's not like you," he added, wrapping his fingers around mine.

I could feel he wanted to tell me something so I stayed quiet. I wanted to hear it. Maybe I needed to hear it.

"The last relationship I had, it took a lot out of me. Writers can be very demanding, emotionally," he said, almost like a warning.

"You're the only one I know, besides Julia I guess. And she's easy to get along with." I said this to him knowing there was nothing easy about what Julia was asking of me.

"Kelly was easy to get along with. That wasn't the problem. But our lives revolved around our work all of the time. We were on constantly. We had no life outside the world of getting our work sold. Our friends were really associates and get-togethers were really business deals and conversations were transactions scripted for maximum profit. Can you understand? All this was exciting at first, but each night when my head hit the pillow, I was more and more alone, and in the dark."

"And Kelly?"

"Kelly? She thrived on it," he said with a smile for a sigh.

"I meant," I hesitated.

"Because you're going to ask me," he joked, "it turned out I wasn't her type."

Where had I heard that before? I wondered what his type was as he looked out into the dark mirror of a sea.

"Last I heard she was living with an actor and still selling scripts out in L.A." After a few seconds of silence, he turned back toward me saying, "Enough about the past!"

"I can't imagine you living with a woman like that."

"Good. I can't either, just like I can't imagine you with David fifteen years."

"That's in . . ." The swaying of the boat made me fix my eyes on his. ". . . David is in the past, too," I said, really meaning it for the first time.

"Vamos, Isa . . ."

"Where do you want to go?"

As if coming out of a trance he whispered, ". . . we can't let this food go to waste."

I looked down at the food and, as if going into a trance, filled my plate and began to eat. We listened to the music, savoring the melody and the food in our mouths, in total silence. It was the kind of silence we both knew how to speak.

"Well?" asked Orlando after a while. "How do you like it? Say something!"

I wiped my lips with the napkin, swallowed my last bite, and said, "I'm speechless."

"Now there's a chef's best endorsement!"

"I've never been spoiled like this. I'm so full. La comida, the music, the *SeaLove*, it's . . ." I was going to say *perfect* but I knew better, when he finished the thought for me.

"For us."

He looked at me with that gentle expression in his eyes and said, "I wanted to celebrate for me, and for you. You've been through so much lately." He took my hand and I felt the weight of Mount Motherhood shift from under me as I shifted myself toward him. He was leaning closer toward me. I let my head lean back against the cabin wall. His face reached for mine. I closed my eyes, and I kissed him. I kissed him like a rock shifts, slowly and steadily, to where it finally wants to settle.

We shifted ourselves around the settee, still kissing. We avalanched ourselves onto the cabin floor where the green blanket had landed, still kissing. We settled on it in slow shifting motion, still kissing. Everything we did seemed a long series of slow movements. In my head, I could see everything my eyes could never take in if open and everything my lips could never, would never, say, not even to a priest.

I became weightless, falling like a smooth stone with no tierra firme to break my fall. I raised my arms and let him smoothly slide my camisole off. He unsnapped the front clasp of my bra and began to caress my breasts. With every gentle pull I felt the gravity of my resistance giving way. Blindly, yet knowing every move of my hands, I pulled his polo shirt over his head and then drew him to me, feeling his skin against mine.

Years of locked-up lust surged through every pore of my being and I did nothing to stop it. Kissing his chest, my lips slid along the curves of his muscles, then glided over the length of his neck, reaching his earlobe. I felt his breath bathe my neck with its warm fragrance. I became aware of his warm jeans as my hands reached to unbutton them. I reached for the depth of his maleness within and instantly knew, became aware of, felt in my hands' tenderness, and in his body's trust, sabía, down to the furthest reaches of my soul, that Orlando was for me.

We finished undressing each other, serenely exploring each other, trying to memorize every breath given and taken and every fold discovered with the touch of a hand or a lip. We felt at ease in each other's nakedness, without shame or fear. We kissed insatiably, letting desire take its fill as we entered each other's skin. It was only then that we opened our eyes to each other, becoming conscious of the silent love between us. His eyes asked, mine nodded. My yes was also to love and lust and to hope and fear and to trying again and maybe losing again and to forgetting everything and remembering only as if memory was a constant fadeout of the present moment, like a Polaroid in reverse. Our bodies slowly undulated and the ripples of our love swayed the SeaLove and I imagined the waves beneath her radiating in ever growing arcs toward the unknown. Falling into each other's passion, our whispered groans floated out of the cabin and over the silent sea. We embraced, as if for life, and I felt his vigor free itself within me. Every cell in my body screamed with delight. Exhausted, we fell asleep in each other's arms, ignoring the clanging bell that had been announcing all along the birth of a love finally allowed to breathe freely.

All I can say is that I woke up in his arms, naked to the core, except for our white socks. And all I can remember is that what I did that night with Orlando felt like what making love after twenty years of marriage must feel like after the puppy love and the lustful love and the power-tug-of-war love and the love-for-the-hell-of-it love are exhausted and your marriage is still whole and then your lovemaking becomes a savoring of the finest thing. I felt that thing with Orlando.

Looking down at our tangled socked feet I felt another thing. I felt a wave of panic hit me as I realized what I had done and what I had gone against. Coño y carajo, as I got up to the deck I realized that every other boater around us was flashlighting the *SeaLove* trying to figure out what the infierno all the bell ringing had been about. I had Orlando get me out of there like a bat out of Hell, except that in this instance, Hell had been Paradise.

⟆

"Forgive me, Father, for I have sinned."

"What is it, my child?" he asked in his still-heavy Irish accent, which right away told me it was Monsignor Rambo behind the little square grid. Right away, without any doubt, I knew God meant business. I lowered my voice and whispered into God's grated ear.

"I have committed adultery."

There was a long silence and I began to wonder if God had a hearing problem, but suddenly I heard Father Rambo's words clear as a bell.

"Isa, is that you? When did you get married? Wasn't your old marriage annulled?"

I was stunned into silence. I never knew a priest could just take off his mask and get personal with you like that, but Monsignor Rambo was not a go-by-the-book priest when it mattered most.

"I am not married . . . but I have been intimate with a man. Once." I managed to say this before my throat choked, but my tears couldn't hold back the feeling of shame at hearing myself say such a thing. I always considered myself a virgin because David was the only man I ever knew in that way. Now I knew Orlando and he knew me too—and I was having a hard time facing this. I couldn't believe the face on my father when I arrived three hours past nine that night.

"Where have you been?!" he asked in his boxer and T-shirt pajama ensemble. "We"—meaning David Jr. and him—"have been up waiting for you."

"Mami, I thought you were in an accident or something. By the way, I got here at eight-thirty," David Jr. said in his rubbing-it-in teenager way, figuring he'd have a three-hour credit on his next curfew.

"Isa, estoy muy viejo and cansado for this. Why didn't you call?"

"Why didn't you beep me?" I asked, shifting the blame away from me.

"No me hables de beep! Your mother refused to let me beep you. Yo no sé what is happening here."

"Where is she?" I asked, slowly making my way to my room followed by my two male watchdogs.

"Sleeping! At nine on the dot, she went to sleep. Durmiendo like a baby!"

"What did she say?"

"Algo de que you were in good hands. Yo no sé qué está pasando aquí. This would have never happened in Cuba!" he mumbled as he disappeared into his room. I gave David Jr. a none-of-your-business don't-you-even-dare-mess-with-this look, which he took in by smiling at me in his boy/man kind of face.

"Isa, can we do this face to face?" Monsignor asked.

What the hell, I thought to myself, it's all out so why not put a face on it. We shifted to the corner of the confessional and sat in two little chairs. I felt him looking at me, because I couldn't look at him, over the little round table. Everything was small and intimate and I felt like I was back on Orlando's boat. The thought of such a thought in the confessional made my face burn.

Monsignor took both of my hands saying,

"Really, the sin you have committed is the sin of Fornication; so has the fellow you committed it with, by the way. Just a thought, mind you, just a thought. Fornication, now that's a bad sin indeed. Yes it is, that Fornication."

Awful word to pile up on somebody's back, but I have to confess that what I did with Orlando didn't feel like Fornication. Pero to hear it with an Irish accent made the word feel heavier than the Great Pyramid at Giza. The back of my Catholic soul was about to break when Father Rambo's next words broke through my burning-in-everlasting-Hell ears.

"But there is a worse sin than Fornication, and that is Fornication without love. Do you get my meaning in this, Isa? Do you love this fellow you Fornicated with?"

For the first time in the confessional I looked up at God's eyes, which in this case were as green as an Irish spring, and I felt myself nodding yes.

"You do, do you? Does he feel the same way about you? Well then, if this fellow has any sea legs to him he'll sail his way to an act of contrition as well."

"What do I have to do?" I asked, wondering how sailing got into this confession, and then I remembered God works in mysterious ways. I got the feeling He wasn't just turning pages here.

"Stop Fornicating, forgive yourself and . . . let him go."

What I said to him next came from someplace inside me that I forgot about long ago.

"But, Father, I love this man."

"Let him go, Isa . . . and see where he lands. God bless you and for your penance do one Our Father and two Hail Marys and, Isa . . ."

"Yes, Father?"

"Take care of yourself."

⎯⁓⎯

Do priests and mothers have some sort of psychic connection? Maybe I should have gone to Mercy's Walter Mercado for relief. I went to confession thinking God would take care of me pero qué me dijo? Cuídate. Qué carajo was I supposed to do with that? Where's the relief? An Irish priest and a Cuban mother were both telling me, qué cosa, they were commanding me, to take care. Take care of what? Of business? Of my kids? Of my reputation? Of my faith? Of myself? Of everybody and their kitchen sink? Coño, after a day's worth of making a living, I moonlight at taking care of everyone else's living. And now I slipped up, I let my guard down, me desnudé in God's closet, and I didn't get any relief. I didn't get what God and mami were asking of me. And then it hit me like only a gallo fino could, fast and furious and on the mark. "Cuídate and let him go," they had said, creating a paradox of the heart only a soul could understand. And my alma was finally screaming with understanding. It understood I was in love. I was in love and I was petrified to the core because of what I had to do, but I had to do it. I had to do it for my kids, for my parents, for myself, and for Orlando, and because it was a calculation I had to take to its result.

I called Orlando the very next day. He was in his bed on the rocking *SeaLove* and I was on my bed in my grounded house. It was five-thirty in the morning and we hadn't talked since that night. I had something to say to him and I said it.

"Orlando? I need to tell you something."

"What is it, Isabel?"

"What happened that night—" I said while my voice lowered itself against my will.

"I can't get it out of my head," he interrupted.

"Me too."

We both stayed quiet.

"You were saying something to me, Isabel."

"What happened that night," I whispered on, "can't happen again."

There was a long and loud silence on the line. That silence was screaming into my heart everything I was fearing to hear. But I went ahead anyway.

"Orlando?"

"Yes, Isabel?"

"I don't know what you want . . . but I want us . . . to wait." I said it.

He stayed quiet, then he said, "Isabel."

I got into it.

"I'll understand if you can't, or don't want to, or it's not a step in your new plan, or you aren't ready for kids, or I'm divorced, or Kelly is still ghosting around, or the timing is off, or the stars were too aligned—"

"Isabel."

"I want us to wait."

"Isabel."

"Sí?"

"That's what I want too. But—"

"What?"

"Can we wait together?"

Chapter 22

—⟨⟩⟨⟩⟨⟩—

Lucinda

*L*ucinda sat in the Adirondack chair at the end of the wooden pier, her eyes closed to the sun. She could hear the tidewater sloshing against the wooden pilings beneath the pier that stretched out one hundred feet beyond the island. Little Palm Island was small enough for fifteen cottages and an intimate restaurant, which was one of its main attractions. The other was its complete isolation from life's calendar. Time was kept by the meals of the day, and by the length of a conversation spoken in whispers. Lucinda faintly heard the voices of a young couple wading in the crescent-shaped beach to the left of the pier. A recent storm had increased the sand's hold on the land against the ocean's relentless pull.

She opened her eyes and let the sun's unwavering light bring the couple into focus. They looked like love ought to look, she thought to herself, alone, in the company of two. She heard, beyond their solitude and from beyond the reefs, the propeller noise of the single-engine Cessna seaplane. Lucinda watched as the seaplane came into sharper focus. The sound of the mechanical gull intruding on the natural landscape reminded her of the day the bank helicopter hovered over la finca. Her pulse accelerated as she watched it circle the island to make its approach. Lucinda stood up. The plane skied onto the water, a quarter of a mile away from the pier. She thought about Carlos inside. This time she had invited him on her terms. He agreed to stay for two nights.

As she waited for the seaplane to slowly reach the boat landing, Lucinda leaned on one of its posts. She could just make out Carlos' head framed by the passenger-side window beneath the seaplane's wing. They had started talking to each other again over the phone. At first, the conversations were about the children. Once in a while they had seen each other at school functions. Lately, they had met a few times for lunch. Because of this, Isa was sure Gabriela was out of the picture, but to Lucinda, the picture had been branded in her mind too clearly to let promises and time blur it out of existence. Suffering needs its space, her father was fond of saying whenever a bad storm damaged his finca or Doña Rosario prepared the almuerzo herself.

At one of their recent lunches, Carlos had made it clear he wanted a second chance. She wasn't surprised, but Lucinda had been skeptical. It was one thing to say it, and another thing to make it so, and yet another to make the thing disappear—that thing that had lodged itself in the folds of her heart like a thick tumor. He had suggested they get away, just to talk. This was different, she thought to herself. There he was, in his business suit, sitting across from her in that restaurant, asking to get away, just the two of them with no Bank around their ankles. She looked at him, and even though the picture of his infidelity filtered her sight as if it had etched itself into the very lenses of her eyes, she agreed, so long as she made all of the arrangements.

Little Palm Island off the Florida Keys had come to her mind. It was a crazy thought. The place was where she had wanted to celebrate their twentieth wedding anniversary. She never told Carlos about it. But now it was a place where she had come to see if another day of marriage was still possible. The thought of a freshly painted Easter egg came into her mind as the little seaplane, with its red and blue stripes painted on its white shell, continued its approach. She noticed what the pilot was doing to get in; it was fragile maneuvering over a choppy sea. Lucinda realized that's why it was taking so long. She also realized the pilot was a woman. The seaplane slowly bobbed its way toward the island.

It was an isolated island with no bridges, no roads, no TVs, no telephones, no kids, and no memories. It was a new place for the both of them, with only a few scattered thatched-roof villas clothed in luxuriant tropical vegetation, a five-star restaurant overlooking the sea, and room service from morning to midnight.

An old college friend, Paul Royall, had recently taken the position as manager of the "small luxury hideaway" as he put it. She had called him a few weeks ago to explain her situation. He had agreed to set everything up for her at the Relais & Chateaux resort. And though it was expensive, Lucinda wanted to handle the charges herself. Paul, who since their New York college days was described as "the red Englishman" because of his inability to brown up even under a tropical sun, gave her an old friend's discounted rate.

At first, they had agreed to fly down together on the appointed morning. Carlos called the night before. He had an unexpected meeting that same morning so he would be arriving on an afternoon flight instead. Lucinda's first inclination was to cancel the plans.

"So early in the game and Carlos is already making excuses," Lucinda had said to Isa on the phone after hearing his reason.

"El punto is that he's still showing up. David skipped an entire country on me."

She took a deep breath at her amiga's words and agreed to go on with the "Resurrection Weekend" as Mercy had put it.

Standing at the pier by the edge of her chair, Lucinda wondered, as she watched Carlos stepping out of the Cessna, whether her heart's palpitations were for a resurrected love or were the drums to a requiem. The second thing she noticed was that he was still wearing his dark banker's pants and white long-sleeved shirt, and that he was not wearing a tie or a jacket. In his left hand, he gripped the black leather briefcase Lucinda had given him three birthdays ago. As he walked down the pier, he talked to the thirty-something pilot, a youthful-looking woman with a ponytail and shorts. Lucinda caught his attention from where she stood. He turned and walked toward her.

"Hola," he said as he wrapped his arm around her waist and kissed her on the cheek. "You've been waiting long?"

"No, I had lunch with Paul," she said as she slightly moved away from his arm.

"Paul?" he asked as they started to walk down the pier toward the restaurant, which was the first structure seen upon arriving at the island.

"Paul Royall, the manager, that friend of mine from college . . . I told you about him."

"Sí, I remember now."

"You had a good trip?" Lucinda asked, feeling as if they were new acquaintances instead of a couple long married.

"These seaplanes are amazing. The island looks beautiful from the sky," he said, then adding as he stopped to look at Lucinda, "almost as beautiful as you."

Lucinda tried to hold back a smile. She was wondering whether he had come here to seduce her, or to pretend nothing was wrong, or to start something new. Julia would probably say all three. He was looking at her dress. Lucinda chose to wear a sleeveless tight-fitting tropical-print dress with canvas open-toe sandals. She had wanted to wear her usual jeans and cotton shirts, but Isa had talked her into setting a different mood for herself with the new attire. Lucinda wasn't sure what mood she was trying to set for herself, but she went ahead with the suggestion. By the way he came dressed, Carlos was obviously still in a business mood, Lucinda thought to herself as he spoke.

"I had no time to pack," he said, looking into the restaurant through its glassed wooden door. "Is there a place where I can buy some stuff to just get by?"

"The Island Store is around that turn." Lucinda pointed at the pathway barely wide enough for two.

"You've been here before?"

"No. I did my exploration while you were in your business meeting. If you'd like, I'll give you the tour."

Their first stop was the island's small shop for a pair of shorts and other beach gear for Carlos. When he was done selecting the items, he approached the clerk to pay. Lucinda noticed him pulling out the bank's American Express card. On the way out the door, Carlos' cellular phone rang. He moved to the end of the store's roofed deck and answered it. Lucinda heard his loud whispers but did not care to listen. She saw him shake his head and hang up. He apologized to her and promised to turn it off for the rest of their days on the island. She shrugged her shoulders and walked ahead.

"Lucinda, perdóname. There's a mini-crisis going on at the Bank because I'm—"

"Because estás aquí? So everything is falling apart at the Bank, right? What a coincidence."

Carlos made it a point to turn off the cellular in front of her. From the store they walked past the free-form pool with its floating red hibiscus flowers. They walked past a few of the raised South Sea–style cottages sprouting from the sandy ground among the full-grown coconut trees.

"This looks more like a South Pacific island than a Florida Key," said Carlos looking up at the palm trees towering over the thatched roofs. "I feel like a castaway," he added as they reached the suite Paul had reserved for Lucinda. She turned toward Carlos as they both reached for her bag.

"Let go of it. I can carry it myself." Lucinda lifted the small suitcase, which had been delivered to the front door that morning.

She could tell by the look on Carlos' face he was impressed by the villa. He followed her in as she walked across the rattan and colonial furnished living room, past the large bathroom with its Jacuzzi tub, and into the bedroom. How many times had she entered a one-bedroom villa on her travels with Carlos? And yet, this time, she was conscious of her feelings as she walked to the closet, putting her bag down. She felt a wanting, a wanting to have him as if nothing had happened, as they always had each other in these traveler's bedrooms. Watching him place his shopping bag on the bamboo writer's desk, she felt another thing. She felt repulsion at the thought of his body in the arms of another woman, a body that had always been there for her intimate pleasures. She noticed the shutters' shadows stripe across his bent-over back as he pulled out the rubber sandals from the bag. She turned toward the shutters feeling sad.

The luxuriant greens of the fishtail palms, the ferns, and the heliconia bushes surrounding the villa seeped in through the wall-to-wall windows in the bedroom. Looking through the slits of the shutters, Lucinda realized the room felt like a tree house. She then lifted the mosquito netting on the four-post king-size bed and picked up the box of seashell Godiva chocolates nesting on the pillows. She read the note from Paul Royall welcoming them to the island. She handed the note to Carlos. It included the time of sunset and sunrise, the weather, and the schedule of activities for the day. Carlos pointed to the Queen Anne dresser where Paul had left a freshly uncorked bottle of White Star champagne on ice. It was framed by two etched flutes. She could feel in her hands the slender outlines of the egret pair on each glass. There was a time when that would have felt romantic, when those graceful birds would have been a drawing of themselves. Lucinda erased the image from her mind.

She filled the glasses and handed one to Carlos. They drank to a silent toast, each not knowing what the other wished for.

"Y ahora qué?" asked Carlos, removing his shoes.

"We should go outside. Paul's note said something about a rainy sunset."

"Can we talk?"

Feeling uneasy, Lucinda unpacked while Carlos began to undress. They ended up sitting side by side at the foot of the bed. Carlos reached for Lucinda's hand. She did not withdraw it this time. They sat looking at the wall of green, sliced by the brown of the shutters, without speaking. To Lucinda, it was as if the immensity of the foliage outside mirrored the space of the silence between them. She noticed the sky slowly turning gray. Finally, Carlos spoke.

"It feels good here, Lucinda, even overcast," he said, pointing to the sky with his face.

"Sí," she answered. She felt something too. In spite of their troubles and their separation, it felt good to be next to each other again. For an instant, it felt right. Her uneasy feeling was suddenly displaced by una nostalgia. Lucinda leaned her head on his shoulder. Carlos caressed her hair. Lucinda stood up to close the bedroom shutters. She turned to him, letting her dress crumple down around her ankles. Carlos held Lucinda by her naked arms and pulled her to him. She let him kiss her and she felt herself kissing him back. There was no time to linger. Fear and remembrance and hope and desire and wanting to possess him again all colluded to overpower her. Lucinda let herself go, but her mind held on to everything she was doing.

They fell back on the bed, passionately groping each other. Desperately and deliberately, Lucinda ran her palms all over his body. She was like a blind lover, reading the Braille of his body, feeling for what his love had once meant. She was trying to recover a lifetime of embraces. Every touch was marked by a longing, a longing for those long-ago encounters before the compromises, the disappointments, and the betrayal had wedged themselves between them. His naked body evoked a familiar pleasure in Lucinda that gushed from deep within her loins. She ached for what was once all hers, but the very force of her delight served to more deeply mark the pain.

All throughout the lovemaking, Lucinda had kept her eyes open; she knew he had kept his closed. Lucinda got up from the bed, put on the guest robe, and sat on the corner lounge chair.

"Por qué, why did you do it? Tell me, Carlos."

"You've asked me that mil veces," he answered, still lying in bed.

"And you've given me a thousand answers but not the truth."

"Lucinda, I don't know what else to say. I was lost—I was confused—I was wrong."

"Were you in love with her?"

Lucinda didn't like his hesitation.

"Lucinda, our lovemaking, it felt like always."

"Ese es el problema. It's not like always anymore," answered Lucinda, thinking of her in-laws and the Bank y esa mujer.

She abruptly got up, adding, "It's late. I'm going to shower."

When she came out, Carlos had put on the blue shorts he'd bought and had the tails of his white shirt tied around his waist. Before she could say anything, he quickly suggested they take a walk.

While they strolled along the palm-lined gravel paths of the island, they made small talk about its landscape, their children, their friends, avoiding the complicated topics pulling at them. On the Atlantic side of the island, protected by a wide marshy sandbar, a long dock paralleling the shore harbored several boats. They lingered there.

"Remember how you always wanted one for yourself?"

"I never got around to it."

They continued exploring the island, wandering onto a more isolated spot, where a small Cheekee hut had been built among the bushes for outdoor massages.

"Why don't you have one done tomorrow?" Carlos asked.

"I don't think there are enough fingers in the world to weed out the tension—in me," she answered, really wanting to say "between us."

They stopped to watch a solitary white ibis probing the wet sand with its curved orange-pink beak as the waves washed up around its long crimson legs. They stood quietly watching the bird make its lonely way along the shoreline. They made their way along the footpath quietly, not holding hands. Back in the suite, Carlos and Lucinda refreshed themselves for the dinner being prepared in the restaurant.

"Good evening! Hello, Mr. and Mrs. Colón. Choose any table you see," directed the hostess. Lucinda let Carlos make the choice. They sat in a dark corner by the terrace window. The candlelight reflected off the framed paintings of the island hanging on the wall next to them. Beyond the restaurant terrace, Lucinda could see the moon reflected on the shallow water below. A guitarist played Caribbean blues as Carlos and Lucinda ordered their meal from the select menu. The seven-course meal took two hours to take in. The flowing in and out of the various meal attendants, all employed in serving every course deftly, gave Lucinda the impression of being looked after, of being nursed. For those two hours, Little Palm Island was giving her a respite from the phantoms haunting her mind. It was a welcome distraction and helped to ease some of the tension between them.

"Funny, how strangers in a strange place can make one feel at home," said Lucinda. They hadn't spoken much throughout the meal.

"It releases us."

"What are you saying with that?"

"We can just concentrate on each other."

She looked out past the terrace, tracing the reflected moonbeam on the sea, wondering where all of this had started.

"Lucinda." Carlos broke her concentration.

"Bueno, I just want to concentrate on these desserts," Lucinda replied, not hiding her smile.

"Una sonrisa! Are you smiling at what I said, or at the chocolate soufflé in front of you?" he asked, smiling back.

"There used to be a time when I'd smile at both. Pero ahora, I'm just smiling at one."

Carlos was about to ask which, but the waiter's hand holding the check inside the leather fold interrupted him. Lucinda, taking the last spoonful of soufflé in front of her, waited. He pulled out his wallet and gestured toward the waiter. The young man explained that meals were taken care of as part of the special package selected. They just wanted them to sign for the billing. Lucinda reached over and signed off on the check. Carlos protested, shoving the Bank's American Express card back in his wallet; he didn't say another word.

"Delicious dessert, wasn't it?" asked Lucinda. Carlos did not answer.

When they returned to the room, they found their bedding turned over. On it lay a note with information about the next day's weather and activities along with a shiny large tulip shell. They went about the suite that first night, each one getting ready for bed, not talking much. Carlos sat in the living room couch wrapped in the provided white robe, his feet propped on the coffee table, reading a magazine. Lucinda lay on the bed, her legs under the beige blanket, looking up at the tulle draping down along the posts of the bed. She wasn't crying, but she felt as if she just had. Reaching out for the lamp chain, she pulled on it.

A while later the motion of Carlos lying down beside her brought her out of the shallow sleep she was wrestling with. For a time she heard his shallow breathing and knew he wasn't sleeping either.

"When did it change for us?" she asked.

"I don't know."

"When did labels become so important?"

"What labels?"

"Banker, Wife, Don, Socialite, Firstborn. They have become tags to our souls just like all those designer tags our clothes carry around. When, Carlos, did our love get tagged?"

"Lucinda, a pesar de todo, I love you."

"In spite of Gabriela?" she said the name out loud for the first time. The sound of the name seemed amplified by the silence of the island. Gabriela's face filled the darkness in Lucinda's mind.

"Ya eso se terminó. Lucinda, why bring that up again?"

"Why did you do it, to us, Carlos, why?"

Carlos turned on his side, away from Lucinda. After a long silence he answered, "I don't know what else to tell you. What else can I do? I'm here, no?"

Lucinda turned on her side, away from him. She did not respond. The last thing she remembered thinking, before the quiet tears brought sleep, was "Yes, you are here, but the answer isn't."

When a hint of light slithered between the wooden shutters, Lucinda woke up, put on her robe, and sat on the porch to watch the sunrise. The morning quiet soothed her mind, cluttered by the noise of a restless sleep. She had prepared for this encounter, but the feelings of betrayal and fear kept diverting her from her goal. This marriage could be saved, she thought, looking at the rocks a few feet away forming Little Palm Island's bayside shore. But the realization that their love's second chance was in his hands, hands that still grasped the tags that defined the life she wanted to reject, took her breath away. Taking deep breaths trying to center herself, she focused on the band of white clouds rising far in the horizon. Her muscles loosened their grip on her peace as she let the sound of the waves rolling over the rocks smooth away the jaggedness of her fears. Their hypnotic rhythm calmed her down until, slowly, she began to feel in control again.

The room-service attendant delivered breakfast right at the appointed hour. Lucinda watched him transform the porch table into an elegant breakfast setting. The white tablecloth stirred in the morning air just as a formation of pelicans flew low over the water. Thanking the attendant, she went to awaken Carlos. In their matching robes, they sat down to eat. The vegetable omelet with rosemary potatoes, fruit salad, croissants, fresh orange juice, and coffee was more than they had expected. Touching her hand under the table, Carlos spoke.

"This is magnificent. Gracias. Last night, I was thinking—of what you were saying. I know how hard this must be."

"Some good has to salir de esto."

"I fixed it so you can keep the Jaguar."

Lucinda looked up trying to swallow what he was saying.

"You can keep the Jaguar."

"I don't want it! I don't need it. I already bought a car. I'll drop off the Jaguar on Tuesday when I pick up the new one."

"You didn't have to do that."

"You still don't get it, do you?"

"What?"

"I don't want a life with the bank anymore. I have a new life."

"What about me?" Carlos asked looking up at her.

"That's up to you," Lucinda answered, holding his gaze.

"What do you mean?"

"I can't tell you what to do. You have to decide."

"I have decided. You know there was nothing between me and Gabriela. That's over. A mistake. It won't happen again."

"It always does, Carlos. Just look at a few of your associates back home."

"You have my word."

"I had your word before, Carlos, at the altar, eh?"

"I'm sorry."

"I'm sorry too! You killed something inside of me, I'm in mourning for our love. Coño, Carlos!"

"Don't say that, Lucinda."

"Es cierto. You want me to take you back pero my trust is gone. It's that simple. I don't trust you. I don't trust your family. I'm barely trusting myself!"

"I want you to let me try again. I want you to come home." Carlos reached for her hand. Lucinda pulled it away.

"If that's how you feel, why are we even here then?" Carlos continued.

"I don't know. I guess I hoped you'd see things my way."

"I want to."

"You aren't who you used to be."

"People change."

"Not always for the good."

"I'm not the only one that's changed."

"What is that supposed to mean?"

"You stopped painting. And you used to be idealistic and spontaneous and—"

"Like Gabriela?"

"That's not what I mean. You left no room for anything but the children and the house, like one of those matronas you make fun of."

"I became a matrona because you became a matrón! Mistress and all—"

"I did it for all of you! I've given you a good life."

"It's a borrowed life! Can't you see that? It's not the life I fell in love with. It's not the life we had planned for each other."

"What do you want from me?" asked Carlos, reaching over the table, wiping the tears on her face. He got up and stood behind her, folding his arms across her chest. Lucinda leaned her head against his left arm.

"I want my life back—our life back, as we started it, before it was seduced away."

Lucinda grabbed a clean napkin from the table and motioned Carlos to sit down.

"Are you satisfied with your life?" she asked, drying her eyes. She saw his becoming wet. The food was long ago cold. He sucked back his tears before answering.

"Lucinda, I'm—"

"Shit, Carlos! Give me a real answer!"

"Damn it, Lucinda!" he yelled, turning his face from side to side. He pushed back his chair from the table. He made a motion to get up, but didn't.

"There's nowhere to go on this island. We made a commitment to talk," Lucinda said.

Carlos didn't talk.

"What are you thinking? Such a simple question. There was a time when that question was a reality check for us, remember?" She reached for his hand and gently held it in hers.

"We used to always ask that question whenever we'd find ourselves where we didn't want to be. Where are you, Carlos? Do you really want to be there?"

"Leave the Bank . . . throw away everything I've worked for?" he asked more to the island than to Lucinda.

"What do you have to show for it? A broken marriage and a house you don't even own."

"You're being unfair."

"You know I'm right."

"Start all over again?"

"I'm doing it."

"What would the family say?"

Lucinda slumped back on the iron and reed chair. She threw the crumpled napkin on the unfinished breakfast dish.

"That's it, isn't it, La Familia?" Carlos asked, looking up at her from across the table.

Before she could answer, Paul Royall strolled up the path toward their cottage.

"How's the island treating you?" He waved at them.

"Good morning, Paul," Lucinda called out, composing herself. "Come, meet—my husband, Carlos." She waved back.

"Hello, it's a pleasure to meet you," Carlos said, politely extending his hand. "Won't you join us for some coffee?"

"No thank you. I just stopped by to see if you were enjoying yourselves."

"Definitely," answered Lucinda. Carlos nodded.

"Everyone has been so courteous and so helpful."

"Good. That's what I like to hear! I also came by to tell you the boat for the snorkeling trip will be leaving in thirty minutes. I took the liberty of scheduling it for you. You still want to go out to the reefs, don't you?"

"Yes. I had forgotten. I'm glad you reminded me," Lucinda was saying, looking over at Carlos. She hadn't told him anything about it.

"How about equipment?" Carlos asked.

"The captain has all that. Just meet him at the Atlantic Dock. Thirty minutes, but don't worry, he'll wait." Paul winked at them as he left to make his inspection rounds.

"Snorkeling? That brings back memories. Skinny-dipping in Las Minitas reefs?" Carlos teased, recalling their early marriage home vacations in La Romana Resort.

Lucinda playfully grabbed at Carlos' backside.

"Do that again and I'll be diving into your ocean!" Carlos responded.

"Qué corny," she answered, turning toward the door.

With little time to get ready, Carlos and Lucinda quickly changed into their bathing suits. When they got to the dock they realized no one else had signed up for the four-hour trip.

"Maybe that's what Paul was winking about."

"You think?" replied Lucinda.

The captain guided them onto the boat. "The Looe Key National Marine Sanctuary is rated among the ten best reefs in the world. You know, it is the only living reef of its kind in the entire North American continent. You're sitting at the bow? It's going to get a bit wet, folks."

As they headed out to the reefs, Carlos and Lucinda sat on the bow of the open-decked thirty-foot dive boat. Its massive engine roared so loudly they had to graze each other's ears with their lips in order to be heard. Lucinda held on to the railing as the boat bounced across the choppy waters. Carlos, seeing her struggling to keep her balance, moved closer and reminded her to ride the waves like a horse, letting her legs absorb the blows instead of her rear. Lucinda grabbed the anchor line and did just that. She felt exhilarated and loosened her hair to feel the wind rush through it as her body found the perfect rhythm. It was almost like being back in la finca galloping on Sonora, she thought to herself. She could feel Carlos watching her with an intensity she hadn't felt in years. She turned to him and broke into a smile. He placed his hand on her thigh.

Ahead they began to see other boats moored next to diving flags. The water beneath now took on a light aquamarine tone as they slowed down over the translucent bottom. The captain moored the boat just off the edge of a large clump of reefs. The chop had now turned to swells, causing the dive boat to rise and fall with every roll of a humpbacked wave. After briefing them on proper dive procedures, the captain helped them get geared up.

Lucinda felt a queasiness in her stomach. She ignored it and rushed to put on her equipment.

"Estás bien?" Carlos asked.

"As soon as I get into the water, I'll be fine." Lucinda waved him off.

"OK folks, you're all set for a go. We have forty-five minutes on this side of the ocean. Swim against the current for a while, that way you'll drift back toward the boat. If you get too tuckered out, give me the signal and I'll go pick you up."

They nodded from behind the masks and jumped into the water, first swimming away from the boat toward the middle of the reefs. Lucinda felt the force of the swells against her as she tried to keep up with Carlos. She grabbed his hand and swam alongside him, watching the colorful explosion of marine life passing beneath them. The ridge of coral lay about ten feet below the surface. In spite of the strong current, they dove to get a closer look, staying as long as they could hold their breaths. Lucinda did not feel better. She focused on the school of bright angelfish darting about, the entire group turning on a dime. Carlos pointed at a solitary barracuda swimming beneath her. Lucinda pointed to the surface. She tried to speak in spite of the water slapping her.

"I'm not feeling well," she managed to say, treading water.

"It must be the swells. Are you seasick? Do you want to go back to the boat?" Carlos pointed to it about 200 feet away.

"No, I'll try a little longer."

They descended again. Lucinda tried to concentrate on the stillness below the surface as she watched the sun's rays give life to the reef. But she felt her body being pulled back and forth by the waters above. Carlos swam ahead toward a pair of small manta rays. Excitedly he turned to Lucinda and gestured for her to follow. She couldn't. The pull of the current made her dizzy and she felt the nauseousness rising in her throat. She tore the mask from her face and furiously tried to reach the surface. That's all she could remember until she realized she was somehow back on the boat.

"What's wrong?" she heard the captain asking.

"Let's go," she heard Carlos order.

"Are you OK?"

She shook her head as again she tasted the morning's breakfast in her mouth. Carlos rinsed her under the boat's outdoor shower, taking her vest off.

"Feeling better?" he asked.

"I don't think so."

"She has a bad case of seasickness. Solid ground will take care of that," the captain reassured them.

The trip back felt endless as Lucinda struggled against the moving horizon and her own ailing body. Carlos wrapped a towel around her and snuggled her within his arms. She rested her head against his chest.

"I'm so sorry. I ruined the trip. I wanted it to be a nice surprise. We didn't even get to go to the second spot."

"Don't worry," he said brushing a strand of wet hair from her face.

"If you've seen one reef you've seen them all. Además," he continued, "I came out here to be with you. I don't care what we do." Carlos lifted her right hand and kissed it softly, twice.

Lucinda tried to smile but she felt too lightheaded and weak. She slept all the way back to the dock.

Once in the villa, Carlos helped her rinse off the saltwater in the outside shower. After he dried her, he walked her to the bed.

"No, no clothes," she whispered because she was too dizzy to sound loud. He tenderly tucked in the sheets around her.

"Just rest for a while. You'll feel better soon."

Lucinda fell asleep still feeling her body swaying in the water. She woke to find Carlos sitting by her side, watching her.

"How long was I asleep?"

"About four hours. How do you feel?"

"Better. Hungry."

"I thought so. I had room service bring a couple of sandwiches and fruit salads. You should see the sizes, they're as big as that barracuda we saw!"

"Por favor, don't remind me of the ocean for a while, eh?"

They both laughed. Lucinda propped herself on her elbows and tried to get off the bed. Carlos stopped her. She slowly lay back on the mound of pillows. The look on his face detracted her attention from the slight dizziness she was feeling.

"What's wrong?" she asked.

"When I saw you so sick in the water, I was afraid, really afraid of losing you."

"How did you get me to the boat?"

"I swam you over. I was so nervous I forgot the damned distress signal the captain showed us."

"Did I faint in the water?"

"When I turned around the second time to show you the rays, your mask was off. You were sinking. Shit, I've never been so scared in my life. I swam over and lifted you to the surface. I kept calling your name, but you didn't answer." He leaned over her breasts.

"It was too close, Lucinda, too close."

She buried his head with her embrace and whispered over his back, "Why did you do it, Carlos?"

His shoulders heaving, she could feel his hot, heavy breaths blowing against her chest, the warm expelled air rushing its way down the length of her torso. In her arms, he felt like a raging storm trying to rein itself in. She held on tighter to him. The realization of what he was saying came upon her slowly, like the lull before a hurricane. Then it hit her.

"Ay, —mi Lucinda—all these years—oh God—el Banco—La Familia—our life—I thought, for the kids, for you—I miss them tanto, I miss you—she means nothing to me—te lo juro—mi Lucinda— estoy perdido—so much—oh God—I don't know, no sé what I've become—what I am—I'm lost—no la amo, I don't love her— perdóname—please, please—I'm losing you, I love you—oh God, I don't want to lose you."

The fury of his tears flooded Lucinda's senses, filling her with his pain and overflowing hers to a point where she felt her soul break open. The rage drained out of her not in a vengeful torrent, but in a slow and steady rain, and she felt herself like water divided into an infinity of raindrops, each drop washing away the doubt from her. She cried along with him. Lifting his head from her bosom, she kissed his face over and over again.

"We need to work this through together. Just you and I," she whispered in his ear.

Hearing her words, Carlos sighed loudly as if the weight of an unspeakable thing had been lifted off his back.

"Where do we begin, this journey to each other?"

"This island, with its sea, with its silence, was a first step, no?"

Carlos lay low on the bed next to her, resting his head on her stomach. He could hear its tightness within. Lucinda stroked his hair. Both fell asleep exhausted and spent from the emotional downpour they had just come through. The only sound heard in the room was that of the ceiling fan spinning cool air down on them.

Lucinda awoke first. Looking down the length of her body, she saw Carlos curled on his side, using her thighs for a pillow, his face toward her. She watched him in silence, feeling his breath on her upper thighs.

She looked away. He opened his eyes.

"I'm hungry," he said after a while, not moving.

"It's getting dark outside," she responded.

"Are you hungry?"

"Sí." She smiled down at him. With a little lift of her legs she shook him off her thighs.

"I meant lunch. You want to eat the sandwiches I ordered about ten years ago?" He smiled back.

"It's our last night on the island. Let's have a grand dinner."

She sat up with her legs dangling off the side of the bed. Carlos crawled up, kneeling behind her. He brushed aside her hair and nibbled at the nape of her neck.

"No hay nada so sweet as making grand love after a grand meal," he said, all the while running his lips down her back. She felt the goose bumps rising off her skin and she felt the thing weighing her heart down slowly rising as well. With a shake of her back, he stopped.

"Want to eat in?" he asked.

"No, let's say good-bye to Little Palm Island on its own terms."

"Qué?"

"Come."

"Adónde?"

"We'd better go shower for dinner." She took him by the hand.

"If you insist. Let's go." Carlos looked at Lucinda with a suspicious glance.

A door connected the bathroom to the open-air shower enclosed by a large bamboo stall. It was wide enough for two people to bathe in comfortably. Carlos grabbed their still-wet bathing suits hanging off the towel rack, stopping before the door Lucinda had just opened.

"What are you doing with those?" she asked.

He had begun to undress.

"If we're going to shower outside, we'd better be decent."

"Give me those." Lucinda threw the bathing suits into the Jacuzzi tub and walked out. She stood under the warm shower first.

"See? Nadie can see through the bamboo," she said as she lathered her hair with the resort's shampoo. She felt Carlos' eyes on her.

"Además, let them see what a Dominican bathing beauty really looks like."

The shampoo's lather glided off her head as she rinsed it under the shower, her eyes closed. Carlos stood naked beside her, waiting. She peeked at him watching the sun setting. He no longer had the thin limber body of the young man she had married. He was fuller, yet still had the broad back and the solid chest she enjoyed so much. She handed him the shampoo. A light breeze sneaked in through the bamboo stalks. They looked at each other, shivering under the sky and the thatch roof overhang, smiling, both remembering the early days of their love when no shower was too small to keep them apart. Carlos took the soap from her hand and bathed her arms, her back, every part of her, as he had done so many times before. She did the same for him. They stood under the shower together, letting the water flow over their heads and off their shoulders, forming a fine mist around them. It was a familiar mist to her, a watery cocoon that had protected their love before they had become too busy, too distant, too sophisticated to speak of such things. She felt it forming itself again. He took her by the waist and kissed her. With that kiss came a deluge of jumbled emotions all tugging at her fear and at her hope. She tried tugging at her tears but their weight was too much. Under the shower, tasting Carlos in her mouth, recognizing him again, her tears flowed down her face along with the water. She could feel Carlos' desire pressing itself against her own body's. They leaned against the smooth bamboo wall, their nakedness taking on the delicate salmon hue of the sunset clouds.

"No, not now, después," she whispered in his ear.

"Está bien, mi Lucinda," he whispered back, tasting the wetness on her ear one last time.

"Carlos, really!" She pushed him under the shower.

"Ha! It's still hot, so forget about a cold shower saving you."

"Then a cold dinner will." And with that, she turned off the water and threw a towel at him.

⟶

"Why are we taking a towel to dinner?" he asked.

"You'll see." She smiled as she took his arm to walk down the path to the restaurant. The hostess led them out to the terrace, down its steps, and onto the beach.

"Give us the table farthest out to sea," Lucinda directed the hostess who took their shoes and instructed Carlos to roll up his pants.

The tide was out, allowing tables to be placed out in the ankle-deep water. Carlos and Lucinda waded to the table she wanted.

Sitting down, their view unobstructed by anything man-made, Lucinda felt as if she was suspended in God's firmament. The blazing orange of the already set sun cast a fiery dome over their heads, matching the firelight of the torches reflected on the watery sand.

"It's as if they were lighting up the sky." Lucinda pointed to the flaming tiki torches planted about.

"I feel like I've left the earth." Carlos took her hand to his face.

Lucinda felt transported a million miles away from Miami, a million miles away from her pain. She looked at Carlos and was startled by what she saw. Looking at him, she saw an image she had not recognized in too long a time. It was an image of Carlos without his suit on, without the weapons of technology—the cellular phones, the laptops, the briefcases—that had kept him on the front lines of the endless war that was the Bank and away from each other. Looking at him, sitting there with his business pants rolled up to his knees, with his stale white shirt wrinkled from exposure to the elements—the sand, the surf, the sea—she recognized her lover once again.

She felt his warm hands on hers. She felt the wet sand between their touching toes. And she felt a relief, a relief from the endless grief she had been carrying, she realized, for years.

The waitress carried over the menus. Carlos noticed all of the attendants dressed in torn and worn-out clothing.

"They look like castaways," he said.

"So do you," she teased.

Looking through the menu, they decided to eat the same things and to go all out. They started with the cured Chilean salmon served atop a wild mushroom pancake topped with caviar appetizer.

"This is enough for a whole meal," Carlos was saying.

"Is this enough for what we need?" she asked, changing the subject.

"It's a good start, no?"

"We have so many more starts to go, to where we were before—"

"Don't, no lo digas. We both know—"

"We know that sex is not a problem, it never was between us. Pero, Carlos, there is still so much pulling us apart."

"And we've made two beautiful children between us. What about them, what do they say about us?"

The thought of Roberto and Brenda calmed her fears. They had agreed to stay these past days at their father's house, their old house. Rosario was happy to look after them. She enjoyed being the nanny she once was. Lucinda had caught herself saying her good-byes to the children. She was about to say "we'll be back," but she said "I'll be back" instead. She had realized how measured her conversations had become. The thought that Carlos was having this conversation fanned her hopes.

The waitress served the black bean soup with sour cream and cilantro along with the Caesar salad. Night had overtaken the island. Its darkness was total except for the circle of lights coming from each table out in the water. Overhead, the stars and their reflection on the sea melted into one continuous band, wide enough to encompass all troubles, thought Lucinda.

"We are good parents, that's not the point," she said.

"We made children together, they came from our love. Imagine, if we don't make it, what will that do to them, to what they represent?"

He saw that she was still questioning.

"Lucinda, the children pull us together. It's a start."

"And if we had no children?"

"On this island we're childless. Look at us, alone under these stars, together. Qué más puedo decirte? I love you."

"Me too," she said, wondering if two innocent children and the respite that was Little Palm Island was enough, enough to drag Carlos away from his detoured life. Looking at themselves from above, as a security camera from some ceiling would film them, she saw a couple whose troubles were colored by nostalgia, the pampering of an island, and a desire (was it wishful thinking?) to start over. That couple would look bright and hopeful on any color film. But she was seeing the romantic scene in the black and white

of a grainy reality. Security cameras don't romanticize their subjects, she thought.

A shipwrecked busboy took away the finished plates from their
table. Soon, the main meal of muscovy duck breast deglazed with
honey and passion fruit vinegar made its appearance. They ate
slowly, letting the reality of their conversation rest, at least for a
while. The richness of the dinner settled upon their anxiety, allowing them to feel the physical sensations once again seducing them.

"If we make it—when we make it, this should be our place.
Ours, alone to come back to and—rejuvenecer," Carlos finally said.

"I would say renacer. Can a shipwrecked marriage float again?"

"Sí, it can and ours will. Lucinda, this is our last night on this island. Let's make it as grand as this dinner—your words, remember?" Carlos reached over the table for her hands.

"Ay! You spilled the flower vase!" Lucinda exclaimed.

"What's a little more water on this floor going to do?" He
splashed up water with his feet.

Their laughter was interrupted by the waitress suggesting
dessert. Carlos interrupted her.

"We already have dessert," he said, looking at Lucinda.

Lucinda signed off on the check, watching him take the den-
drobium orchid sprays off the table. He was flirting with her and
she liked it. The scene in her head was playing in color once again.

After drying their feet, they leisurely took the long way around
back to their villa.

"Here, let me do this." Carlos stopped her, placing a tiny white
orchid behind her ear.

"Y las otras?" She pointed at the orchids in his hand.

Carlos shrugged his shoulders and continued on the walk. He
led her to the massage table, tucked away behind the palms and
the croton bushes. She sat on the table, looking up at the night sky.
Carlos began massaging her shoulders. Lucinda closed her eyes
and let his touch reach her.

"Let me ask you something. How did you manage to—to do it?
To go your own way?"

"With a little help from las amigas."

"I mean, the decision, you know, to leave—"

"You? I left everything that made you leave me."

Carlos' hands dropped. He sat beside her.

"You left that old statue of Don Quixote in the studio. Why?"

"Una locura mía."

"You know, when you called about this Little Palm Island, I was in the empty studio, with that crazy statue looking at me."

"Did it speak to you?"

"I'm here," he whispered.

She saw the expression on his face. It was a mix of love with pain. Lucinda knew its source.

"You know I can't go back. No puedo, it's not me anymore."

"Yo sé."

"I've been seeing a counselor, a marriage counselor." Lucinda could feel his tension. She recalled what Mercy had said about it, what she told her at their last breakfast.

"Shrinks and males, especially Latino ones, qué va! Talk about the quickie way to a divorce. Let me tell you, mentioning that word to a Latino causes male frigidity. They freeze up and shrink! Oye meng, what good is a shrunken male? Piénsalo bien!"

Lucinda had thought about it. If this was going to work, she couldn't shrink away from any truth. Pain is truth, she had come to realize.

"Her name is Nicole, Nicole Hospital. She's very good at the truth."

"What kind of a name is Hospital?" he asked. She noticed a smile slowly forming itself on his lips.

"After the first time I met with her, I made up my mind not to go through that again."

"What changed your mind?" he asked, not smiling.

"When Brenda asked about her, what she did. Sabes what Brenda called her? A happy-maker. It broke my heart to hear our daughter's hope in that nickname."

"I can see how it broke your resistance."

"One visit, Carlos. Come once with me to see her."

"Dr. Happy-Maker? It's not like I haven't been to a hospital before," he said with teasing eyes.

"That means you will?"

"If I say yes, will you?"

"To what?"

He kissed her fully, getting his fill of her mouth. She felt the desire rising within and she let him, encouraged him to take his fill of her. She whispered yes into his mouth.

"Wait, wait. Let's go inside," she said, not wanting to share him with the night, with the island, not even with God.

They made their way to the villa, but not before Carlos had gone back to the massage spa. He had forgotten the orchid sprays.

Coming out of the bathroom with nothing on, because nothing was needed, she walked into the bedroom to find Carlos standing by the bed, robed. He pointed to the orchids strewn on the bedsheets. The little orchids reminded Lucinda of delicate butterflies with milky white wings, like those that fluttered around the herb garden she had started to grow. They looked like they were nesting on the bed. She pointed to the one still nestled behind her ear.

She approached Carlos, undoing the robe, sliding her arms around his waist, feeling his warmth engulfing her. They stayed that way, embracing by the bed, until she reached up with her lips to touch his. With her hands she worked the robe off. He stepped over it, gently nudging her to the bed. She lay herself on it, feeling the coolness of the tiny flowers against her back. Carlos was over her, kissing her face and then her breasts and then her face again. She looked up and noticed the milky white of the tulle glowing from the soft ocher of the lamps. Everything in the room, the lampshades, the off-white curtains, the white bedsheets, his face, the wood of the furniture, all took on the tone of honey. Everything became thick and translucent to her. She felt herself inside the honey looking out at everything. And everything had become soft and sweet again.

Lucinda was tasting his neck, his shoulders, his chest. She pulled at his nipples with her mouth. She kissed him hard and then softly. She grabbed his hands and placed them over her heart.

"Do you feel that? It still beats for you," she risked saying aloud, challenging her fears.

He took hers to his own heart.

"Ahí está. My love for you. Para siempre."

He lay her back, quieting her lips with his finger because he had gotten up. She lay there, watching and wondering as he gathered the orchids.

"Close your eyes."

She could see in her mind's eye what she was feeling. He was gently placing one orchid on each breast. She felt the sweet sensation of his finger pressing one into her bellybutton. He sprinkled a few over her midriff and she learned what butterflies landing all over her body must feel like. She felt Carlos' lips brushing her thighs, fluttering over the dark femaleness that was between her legs. Then she felt his fingers weaving the tiny orchids there. Her body vibrated from the delicious sensations his hands grazing her inner thighs were causing. He reached over her; she sensed his soul hovering, and she felt him lightly tucking the orchids within the hair fanned on the pillows, surrounding her face.

She opened her eyes to his garden. She searched for his face among the flowers and she rediscovered her lover. His eyes open to her, she saw the fullness of his love for her and she saw the measure of his wounded heart and she knew then and there that their love, from then on, would carry a scar.

His eyes were searching hers too. She knew what he wanted to find in them: forgiveness, and a wanting, and a possessiveness, and . . . an unstained desire as it all had once been. She gave him all except for that.

Carlos moved, as if to go inside her, but she stopped him. Propping her head on the pillows, she motioned for him to crawl up to her. In one hand she held three of his orchids, and in the other she held the fullness of his desire now completely in front of her. She carefully twirled each flower among his dark strands, as if the orchids were tender seedlings for all that was wanted. She knew the meaning of his flowers.

Looking up at him, she kissed his maleness. Then lying back, she unfurled her soul to him; he lowered himself, gently flowing into her. The image of the flowers between them excited her desires along with his eyes. He hadn't closed them. She moaned at the moment of her ecstasy from the pleasure she had finally allowed herself to feel again. But her soul screamed from what she saw in his eyes: an innocence trying to unbury itself.

Lucinda closed her eyes, blanketed by his limp body, wondering how she could be feeling so satisfied and at the same time so hurt. For an instant, she feared which would win out, but the feeling of the limp orchids pressed between them pressed the fear out of her sleep. She fell asleep to the rhythm of his deep breathing.

⎯⎯⎯

The morning air was still. The hazy sunlight glared off the petrified surface of the water, making every object in the scene emit an unbearable white light. Carlos and Lucinda squinted through their sunglasses at the pilot. She placed their belongings in the back jump seat of the plane and then helped them through the tiny door. The narrow fuselage allowed for five seats. Two, including the pilot's, just behind the engine, two behind those, and the jump seat in the cone at the rear of the plane. The burgundy leather of the seats was cracked from age and overuse. It was an old model. Having done most of its hauling in Alaska, it was now retired to the sub-tropics of the Florida Keys, where it shuttled guests and baggage from Miami to Little Palm Island and back. Lucinda and Carlos sat side by side in the two middle seats. Paul Royall waved to them from the dock as the engine cranked to life.

The loud roar of its pistons immediately exposed the plane's thin skin and its tiny size. The pilot turned around and yelled at them.

"Make sure the harness is clamped! That's right! See those headsets between your legs? Put them on! We'll communicate by radio from now on!"

She gave a thumbs-up to their successful efforts at wearing the headsets correctly. She did a voice and volume test on them, and when she was satisfied that Carlos and Lucinda were satisfied, she started on her takeoff run. Slowly at first, she checked the gauges on the cluttered instrument panel. Finally, when there were no boats within crashing range, she throttled for the skies.

The plane's hulls sliced at the smooth water, leaving an ever-expanding set of elongated V-shaped wedges until suddenly they stopped. The pilot motioned they were off the water. When she gained sufficient altitude, she twirled her index finger in the air.

"Want to circle the island before we head to Miami?" Her voice crackled over the radio.

"Can we?" Lucinda asked.

"It was Paul's idea."

"Let's go," Carlos said.

The little seaplane banked back toward the island. In the glaze of the morning sun, Little Palm Island looked like a green drop-shaped pearl with a hazy halo all around it. This is the way she wanted to remember these days, as if a dream could exist, Lucinda was thinking. She held on to his hand in her lap. He mouthed the words I-love-you to her.

"Me too," she answered, speaking into the headset.

"I didn't get that. Could you repeat?" asked the pilot.

"Take us home." Lucinda smiled at Carlos.

As the plane circled back to its Miami heading, the pilot pointed to the low, gray bank of clouds far in the distance.

"Thunderheads. The trip may not be as smooth as we planned."

Lucinda could feel Carlos' grip tightening in her hand.

Chapter 23

———◦◦◦———

Julia

"Hello?"

"Profesora? It's me, Manuel."

"Yes, Manuel. What is it?"

"Did you get my E-mail about coming tomorrow to the camp?"

Julia instantly remembered she had forgotten about Manuel's invitation. Since that night with Beatriz she had forgotten about a lot of things. She had kept herself busy with the final preparations for the book, her class lectures, the endless grading, and with helping Lucinda at the studio. She had even attended Mercy's "Liberation Party" for her mother's return from Cuba. All these things kept intruding upon her thoughts. The little details of her daily life were under siege. The assault on her heart had been relentless ever since that night with Beatriz. Beatriz herself had been coming in late from the extended performances at the café. Life had gotten busier as if on cue, and both were letting its flow take charge, at least for a while. And now Manuel, her culturally charged student, was on the phone line.

"Yes, I did. I don't think I can—"

"So why are you the advisor to the Mexican American Student Association anyway, just to give us your stamp of approval?"

By now, Julia was used to Manuel's directness. Partly because it

reminded her of her own college days, when passion moved mountains, and partly because she admired Manuel's thinking, which was
insightful and original, she put up with him.

"Profesora, come with us to Homestead, to the Emiliano Zapata
Migrant Camp. Get a taste of La Raza, before you disappear into the
Great White Way."

Julia was thinking of how Manuel had taken it upon himself to
safeguard her Mexican side. As he put it, he was her "brown knight
in shining armor."

"Manuel, what do I have to do?"

Julia knew she had to invite Beatriz along. There was something
else she wanted to protect for herself, something she had to shine
a light on before it disappeared into the Great Safe Way.

Later that day, as she made her way home from the night class,
Julia wondered if what she was feeling could be put into words.
She wondered what actions these words, if she could say them,
would bring. Regardless, she was going to ask Beatriz to come to
the camp with her.

My God, what are you thinking? No, what are you feeling that is
driving your thinking? Up until Beatriz, your passion was the fruit
of your thought, and now, thought was the fruit of your passion.
You want to follow your instincts, not your mind. Your instincts tell
you to make the leap, a leap of love across alien waters so familiarly
foreign. The nerve of it. Do you have the nerve to do it? To actually
follow where your heart is beating to go and where a kiss was the
prelude to a passion finally allowed feeling? But what if you don't
make it across? What if your will doesn't match your desire? What
if all there is is the kissing of another woman? A "carried away"
episode weighed down by your own fear. Of what? What does it
mean to be gay? It means nothing you say to the invisible Devil's
Advocate stalking your mind. It means nothing because all meaning
is blinded by Beatriz. What about the things that matter most: your
career, your friends, your family? Do they survive such a leap? What
about the hard work done shaping a life for yourself? A construct
of the mind in three-dimensional flesh so secure that nothing, not

even Felipe, could shake it from its foundation. But now, in an unexpected longing, everything you rely on is on shaky ground. Everything is at stake. Can you risk it all this once? Will you?

Beatriz had said yes to the trip. They drove to Homestead the
next morning.

"You took a risk with the women, Beatriz," said Julia, "and yet,
they responded to you like you were an insider."

"Sí. At first they looked at me like I was crazy. But once they
started stretching and loosening up, you could tell they trusted me."

"It's easy to. You're a natural."

"At dancing or teaching?"

"All of the above."

"Gracias, chica. I like to be helpful. Stretching is so important, especially when you are pregnant." Beatriz picked up a glass of water
from the table. They were sitting at a corner table in the restaurant
next to a colorful Diego Rivero wall mural.

"I'm tired," Julia said.

"It was a long day."

"I know, sorry about that."

"No, está bien. I enjoyed it," responded Beatriz.

"Manuel did a good job organizing the activities." Julia was obviously proud of her student.

"How often do you do this?" asked Beatriz.

"Honestly, this is my first time, but the kids come down about
twice a month, depending on the needs. Sometimes, they help with
chores around the trailers or with painting the houses; other times
they work in the fields; often, from what Manuel tells me, they help
the high school kids with tutoring and such."

"Es una buena idea."

"I think so. A few years ago, before I became their faculty advisor,
the group campaigned for the county to set aside the land across
from the camp for a park."

"I see they were successful."

"Manuel had a lot to do with it. He was only a freshman then."

"He's quite a character."

"You noticed. He means well."

"Seguro."

Their conversation was interrupted by Claudia, Julia's former student and the daughter of La Quebradita's owner, who was proud of the fact that he could send his children to the University of Miami and pay their tuition in full. La Quebradita was Julia's favorite Mexican restaurant in Homestead.

"I'm so glad you came tonight, Profesora," said Claudia as she set a bowl of tostaditas and salsa with two ice-cold Tecate beers in the middle of the table.

La Quebradita was an unpretentious family restaurant on the corner of Main Street, across from the old Baptist Church. Its decorations were real, things a tourist would not recognize, as Manuel had pointed out when he first told Julia about the place. The food was tasty, plentiful, and authentic. Julia occasionally drove the forty-five-minute ride it took from Miami for a reminder of her grandmother's cooking.

"My cousin has a Mariachi band," continued Claudia, "and they're going to be stopping by in a little while. Do you like Mariachi music?"

"Of course." Julia looked over at Beatriz, who was looking over the selections on the menu.

They ordered the house specialty: mole with rice, corn tortillas, and salsa de chile guajillo with lots of cilantro. Julia also asked for a side of guacamole.

As they waited, Julia watched Beatriz dab the rim of the beer can with lime and then salt. She brought the red can to her open lips and took a long slow drink.

"Perfecto, after such a hot day!"

"Where did you learn to do that?" asked Julia.

"I get around, chica."

"I can see," Julia said. "Thank you for coming with me. I liked having you there."

"I'm glad I came. Those women had amazing stories of survival.

I learned a lot. I don't know if I could have overcome the obstacles they have."

"You are a strong woman."

Beatriz lowered the beer can from her lips. She placed it on the table and slowly began to rub the condensation from its sides. She didn't respond to Julia.

"Beatriz."

"Qué, Julia?"

"Beatriz, about the other night—"

"We don't need to talk about it. Sometimes things happen."

"No, Beatriz. You don't understand."

"What?"

Julia stayed quiet for a few long seconds, then she said, "I want you to stay."

"What do you mean?"

"I want you to live with me."

"I am living with you, Julia."

"No, I mean I want you to stay."

"Stay?"

"Yes, I don't want you to find another place."

"I don't know—" Beatriz started to say, her fingers still rubbing the can.

Julia was beginning to formulate a script in her mind, a thought wrapped in proper semantics, something her editor would accept at first glance, something correct and easy to read aloud, something well crafted, but instead she said, "I don't want you to find another one, any other one."

At this Beatriz let her fingers slide from the can. They rested on the beige tablecloth; she could feel her pulse at each fingertip silently beating against the table. She gave Julia a long look. It was not a hard look. It was more a look of fearful gratitude, and Julia noticed it.

"I don't think you've thought this through."

"I'm tired of thinking," Julia said. "All my life I've been thinking."

She leaned over, reaching for Beatriz' hand but stopping at its fingertips.

Beatriz' fingers went back to her beer can. She looked straight at Julia and asked, "What about Felipe? I know about the phone calls, the postcards."

"Beatriz, no," said Julia, fully realizing how much Beatriz knew about her. "There's only a friendship left."

"Then why keep it from me?"

Julia could not answer. She wanted to say so many things, things that only her heart could come up with, but her mind was still thinking like a dam, holding back, creating a huge reservoir of emotions.

"It's your life. I'm just pointing out how you still have strings connected elsewhere."

Finally Julia was able to say something.

"He's not what I want."

"I don't want to be an experiment, Julia."

Before Julia could answer, Claudia walked up with their meal.

"Be careful, they're hot." She placed the steaming plates before them.

Just then the trumpet sound of the Mariachi band instantly charged the room as the musicians walked in. Behind the trumpet players followed a violinist and three guitarists. In their black shiny bolero jackets, pants, and large-brimmed hats, the musicians strolled around the tables, playing Mexican folk songs. As they neared Julia and Beatriz, Claudia's cousin began to sing "Cucurrucucu Paloma." The band stopped at their table. The musicians surrounded the women with their song. Julia felt a knot forming itself in her throat as she watched Beatriz singing along, fully absorbed in the music. It was Julia's own music, the music of her stored-away childhood, the Raza of her grandmother, her Raza, and Beatriz was singing it like only an insider could.

"Música follows us, chica, wherever we go," Beatriz said, holding her beer up for a toast.

They didn't get to talk much the rest of the meal. By the time they made it back to the Land Rover, it was almost midnight. They settled into the quiet rhythm of the highway.

"I have to go to Mexico, soon," said Julia, breaking the cocoon of sound the humming of the rolling tires made. "I've been invited to be on a national TV show, to talk about the book. My agent sent the producer a copy of the galley."

"That's nice," Beatriz said without much enthusiasm. "How long will you stay?"

"Two or three nights."

"That's nice."

The lights of the car created a tunnel in front of them, giving Julia the sensation of being in a deep ocean, the car being one of those small research submarines, searching the unknown depths for something recognizable. She turned her face toward Beatriz.

"I want you to come with me."

"That's nice," she answered, looking out her window, seeing Julia's reflected face looking at her.

—∿—

They were greeted at the airport in Mexico City by an associate producer of *Impacto Latino* who had a limo ready for the drive to the hotel. Reservations had been made at the María Isabel Sheraton on Reforma Street next to the American Embassy. As the car circled the statue of La Glorieta del Angel de la Independencia, Beatriz strained to look out the window and up at the gold-plated angel on top of a high pillar holding a torch. Julia explained how the statue represented the spirit of independence, Mexico's painful birth from the clash of Spanish and Aztec cultures. The torch always reminded Julia of the Statue of Liberty. Why was it countries always revered such massive symbols of freedom, yet found it so difficult to allow it in the simplest of forms, such as a heart's desire, thought Julia as the limo passed the familiar streets she used to walk down with Felipe as her cultural guide.

The car passed Reforma, Independencia, Revolución, street

names steeped in history, but now, with Beatriz at her side, full of double meanings. That's why she was there after all, to talk about reforma and independencia and revolución for Latinas on the border. She looked at Beatriz and admired the way she savored the moment. She is una auténtica, Julia thought. She should be the one interviewed on the talk show, she and the pregnant women of the Zapata Migrant Camp, she said to herself as the driver pulled into the hotel.

"Julia Velásquez, it is a pleasure meeting you. Welcome." It was Jorge Torres, *Impacto Latino*'s producer. Julia took note of his dark blue pinstriped suit, which, to her, made him look shorter than he already was. With his pinstripe mustache, he looked at her like Danny DeVito. Julia shook his extended hand and introduced Beatriz. He explained the agenda for the two days. They would spend the first day getting acquainted with the show and its host, going through the outline of the interview, and editing the images the show's researchers were planning to air along with it. The actual live show would take place that evening before a packed studio audience. On the second day, as agreed in the contract, she would give extended commentary for a documentary on Latinas the producers wanted to package and sell throughout the Americas.

"We find your book to be very well written and timely. Your essays really capture the mood out there. I am most confident your work will be broadly accepted. We want to be first in making that happen. No doubt it will have un impacto!" Jorge Torres said as he was getting up from the lobby sofa where all of this planning took place.

"Is the world of television always this hectic?" Beatriz asked with a look of jet lag in her eyes.

"We prefer to call it exhilarating. Ah! I almost forgot! Here, you have a one-thousand-dollar limit on it, courtesy of *Impacto Latino*. Enjoy your spending!"

He placed the Visa International card in Julia's hand. Her name was already printed on it.

"Híjole!" he exclaimed, looking at his watch. "We need to be at the studio in two hours! Don't worry about looking good, we're just going to go through the motions, like I explained. See you at ten, the driver will wait for you!" He left in a rush, a cab waiting for him as he waved one last time.

Julia spent the day well into the afternoon ironing out the show's kinks, especially the film footage, with Jorge and the director. Beatriz stayed at the hotel sleeping in the morning and sightseeing along the Zona Rosa, Mexico City's exclusive commercial and residential district. She had ordered room service for breakfast and then again for a late lunch. Julia had left a message for her while she was out. She told Beatriz the show would go on the air at seven and she'd try to be back at the hotel by five so Beatriz should be ready early just in case.

Beatriz was ready by four-thirty, sitting on the balcony, enjoying the clear view in the distance. She remembered that Mexico City was built up in a huge valley plateau surrounded by tremendous mountains. On most days, the city's pollution would obscure any distant view, but the city was making progress toward cleaning up its air with strict anti-pollution laws. A clear day made up for all of the restrictions placed upon its residents, so had said the room-service waiter Beatriz had befriended. She took a sip from her margarita, not the fruity frozen concoction served in los Estados Unidos, no, the waiter had insisted on bringing her the real thing. The mix of the salt with the tequila and lime made her lips purse. She heard a knock on the door, finished the drink in three swallows, and grabbed her purse.

"Por favor, firme aquí," the delivery boy instructed. Beatriz signed, took the box with the envelope attached, and closed the door. Its cover had a clear plastic window. She first noticed the long spray of green orchids arrayed along the full length of the two-foot box. They were delicately pillowed by puffs of white cotton. In the moment that it took to turn the little dangling envelope around, Beatriz realized the flowers were not from Julia. She saw Julia's name neatly typed. It was only her first name.

She leaned against the door looking at the tiny envelope dancing on its string. She placed the box on the rectangular table, accidentally knocking over the replica Aztec bowl to the ground. The candy mints bounced on the tiled floor like raindrops off a cool tin roof. Just as she was beginning to pick up the pieces of the bowl, the phone rang. Quickly she scooped up the remaining fragments, placing them on the table. The phone kept ringing, making her ignore the mint drops on the floor. The thick heels of her shoes crushed them as she hurried to the phone.

"Sí, sí, I'm ready!" she answered Julia's concerned inquiry.

"You got my message? Good. I won't be able to get to the hotel so I'll just have to wear whatever they have here. They've sent the car to pick you up. I've got an incredible headache."

"You got a box of green orchids delivered to the room."

"My favorite flower. Who from?"

"It doesn't say. But there is an envelope."

"Can you open it for me? It's probably from Jorge Torres, the producer. I want to be able to thank him in case I see him after the show."

Querida Julia,

I hope all goes well for you tonight. It is good to know we are on the same soil again. Maybe we can work it out soon enough.

Te quiero,

Felipe

Neither spoke after Beatriz stopped reading. The silence spoke between them. Beatriz sat on the clay-colored leather couch, still holding the card in one hand and the phone in the other. Julia leaned against the wall in the hallway to the dressing room of the studio. Busy people passed by on their way to preparing for the show's start. They reminded Julia of the busy Mexico City streets she was always hesitating to cross. She hesitated before talking to Beatriz.

"I had no idea—"

"Don't say nada más, Julia."

"Beatriz, no—"

"Listen, Julia. You have a show to get ready for. I have to think—"

"Beatriz, don't—"

"What, think? You're the thinker! You've thought this out, no? Maybe for you thinking about love is better than being in it."

"It's not what you think," Julia heard herself saying, realizing the cliché of her words and not being able to do anything about it. There was no time.

"I don't know what's going on, Julia. Yo no sé."

The intern to the makeup artist popped his head out a door and pointed at his watch. The production assistant was coming down the hallway with a rack of clothes for Julia to try on. She took a deep breath and said, "Beatriz! Just come, be in the audience. I want to say so many things tonight. I want to say so many things to you. Beatriz!"

But Beatriz hung up without answering. Julia got absorbed into the mad rush of endless details in getting the show ready for a flawless start. She let the various handlers handle her from room to room, from script change to seat change. Her thoughts were diffused into the infinite universe that was a one-hour show seen in a small electronic box. She tried to see the faces of the audience members filing into the studio, but the lights aimed at the set blinded her. The only purpose allowed now was to get her thoughts into the millions of homes about to see and hear her thinking. To the people around her, that is all that mattered. Her thinking had to be flawless. But sitting there, in the efficient guest chair on the set, all that mattered to Julia was Beatriz. She looked out into the audience once more, and as the house lights were tested, she saw her. The lights were dimmed, but she definitely saw Beatriz about to sit in the back row. The lights were raised again and Julia scanned the row quickly. There she was. As the house lights flickered, signaling the show was about to begin, the host came out and began to warm up the audience. He introduced her and made a few funny remarks about the show's producers. He then pointed to Jorge Torres in the front row. As he stood up, taking an exaggerated bow, Julia took an exaggerated second look at the man sitting next to him. She was sure it was Felipe. The small studio went dark as the show's theme music played and the announcer said, "Desde la capital de las Americas, *Impacto Latino!*"

The interview was going well enough though the spotlights were blinding Julia's searching eyes. She was sure it was actually him, now probably looking up at her, hanging on to everything she said. Even though the host was following the line of questioning they had agreed on, Julia was feeling uneasy, even nauseous. She was straining to keep her usually low and smooth voice in control. She sounded gravelly and had to clear her throat on numerous occasions. The talking continued on through the commercial breaks and even during the film footage spots. The host was constantly editing the script at every chance he got. But during the last commercial break, Julia excused herself. She rushed into the bathroom and locked the stall behind her. Cold sweat began beading itself along the sides of her neck. The whole place felt cold to her skin. Julia leaned on the Formica divider and looked up, the drop ceiling menacing her, reminding her of how boxed-in she felt. She closed her eyes but could still see both of them clearly.

Sitting in the audience were Beatriz and Felipe, a multiple-choice question making its demand right in her face, glaring itself into her mind's eye while the host grilled her thoughts in front of millions. Someone knocked on the door, rushing her to get back on. Julia wiped the freezing sweat and rushed into the light.

Something felt different. The lights became hotter, the sweat glistened more, her voice grew coarser, and the host became aggressive. He asked questions not planned. Julia handled herself as best she could, but the efficient guest chair began feeling more and more like an electric chair to her.

"Julia, let me ask you one more question," the host was saying, smiling as he looked over his glasses at her, then at the audience. He opened his copy of her book to an already marked page. Julia noticed it was the chapter on relationships she had written with Beatriz' help. She looked up at him when he asked, "Are you gay?"

There was a slight yet audible gasp from the studio audience. Julia restrained her own desire to gasp. Everyone she knew was watching this show. Her mother, her father, her students, her colleagues, her amigas, and Beatriz with Felipe in the audience all came to her mind. Her mind went into warp drive trying to see where he was coming from and where he was headed with such a question. She became more aware than ever of the camera's unrelenting stare. She looked at her book in his hands, a book that held her hard-earned thoughts, which now, she realized, were about to be twisted. The urge to panic was mollified by the equally strong urge to protect her words. Julia sought refuge in her profession. Her years of teaching held her up and she leaned on an old technique from her intern days. She threw a question right back at him.

"What do you mean?" she asked in a beautifully calm voice, hoping that he would fall for what she wanted to give him, a chance to display his thoughts, which he no doubt saw as very astute.

"Well, it seems to me," he said, leaning back on his chair—Julia knew he fell for it—"that your views on Latinas on the sexual border are very provocative, especially for the Latino world. I mean, some of the things you say, well—"

"What is it that I say?"

"Well, that 'Gayness' is an artificial construct, a cruel label much like 'Black Sambo' and 'Feminazi'—"

"Or 'Gringo' and 'Wetback.'"

"Yes, yes, more revealing of those that use it than those that are called it. It seems to me, Julia, that you are advocating a sort of color-blind policy toward sexual preference, especially in the Latino world. Are you?"

"What I'm saying is that love is indeed blind."

"That is an old cliché for a writer to be hiding under."

"Who says I'm hiding?"

"Well, indeed, you write here with a very authentic voice, as an insider, an intimate in affairs of the same-sex heart. So," he asked once more, folding his hands on her book now resting on his lap, "are you gay?"

"Why are you limiting yourself to only a few pages of that essay? That essay has more to do with relationships than with anything else."

"You didn't answer the question."

She knew what she wanted to say on international TV. The director held up a sign with the number of seconds left in the show. Julia took her time answering. She leaned in on the host.

"Your question is as irrelevant as me asking you whether you are 'hetero,'" she said, hoping he would take the bait one last time.

"Are you asking me?" He sounded a bit defensive and anxious for her to really ask him. But Julia did not fall into his trap. He was already in hers. There were only a few seconds left.

"No. You're missing my whole point. To me, labels are not important. In fact, labels distort. Labels damage. The important thing to know . . ." Julia paused for effect, looking out into the audience, especially toward the back row. She could feel the audience sitting at the edge of its collective seat. "The truly significant question to ask in affairs of the heart is not are you gay, or are you hetero, or are you bi, but are you"—here she paused again, letting the silent moment cast its spell and hoping that Beatriz would catch her words—"truly in love?"

The host looked at her in silence. The waving arms of the frantic director told him time was up. The loud clapping of the audience made the host strain to get his signature sign-off in before they went off the air.

"Julia Velásquez, ladies and gentlemen, a writer with provocative views and sin duda, con un *Impacto Latino*!"

The sound assistants began taking off Julia's body microphone along with the host's. The credits were still rolling as they both stood up.

"Julia, thanks for a great interview." He looked over his glasses, still smiling for the camera. Julia did not respond.

"I am just doing my job. And, I'm very good at it," he added.

"It's good to know someone who is so proud of the shit they do." Julia excused herself, stepping down off the set. The host's bewildered look followed her. Julia smiled, in spite of her still-raging headache, thinking what Isa's reaction would be on hearing about this.

"By the way, are you in love?" he loudly asked as Jorge Torres and Felipe reached her. Beatriz was right behind them. Julia looked over Felipe's shoulder at Beatriz.

"Yes. Yes, I am."

Felipe was smiling at her words. He embraced Julia while Jorge Torres shook her hands congratulating her. People began to gather around them. Beatriz just looked on.

"Felipe tells me you two go way back. So do we. Qué mundo más pequeño!" said Jorge Torres. Julia was mindlessly thanking the many people complimenting her.

"Did you get the orchids? Were they green?" Felipe managed to squeeze in.

"Yes, thank you," Julia answered, looking at Beatriz. Felipe took her by the hand and began leading her through the small crowd. Jorge Torres and Beatriz followed.

"Let's celebrate! I know a place we can—" but Jorge Torres excused himself from Felipe's planned evening. He had to meet with the researchers for the next day's filming.

"I am so sorry. Perhaps tomorrow the four of us can get together after the taping. Did you like Julia's performance?" he asked Beatriz.

For the first time, Felipe looked over at Beatriz, then at Julia. He had his arm wrapped around Julia's waist. She introduced them as Jorge Torres was leaving.

"Bueno pues, you come along too, Beatriz," he said in a very polite tone. Julia could not talk. She obliged the hungry thinkers pressing her with questions along the way to the exit. She tried but was not fast enough to counter Beatriz' polite decline of Felipe's invitation. He whisked her past the crowd.

"We have a lot to talk about. It is so good to feel you in my arms once again, Julia," Beatriz heard Felipe saying as she was walking up the aisle to the exit door. Julia caught a glimpse of Beatriz before the rest of the crowd engulfed her view.

Julia and Felipe took off in his rented car toward a quiet little intimate place he had chosen for her, where they could "talk in peace."

—∿—

Beatriz took off her elegant clothes as soon as she got into the hotel room. She put on a short blouse with capri pants and sat on the couch barefoot. The only light in the room came from the television set she clicked on with the remote. *Sábado Gigante*, America's most-watched variety show, was on. The silly antics of its host, Don Francisco, gave her an excuse not to think. After thirty minutes or so, the hypnotic glow of the TV numbed her senses to sleep, but she was not sleeping. Her mind was penetrated by the show's next segment, a mini version of a talk show. Don Francisco was talking into the camera.

"Y ahora, accepting homosexuality in the Latino world. But first, a word from Quaker Oats!"

Beatriz clicked the visual noise off. The room's darkness allowed her to notice the city's millions of tiny lights spread throughout every part of the valley. She imagined every light illuminating a conversation, millions of people saying things to each other late into the night. Beatriz stayed as she sat looking out the window for an hour, trying to eavesdrop into every word being said by the glow of a light. But the only conversation she could hear was the one Julia was having with Felipe somewhere among those points of light. The image of them embracing still glowed in her memory. It was a warm embrace, especially after she had said she was in love.

Beatriz stopped looking out the window. She made her way to the phone and dialed the front desk. She jotted down the name and address given. She slipped into a pair of heeled black sandals and walked into the city-lit night. It was a short walk from the hotel to the bar. The music invited her to sit down. Music had been her constant companion throughout her life's lonely times. And now she was alone again, in another capital, with another possibility denied. The music insisted, so she ordered a drink.

—m—

Julia got to the hotel at two in the morning. The drinks had not helped. Her splitting headache refracted itself like a mirror image inside another mirror. It felt endless, that time with Felipe. But walking into the room felt like walking into an aspirin bottle. Beatriz would be her relief from the pain she was feeling.

The first thing she noticed when she turned on the lights was the sofa. It was still a sofa and not Beatriz' bed. She walked into the bedroom. The bed was still made. Beatriz' clothes were still on the chair, her suitcase still open on the floor rack. She turned on the table lamp and noticed the phone off the hook, the receiver lying on top of the notepad. Julia slowly placed it back. She noticed the hotel's logo letterhead on the pad, then recognized Beatriz' scribble. Julia took the notepaper and dialed the front desk for a cab.

The taxi turned down a side street five blocks from the hotel. Julia entered the foyer of La Cueva Argentina and was directed toward a metal spiral staircase in the back. Slowly winding her way down the dark stairwell, Julia stroked the stone walls. They gave the place the uncanny feeling of a real rock cave. The cavern-like room downstairs consisted of various cavities full of tables and chairs, connected by hollowed-out arches in the stone walls, all leading to the dance floor in the last cave. Behind the dancers stood the small band of musicians all dressed in black tie. Her eyes adjusted to the black rooms and still she didn't like the feeling of being caved in. It reminded her too much of her life at that moment. She needed to find Beatriz, but in that dim darkness, the faces on the crowded dance floor blurred into one. She passed through the crowd and under the archways from cavern to cavern. Finally, she spotted Beatriz' silhouette. She was sitting alone watching the dancers.

"Hello," Julia said as she approached the table.

"What are you doing here?" Beatriz responded, not turning around.

"I wanted to see you."

"Aquí estoy."

"Can I sit down?"

Beatriz pushed back one of the chairs. A waiter came up and Julia ordered a glass of water. The drinks with Felipe were still lingering in her brain, along with what she had said to him. She sat down, following Beatriz' stare toward one of the elegant couples on the floor. They were dancing a tango.

"How did you discover this place?" Julia said turning to her.

"Necesitaba música," she said to the dancers.

Julia wanted to say she needed her, but instead she said, "I have a terrible headache."

Beatriz didn't speak.

Julia fumbled in her purse for two aspirins. They sat across from each other listening to one tango after another. Julia watched as couples in their finest clothes played melodic games of dominion, their postures suggestive of a sensual foreplay. The men in black dominated the scene with their desires. The women, dressed in jeweled colors, dominated the men with their well-placed curves, their gestures suggesting surrender but really enticing the men to give in. The accordion pumped heartache into the air, Julia thought to herself. The cave was flooded with melancolía. Even the stones sang of betrayals and abandoned hopes. Julia looked at Beatriz.

"Beatriz," Julia finally said forcefully, "we need to talk."

"Y Felipe? I thought you'd be spending the night with him."

"You don't understand." Julia reached across the table and grasped Beatriz' arm. "Look at me."

"I'm tired of trying to understand," Beatriz answered as she pulled her arm back.

"I'm finished with Felipe."

"You looked like you were just starting."

"There's nothing. My future is not with him."

"I've heard that before."

"Is that why you didn't come?"

Beatriz didn't answer and looked away again.

"Listen, Beatriz, I just finished breaking a man's heart, what do you want from me?"

For the first time Beatriz looked at Julia with intention.

"It's over." From the lilt in Julia's voice it was obvious she was struggling to find the right words. But she knew what she wanted to say. "I want a life with you."

"Isn't that what you told him?"

"I've never told him that."

Beatriz looked at Julia, her eyebrows slightly raised with relief, but just as suddenly she squinted her eyes, measuring what Julia had just said.

"Are you ready to give us a chance? Do you know what that could mean?"

"Sin duda," Julia whispered, reaching for Beatriz' hand. Beatriz stared at Julia's hand over hers on the small square table. The musicians tore into their silence with one last tango, a classic Carlos Gardel number.

Beatriz walked around the table. She extended her hand.

"Now?" Julia nervously asked.

"Sí, just like we've practiced it at home."

Julia looked toward the dance floor. It was packed with couples, their bodies intimately whispering desires of the heart with every dance move executed. Noticing that all the couples were men with women, Julia balked.

"I can't."

"Yes you can," directed Beatriz, offering both hands to Julia. "Vamos," she insisted as Julia slowly rose from the table.

Beatriz took off Julia's black knit jacket covering her short sleeveless dress and threw it over the chair. Julia took Beatriz' hands, which slowly guided her toward the crowd. At first, no one noticed.

Beatriz firmly pulled Julia by her waist into a close embrace while taking her right arm and extending it fully to the side. She pressed her hand against Julia's. She could feel her own pulse rising against Beatriz' hand. She realized there was no turning back. Julia breathed in the musk oil scent of Beatriz' perfume, a smell she had grown to anticipate. The tempo started out slowly. With their upper bodies erect, Julia and Beatriz glided across the floor in long strides and smooth flowing movements. They both wore high-heeled shoes. Beatriz' full hair flowed loose down her back in contrast to Julia's. Hers was pulled up high in a French style bun, exposing wisps of curls along the nape of her neck. Beatriz cast her spell as she led Julia in a series of sharp moves. She fell into Beatriz' rhythm, abandoning her will to resist any longer. They flowed like a pair of gazelles over the polished wood. Julia noticed a few of the couples stopping to watch. To her, they seemed frozen in postures, like in a Mariano Otero painting, each caught in a still life of movement and murmurings. Julia saw heads tilting toward each other, lips moving in whispered commentary as she and Beatriz danced. Julia saw many eyes following in their wake. Then she noticed a few smiles blossoming in admiration. Julia and Beatriz moved elegantly and sensuously across the floor, the other couples giving way. Julia imagined herself as a sleek motor launch, skimming over a smooth sea.

The crowd soon lost interest as they too were swallowed by the music and the resonant voice of the singer, now standing among them with a microphone in hand. The couples glided past one another, like ships in the night, each aware of all others yet each headed in its own direction.

Facing the same direction, Julia and Beatriz stood side by side, their hips touching. A sensation of tension and pleasure jolted through Julia's entire body. She felt her whole body vibrating, slapped, like the sharp chord on a guitar. They slightly turned inward, grasping each other's hands, fully extending their locked arms once again. Beatriz pressed her cheek against Julia's face, making their bodies come so close they formed a mirror image to each other, their breaths, in rapid half-suspended bursts, mingling. Julia could taste Beatriz' bouquet. She realized her headache was gone.

The soft murmur
of your breath
caresses my dream.
Life laughs
when your black eyes
want to look at me.
And refuge is mine
in your gentle smile
like a song
that calms my wound,
everything, everything is forgotten.

The singer crooned his words of tango into the cavern, each syllable echoing off the rock walls into Julia's heart. The tempo quickened in a sudden, seething shift. The cave vibrated with pleasure. Julia followed Beatriz' swift steps, back and forth, back and forth. Their thighs touching, Julia raised her leg, wrapping it around Beatriz' waist. Julia ignored her short dress, now made shorter by her posture. Beatriz placed her hand under Julia's raised thigh. Face to face, they looked into each other's eyes. Nothing could obscure the thrill her heart was pumping through her veins. Beatriz began stepping back, passionately taking Julia with her. Julia leaned in on Beatriz, allowing herself to feel the contours of their bodies settling into each other; her excitement pulsating to the farthest reaches of her desire. She felt the floor moving beneath her. She held her breath.

La noche que me quieras . . .

The night you love me . . .
from the blue skies
the jealous stars
will watch us pass by.
And a mysterious ray

will nest in your hair.
A curious firefly, you will see
you are my consolation.

With two quick steps, Beatriz pivoted under Julia's raised arm. Julia mimicked her by taking two quicker steps while staying in place, making her look like a toreador. Beatriz laughed with abandon and spun Julia. As she turned, Julia caught a glimpse of flashing eyes. She ignored the man. No angry eyes could extinguish the sensations she was feeling from having Beatriz in her arms. The tempo slowed. Beatriz rested her forehead on Julia's flushed cheek. They slowly lowered themselves, each stretching a leg back, inches off the floor. In a very deliberate way, rising simultaneously, finally standing once again, Julia thrust Beatriz away from her, holding her at arm's length. She could not hold back the smile exposing her pleasure. Quickly Julia pulled her back, holding the posture for a few seconds, feeling Beatriz' warmth throbbing against hers. At the music's final fury, she forced Beatriz back against her arm. Beatriz abandoned herself to the movement, arching her back toward the floor, her long hair collapsing over the wood. Julia leaned in, and she could not but let her lips taste Beatriz' exposed neck.

El día que me quieras . . .

The day you love me . . .
the chirping bird
will sweeten his chords.
Life will bloom
pain will no longer exist.

The music stopped. Beatriz, her face flooded with color, whispered in Julia's ear, "Es el día que me quieres?"

"Sí, Beatriz, I love you."

Chapter 24

—∞∞∞—

Mercy

I can't go."

"Why not?"

"I'm watching TV. The ALMA awards are on," I was telling Isa on the phone. She couldn't believe I turned her down to go out for some ice cream and she couldn't believe I was watching TV. It's true, I never watch TV even though I have one of those HDTV home theater jobs that needs an entire wing of the apartment just to get the whole picture in. But when I watch TV, I have to watch it all the way. Además, Tony was watching with me.

"Tony is with you, watching TV?" I could tell by her voice she doubted it.

"Sí. Just hanging around. That's all we're doing . . ."

I motioned Tony for some more popcorn. We were sitting on the floor, eating popcorn and drinking Cokes and watching the Latinos in the American Latin Media Awards kicking butt. Bueno, Jennifer Lopez was strutting hers all over la pantalla. She's giving another Latina media icon, Iris Chacón, a run for her rear. And you know what I say? I say more maximus buttocks for the both of them. It's good for America. People here have been retaining their anals for too long, let me tell you. So what if I sound a little proud? I'm orgullosa, and sabrosa y qué cosa!—I'm savvy too. Oye meng, all I know is that by the year 2000-something, half of America will be Latino surnamed. Say that out loud in certain circles and you know that if looks could lynch, you'd be swinging from the nearest suburban Junglegym play set. Don't get me wrong, I love Americanos, especially the big-hearted ones. It's the small-assed ones I can't stand.

Tony has some Americano in him. He's got a nice rear too, especially as it was framed by the glow of the TV he was bending over in order to raise the volume because I was talking too loud to Isa.

"Have you accepted his hand?" she was asking me.

His hand? I'd go for two handfuls of his rear right now but the bowl of popcorn and the phone were keeping my hands occupied at the moment.

"Nope."

"Are you?"

"Yep."

"What's stopping you?"

I answered the call waiting that stopped me from answering Isa and then I got back to her.

"Mamá. I have to drive her to la clínica tomorrow. She's not feeling well."

I noticed Tony paying attention to the conversation for the first time.

"She hasn't been the same ever since Cuba. The strain must have been too much," Isa was saying.

She hasn't been the same ever since Tony. Every day it's a different ailment. Juana's Pharmacy has tripled its profit margin solamente on mamá's medications since Tony popped the question. I haven't popped the answer to him since.

"Sí, claro," I mumbled to her.

"Don't you think too much has happened too fast? Maybe that's why you can't give him an answer. Maybe you want to take your time on this?"

"Take my time?! That's easy for you to say. Don't forget, I just got off the banana boat, unlike you who've been playing in Coca-Cola Land for more years than I've had men."

"Mercy, you got off the boat twenty years ago."

"Well, time flies in America, let me tell you."

Isa was being motherly and trying not to be metida in my affairs. I shouldn't have been so testy with her. It's just that in all the affairs I've been in, she's been there for me, pero with Tony—actually, there hasn't been any affair, no end-play because there hasn't been any fore-play. All we've done is kiss and hold hands and eat. Oh sí, and he proposed matrimonio to me. I've never been proposed to without some sort of proposition messing things up first, something like, how about the sofa?

Tony hasn't even seen my Victorian-inspired boudoir yet. Qué cosa, he hasn't even come to eat at mamá's Kendall House of Approval. Mamá hasn't been very mothering to him, let me tell you.

I gave a halfhearted answer to Isa's mothering questions and we hung up. Tony and I spent the rest of that Sunday evening watching the awards show and eating his homemade mango ice-cream sundae, which was delicious. And he asked the question once again. I gave him a halfhearted answer. Something was keeping me from giving him the other half.

The next morning I was late to my job because mamá didn't call me with her usual "God bless you" wake-up call. Oye meng, when mamá doesn't call to bless me, algo apesta in Denmark. Lo que me'spera, I thought to myself, rushing out of my building like I was on fire.

I had a gazillion messages waiting for me at the office. Only one got my attention. It was from a representative of Ricky Martin, the Puerto Rican singer with the crossover voice and a look that makes you want to say, "Don't ask, I'm already naked" to him. His rep got my name from Charlie Jones, the owner of The Blue Rhythm Room on South Beach. Coño, what a little leg work can do for referrals in this business. Charlie was a big-shot blues club owner from Chicago who wanted a piece of Ocean Drive as bad as I wanted to sell him one. Everybody had told him black blues wouldn't make it on the Drive. When I showed him otherwise—I spent three nights club hip-bopping all over, showing Charlie the Afro-Latino-Black-

Caribbean-American stew side of Miami—bueno, like I was saying, he went against everybody's advice and took mine. Now his joint is jumpin', as my Afro-American friends like to say.

I have a dream that one day we'll all get off the hyphen, but let me tell you, in present-day America as seen through Miami, hyping the hyphen sells. Everybody and their blank-madre is looking for me to sell them a piece of the hyphenated action. Ricky's rep wanted to look at small hotel properties for a joint venture with Noble House Hideaways. They think that with his marquee, the rich twenty-something jet-set from Latin Land will come flying to Deco Land and swing from its palm trees, their excess cash raining down along with a few of the coconuts. Oye meng, Noble House would be a great catch for my business. They concentrate on exclusive small properties, like Little Palm Island. No such thing as coincidence, let me tell you. Lucinda told me all about that place somewhere in the keys. By what she said, Gilligan's Island couldn't hold its own against Little Palm Island. The place can hold me in its palms anytime it wants, let me tell you. Maybe when I give Tony the OK, we can finally palm each other up honeymooning there. It did wonders for a cracked marriage, no?

I dialed Ricky's rep and got the OK and spent all morning showcasing hotel listings to her. I didn't want to forget to thank Charlie Jones for the tip, so when I got back to the office after lunch, I had my assistant send flowers to his place. It pays to be polite and persistent. Mamá was being persistent, but not polite, when I finally remembered that I had forgotten about her.

"Where have you been? Me voy a explotar como una olla de presión! My blood pressure is too high. I can feel my temples bursting!" Mamá was saying as I opened the door to the Z3.

"No, no, no! You want to fry my brains out? Qué va! Put the top up this instant," she commanded while I drove her from Kendall to her favorite clinic in Little Havana.

It took one hour of driving and a hundred complaints from mamá to get to Lincoln-Martí Health Clinic #23 on the corner of Eighth y Fifteenth across from Rivero Funeral Home. Talk about an incentive to avoid Cuban food. Well mamá wasn't being avoided, let me tell you. Coño, she was being treated like a queen. All I saw her do was flash her Medicare Express card and Pandora's box, or however you say it, opened up for her. The way the nurses handled the paperwork and ushered her from room to room, you'd think they had the "Viejita that Lay the Loaded Medicare Checks" in their care. They loaded mamá onto every machine in the clinic to find any conceivable health problem they might cash in on. I think they even gave her a pregnancy test.

Let me tell you, mamá was in the grip of an HMO novela, and like only a true soap opera queen could, she was playing La Víctima to the max. Finally, when they ran out of machines, they sat us in a waiting den to wait for la consulta with El Doctor. That's the way mamá has always referred to her doctors. And like a true Cuban viejita to be, she defers to whatever they say. Bueno, we waited in that den for a long time—I guess her Medicare Express card reached its limit—and she had plenty to say. I found out on that visit that my deferring to mamá had a limit on it too, let me tell you.

"I'm exhausted. I hope what I have is not too serious," she said, sitting on the chrome and vinyl chair along the wall with half the over-sixty-five-aged population of Latino Miami sitting next to her. An old gentleman with loose eyes gave up his seat for me.

"I hope they get a serious prison term—"

"Qué?"

The TV up in the corner of the ceiling was drowning out any hopes at a decent decibeled conversation. A rerun of *The Rockford Files* was playing in Spanish. James Garner sounded so natural in a thick Mexican accent.

"I hope you're OK, mamá," I said to Jaime on the TV. Mamá stared up at that TV like if waiting for a signal to start a boxing match. The commercial break was her gong.

"OK? How can I be OK con what you have done to me?" She grabbed a *Time* magazine from the Formica and aluminum table in front of us.

"Mamá, what are you talking about?" I asked, looking over a *People en Español*.

"No entiendo nada. I spend a hellish time in a hellish Cuban prison, I'm feeling hellish, and now this from you!"

She was furiosa, turning the pages of *Time* as if Old Man Time himself wanted to get to the end of it pronto. We traded magazines, seeing as how mamá couldn't read English to save her own bank account.

"Qué tú haces con un puertorriqueño?"

So, she was being truthful. So, I told her the truth.

"Nada. I haven't done a thing with— His name is Tony, Tony!"

"No me explico. To leave Cuba en el '80, to start de nuevo in another land, to get this far, and for my only hija to fall in love with a foreigner! A foreigner!"

"He's a natural-born citizen. You and I are the new ones," I tried to whisper. I didn't want to distract the viejitos from Jaime up in the ceiling.

"He's a natural-born lobo, eso es lo que es! He is not a Cuban." She beady-eyed me.

She threw the *People* back on the table. I noticed its cover title, "En medio de la tormenta." It was a summer issue from 1998 on a celebrity divorce. My *Time* magazine was from 1980. Reagan had just won. I looked at both covers, side by side there on the coffee table. Oye meng, I can tell when signs are giving me signs.

"Mamá! If it wasn't for him, you'd still be in Cuba."

"Sí, y libre de este mal! And from that Carmen too. How dare she stuff my face with that foreign food! How could you do this to me, tu única madre?"

I looked up at James Garner on the TV, who was questioning a suspect real intense, and let me tell you, I looked at mamá real intense and I don't know what came over me but I let it.

"Mamá, oye bien lo que te voy a decir. A guy like Tony comes around only once in my kind of life! He is a gentleman and he is no one's fool and he is funny and he is sweet and he is sexy and he is in love with me. With me! Coño! For once a man has said those

words to me like he means them. Do you know what that is worth
out there, out there in No Woman's Man Land? To find a man who
is self-made and who's made me the center of his universe? No
tienes idea. You don't have any idea of how I feel—"

"Oh no? I had such a man as you are describing. He was your father, tu padre, God rest his soul! What about him?"

"He would be happy to see what I have accomplished in such a
short time. Mamá! How could you bring him into this?" I yelled over
Jaime Garner's finger-pointing Mexican-voiced accusations on the
TV.

"He gave his life for us, for his cultura!" She started to sob. The
others in the waiting den stared.

"It was, was my dream for you to marry a Cuban to honor him,
to continue our roots in this soil we've had to borrow . . ."

She pulled a hanky from her black vinyl purse. Let me tell you, I
started to cry at the sight of my mother, little and frail and scared
among all those viejitos, and I cried because of what she was telling
me.

"I gave up my homeland and my husband. Do I have to give up
my Cubanía también?"

I blew my nose. Es que when I cry, my nose takes over and I drip
like a granizado in July, or like a Mr. Coffee in January, depending on
which side of the hyphen I wake up on.

"No, mamá, you have nothing to lose with me falling in love—"

I stopped because my father's image made itself in my head and
I realized he looked a lot like Tony. Another sign.

"You have everything to gain, everything!—especially a daughter
who is al fin really loved. Gracias a Dios! Is that such a bad thing? I
think papá would smile at that."

I saw a few of the viejitos smiling at me. A lot of them were also
adjusting their hearing aids.

"It was my esperanza, ever since we were forced to abandon la
Patria, for you to marry a Cuban, un cubanito decente, and make
more cubanitos to keep the culture alive. Look at the Judíos! Esos
sí saben bien. They stick together!"

"Señora Virtudes! El Doctor will see you now!" The voice came over the loudspeaker with a vengeance, causing three of the viejitos to jump off their seats. They probably raised the volume on their hearing aids too much or something.

Mamá raised herself off the chair like every bone in her body was leery or however you say it. She shrugged me off and walked herself down the long corridor to El Doctor's office like she was Dorothy walking to see the Great Oz all by herself. Let me tell you, I was praying he'd find something, even an ingrown hair, to keep mamá occupied for the rest of my courtship.

I waited by keeping my mind occupied with what had just happened. Something was different between us. I couldn't put my Pink Soda–painted–fingernailed finger on it. Then it hit me while I was picking up an old issue of *Latina* magazine. Right there, in big evergreen fresh letters, was the title "Time for Your Romance," and I knew, let me tell you. I knew like when I first came to this country that I'd grab a handful of its sweet pesos for myself before I turned thirty. I knew like from the first day papá didn't come back that he'd send me un special hombre one day. And then, sitting in that HMO cash-cow den, I knew, por primera vez, that I was the one fighting for my future man and not mamá. Coño, I felt happy and she didn't. That could only mean one thing, I was in love for sure.

"Acute gastritis! Qué condenación!"

I could hear her moaning down the corridor, walking toward me like she was pregnant. Curse, more like a blessing, let me tell you.

I was telling all this to Tony on the phone the next day. Bueno, I skipped the parts about him.

"It's a shame, your mom having all that pent-up gas inside. Can't they poke a stick in her, you know, relieve the pressure?"

"Tony!"

"Hey, you gotta do what you gotta do. Take it from me, there's nothing worse than a bloated tire to throw things off. Could you imagine a bloated mother-in-law?"

"Tony!"

"So, my little petard—"

"Stop calling me that!"

"What? You're the one that farted on me that second date. It was a cute little fart. I'd call it a 'fartette.'"

"Will you stop it," I was saying between my risa and my embarrassment. It was true. He had me laughing so hard that time, I forgot about control. He never forgot about anything embarrassing, let me tell you. Tony had a way with making a moment you might want to forget follow you forever in a little nickname. Oye meng, I loved it.

"Am I lying, my petite petardo?"

"What do you want?"

"You. You wanna go out tonight?"

"Where?"

"You choose."

We ended up in the Blue Rhythm Room on Ocean Drive. And we ended up dressing alike. No such thing as coincidencia. He was wearing his black pants with a dark blue silk shirt open at the collar and I was dressed in my "little black dress" except it was a glistening dark blue and it was open, way open at the back.

We sat way in the back of the midnight blue–painted room. Little silver lights shaped like stars glistened from the roof. The shiny black floor made you feel like you were walking on water. We ordered two Cuba Libre Bacardi and Cokes in honor of mamá and let our feet jump to the dirty, in your solar plexus, thick as molasses blues rocking the room. Let me tell you something, I'm a café-con-leche Cubana, but the way these blues make my spine sizzle, I know I have lots of café in me. When I was a little kid back in Cuba and my abuelita was still around telling me her Afro-Cuban Aesop's fables, I was sure she came from somewhere in Africa. Oye meng, I don't let those Frenchified Cubans I bump into at Miami's Latin society balls get away with it. The way they dance a rumba or a mambo, let me tell you, points to a more-café-con-less-leche abuelita living in some walk-in closet inside a Paris-style mansion somewhere in Miami. One thing I can't stomach is seeing Latinos trying to whitewash their roots. Who wants to look like Michael Jackson?

Tony was looking at me kind of funny from across the little

round table we were sitting at. The star-shaped centerpiece candlelight reflected off his ebony eyes. Coño, he *was* looking at me starry eyed.

"What?"

"You look magnífica," he said in an exaggerated Italian accent.

"Gracias."

"Can I sit next to you?"

"Why?"

"I need that lovin' feeling." He smiled at me while scooting his chair around to mine.

I don't know, ever since I first sat next to him in his car, back in that Stephen King of a spooky suburb, I had a special feeling. It was a rush of warmth, like from a fire, like when everything past the fire's circle is cold and dark but inside it everything is warm and creamy colored. I get it every time Tony is around. I call it the fireplace feeling. But I got a feeling Tony wasn't looking at me anymore.

"Who's that guy? He keeps looking at you." Tony pointed toward another table. I felt a "put the fire out" cubo of water splash up my spine as soon as I recognized Ramón, my old clay-potted boyfriend.

"He's an old flame. Tony, don't worry about him."

"Me? He's the one that's gonna get a dousing if he doesn't shut his eyes down."

That's when Ramón decided to roll over to our table. He still looked like he could fit inside those air ducts, let me tell you.

"Mercy, mi cielo! How are you, mi corazón de melón?" he asked, not paying attention to Tony. Tony sat back and just looked at him.

"I'm fine."

"Me too. You know, they made me the head duct inspector for the greater Miami area." He said that like he had been given a principality or something.

"Qué bueno," I said, trying to brush him off by saying little. What was there to say? Looking at Tony next to Ramón, qué cosa, it was like God was saying, "You want Tiffany or you want tinsel?"

"So, when can I see you again?" Ramón asked.

"My name is Tony." My Mr. Tiffany wasn't glowing, he was glowering. "Her fiancé, you know, boyfriend. Capisce?" he added, not taking his eyes off Ramón.

Ramón looked over at me, then at Tony, then back at me.

"And tu mamá?" I couldn't believe he asked. "Tell her I'll drop by for some of her potaje. Man, do I miss her!" he just had to add.

His smile reminded me of the shine coming off some cheap ring. Mr. Tinsel checked the time—I noticed he still had the imitation Rolex—and gave me a small good-bye wave and a wink. Now when a guy waves and winks at you, what does that spell? L-O-S-E-R, and to think que I was spellbound in his arms once. Let me tell you, there's nothing, nada, like being dumped by a guy to give you that wide-eyed fish-lensed broken-spelled view of his comemierdería, or like Julia would translate it, his shittiness.

"That guy's full of shit."

"It was nothing, the thing with him," I said, reassuring Tony but more like realizing it for myself.

"Look, Mr. Ca-ca is giving me the thumbs-up," said Tony. "Yes, Mr. Ca-ca, and here's a thumb back up your—ah, forget about it."

Tony wrapped an arm around me and I nuzzled up to his neck. We sat there letting the blue rhythms wash over us like a crashing wave, and as the music drifted away, I feared nothing. I felt safe and secure under his wing.

The Blues Band of Distinction got into a really caliente and saucy B. B. King number about a chica who couldn't be pleased, no matter what her guy got her. Let me tell you, I've never had that problem because I've never had a guy give me much, until Tony.

I saw him, through the corner of my eye, reaching beneath the table into his pocket.

"Look what I got for us," he was saying as he placed the little black box on the little black table and slid it, real slow, toward me.

Real slow, I got off his shoulder and just stared at it, almost invisible in the blackness of the room. I ran my Mesa Red–painted-fingernailed fingers over its black velvet and I felt what Elizabeth Taylor must have felt when Richard gave her that hunk of a jewel that told the world they didn't care what the world said, or did, or wanted from them. That's the kind of love I wanted, the leave us alone if you can't take it kind, let me tell you. For some reason, Julia's face got into my mind but I took it out pronto.

I took the little black box in my hands, precious by the way Tony looked at me, and opened it. Green, green and white in a sea of gold burst out at me. The two of them, sitting there in their little gray cushion, looked married. Heck, they looked like they've been together for years, cut from the same emerald and from the same diamond and banded from the same hunk of gold.

"Well?" he asked looking at the rings.

"Why two?"

"One for you and one for me. We can skip the engagement part. Well?"

I took them in my hands and let the diamonds and emeralds roll in my palm. I could feel my heart rolling all over inside my chest, let me tell you. I never had such a feeling come over me from pieces of rocks and metals, pero how long have I been waiting for these? Mucho tiempo, because papá was being picky with his final choice and now I had to look at Tony and give him my final choice and deep down there could be no hesitation because I didn't want to mess this one up. I looked at the rings and then at Tony.

"Well?" he repeated.

I counted to ten and no interference came through. Bueno, mamá's face made a try but I squeezed it out of the picture.

"Yes," I finally answered him.

"It's about time." He smiled at me.

"And my mother?" She had squeezed her way back into el cuadro.

"About time she came to ma's for dinner, you know, make it official or something." Tony gave me his sly leave-it-to-him smile.

I left the Rhythm Room, but not before flashing my ring at Ramón, who was standing by the door, scoping. I knew what he was really up to: hoping. He gave me a happy-for-you look and then pointed to a brand-new prospect walking toward him. I put my arm around Tony's waist and walked out the door, my heart dancing to his rhythm.

We walked a while down the overcrowded sidewalk of Ocean Drive on the hotel side of the street. It was packed rear to rear but Tony and I kept on walking arm in arm. Let me tell you, we were walking on Nike Air. We were hang-timing over the crowd like Mike. I was so high—and I only had that one rum and Coke, which was a record for my nighting-out life—I could see below me all the little heads of all the little people scrambling around each other. They looked like refugees trying to find someone to take them in. Bueno, my refugee heart finally found someone to take refuge in. Tony squeezed me by my waist and I looked at the expression on his face and, let me tell you, I could tell my love fulfilled him just like a great pasta meal.

"I hope Mamá Mercy likes pasta," Tony was saying to me two weeks later. We were in his mother's place waiting for my mother to come out of the bathroom before the food was served. She was in there a long time. It took me an entire week to convince mamá to eat at my future mother-in-law's house. She took the news of our wedding like a patriota faces a firing squad.

"Qué remedio is left to me? I would never abandon the cause. And Mercy, you are La Causa in my life. Para eso vivo yo!" she had said right before getting into the car for the great meal. I could swear she gave a salute to her invisible compadres-in-arms.

"What's that in the bag?"

"Dessert."

"Let me see," I insisted. Ever since her little "Cristo sí, Castro no!" crosses Cuba episode, I've gotten suspicious of every bag mamá carries.

"Tony said his mother took care of everything," I said, referring to the bagged dessert.

"Tony says a lot, pero he cannot tell me about proper Cuban hospitalidad."

"Está bien, mamá."

Tony took to calling every day at her house asking for me, and claro, I was never there, but it gave him an excuse to get her ear. It was his plan to seduce her over the phone. He kept complimenting her about her mothering skills. He told her how there was so much of her in me, about how he could use her help in making me happy. I don't know what happened, but he took to calling her Mamá Mercy.

"We're here."

And now we were all waiting for her to get out of the bathroom.

"Mamá Mercy, you all right in there?" Tony knocked on the door.

We heard the long sound of the bathroom spray can. Tony looked at me.

"Gastritis," I reminded him.

"Oh, yeah."

We walked back to the dining room where Tony's family was waiting. I looked at the soup bowls Carmen was filling.

"What's the appetizer?" I asked.

"Broccoli and chili pepper soup. Ma's specialty."

"Don't tell my mother!" I whispered as she sat down opposite Carmen.

"This soup is very tasty. Qué es?" she asked.

"Vegetable soup!" Tony got in. His mother gave Tony a questioning look and shrugged her shoulders.

By the end of the meal, Eddy, Tony's father, was telling us how every piece of furniture was made by him. Andy, his brother and partner, was telling us how he wanted to increase business by selling ad space on the tow trucks to bathing suit companies. Suzi, his sister, was telling us how smart her boy was and how dumb his father was. And Carmen, let me tell you, she cut through the whole domestic picture with her observation.

"Mamá Mercy, honey, you don't look so good," she said, all the while cutting the pudín de pan mamá had insisted on making. Everybody stopped talking and stared at my mother. You could tell they were remembering what happened at the Liberation Party.

"She's gonna blow," Tony whispered to me.

I was hoping she didn't blow it.

"If you only knew, Carmen." Mamá rested back on her chair. I practically fell off of mine.

"What?! What is it?" Carmen leaned over the table.

And then mamá told her of her ailment and then Carmen shared some of her own problems of the intestinal kind and then everybody started to blab about their own gas stories and remedies and let me tell you, thank God no one smoked because if you lit a match in the middle of all that gas talk, you'd be seeing what the inside of the sun would look like. Coño! Talk about your getting-to-know-each-other-for-the-first-time family talk! I don't know, pero oye meng, why is it that talk of the earthy kind brings the defenses down?

Tony brought the house down with his retelling of my little passing gas episode and that triggered mamá into revealing that in the blimp department, I came out just like her. Then Eddy started telling us about his blimp duty in WWII and how important it was to maintain proper pressure. That's when Carmen took it upon herself to demonstrate the proper way to relieve the buildup by crossing the legs a certain way and that's when I made my way out to the carport for some real hot air.

I sat down on one of the rocking chairs Eddy told us he made and rocked. I heard the family's hot air talk drifting over me from the window and for the first time I felt contentment like I always imagined it would be: no hustle, no sell, and no bull to cover up. And then it hit me. My little oyster of contentment had a little grain of sand in it. Something I had said to Tony was scratching it. I dropped off mamá after the dinner and drove back to the beach with irritation in my heart.

Now I'm not one to linger over anything I've ever said and I don't hold regrets, pero that one thing I had told Tony way back at one of our romantic "car parts exchanging" rendezvous was making me regret I ever said it.

"What did you say to him?" Isa was asking me.

It was the day after and I was trying to get myself out of una depresión that was setting in. I was calling from the last hotel Ricky

Martin's rep wanted to look at. She was taking too long to make up a sale for me. I had a corazonada this wasn't going to fly. We were in this dust-caked place for over an hour. It was a work in progress, an old Art Deco number looking for a second chance. The rep was looking at its ocean backyard. I was looking to Isa for something. But even if you bribed me with a Trump real estate deal, I couldn't say what, let me tell you.

"I really put my spike-heeled foot in it. Isa, todo is going so well with Tony, but I can't get this out of my mind."

"It can't be that bad."

"It is."

"Whatever it is, he's still going to love you. I mean, the way you've taken to each other, your mother even likes him! What can stop you now?"

"Isa, I told him I was a virgin."

I could hear her swallowing. "Estás loca?!"

"I didn't want to lose him!"

"You are crazy!"

"It's not like he's from *Pleasantville*. I'm sure he's seen some color by now."

"Sí, but not your color, right? Tell him."

"I just don't want him to know about my Technicolor past."

"Mercy, you want a church wedding, no?"

"It's my dream." I always pictured myself in a Chaste White—well, Chestnut Beige—full Victorian gown, with baby roses in my hair and everything pastel-ish.

"Confiésale everything!"

Coño, love was making a nun out of me.

Epilogue

———∽∞∾———

Isabel

Ten Months Later . . .

The trek up to the Utopia Ballroom on the second floor of the
Galaxy Hotel on Miami Beach didn't feel much like utopia. The
hotel was being renovated. I struggled in the hallways as my heels
kept getting tangled up in the plastic sheeting protecting the tile
floors from the new paint job still in process. Finally in the elevator, I couldn't stop sneezing from the construction dust. Utopia
under construction—that pretty much explains Mercy's life. She
had suggested the place. One of her clients owned it and offered
her a good discount as a baby shower gift.

Since marrying Tony, her world had turned into a utopian domestic dream, with a few nightmarish intrusions from her
mother. These came under control when she found out she would
be an abuela.

I opened the doors to Utopia and ran into Carmen loaded with
food trays.

"Carmen, what is all this?" I asked. She was dressed in tight pink
capri pants with a matching shirt. She looked like bubble gum.

"Just a few little things I cooked up, Isa—you know, pasteles,
empanadas, jamón relleno . . ."

"Carmen, that's sweet of you, pero I thought Mercy's mother
was handling the food?"

"Honey, Mamá Mercy can barely handle my Tony! This is nothing for my future grandkids."

She disappeared into the back kitchen, looking like a doting abuela loaded for bear, like David used to say. By now it was common knowledge around our circles that Carmen couldn't arrive anywhere empty-handed. To her, food was the fifth column in the war of social graces. Mamá Mercy wasn't too pleased with this situation.

"Otra vez! There she goes, putting her cazuelas everywhere!" Mamá Mercy was saying, storming out of the kitchen in her floral print dress.

"She's just being nice, Tía. You look very beautiful!" I tried to deflect.

"Ay, hija, gracias. I think we have too much food now, thanks to Carmen."

"Don't worry, in an hour it'll be too little." I surveyed the crowd of women. They were talking ferociously. Every woman Mercy knew was invited to her baby shower. The room was full of fast talk and smelled like a fragrance factory.

I looked around the room. I couldn't recognize it from the day I had stopped in to drop off the deposit. Lucinda, who was in charge of the decorations, had transformed the place into a glowing Victorian garden. In the middle of the round tables, she had placed small delicate arrangements of lavender dendrobiums, yellow oncidium orchid sprays, and miniature roses of every pastel shade imaginable. Queen Anne's lace made the centerpieces look like they were floating on clouds. At Mercy's head table, Lucinda had used the same flowers but in a much larger arrangement resembling a window box overflowing with abundance. Each chair was wrapped in a satin cover with a large pastel pink bow at its back. The tablecloths dripped with maidenhair fern—Julia's idea. The entire room was one giant Victorian overflow.

"What do you think, mi amiga? Did we do justice to Mercy?" Lucinda, standing by the cake table, asked me. She had her hair up, loosely held together by pins to which she had clipped small white orchids. She was looking radiant. Ever since Lucinda's "Resurrection Weekend" with Carlos at Little Palm Island, she's been orchid obsessed. I remember when she just used to grow them, pero ahora, it's like she even sleeps with them. Qué sé yo what's going through her head. I know she's been sleeping with Carlos. Bueno, he's been staying at her place more often than not.

"I think Mercy is a very happy mujer. Look at her." I pointed to my little cousin, who wasn't so little around the middle. She was sitting at the head table, tight as a blimp and smiling away.

"Can you believe this? Our Mercy seven months pregnant and with twins?"

"His-and-her babies. Only Mercy could pull off such a sweet deal!" Lucinda and I both laughed at the thought of what Mercy must've put God through for the two-for-one deal. I looked over at Lucinda wondering what she has been through. It's funny, how ten months can take in a lifetime. But Lucinda has kept her head on straight throughout, even with the few surprises sprung at her.

Their marriage comeback was still on shaky ground. It didn't help when Gabriela showed up at the bank those few times, trying to get hold of Carlos. She had even gotten Lucinda's home phone number and had dared to call him there. Incredible, how a man's mistake can double back on him. It took Carlos three more months to "divorce" his mistake. The only thing that kept Lucinda interested in keeping on was his wanting to go with her to see Nicole, the "happy-maker" marriage counselor. I give him credit for that. It takes two to save a marriage, and these two were holding on like this Dr. Hospital was the only lifeline left to it.

He's been trying to leave behind part of his life. He put the Coplum house for sale and has been throwing out feelers to his clients to see if they would be interested in working with a private financial consultant. When La Familia back in Santo Domingo got wind of this, it was enraged and lawyers were engaged. In the end, Carlos is going to have to divorce himself from his parents too. But I've learned that a man has got to be measured by his actions. Forget about words. Words from a man are like cut flowers—beautiful at first, and then they wilt. Let me see a man's actions, and I'll tell you his truth. I learned that the hard way with David and the easy way with Orlando. Lucinda al fin got more than words. Carlos was acting in ways he had forgotten how to act and Lucinda was recognizing him all over again. The kids were more settled too. You want to see how a marriage is doing? Look at its kids when they're not looking.

"Isa, your mother is looking for you." Lucinda pointed.

"Where have you been? We've been waiting for you to start the games."

"I was tied up at the office."

"I can't believe you went a la oficina today!"

"Ya mami, we already discussed it," I answered, rolling my eyes at Lucinda.

I followed mami to where Mercy was. Sitting on that large white fanned-out wicker chair, she looked like a contented female fertility goddess. We exchanged kisses across her large belly.

"Let the games begin!" she yelled over the crowd.

We played a bunch of silly games for about an hour. There's nothing like a baby shower to bring out the baby in people. I was having fun seeing my little cousin lose every round of musical chairs even to the viejitas. Finally, the last game came. It had to do with guessing Mercy's circumference.

We stood Mercy in the middle of the room like the mother goddess she had become. Julia and Beatriz grabbed the ribbon rolls and scissors and went around the tables asking people to cut a piece of ribbon the size of Mercy's belly. When we were done, we took one ribbon at a time and wrapped it around her huge belly to see which one was the most accurate. Mercy was having a blast.

"What is this? I'm having twin babies, not Tweety Birds! Too small!

"Oye, Carmen, remember, I'm Cuban. Everything we do goes double. This isn't even enough ribbon for one kid!

"Well, all it took was one Puerto Rican sperm to give you two kids. That's my Tony!"

"And I know my Mercy! Here, try this one." Mercy's mother thrust her ribbon at Beatriz.

"Mamá, close pero no cigar!"

"Lucinda, me ves con barriga de planeta? This is huge!"

"Mercy, if your belly represented the earth in 1492, Columbus wouldn't be sailing, he'd be wallowing in the ocean blue!"

"Qué poeta." Mercy faked a smile back at her.

Beatriz won. I guess being a dancer helped. Julia handed her the prize the size of a watermelon. When Beatriz slowly pulled out a giant box of Tide laundry detergent, the crowd burst out laughing. Beatriz and Julia exchanged a quick loving glance, so quick it was missed by everybody, but not by me.

I have to admit that Julia and Beatriz had the guts to take on their love. It took a little while for the rest of us to get used to it. Lucinda was never taken aback by it. I guess in love wars there is solidarity when soledad is the enemy. Lucinda had seen Julia's loneliness, even with Felipe, long before me. And ever since Beatriz, Julia hasn't been lonely. Its shadow is long gone from her. Looking at them helping Mercy, they fit, like an old couple that still looks good together. Well, that's what I see when I see them together, even though I still get a few mariposas in the belly when I let the fears flutter. What the hell, it takes time to make a move, right? I think I'm getting there.

It took Mercy a while longer to get used to Julia's "there." Her fear was that Beatriz would turn out to be the Yoko Ono to our Beatles get-togethers. That's how she put it. But I know my little cousin better than she knows herself. All it took was Tony to put Beatriz in the proper perspective. "True love looks the same when you squint your eyes, no matter how it's packaged." Those are her fighting words for whenever Mamá Mercy activates her anti-Tony missiles. I repeat them to Mercy whenever she takes aim at Beatriz.

It hasn't been easy for Julia. Many have taken aim at her since her return from Mexico, even though her book is a best-seller. There have been a few "elegant" punches thrown her way by some colleagues and other friends who hold her love against her. She handles them much like she did that host back in Mexico, like a jalapeño pepper, cool on the outside but burning hot on the inside. She's left a few with swollen lips, metaphorically speaking. This passionate side of Julia has taken us amigas by surprise. Es verdad what Lucinda says, ever since her TV episode, Julia has come back a changed woman, in more ways than one.

Julia left Mercy with Beatriz and joined me by the cut crystal punch bowl.

"By the way, Isa, I never did ask you. Did Mercy ever tell Tony about not being a virgin?"

"Qué tú crees? Instead of confessing to him, she confessed to my priest, Father Paquito. They had to call 911 to resuscitate him! It was too much for the young kid's ears."

"You're joking, right?" Julia asked, serving us both a cut crystal cup of the punch.

"No! She said that made her a spiritual virgin."

"A virgin to a higher power?"

"More like a virgin cubed. Anyway, she said it wasn't any of Tony's business."

"Y qué le dijo on her wedding night?"

"Nada más that she was a tampon woman."

"More like a tampered-with woman, esa Mercy!" Julia smiled as she walked to the kitchen to help out.

Mercy was still in the middle, now sitting in the high-backed wicker chair. It was time to open the presents. All the women gathered around. Las viejitas were on the outside of the semicircle. The kids sat closest to her. I looked at her, surrounded by her loved ones and all those kids, and all of a sudden she matched. She looked rooted among the kids.

"Tía"—that's what Sam called my cousin—"tremenda mother!" I heard him saying. It was true. Mercy had become the mother of all mothers. I suppose Tony's kid-loving personality and her twinning had something to do with it. I went up to help Beatriz, who was handing her the gifts one by one.

And one by one, everyone ooh-ed and aah-ed each time she held up two sets of tiny shoes, two sets of matching his-and-hers sailor suits, two sets of unisex bonnets. They even aah-ed when David Jr. just mentioned the number two before anything was opened. Las viejitas almost fainted at some of the after-pregnancy, after-dark lingerie some of us gave her. I saw mami take a double shot of the spiked punch when Mercy held up the matching his-and-hers thong pajama briefs. It was a gift from Beatriz.

"Pajamas? En mis tiempos those would have been training bras!" mami said.

Everybody laughed at the thought. When I tried to lift one of the larger boxes, tía rushed up.

"Let me help you. It's glass. I don't want it to break."

I could tell by Mercy's face she was imagining some fancy glass bowl or Lalique figurines. When she opened the package her jaw dropped and she let out a laugh.

"Qué es?" everyone yelled out.

Mercy lifted up one of the small thin bottles with a honey-colored fluid inside. She opened it and everybody got quiet. You could see the nostrils flaring and hear the air being breathed in. We all recognized the fragrance.

"It's a year's supply of Agua de Violeta!" Mercy's mother proudly exclaimed. It was more like a lifetime supply.

"They wouldn't be Cuban babies without their Violet Water. I used to bathe you in it." Mercy's mother beamed with Cubanía. Every Cuban member of my family has been genetically imprinted with this baby cologne. To my family, Agua de Violeta is the Johnson's baby powder smell of childhood.

"Open the one from me and Eddy!" Carmen pointed to a tiny box wrapped in pink and blue paper.

This time the crowd shouted with delight at the sight of the twin azabaches. The cut, pea-sized, black stones mounted on 18-karat gold safety pins were worn to ward off evil eyes. All the viejitas in the room were in agreement as to the necessity of such a piece of jewelry, especially for twins, seeing as how they were symbols of good luck and therefore already targets for the forces of negatividad.

"That's right, that's right. Good Puerto Rican babies need good protection!" Carmen was beaming back at Mercy's mother. Mercy was now opening her fifth box with an azabache in it. At this rate the babies would be protected for a radius of 2,000 miles. Even the Pope would have a hard time getting at them.

I saw Carmen walk over to the CD player and joined her.

"Mija, esta música is giving everybody a hard time staying awake," she was saying to me as she replaced the *Yani Live at the Grand Canyon!* CD with Marc Anthony's salsa tunes. Mercy was right about her mother-in-law. Everybody had a hard time sleeping around her.

"You always carry CDs in your purse?" I asked Carmen.

"Claro que sí! You never know when you might need a little salsa to cheer things up. Además, whenever I get a chance I practice for my class."

"Una clase?"

"I talked Eddy into learning salsa. Every Tuesday we go to Borinquen Banquet Hall. He takes the beginners class, you know, Italian men have it hard around the hips. I take an advanced one. I'm even learning casino and rueda! You should see this boricua menearse," Carmen said, shaking her hips. "I always request one of the young instructors for a partner. I don't want any of those viejos with guayaberas and flabby stomachs. Claro, I don't tell Eddy nothing."

She pulled Beatriz off to dance. Mercy se sacó la lotería with her Neoyorrican mother-in-law. I stood next to Mercy, watching her open more gifts. She was talking to one of the cousins.

"You'll be staying home with the babies now, no?"

"Al principio sí," Mercy was saying as she smiled, rubbing her belly. "Tony loves to rub my belly. Look, here's one of the feet. You want to feel?" she asked, putting the double set of rubber duckies down.

"No, thanks. And later? Are you giving up realty?" the cousin continued. I knew the answer to that one.

"Estás loca? No way! In a few months I'll be back in shape hitting the sidewalk again, or at least the cellular."

"And the babies?"

"Mami and Carmen have already worked out a schedule, more like a treaty, between them. So I have no problemas in that department. Qué cosa, as soon as the babies are big enough, I'll take them with me, let me tell you."

"To work?"

"Oye meng, there's nothing like the smile of a sweet baby to make a sweet sale. Imagínate twins? Walter Mercado was right, two is my lucky number!"

I could tell the cousin wasn't about to stop probing, so I saved Mercy with an announcement.

"Cake is served!" I yelled out, pointing to the pink and blue, triple-stacked cake, topped with a stork carrying two sacks.

Carmen and tía had meticulously arranged the plates, cups, and napkins. People began to gather around the cake, waiting for a slice. I walked over to Mercy, now sitting at the head table caressing her belly, and offered her some cake. I had cut an extra large piece.

"Look, Isa, she's hiccuping." Mercy pointed to the movement on her belly.

"How do you know it's her and not him?" I asked.

"A mother knows her child," she solemnly informed me. Why is it that young mothers forget that old mothers know everything they're just reading about? We're just too worn out to make a big profound deal over it.

I looked at her earnest eyes and said, "Of course." I was remembering myself as the wide-eyed and know-it-all mother I once was. I'm still una buena madre, my boys attest to that, but I'm a wiser mother now. I'm wise enough to know that kids come already packaged and programmed. All we are left with is the tending part. In the end, love is a tending thing, to paraphrase a well-worn line.

Orlando was tending to me. For the last few months he's been busy with his PBS project and he's been attentive to me. That used to be a paradox when it came to the male in my life. I still work hard and I still give Orlando a chance, something I thought I would never do again for a man. We've taken the boys out on the *SeaLove* a few times. David Jr. is still teaching Orlando how to fish. We still haven't figured out how to make my house float in the marina or how to dock his boat in the yard, but we're definitivamente heading in the same direction. We're counting the nautical miles toward spending endless nights together. We just aren't doing any overnighters—por ahora.

Julia and Lucinda were making their way toward us, each with a plateful of cake. We stood around Mercy, on her wicker throne, surveying Utopia.

"Well, Mercy," Lucinda asked, "what do you think?"

"It's beautiful. It's like a dream come true over and over again."

"We did it for you," Julia said.

"I've never been so happy, well except on the day Tony gave me the little black box with—"

"The two rings," I interrupted. "You've told us the story a million times."

"But you know why I'm so happy now?"

"Why?" asked Lucinda.

"Because of us." She reached out for our hands.

"The baby hormones are making you sentimental," one of us said. We were all holding hands by now.

"All of us have it," she said, turning to Julia and then looking at the rest of us.

"Have what?"

"Coño, a little love!"

We laughed as only women on the front lines can, fearlessly.